Einstein's Daughter
The Story of Lieserl

Chris Vuille

Copyright 2013 by Chris Vuille and Supernova Press
ISBN-13: 978-1491267745
ISBN-10: 1491267747

Einstein's Daughter: The Story of Lieserl

Chapter One

September 4, 1939. An airfield outside of London

The Vickers Wellington bomber was sitting on the far corner of the airfield, a dark shape silhouetted against the cold stars of a cloudless sky. The crew traded casual banter with the mechanics checking the plane, while two gray-suited men strode toward them in the company of an airman wearing a baggy jumpsuit and parachute pack. The airman was tall and athletic, his blond hair reflecting the faint light. He carried a helmet in one hand and a rucksack in the other.

His name was Wolfgang Weisz.

They stopped in front of the airplane, Weisz putting his gear down. Goudsmit, one of the suited men, was tall and slender, with a high brow and diffident manner. "The most important thing to look for is evidence of a separation system," he said quietly in a musical Dutch accent. "Large coils of wire, Geiger counters, big magnets, anything that might be part of a mass spectrometer. They could have taken one from the Curies."

Weisz nodded. "Or thermal diffusion tubes."

"That's right," said Goudsmit. "Anything like that. That's important."

The man with Goudsmit, James Muellar, was tall and thin-lipped, with dark, bushy eyebrows shot with gray like his hair. He wore a terminally bored expression. Taking a thin packet of photographs out of his pocket, he held them out to Weisz. "This is a new acquisition," he said, his accent from the Scottish highlands.

Weisz took the photos and began going through them, using a small pocket flash while the other two men stepped closer to him so as to shield the light from distant, prying eyes. Most of the photographs had been taken at long range, but a few had been snapped in a restaurant from a nearby table. He saw a good-looking blond with highly arched eyebrows and dark, luminous eyes that seethed with intelligence. She had a round, pleasant face, like a cat.

He clicked off the flash and handed the photos back to Muellar. "She's beautiful. She's really a scientist?"

"Heisenberg's assistant, Lieserl Meier," Muellar said. "And you are damned right she's a scientist. Too damned good a scientist."

"She's the main target? Not Heisenberg?"

Muellar glanced at the Dutchman. "Doctor?"

Goudsmit coughed uncomfortably. "She's very brilliant, probably much more so than Heisenberg. I haven't met her, but I've read her work and it's excellent. It is said she's cold and calculating, a machine that does physics. Not a normal woman, by any means. So yes, she's definitely a threat. Both of them are."

"There's no room for sentiment in this operation, Weisz," said Muellar. "Be prepared to kill her, if necessary."

"You were going to dispatch a bombing run..."

"Yes, but I can't always get the Air Force to cooperate. Those bastards don't even listen to Churchill."

"Right, of course," said Weisz, a catch in his voice. "I'll take care of it. Whatever has to be done."

"Good man. See that you do."

Goudsmit clapped Weisz on the shoulder. "Good luck, Wolf."

"Thanks." Weisz shook hands all around, then picked up his gear and turned and walked briskly over underneath the plane, handing his helmet and rucksack up through the belly hatch and then climbing in, getting a hand up from his friend Will Polk.

Weisz sat opposite Polk, who was in the tiny radio room with a headset on, talking softly to mission command. Through a window Weisz watched as the pilot finished his slow, methodical examination of the plane, rechecking the tires, testing the ailerons, elevators, and other control surfaces for loose play, anything that might cause a problem once they were airborne over enemy territory. To Weisz, it seemed to take forever. He briefly squeezed his eyes shut, forcing calm, clamping down on the nervous worry that would show on his face and make him stand out in a Hamburg crowd.

Across the field, other pilots and their mechanics were finishing the preflight routines on their own bombers. He could hear the clank of metal against metal, distant creaks and disembodied voices. With his helmet on, he could hear the sound of his own breathing.

Finally the Hampdens and Whitleys, the Blenheims and the other Wellingtons, began cranking up their engines and trundling down the runway one at a time, taking to the air, roaring away into the thickening night. Through his small oblong window Weisz watched them go, feeling the knot of tension growing in his belly.

The pilot came up through the hatch at last and exchanged a few confident words with the rear gunner and other crew members as he checked out the inside of the plane and then made his way forward to the cockpit, joining the copilot who was already strapped in. An airman outside took away the chocks, and a moment later the engines began to turn over, the twin propellers cutting the night air. They ramped up to a full-throated roar like a beast bent on vengeance, and with a sudden jerk the Wellington began accelerating down the runway. Weisz sunk back in his seat. Red flares shot through the night to mark the path. The thick-waisted, lumbering craft bounced once and pulled up into the air.

The Wellington passed over a darkened London and on over the English Channel. Looking outside his window, Weisz could see sparks flying off the roaring engines and reflections on the wings, but otherwise nothing but blackness, broken here and there by the faint sparks and dim outlines of other planes in the formation. Over forty aircraft flew toward their targets, the Blenheims toward the Jade Estuary and the *Admiral Scheer*, and the rest to the shipyards at Wilhelmshaven in the Elbe estuary, where *Sharnhorst* and *Gneisenau* were moored.

For the next couple hours Weisz had nothing to do but wait. Under his helmet his forehead was damp with sweat, although the air in the cabin was cold. He thought of the war, of Hitler's mad expansion, taking Czechoslovakia, Austria, and then Poland. He thought of his mission, playing out his possible futures, what he'd say and do. He'd left letters behind, one for his mother and the other for Carrie Brighton, a Welsh girl he'd proposed to only two months before. She'd turned him down, but they'd gone on seeing each other until he'd been drafted into service. He'd come to the airstrip straight from her warm bed.

Lodging his head against a brace in the fuselage, he fell into a fitful sleep, not sure whether he was dreaming or awake.

On *Scharnhorst*, in the Elbe Estuary

Alarm bells rang all over the ship as young German men ran for their battle stations.

Admiral Franz Haberditz, rubbing the sleep from his eyes, walked onto the bridge of the battle cruiser *Scharnhorst*, peering out over the dark waters of the Elbe estuary off Brunsbuttel. He couldn't believe his bad luck: there as a visitor merely to observe some drills and report back to Grand Admiral Raeder, he found himself under imminent attack in the middle of the night, well before dawn. The sky was murky and overcast, a low ceiling that was ordinarily not the best weather for an air raid. Signals flashed back and forth from *Scharnhorst* to its sister ship, *Gneisenau*, as their crews prepared for action.

Vice Admiral Guenther Lutjens, commander of the *Scharnhorst*, was on the phone talking to the radar officers in the computer room. He hung up and turned as Haberditz walked up to him.

"They'll be here within the next few minutes, probably Hampdens or similar craft, in two waves. A good exercise for the antiaircraft crews."

Haberditz's upper lip curled slightly, his thin blond moustache accentuating his displeasure. Not a trace of fear was in Lutjens' voice, and he hated him for it. "I hope your gunners can hit something besides a drone, Admiral."

"I have every confidence in them," Lutjens replied in a quiet, gravelly voice.

"Any of them face live combat before?"

"The drone exercises have sufficiently prepared them for a real attack."

Haberditz smiled. "Vice Admiral, as you surely know, the drones don't shoot back."

Lutjens frowned and turned away. Haberditz knew he wasn't one for words, but felt slighted all the same. Always the perfect officer, correct, loyal to a fault, although he wasn't a member of the Party, and that had to be counted heavily against him.

Scharnhorst and *Gneisenau* were going through their final teething trials, outfitting for raider operations. If they survived the current attack, the powerful ships would soon be on their way into the North Atlantic, to seek out the Allies' ships and send them to the bottom of the sea.

But Haberditz, to his great relief, would not be going with them.

Haberditz was a dashingly handsome man, tall and broad, square-jawed, with the perfect Aryan long head and blond hair. His blue eyes sparkled with intelligence, although the glint in them was often hard and calculating. A veteran of the Great War and member of the Nazi party, he was one of the highest-ranking officers in the German Navy. He searched the black skies for the British aircraft, wanting more than anything to run downstairs, deep inside the bowels of the ship where he'd be relatively safe.

At one time in his life he'd been a man of action, reveling in the thrill of naval engagements. Now he preferred a gambling hall with a beautiful prostitute draped on each shoulder. His harrowing escape from death at the battle of Jutland toward the end of the Great War had cured him of the arrogance of heroism. In the *Bismarck* or *Tirpitz*, whose hulls had already been laid, he might have felt a measure of security. At the moment, however, the British Navy was still the most formidable force in the world. Would *Scharnhorst*, a heavy battle cruiser, stand a chance against the likes of *Repulse* or the mighty *Hood*?

Lutjens was an altogether different type of man, and Haberditz had nothing but contempt for him. Lutjens wanted to be a hero, like a Greek demigod out of mythology. Because he wasn't a member of the Party, however, he would never be given a major fleet command. That duty would remain in the capable hands of Admiral Wilhelm Marschall, who flew his flag on *Gneisenau*. Haberditz liked Marschall even less than Lutjens. Cursing his bad luck, he grabbed a pair of binoculars off a hook and scanned the opaque skies.

Then the flak batteries opened up, and the night came alive with the sound of gunfire. A great dark shape appeared briefly in a break in the clouds, followed by a whistling of bombs.

On Board the Wellington

"Five minutes," came Will Polk's voice, disembodied and nearly drowned by the roar of the engines, but then Weisz felt his calloused hand firmly squeezing his shoulder.

Weisz roused himself, rubbing his eyes. It seemed he'd just boarded the plane. He felt hollow and unreal, as if he were still dreaming. He unbuckled his seat belt and stood up in a crouch, holding a stanchion, the vibrating deck insubstantial beneath his feet. Somewhere far below was the Elbe estuary with half the German Navy in it. Butterflies danced in his stomach, and for a bad moment he felt sick. He took a couple of deep breaths.

The flak batteries opened up on them, spotlights swiveling, seeking to catch the planes in their glare, brilliant flashes of light on the ground and in the air as the guns hammered away. The plane bucked and shuddered as the captain took evasive action.

An explosion to the rear nearly knocked Weisz off his feet. He glanced back, seeing flames. Grabbing a fire extinguisher from a bracket on the bulkhead, he rushed past the bombardier to the tail section, pointing the extinguisher at the fire and squirting foam. The flight surgeon pushed past him, ignoring the flames, heading for the gunner in the rear turret.

Weisz went back to the jump hole. Polk was checking his gear. He straightened and clapped Weisz on the back. "Better assume the position, laddy," he said over the din, a friendly smile on his face.

Another hail of flak came at them, then fell off as the Messerschmitts attacked, knifing into their formation, guns blazing. The captain jerked the plane all over the sky. Weisz staggered, grabbing an overhead pipe. They were nearly over their target, the shipworks in the harbor on the Elbe estuary. Somewhere far below lurked powerful battle cruisers and their support vessels, and near them the fuel and supply dumps.

Suddenly the plane went into a dive, leaving Weisz's stomach behind. Were they going down? Then the pilot just as abruptly leveled off at a much lower altitude. The bombardier, gazing intently through his sights, loosed the rack of bombs, which fell in a whistling stream out of the belly of the plane.

"Your turn, young fellow!" cried Polk. He opened the jump hatch to a rush of freezing air. Weisz could hear the explosions following the silent blossoms of fire lighting the harbor and the streets of Wilhelmshaven, fires erupting in the warehouses and the older wooden buildings. He saw a Hampden tumble down out of the sky and hit the ground, going up in a gigantic ball of flame.

Polk clapped him on the back again. "Give my regards to Adolf," he shouted, his lips an inch from Weisz's ear.

Weisz gave him a thumb's up and took a step forward to jump just as another explosion buffeted the plane. He tumbled backwards to the deck.

Weisz turned over and got to his knees, stunned, staring out a gaping hole in the side of the plane, Polk nearby, sprawled in flames. Weisz crawled over to him, slapping at the fire with his hands and putting it out. He grabbed the man's shirt and tugged at it. "Will! Are you all right?" he shouted as the plane tilted at a crazy angle.

Then he saw that Polk's arm was gone, blown away just below the shoulder.

Rising, Weisz grabbed a bench to steady himself against the shifts and jerks of evasive action. "Flight surgeon!" he yelled against the din. "Man down!"

He dropped back to his knees and ripped open Polk's shirt, then with his pocketknife he cut a strip of fabric for a tourniquet.

Polk opened his eyes and stared wildly at him. "What the devil are you doing, Weisz? Get your arse out the hatch!"

The flight surgeon was still working on the rear gunner. Another Messerschmitt roared by, a staccato burst from its machine gun stitching a line of holes in the fuselage. Weisz said desperately, "I can't leave you like this, Will."

Polk's blood-spattered face twisted into a demonic grin. "Like bloody hell!" He stuck his hand on Weisz's chest and gave him a terrific one-armed heave.

Weisz, taken by surprise, fell backwards through the open jump hole. He cried out in terror as cold air rushed past him. Frantically he felt for the ripcord as he plummeted down. Locating it, he remembered to count slowly to five before pulling it. His parachute's black canopy issued from the pack and beat the air for several breathless instants before deploying above him, filling up with a jolt. He floated earthwards, the city in flames stretched out beneath him.

A Messerschmitt flew at him out of nowhere, machine guns firing. Passing him, its wash pulled him laterally and nearly twisted his lines as the plane went after a crippled British bomber. Weisz drifted down, hoping that any other German aircraft, even if they saw him, would choose to ignore a single paratrooper in favor of bigger game. To his left he could see capital ships outlined in their own antiaircraft fire. Even some of the big guns were engaged, fire and smoke belching from their gaping maws like dragons out of a monstrous fable.

He'd wanted to come down in open fields south of the town but hadn't jumped at the right moment and was heading for the water. Flak filled the air, shells bursting all around him as the ragged formation of RAF bombers began turning around, peeling off to the north and south, heading back toward their bases in England, hounded by the German fighters. Dangling from cords in the air, he envied the survivors, returning to the relative safety of London.

A terrific explosion deafened him, a hot pain lancing through his lower left leg. He cried out. Burning debris fell all around him, hitting his canopy. Craning his neck, he saw his parachute had caught fire. He felt his pant leg getting wet and sticky with his blood. Pulling on his lines, he tried to angle his drop further to the east. He had to get down to the ground; he couldn't tell how serious his wound was. The blood was filling his boot and his chute was beginning to luff. He plummeted downwards.

He hit the frigid waters of the Elbe hard, the wind sailing out of him. He floundered, gulping water and choking as the burning chute collapsed into the water, extinguishing the fire. The parachute lines went around him, his arms caught in a tangle of cords. He fought them, going underwater. Where was his other knife? Had he dropped it on the plane? He felt his belt, found the sheath, but it was buttoned down tight. He sunk lower into the water, holding his breath as he unsnapped the cover. Taking it out, he started cutting lines, his lungs hot and straining against the confines of his rib cage, ready to burst.

Free, he kicked hard, reaching the surface and pulling in a welcome gulp of air. Wrestling off his backpack and dragging it behind him, he swam towards shore in an improvised sidestroke. Above him the battle still raged.

Reaching the rocky shore, he stripped off his pants and checked the wound. A small piece of shrapnel had penetrated his left calf and it hurt like hell. He probed the puncture with the tip of his knife, gritting his teeth, working a fragment of metal out of his flesh and flicking it away. Cleaning the wound with river water, he applied an antibiotic powder and taped it up.

He stripped off his flight suit and buried it. Pulling a set of civilian clothes out of a waterproof pack, he dressed. He heard patrols going by on the road on the rise above the beach. Standing, he tested his leg and found he could walk, although he limped. He moved carefully along the beach for half an hour before climbing unobtrusively up to street level. He'd spend the rest of the night somewhere in Wilhelmshaven, then make his way to Hamburg where he had contacts. Soon thereafter he'd go to Berlin and begin scouting his targets.

The Walther PPK felt reassuring inside the inner pocket of his coat. He hoped he wouldn't have to use it against civilians, but knew he might not always have a choice. He thought of Will and gritted his teeth, cursing under his breath. His friend was probably already dead, maybe the whole crew: more blood on Hitler's head, more death to avenge.

Scharnhorst

The English bombers were phantoms in the dark skies, even under the cloud cover, revealing their presence via an angry buzzing that filled Admiral Haberditz with dread.

The flak guns and lesser caliber weapons opened up, and the din was terrific. The bombers came in low, boldly ignoring the barrage, discharging their deadly payloads. Bombs dropped all around the two battle cruisers, one explosion after another sending towering geysers of water into the air.

One of the Wellingtons, hit by flak, plummeted into the sea, exploding as it hit the water. But the other planes kept coming, circling around for another pass as Haberditz cringed on the bridge and cursed the inaccuracy of the gunners.

A fresh wave of bombers came, again greeted by a hailstorm of flak. One of the bombers roared low over *Scharnhorst* and was shredded by antiaircraft fire, crashing in the sea on the opposite side of the ship before exploding. Haberditz could feel the awful heat of the flames, even at the distance of a soccer field. He breathed a sigh of relief when he saw that several German planes had joined in the defense, screaming into battle against the remaining British planes, braving flak from their own ships and that of the coastal batteries.

The pilot of one of the Whitleys managed to bring his wounded plane around, thick smoke issuing from the right engine, its blunt, blocky nose drooping down. As Haberditz watched in horror, the pilot started a suicide run straight at the bridge.

Haberditz cried out and dove for cover. The gritty Brits sprayed the bridge with machine gun fire, then pulled up at the last possible instant, releasing a bomb which arced down onto the fore turrets.

The bomb bounced off the deck, failing to explode, and skipped over the side. The Whitley barely cleared the bridge, roaring over Haberditz who was cowering with arms thrown up over his head and neck, curled very nearly into a fetal position. The plane careened off to the right, twisted as the other engine burst into flames, and plummeted into the sea.

A moment later the attack was over. The Heinkels and Messerschmitts disappeared over the North Sea, still pursuing the surviving British planes. Haberditz stood up and dusted himself off, straightening his cap and clearing his throat, hoping no one had noticed him crouching down on the deck. It only made sense to take cover, but he regretted that it may have appeared cowardly. He stepped over to Lutjens, who was still standing, unflustered, staring at the fires through his damned binoculars.

"A good exercise," Haberditz said, forcing his voice to be cool and steady. He wanted to appear at ease, although inwardly he felt a terrible need to get off the ship before the British returned. "The gun crews need all the practice they can get."

Lutjens turned to him and nodded, his face dour. "Yes, of course." He looked away a moment, clearing his throat, a trifle nervous. "There are certain issues that may require careful attention. With your party connections, and presence in Berlin..."

He trailed off, looking at Haberditz in a vague, questioning kind of way. Inwardly Haberditz exulted: Lutjens was going to ask him for a favor! "Yes, Vice Admiral?"

Lutjens cleared his throat again. "As I was saying, your party connections could be useful in communicating important information to the right people. I would like to suggest that I have the requisite expertise to lead the fleet successfully in major operations throughout the Atlantic. At some point it may be appropriate to make use of that expertise."

Haberditz nodded sagely. "Of course. I will keep that in mind the next time I speak with Grand Admiral Raeder."

"Admiral Marschall, while a competent fleet commander..."

Haberditz shook his head and held up a hand. "Please, say no more. I perfectly understand. I'll see what I can do."

"You always were more adroit in such matters. I thank you for your consideration."

Haberditz gave a self-deprecating chuckle. "Don't thank me. I'm only doing my duty, and finding the best fleet commanders is one of the most important of those duties." He paused, pretending to reflect. "The *Bismarck* and *Tirpitz* will be available in a few months, perhaps early next year. We need to speed up their development. They'll need a good fleet commander, although a little more experience with battle cruisers like *Scharnhorst* and *Gneisenau* might be in order."

"Yes, well, Admiral Marschall is in command at the moment."

"At the moment, yes. As for the future, we'll have to see." He shrugged and changed the subject. "Getting the ships ready is the most important thing."

Lutjens almost smiled. "Your expertise, Admiral, has always been overseeing their construction. That's more important than sailing them."

"You're much too modest," Haberditz replied. "But I admit I will envy you, sending our enemies to Hades out on the North Atlantic."

"With *Bismarck* and *Tirpitz* we'll be able to challenge the British Home Fleet. When that day arrives, I hope to be called upon to render service."

"A message for you, Admiral," said a dark-featured young sailor, handing a yellow piece of paper to Haberditz.

Haberditz frowned, nearly tearing the message out of the sailor's hand, dismissing him abruptly. He did a double take, trying to read the sailor's nametag, not catching it.

"Who was that man?" he demanded irritably after the sailor had departed.

Lutjens was distracted, looking across the bay toward *Gneisenau*. "Josef Freiburg," he said over his shoulder.

"You should have him dismissed."

Lutjens turned towards him and raised an eyebrow. "Why is that? Did he offend you?"

Haberditz's handsome lips curled ever so slightly. "I thought that should be obvious."

Lutjens nodded curtly. "I'm sorry, but that's one directive which I'm not interested in implementing. I have no desire to lose excellent seamen for political reasons."

"He won't hold up in the pitch of battle. And he'll poison the rest of the crew with his very presence. Morale is critical, you know, and a Jew..."

Lutjens tightened his lips, his eyes darkening. "Thank you, Admiral. I'll take your recommendation under consideration. Now, if you'll excuse me..."

He turned away, and Haberditz wondered whether he'd made a mistake in obliquely agreeing to arrange Lutjens' advance to full command of a major fleet detachment. The man didn't seem to understand the facts of racial differences, nor the trouble that lesser breeds had caused the Reich and other countries throughout the centuries. They had controlled the banks, the flow of currency, and they'd bled the Volk dry since the time of the Romans. Strangely enough, these same Jewish bankers had financed the Bolsheviks! Many good Germans blamed the Jews for Germany's defeat in the Great War, and Haberditz had no doubt they were guilty as charged. The situation had become intolerable, and he quietly thanked God that Hitler had taken firm steps to put them in their place.

Haberditz himself occasionally lent his hand to the effort. When unions had threatened to cause trouble in the shipyards, he'd spoken to his friend Himmler and the SS had arranged some accidents. One leader had been beaten to a pulp, another had suffered a broken arm. A third ended up dead after a brawl in a bar, his throat slit. On another occasion a rival Jewish-led shipping company tried to steal a contract by spuriously underbidding. Haberditz set up the company vice president with a beautiful prostitute, and when the man succumbed to the woman's charms, obtained photographs and blackmailed him. Meanwhile, a gang of hoodlums set upon the president's teenage son and gave him a sound thrashing. The company's bid was subsequently withdrawn. It was gratifying that the elimination of one or two loudmouths often silenced the rest, bringing them back to discipline and service.

Later, of course, the company closed down completely, their chief officers and families deported from the country, their assets seized and put in the hands of patriots. Rather harsh, but that was the way it ought to be. That was right, that was German. The war effort was too important to be derailed by malcontents and mongrel races.

Lutjens stood over at the railing, peering through his binoculars as if glued to them. Haberditz frowned at him, snorted, then ripped open the telegram and began reading. It was from the Reichsmarschall of Industry, Albert Speer, who was also a personal friend of his family. He was a good man, technically highly competent and extremely rich. The war was making him richer.

RETURN TO BERLIN STOP MEETING WITH H AND THE CLUB HIGHEST PRIORITY STOP

More antiaircraft fire started up as one of the crews began testing their guns. Haberditz took out a gold-plated pocket lighter and lit the communiqué on fire, dropping it to the deck. "H" would be either Otto Hahn or Werner Heisenberg. It probably wasn't Hahn, because he was fainthearted about force and might not cooperate. Heisenberg, on the other hand, had been thoroughly investigated by the SS, charged with treason and homosexuality, and would have been executed had it not been for undue influence. Heisenberg's mother, it turned out, was an old friend of Himmler's mother, and after the ladies had a little heart-to-heart over tea Himmler had dismissed the charges.

Still, the scrutiny had scared Heisenberg badly, so he would be less likely to cause problems. Although he wasn't a Nazi, he was a German patriot who wanted to help win the war.

For Haberditz, the presence of his wife Bertha was the only bad thing about going to Berlin. She had been beautiful at one time, and some still saw her that way, although Haberditz did not. She was very straitlaced, a traditional German wife, and he found her boring. She cooperated in bed to the extent of spreading her legs, but that was all. Maybe he could sneak into town and stay with one of his girlfriends. He thought of Marjot's thick red lips and eager thighs, and smiled. She played rough; she knew what he needed.

He turned and saw Lutjens on the phone, calmly talking with the gunners when he ought to be screaming at them for their incompetence during the engagement. They had taken much too long finding their range, and it was only a matter of luck that the bomb on the foredeck hadn't exploded and crippled the ship. It was obvious Lutjens understood very little about discipline. In war, as in love, you couldn't afford to let anyone off the hook.

No, Lutjens was soft, and perhaps it was better that he would be sent out on one of the first forays, fodder for the British gun crews. There was bigger game afoot, maybe even a way to win the war, and it had nothing to do with Naval engagements and everything to do with the latest scientific discoveries, with German science. The key player was Heisenberg, with experimental support from Hahn if he would cooperate. It was a shame they'd allowed Lise Meitner to escape the country, but she wasn't a German, and in addition was part Jewess so it was just as well. Hahn, at any rate, had done all the truly important work; she'd been little more than a laboratory assistant. But they were scientists, a very odd group, usually blind to political realities, always fascinated by things of no interest to anyone else. It was hard to keep them focused on practical matters. Haberditz had to get them to speed up construction of the reactors and then get working on the *wunderwaffen*.

Thinking about powerful weapons somehow reminded him of Heisenberg's assistant, Lieserl Meier, and he wondered whether she'd be at the meeting. She was a beauty, that one, and according to Heisenberg she was dedicated completely to science, unmarried and uninterested in men.

If she were a lesbian, that would make seducing her a challenge. More likely she was simply frigid and needed someone worldly and knowledgeable to open her up. Haberditz loved a challenge, especially when the objective was beautiful and intelligent. Stupid women like his wife left him bored and impotent. If the assistant were in Berlin when he arrived, perhaps he'd forego his frolic with Marjot in favor of wooing her. A Nobel Laureate protégé would make a fine addition to his collection of conquests.

Lutjens was coming back over, obviously wanting to discuss the attack further. Haberditz looked away, hands clasped behind his back, and wondered how soon he could get off the ship and back on solid ground again. Thinking about Meier made him eager to get going. And he wanted to arrive in Berlin in plenty of time to see the Fuehrer before the meeting with Heisenberg and Speer. Hitler, who loved big warships, would be happy to get a personal report on the preparations for the forthcoming attacks on British shipping. And possibly, if he were in the right mood, he might acquiesce to supplementary funding for the secret project, and so instruct Speer.

"One of the flak crews had a jammed gun," Lutjens explained as he walked up.

Haberditz snorted. "And the others couldn't hit crippled geese with a shotgun. You're lucky you had nothing worse to face than those clumsy bombers. If they'd been carrying torpedoes we'd all be swimming right now."

Lutjens nodded soberly. "The armor plating will be stronger on *Bismarck*. The torpedoes will be ineffective against them. But *Scharnhorst's* speed, on the other hand, will allow excellent evasive maneuvers on the open sea."

Haberditz's lips turned down. Lutjens was always so damned serious, it was like talking to a textbook. "I'm glad that you're so confident."

"In the near term the British are obviously far superior," Lutjens went on. "But in two years time we'll have a fighting chance."

Haberditz clapped him on the shoulder. "When I'm dining in the finest

Berlin restaurants and drinking champagne with my mistress, it will warm my heart to think of you out there on the North Atlantic, eating ship food and breaking icicles off your lower lip."

"Just doing my duty," Lutjens replied evenly.

"Yes, of course. Striking a blow for the Volk. Thank God for that."

"I depend on you, Admiral."

"Yes, I know. And on your flak gunners."

"We have little to fear against the bombers. Their accuracy is poor."

"Unlike the Stukas..."

"That's one of our advantages," said Lutjens, nodding. He was smiling slightly, an easy, superior smile born of dedication to duty and competence, a smile that made Haberditz hate him even more fiercely.

"I don't imagine the British will take very long to emulate us."

Lutjens shrugged slightly. "It doesn't matter. We've shown our defenses are adequate. With *Bismarck* or *Tirpitz* we will be invulnerable to air attack."

"Yes, of course." Haberditz was familiar with the thirteen and a half inches of hardened steel armor the new ships would carry below the waterline, designed to withstand a direct hit from a torpedo. But he wasn't planning to be on either vessel, and his most pressing concern was getting off *Scharnhorst* before the British came back. "You'll have to excuse me, Admiral, I have important business to attend to back in Berlin."

Lutjens saluted him smartly. "Of course." He gestured at a nearby sailor. "This man will see you to the launch. I hope you found today's performance satisfactory."

"Yes, indeed. I shall so inform Grand Admiral Raeder."

Lutjens nodded only slightly, but he was pleased. "Thank you, Admiral."

Haberditz followed the sailor down to the launch, and soon was on his way back to land, feeling much better now that he was off the ship. It was like a big, floating target, and unlike *Bismarck*, had relatively little armor.

He thought of Marjot again and his breath quickened: there was nothing like infidelity to get the blood moving.

Einstein's Daughter: The Story of Lieserl

Chapter Two

Kaiser Wilhelm Institute, Berlin, March 4, 1940

Werner Heisenberg rose from his chair confidently, striding to the front of the conference room with easy grace. At thirty-eight, he was tall and still athletic, with reddish-blond curly hair and boyish good looks, every bit the Aryan. He exuded a dry warmth, however, and he usually sported a guarded twinkle in his eyes and a touch of arrogance on his lips. Most scientists considered him the best theoretical physicist in the world after Einstein, but in fact he was younger and more innovative, creating new fields of knowledge such as quantum mechanics, while Einstein dabbled around in abstruse mathematics, looking for a unified field theory using old-fashioned ideas.

Standing before an audience of about a dozen military men and the same number of scientists and technical personnel, he was a commanding and dynamic presence, and Lieserl Meier couldn't take her eyes off him. She'd studied with him for a short time at the University of Gottingen until he'd left for a position in Leipzig. Later she became his assistant at the Kaiser Wilhelm Institute. To her, he was the greatest man on Earth after Einstein, and on occasion one of the most infuriating.

"I'd like to begin our discussion today with a review of our progress towards a nuclear reactor," he began in his warm and dry voice, with perfectly modulated enunciation. A large drawing pad stood propped on an easel at the front of the room, and he turned the flap back, revealing the first diagram. "As you can see, the B-1, from our Berlin series of experiments, failed to perform up to our expectations, as did the B-2, although in that case the neutron activity was considerably higher."

He went on for some time in a purely technical lecture, flipping through the drawing pad with its arcane diagrams and dense mathematical symbols, discussing the difficulties of separating U-235 and U-238, hinting at the possibility of finding other isotopes or even new elements that might also be fissionable. It was all very low key, with the military men in the audience yawning in their seats and in some cases actually nodding off.

Finally a bookishly handsome, rather dark gentleman cleared his throat, the industrialist Albert Speer, one of Hitler's closest confidants. He was a slender, athletic man, a former architect, with the mannerisms of a clerk and an unassuming air that belied his high intelligence and awesome temporal power. Impeccably dressed and clean-shaven, balding and wearing glasses in functional thin metal frames, he stood up and waited patiently for Heisenberg to complete his thought and recognize him.

"In your opinion, Dr. Heisenberg," he said in his precise, tenor voice, "is there any near-term possibility of obtaining a very rapid disintegration of uranium, a chain reaction sufficient to produce a large explosion?" He sat modestly back down.

Lieserl held her breath. Heisenberg, to his credit, remained completely calm. And there wasn't any reason why he should be nervous; he was as far advanced beyond them, intellectually, as they were beyond small children, except for Speer, who was university-trained and very sharp. Yet there was so much to lose, all from a choice of words. Too little promise, and Speer would dismiss them, disperse them to factories that built conventional war machines, perhaps even send some of them to the front. Too much promise could turn out just as badly: with sufficient resources, they could build a weapon of awesome destructive power, delivering the world into Hitler's hands.

"There is most certainly a possibility," Heisenberg said with measured confidence. "Perhaps I could even go so far as to say a likelihood."

General Keitel, who had been nodding off, perked up. "How soon?" he said in a hoarse voice.

Heisenberg shook his head. "That's impossible to say. Unless massive resources are given us..."

The general interrupted him. "And if these massive resources were made available, could you produce for us a *wunderwaffen* in, let's say, nine months?"

Heisenberg smiled in a way that was nearly condescending, a fault that he'd never succeeded in mastering. "This is science, General. No one can guarantee anything."

"A guess, please," insisted Keitel. "Surely you can hazard a guess."

"If I were forced to make a guess based on our present state of development, then that guess would have to be 'no'. Nine months is not sufficient time for the conduct of such a project. We're still understanding the fundamental physics: once that's complete, we can go on to practical applications."

Speer rose deferentially from his seat again, holding his pen up as if to stroke a word in the air. "Practical applications such as a reactor. A reactor could be ready fairly soon, isn't that so, Doctor?"

Heisenberg nodded. "There is most assuredly every reason to anticipate that our series of neutron multiplication experiments will eventually lead to a power plant. I am very ably assisted, particularly by Drs. Hahn and Meier, and have every expectation of success."

"Within nine months," repeated Speer.

Again the slight smile came to his lips. "That, I still cannot guarantee. It's possible, of course, much more so than a weapon."

"I see," murmured Speer. "One more question, Doctor. How much money do you need?"

"Need?" Heisenberg's eyebrows rose. "That depends."

"How much money do you need now to assure rapid progress, whether or not you arrive at a reactor or a bomb?"

Heisenberg glanced down a moment, then looked up and said, "Half a million marks."

Speer exchanged a glance with Keitel, both men frowning. Looking back at Heisenberg, he said, "I can give you much more than that."

Heisenberg looked a trifle flustered, covering his confusion with a smile.

"That's very generous of you, Herr Speer, but half a million marks will be more than sufficient for the next few months."

Speer leveled a shrewd, appraising look at the physicist. "You'd have no use for, say, fifty million marks? Or even one hundred million? I can get that much for you. Easily."

"Well, naturally that would be wonderful, but in point of fact we're still engaged in preliminary experiments. We're not ready to scale it up, yet. So in the meantime, half a million marks will do handsomely."

Speer nodded. "If that's what you want, you shall have it." He sat back down in his chair, looking disappointed.

Lieserl watched the industrialist curiously out of the corner of her eye, wondering at the exchange, at his obvious displeasure at the figure, a low one for a man used to dealing in hundreds of millions, even billions of marks. Speer ran the war industry, and at a word from him factories would spring up overnight. It was obvious to Lieserl that he'd been looking for another answer and had been disappointed at not getting it.

Heisenberg, she decided, had played out the exchange adroitly, holding out promise, but putting the fruit of the work just beyond the horizon: close enough to maintain interest, too far to make it seem relevant to the war effort.

Heisenberg ended his talk and took a couple half-hearted questions from the floor before the meeting broke up. Most of the military brass left quickly, looking unhappy and put out. Lieserl wasn't sure about Heisenberg's politics: one day he spoke quietly of the terrible responsibility they'd all bear if they were successful, the next day he wistfully hoped for German victory. He walked a fine line, trying to save as many German scientists as he could from service at the front. Hitler's generals wanted results. They wanted a reactor that would make the refueling of ships and trains, perhaps even airplanes, unnecessary. They wanted a *wunderwaffen*, a bomb using uranium or some similar radioactive substance, a weapon that would be capable of leveling cities. And Lieserl had no doubt Hitler would use such a weapon for exactly that purpose, starting with London.

By working with Heisenberg she was walking the same fine line: she had to produce results, but at the same time keep the power of the atom out of Hitler's hands. She wasn't a Nazi, and never would be. She could never agree with what he was doing to Germany and its people. The very fact that Hitler's chief scientist, Stark, denigrated relativity as Jewish science was sufficient reason for rejecting everything about the party and the man behind it. To Lieserl, Einstein was the greatest man who had ever lived. How was it possible to deny the truth of his brilliant discoveries just because he was Jewish?

A last small group remained in the lecture room, Heisenberg talking privately at some length with Speer and a very handsome officer of the Kriegsmarine. Lieserl waited patiently a few steps away, gazing out the window at the manicured lawns on the grounds of the institute, thinking about her calculations. She was a tall, willowy blond with an oval face and great dark eyes that were powerful and full of dreams. Her chin was strong, her nose flaring, and although she was forty she looked a decade younger. In contrast to her striking looks, she wore a rather severe gray skirt and coat, an ensemble that was quite conservative but which somehow managed to accentuate her fine breasts, of modest proportions but elegantly shaped beneath her white silk blouse.

Heisenberg turned and looked her way. "Dr. Meier, would you kindly join us for a moment?"

She walked across the polished wooden floor and joined him next to the fireplace, where flames leaped warmly. "Yes, Werner?"

"I'd like you to meet Admiral Franz Haberditz, one of the highest-ranking officers in the German Navy. He has strongly endorsed our work on the reactor and supports continuing our funding for the B series of reactors."

"I'm very glad to hear it," she replied archly, appraising him in a critical glance. "Does the Admiral enjoy the confidence of the Chancellor, as does Herr Speer?"

Speer replied for Haberditz with crisp, understated irony. "The Admiral and I have sufficient influence between us, I believe, Herr Doctor. We're practically members of his family."

Lieserl's upper lip curled slightly. "A rather odd family, I'm sure, although I imagine membership in it is worth quite a few Reichsmarks."

Heisenberg cast her a sharp glance, and Speer stared at her with his dark eyes, quietly offended. The ensuing awkward silence magnified the crackles coming from the fireplace.

Haberditz stepped in smoothly. "Hitler has his preferences, and some may occasionally find issue with one or another of his views. But he's our leader, and one way or another we must all work with him and support him. Provide guidance, if you will, for the good of the country."

"You're a silver-tongued devil, aren't you," Lieserl replied with a sly smile to soften the jibe.

"I believe I know a number of other ladies who would beg to agree with that remark," joked Speer, and he laughed shortly, the offending remark forgotten.

"Thank you for the observation, Albert," said Haberditz grandly. "Your unflagging sense of humor is surpassed only by your lack of discretion."

"May I suggest," murmured Heisenberg quietly, "that we adjourn to Herr Goering's country estate? We can continue our discussions in a more informal setting, and perhaps obtain some insights from the Field Marshal. Shall we, Albert?"

"By all means."

Outside it was near sunset, and a soft, fine rain was falling, cooling off the air. Speer's chauffeur was waiting patiently next to a black Mercedes. Haberditz, although he had his own car and driver, nonetheless attached himself to Heisenberg and Meier, arranging for his driver to follow. They roared off through the wet streets of Berlin, following Speer, who had an escort of SS officers on motorcycle. Soon they were on the autobahn, heading out of

Berlin to the northeast.

Haberditz sat in the passenger seat up front with Heisenberg, smoking one of his Turkish cigarettes, talking animatedly about the warships under construction in the shipyards of Hamburg while filling the car with rich, sweet-smelling smoke. "It's only a matter of time before our fleet is superior, at least in quality, to that of the British," he said. "The *Bismarck* and *Tirpitz* will be christened in another year."

"What about the *Graf Zeppelin*?" asked Heisenberg.

Haberditz shook his head and sighed. "Unfortunately, Goering is maneuvering to cancel it. Claims the Navy doesn't need an air corps, conflict of interest or some such."

"The British have several carriers. Surely that's argument enough."

"Yes, I certainly agree with you. Their carriers will be quite effective. Not against *Bismarck*, perhaps. Armor's too thick." He puffed on his cigarette, the coal glowing in the darkness. "Goering thinks he knows everything, and he has altogether too much influence with the Fuehrer." He glanced at Heisenberg. "Once you get your reactor working, on the other hand..."

"A bit speculative at this point, I'm afraid."

"Come now, professor, you're much too modest. I have full confidence in your abilities. You are, after all, the premier physicist in the world."

"Except for Einstein," said Lieserl from the back seat. "And, of course, Bohr."

Heisenberg glanced over his shoulder. "Bohr is a deep thinker, I'll grant him that."

"As for Einstein," Haberditz said, "isn't it true he hasn't produced much in the way of new physics for nearly two decades?"

"Yes," Lieserl said. "That's true. He's a formidable physicist, nonetheless. Even his failures are far more noteworthy than most theoreticians' successes."

"I would have to agree with that," said Heisenberg. "Although it's also true he's gone off on his own track. His view of the quantum, for example."

"The foremost *Jewish* physicist," supplied Haberditz. "That you could grant him without any question. Brilliant, perhaps, but not in the class of someone such as, say, Stark, or yourself, for that matter."

Lieserl snorted. "Stark is an idiot."

Haberditz shifted in his seat so he could look back at Lieserl. "One certainly knows where one stands when you're around. And Stark isn't as bad as you say. He did win the Nobel, after all."

"You wouldn't know it from talking to him. Or rather, you'd hear it with his every other breath, all hot air and past glory."

Haberditz smiled pleasantly at her. "Honest to a fault. But that can have its advantages. What is your honest assessment of our chances for a reactor, Dr. Meier? Could it be ready in time for installation in the *Bismarck*?"

"Professor Heisenberg has already accurately assessed the situation, Admiral. We don't even have access to sufficient amounts of heavy water, now that the Norwegians have cut us off."

"*Norsk Hydro*, yes. Well, that situation will change in the near future, I believe. They're hoarding an important resource, and that can't be tolerated." Haberditz took a last drag on his cigarette, stubbing it out in the ashtray. "If you are successful, well, you will be the envy of every scientist in the world. And I can guarantee that our influence on the course of war policy would be quite strong, as a consequence. Wouldn't you agree, Dr. Meier?"

"As a woman I have little interest in politics, particularly the politics of war."

Haberditz nodded judiciously. "Yes, of course. War is man's estate, and rightly so. And if I may say so, you are far too intelligent and beautiful to serve as cannon fodder in a blitzkrieg."

Lieserl didn't deign to thank him for the compliment. A silence fell over them as Heisenberg drove rapidly through the country northeast of Berlin, following Speer's car and the SS escort.

The Goering Estate, named Carinhall after Carin, Goering's tragic, deceased first wife, was located on the Schorf Heath, a rolling Prussian terrain of forest and lake that stretched almost all the way to the Baltic Sea. The estate was at the top of a large bluff overlooking one of the lakes, *Dolln See*. A tall, masonry wall surrounded the house, which was guarded by squads of air force troops and antiaircraft emplacements. Security guards at the front gate checked them carefully before allowing them to proceed onto the property. A curving gravel drive ran through spectacular rows of oaks along the lake and up to an imposing Bavarian palace built around an immense Norse hunting lodge with thatched roof. Oversized, ornate buildings squatted like giants among the opulent gardens, fountains, and sculptures.

Heisenberg pulled up in front of the mansion, which was fronted with fluted marble pillars of Greek tradition. Footmen in gaudy gold and green outfits stepped forward to open the car doors.

Haberditz glanced at Lieserl. "I take it you've never been to the Field Marshal's home before."

"No, I haven't. It's magnificent, although overwrought." She couldn't help but be impressed despite knowing that Goering had built it by soliciting payoffs from the armaments industry and by looting the German treasury.

"He throws the most incredible parties here," Haberditz went on. "Last Christmas he entertained no fewer than four hundred guests. No one felt crowded. Every time you turned around a servant was offering you something."

"It's a shame we can't use one of the buildings for a laboratory," Heisenberg said with a slight smile.

"Get that reactor working and you'll have all the laboratories you could ever dream of," Haberditz replied. He leveled an annoyed, penetrating stare at the scientist. "Which reminds me: why didn't you take Speer up on his offer of additional funding? He was practically handing you a blank check."

"I could have," Heisenberg admitted, "but if I had nothing to show for it after nine months, I would have soon been digging trenches on the western front. And you'd have been running the harbor police in Danzig."

Haberditz grunted in displeasure. "Never, ever, turn down money for any reason. Tell them what they want to hear and make excuses later, if necessary. That's the most important rule of all. Now if you run short I'll have to wheedle some out of the *Fuehrer*."

The footmen opened the car doors for them. They got out and joined Speer and several other recently arrived guests on the front portico. Speer was smoking a cigarette, giving quiet directions to the servants, smiling and shaking hands with new arrivals.

"Did you bring Goering any good champagne, tonight?" Haberditz asked.

"For you and the Field Marshal, nothing but the best," Speer replied. He made a grand gesture toward the imposing entry to the mansion. "Shall we?"

The spacious entry hall of Goering's home, graced with Van Goghs and Cezannes, opened into a magnificent ballroom, complete with crystal chandeliers sparkling with hundreds of lights. The floors were a checkerboard of large, black and white squares of Italian marble, and at the far end of the room a small ensemble of musicians played a piece by Bach. A vast wall of glass overlooked the *Dolln See*, a backdrop for the cream of Berlin society, elegantly dressed and dancing to the music. Numerous sculptures, including a Rodin, stood in small galleries about the room, and on one wall was a massive fresco of Europe.

An imperious, obese man dressed in a Roman toga, jeweled sandals, and sporting a laurel wreath was holding forth not far from a punch bowl and buffet. He was confident and loud, beaming and too sure of himself. Catching sight of Speer and Haberditz as they entered the ballroom, he waved nonchalantly in greeting.

"That's Field Marshal Hermann Goering, the commander of the Luftwaffe," Haberditz told Lieserl. "A very powerful and brilliant man, if somewhat eccentric."

"I know who he is," Lieserl replied sourly. "Somehow his face appears in every newsreel."

"If you should speak to him, be careful what you say, he has a very generous soul but can be ruthless when he takes offense."

"Like any megalomaniac."

Haberditz smiled ruefully. "Please, Doctor, that's precisely what I mean. And you must admit, he's done a great deal for the economic vitality of Germany."

Lieserl nodded grudgingly. "Yes, I must admit that."

"You see, he's not all bad." He turned to Heisenberg and Speer. "I imagine you two have some business to attend to with the Field Marshal."

"Yes, always," replied Speer.

"I won't be gone long," Heisenberg told Lieserl. "I'm hoping to get an opportunity to brief him on the latest developments."

"Certainly," Lieserl said coolly. "Don't concern yourself with me."

"I'll keep Dr. Meier entertained," Haberditz supplied.

Heisenberg and Speer moved off in the direction of Goering and the punch bowl. Lieserl watched them join Goering's entourage, her eyes narrowing as she examined the group. "Who is that jolly-looking fellow Goering is talking to?"

"Oh, him?" Haberditz smiled as if at a private joke. "That's General Ernst Udet, *Reichsfuehrer* of aircraft procurement for the *Luftwaffe*. Speer and Heisenberg are no doubt going to ask him about four-engine bombers. They'd need them, you know, if they are to win the air war against Britain."

"He doesn't look like much of a military man, other than the uniform."

"He isn't, at least not at heart. He was in Goering's squadron in World War I, shot down a lot of enemy planes. After the war was over he went to the United States and became a stunt pilot, doing county fairs, giving rides to children, walking the wings, that sort of thing. Goering calls him the flying clown behind his back. Not very sporting; he does a reasonably good job at his post, I hear. He runs herd over Heinkel and Messerschmitt, and test flies all the new models himself."

"I see. An interesting and charming man."

"If you like airplanes. I personally prefer the great floating fortresses, something big enough to carry that bomb you're working on."

"Reactor," Lieserl corrected him. "We're working on a reactor. A bomb is another order of magnitude more difficult to achieve."

Haberditz shrugged and took a gold case out of an inner pocket, withdrawing a cigarette and tapping the end against the case. "What's a reactor other than a slow bomb? If you can make a reactor you can make a bomb, but you'd probably have to carry it in a ship. It would be far too massive for an airplane."

"Yes, of course. Several tons, as a minimum."

"Oh? That's surely too heavy for a stuka. Although still under development, the Heinkel-177 might just manage it."

Her upper lip curled in distaste. "I seriously doubt it, Admiral. If you'll excuse me, I think I'll get some punch."

Haberditz threw out his right arm in a grand manner. "I'll accompany you, if you don't mind."

She nodded curtly, and Haberditz escorted her to the buffet, where a waiter served them some punch in fluted crystal. Lieserl found the punch too sweet and too strong; it was a mixture of juices heavily spiked with vodka. Goering, spotting them, strode over to get another drink, his retinue drawn slowly along as if by the gravitational force of his great bulk.

"I propose a toast," Goering said loudly. He was a big man, very stout, with a massive head and florid face. He raised his glass in a dramatic flurry of robes, bejeweled rings flashing on his sausage fingers. "To the *Fuehrer*! And to the Fatherland!"

There was a chorus of *heil Hitlers*, and everyone drained their glasses except Lieserl, who stood conspicuously sipping her drink. Goering noticed, and raised one enormous eyebrow, looking at her like a sly ape. "Your drink's too strong, Madame?"

"Stronger than I prefer, yes."

He walked over to her, managing just barely not to waddle, looking her over frankly. "You're one of the scientists, aren't you? Heisenberg's beautiful assistant?"

"Yes." She found him almost charming, like a child who had somehow acquired an adult's body. His large head and fleshy face contributed to the impression.

"Even scientists need a drink now and then, wouldn't you agree, Doctor?"

Lieserl lowered her glass. "Strong drink clouds the reason, which is inimical to scientific investigation."

Goering turned to Heisenberg and assumed a comical, rueful expression. "Is she always this difficult?"

Heisenberg smiled slightly and nodded. "Science requires a certain stubbornness of character. She's quite good, I assure you."

"Good? Yes, of course, but good for what?" Goering looked back at her, his eyes roving over her body with such familiarity and boldness that Lieserl scowled. The Goering child had suddenly grown into a rude and leering teenager. "We could send her to the front; in no time she'd be drinking like a fish. Or should I say, like a Pole!"

The men all laughed politely. Lieserl was on the verge of delivering a blazing retort when she caught a warning look from Heisenberg. She glared at him, but bit her lip and held her peace.

"I can think of others who might do well on the front line." Goering went on, looking meaningfully at Heisenberg. "Particularly if they don't prove themselves useful in other ways."

Heisenberg smiled confidently. "As you know, Field Marshal, we have numerous experiments underway and have every expectation of success."

Goering downed his drink in a gulp, then eyed Heisenberg sourly. "I've heard varying opinions on your progress."

Heisenberg's smile graduated to a studied frown. "May I respectfully suggest that you leave science to the scientists."

Goering hesitated as if he were going to take offense, then made an expansive gesture with his wine glass. "My apologies, Dr. Heisenberg. Science is your job, not mine, and I thank God for that. But my job is destruction. That's all, just destruction, nothing else. I destroy people and I destroy nations. I wish I could say that my *Luftwaffe* and I could do it alone, but alas, we depend on German science. You'll make it easier for all of us, if you would just get your noses out of your beakers and into the bombs. Give me the destructive power, and I will deliver the destruction!"

Haberditz leaned forward. "You won't take England with bombers, alone, Field Marshal. You need the German Navy for that."

Udet chose that moment to speak up, rocking back on his heels as he raised a finger. "With the new aircraft carrier..."

"Which shall never be completed," Goering said brusquely, cutting him off. He looked sternly at Udet. "There's no point in creating a separate naval air force, that would be totally redundant. Wastes valuable resources." He shook his head and held up a pudgy, cautionary finger as if scolding a naughty schoolboy. "Ernst, I thought you understood that. Besides, a sailor wouldn't know what to do with an airplane. With a whore, maybe he'd have some idea, but that's another question!"

Everyone in his retinue laughed, some of them too hard, and Goering joined in with a loud guffaw, pleased with himself, holding his arms out, turning this way and that, sharing the moment.

Haberditz cleared his throat as the laughter subsided. "Surely one or two aircraft carriers are essential. They could carry air power to within easy striking distance of all of England, even within range of their great naval base in Scotland, at Scapa Flow. We have only to complete *Graf Zepelin*, and the proof will follow."

Goering stared at him in surprise, and then his face flushed, and he held up his beefy fist and shook it in Haberditz's face. "For the cost of a carrier, I can build ten thousand *Stuka* and create the most terrible force the world has ever seen, an invincible weapon! And no one, least of all naval commanders of questionable loyalty, could stand in my way!"

"A trifle strong, don't you think, Hermann?" said Speer calmly.

Goering's great head swiveled and he contained a much more powerful outburst, his face reddening with the effort. "These days you have to be strong or they trample you."

Haberditz smiled, conciliatory. "At least I'm a member of the party."

Goering looked back at him and snorted. "Yes. But too many of your fellow officers are not." He rounded on Lieserl. "Forgive me, Doctor, what kind of host am I? I had no wish to bore you with unpleasant political discussions. I also apologize for skipping your meeting this afternoon. I'm afraid I was stalking a rather impressive elk most of the day."

"He has revolutionary programs designed to protect endangered species," offered Heisenberg.

"Does that conservation program include the Jew?" Lieserl asked, her eyebrows arching innocently.

"The *Jew*!" roared Goering. He turned his great bulk, offering the joke to his retinue. "Did you hear *that*? A conservation program for the *Jews*!" He shook with laughter, joined by Speer and several others. Then he turned back to Lieserl and said, "You are indeed a woman of wit, Dr. Meier." He sighed. "As are many of my senior officers, although most are only half right."

A cute, bouncy little girl of about three with blond hair and bright pink cheeks came running over to them, dodging the guests, and Goering lit up when he saw her. "Edda! Edda my darling little girl! What are you doing here?" He reached down and picked her up. "Dr. Meier, have you made the acquaintance of my beautiful daughter?"

"No, I haven't." She offered her hand to the little girl, who grasped a finger and solemnly shook it. "I'm pleased to meet you," Lieserl said with a nod.

Goering kissed the girl on the cheek, and smiled proudly when she kissed him back. "Where is your mother, Edda darling? You know better than to bother Dada when he's working." He looked up abruptly, scanning the room. "Does anyone see Emmy? Emmy!"

A rather plump blond woman with a round face came hurrying across the room. "Edda! What are you doing here? You're supposed to be in bed!"

Goering put the little girl down, gently pushing her. "Go to Mummy, that's a good girl." He turned to Lieserl as the little girl scampered away. "What do you think of her?"

"She's beautiful."

Goering beamed. "I'm the luckiest man alive. After that shot in the groin, it's nothing short of a miracle!"

"I take it you were injured," Lieserl said carefully, amused at Goering's candor.

Goering seemed to swell with pride and exhibitionistic pleasure. "Yes, of course, don't you read? It happened during the *putsch*, way back in the twenties, that fiasco of a revolt that ended with the *Fuehrer* in prison. Some bastard shot me in the groin; I thought I'd be impotent the rest of my life! Thanks to Carin, and now Emmy..."

He broke off in mid sentence and gestured at the fresco on the wall. "Ladies and gentlemen," he said loudly, making it an announcement. "I take it you noticed my map of Europe?"

Heads turned, and the music softened. "There seem to be some inaccuracies," said Heisenberg.

"Conservative projections," Haberditz provided. "Isn't that so, Field Marshal?"

"You are damned right, Admiral. For once." He grinned, his eyes bright and bulging and glassy. Striding over to the wall, he jabbed a bejeweled finger down on Poland, already colored green, the same as Germany. "Poland is ours. Norway and Denmark, no contest, they're ours for the taking if we want them. The Swedes love us already, thank God. I don't know what we'd do without their iron. As for the rest of Western Europe," Goering smiled winningly, "let me just say that if I were a frog, I'd be taking German lessons!"

Heisenberg looked worried, his high brow wrinkling. "I hadn't any idea Denmark was of interest to us."

"They're on the way to Norway, which is critically strategic," supplied Haberditz. "The fjords, you see, would be useful as navy bases in any operations against England."

"Yes. Another good reason why *Graf Zepelin* can lay rusting." He paused, looking his audience over. "Ladies and gentlemen, our lives are going to get much more interesting. That much I can guarantee."

"And what of the east," murmured Haberditz, "and the great Russian Bear?"

Goering stared at him. "Yes, perhaps it will be necessary to deal with him. You won't be much use in that, unless your ships can sail across the steppe."

"I understand you have a treaty with Stalin," said Lieserl.

Goering nodded and waved his hand vaguely. "Yes, of course, a deal with the devil, himself. But at some point somebody will have to teach that Bolshevik bastard a lesson." He turned, arms raised questioningly. "Can any of you brilliant scientists explain to me how England could possibly object to our attacking Russia? Doesn't it make sense they'd take our side in such a struggle?"

A sudden chorus of screams interrupted the music, and Goering craned his neck, looking for the source of the commotion, all eyes following his. Lieserl, shocked, spotted a full-grown female lion just entering the hall.

"Don't worry, don't worry!" Goering called laughingly. "She's perfectly harmless! Besides, she just ate an hour ago!"

The lion loped across the ballroom floor, scattering the guests. She ran up to Goering, jumping up and placing her paws on his chest, inadvertently knocking his wineglass out of his hand as she licked his face. The glass hit the floor and shattered.

"Yes, yes, pussycat!" Goering laughed at all the frigid stares as he petted the lioness, scratching behind her ears.

Lieserl felt an instinctive desire to back away, but controlled herself. Somehow the lion completed her opinion of the man: he was a showman; he belonged in a circus.

Goering glanced around the room, amused. "So none of you has a lion for a pet?" Again he searched the crowd. "Emmy!"

Emmy came back, this time without Edda. "Please take my girlfriend out back. She's frightening the guests."

"Hermann, you're such a show off!" Emmy chided him.

"My wife doesn't appreciate me," he said mockingly, shaking his head. "And I don't understand her. I ask you, how can two such totally different species ever get along?"

Lieserl cleared her throat. "So you would risk a two-front war?"

"What?" He swiveled as his wife led the lioness away by the collar. "Oh, yes, of course, as I was saying, no, not really, that is, it would be nice to take care of that blackguard Stalin, but impractical, of course. In any case, we have more immediate plans, and then consolidation will take some months. The French may put up a bit more resistance than the Polish." He laughed from his belly. "They sent their cavalry out against the Panzers! Can you believe it? Like lambs to the slaughter!"

The conversation drifted into an analysis of the Polish offensive and the lack of retaliation by the Polish air force, which had strangely dropped out of sight. Goering launched into a long-winded explanation, half lecture, half tirade against his enemies.

Haberditz drew Lieserl aside. "I'm afraid he lacks tact."

Lieserl nodded. "Like most members of the party."

"We're not all so strident. Take myself, for example."

She looked at him questioningly. "Well?"

"I believe in moderation. True, I support a centralization of power in a strong leader, and naturally I support the *Fuehrer*, but I don't necessarily agree with all of his policies."

"If you agree with even one of them..."

"Come now, he's given everyone a job, controlled inflation, cleaned up some of the less responsible political parties..."

"Destroyed them all, you mean. Killed all their leaders and thrown everybody else in concentration camps."

"Many of them were communists. Even you must agree that..."

"Please, admiral. Politics bores me. Remember? Part of man's estate, along with your damned wars."

He blinked and raised his eyebrows. "I agree, of course. Unfortunately, politics and wars are sometimes a necessity, even for scientists." He gestured toward Heisenberg, who was still deep in conversation with Goering and Speer. "He understands that better than anyone."

"I don't know how someone of his ability can stand it."

"Tedious, I'm sure." He raised his eyebrows, gesturing at the dance floor with a nod of his head. "Will you honor me with the next dance?"

"No, I'm sorry, I haven't danced in years and I'm not going to start, now."

"It's high time, then."

She shook her head firmly. "I'm afraid I'm not in the mood."

"Mood! There's woman's estate, if there ever was one, that and children. How about a stroll in the gardens, then?"

"No." Suddenly the party seemed oppressive to her. "I can't stay here. I have work to do. Can you get me out of here?"

He raised his eyebrows again at the swift turn of events, but smiled, eager to please her. "Of course. My driver's waiting outside with my car. Are you going to your lab or home?"

"The laboratory. To my office, actually. I've some papers I'm working on."

"Perhaps you'd like to join me for some coffee, somewhere? I know of a very nice restaurant..."

"Absolutely impossible, Admiral. I have much too much important work to do."

"Just half an hour, that's all. I have something of a scientific background, too, you know. I'd be interested in hearing about your work."

"If you're not a scientist then you wouldn't understand a word I said. Now, do you have a car, or don't you?"

"Yes, of course. We can leave immediately, if you wish."

Shortly thereafter Lieserl and Haberditz were sitting side by side in the back seat of his Mercedes, racing toward Berlin. "Where do you live?" he asked her after an awkward moment of silence.

"Just a few blocks from the Institute."

"No, I mean, where's your home? Where are you from? Are your parents still alive?"

"My father died in the Great War. My mother lives in Hamburg."

"Same family name, I assume?"

She looked at him suspiciously. "Of course. I've never married."

"Married to your work, I suppose."

"Yes, in a manner of speaking."

"There isn't anyone you're waiting for?"

A lump formed in her throat. "No," she said, bitterness briefly welling up inside her. "My personal life is no concern of yours, Admiral."

"No, no, of course not." He thought for a moment, gazing at her thoughtfully while he smoked. "You know, I could probably arrange to set you up in your own division, give you some assistants and additional funding. Interested?"

She gave him another guarded look. "Possibly, although that would seem a little strange at the moment, when I'm constantly interacting with Heisenberg. What would be the point?"

"Let's just say that I recognize your creative potential. It's been a while since Heisenberg's Nobel, and you also have more of a practical bent, it seems to me."

"I would have to think it over."

"Of course, you'll have to moderate your behavior."

She smiled ironically. "I think I see the catch. You want me to quietly agree with people who are no better than common criminals."

Haberditz cleared his throat, and leveled a stern but amused look at her. "There you go again, Doctor. It's a new Germany we're living in, and I won't deny there are certain goings on that are sometimes hard to understand. That's the nature of any truly revolutionary endeavor."

"We'll see." Lieserl changed the subject. "I rather liked Udet. He seems to have a gentle nature."

"Yes, everyone is very annoyed with him. He'd rather be doing stunts in a biplane, walking on the wings and so forth, and probably isn't the ideal man to run aircraft production. But he's an old friend of the Field Marshal, flew in his squadron in the Great War."

"Is he a member of the party?"

"Nominally, as I am. It costs nothing to put up a front, and there are benefits."

"I see little benefit in selling one's soul to the devil."

Haberditz smiled ruefully. "You're incorrigible, Dr. Meier; simply incorrigible. It's important to keep those little thoughts to yourself, no matter how true they might be. Especially if you should find yourself engaged in a similar transaction."

She elected not to rise to the bait. "You seem to be straddling the fence.

Using the party membership for your own ends."

"Yes, you might say that. I certainly can't claim to agree with everything Hitler is doing, although I go along when it appears things can't be changed. I see the advantages of not making a fuss about the details, in hopes of exerting a positive influence when it really matters."

"Thank God for that. Maybe there's some faint hope for Germany, yet." She glanced at him, wondering if, in some ways, he was worse than the dyed-in-the-wool Nazis.

Half an hour later they arrived at the Kaiser Wilhelm Institute. Haberditz got out of the car and accompanied Lieserl to the door of the nuclear physics laboratory. "I want you to know that I stand ready to help you in any way I can," Haberditz told her. "I have some considerable influence in certain circles, and would be pleased to use it to your benefit should the need arise."

"Thank you, Admiral. I'll remember that. I hope it won't ever be necessary."

"As do I. Until our next meeting, then."

He bent in a gallant bow and left her. She remained standing, watching him thoughtfully as he climbed in the back seat of the car and ordered his chauffeur to drive away. He was a strange man, and not altogether repulsive, despite his party affiliation. Maybe he was only doing what he had to do to survive, as she was doing. Since the Nazis had come to power everyone had to lead a dual life; everyone had to compromise.

She had compromised herself, as well, working for a regime she detested. She'd had a chance to flee with Lise Meitner to Sweden but had elected not to go, mainly because of her mother, who was still in Hamburg. In any event, Heisenberg had convinced her it was necessary to remain and fight, to work quietly and tirelessly for change. She'd always looked up to him, following his lead since their wonderful days together in Gottingen, even after he'd finally married someone else.

Putting her troubled thoughts out of her mind, she walked up the steps of the Institute.

* * * * *

Haberditz, sitting in the dark back seat of the Mercedes, was busy thinking about what he could do to lure Lieserl Meier into his bed. The game was off to a good start. It excited him to think she might still be a virgin, that he would be the first to break down her wall of frigidity and show her what it was like to be with a man. He slowly stripped her in his mind, over and over, imagining her white body naked and exposed before him, vulnerable. A tightness grew in his groin, and he took long drags on his cigarette, enjoying the sensations. The only problem was winning her over, but that was part of the fun.

He would do nothing at first, other than make her notice him casually, visit her at the institute on occasion. She was obviously very cold, perhaps a lesbian, and would have to be warmed slowly over a period of months before he took her. Perhaps he could induce her to put on a show with Marjot. She didn't seem like the type to respond to flowers and boxes of chocolates. More, she was a woman of action and would admire a man of strength and purpose who knew what he wanted. And, if his charm didn't kindle the fires, there were other methods of persuasion available to him.

As the Mercedes raced through the darkened streets of Berlin, he thought of her mother in Hamburg. He needed to know more about Meier's family, and made a mental note to call Himmler.

Chapter Three

April 9, 1940, the North Sea off Norway

Vice Admiral Lutjens, on the bridge of *Gneisenau*, stared at the gray foaming seas. Snow squalls lashed the decks, and *Scharnhorst* was only barely visible, a mile off the starboard beam. The seas were heavy, the weather worsening. He turned to the helmsman and ordered him to reduce speed to twelve knots.

Somewhere a few hundred miles to the east were the fjords of the Norwegian coast and the fleet of ten destroyers he'd escorted there for the campaign in Norway. Admiral Marschall, meanwhile, was in Berlin, thanks to Haberditz, who had insisted he personally attend a high-level meeting with Raeder and Donitz. Marschall had taken pains to instruct Lutjens on the conduct of the operation, to the point of offense. It irked Lutjens to think the man didn't trust him under fire.

Cruising aimlessly off the Norwegian coast in bad weather, as bait to draw the British away from the real action, wasn't much of a mission, but it was better than nothing.

Suddenly there was a sound like a ripping of bed sheets, followed by a pair of terrific explosions that sent a tower of water into the air on the port side, another gigantic plume shooting up to starboard.

"Full speed ahead," ordered Lutjens instantly. He whipped his binoculars up and peered through them, searching the mists.

Captain Forster, his own binoculars up, pointed. "It's the *Renown*, off the stern to port. Permission to engage!"

"No!" Lutjens snapped. "Under no circumstances. Return fire, but put distance between us and the enemy as quickly as possible."

The captain gave the orders, and the eleven-inch guns swiveled in their turrets and locked in. A few seconds later came a thunderous roar as the one-ton shells shot away.

Another ripple of fire came from the distant fore turrets of *Renown*, and Lutjens held his breath as he waited, counting seconds. That was the worst, waiting for the shells to fall.

Again an extended ripping sound, something like a passing express train, then a deafening explosion off the starboard quarter, another shell scoring a hit, taking out the forward fire-control position, sending splinters all over the deck. At Lutjens' order, a signalman sent a coded message with a signal light, and *Scharnhorst* broke away so the sister ships wouldn't present a single target. Both ships continued to return fire. The powerful battle cruisers churned through the boiling seas, straight into the face of a gale.

"With *Scharnhorst* we can take them!" shouted Forster angrily. "*Renown* is an antique!"

"I have my orders and you have yours," Lutjens replied stonily.

Another salvo straddled them, sending up foaming white waterspouts on either side of the ship. *Gneisenau* pounded through the frigid waters of the North Sea, the giant swells breaking over the decks, the gun batteries roaring every twenty seconds. Lutjens stood quietly on the open bridge, one hand holding the railing and the other his binoculars, his ship passing through a nether world where roaring guns marked time.

As the distance between the ships slowly opened, the British gun crews became more erratic. Finally, a tense half an hour later, the bombardment ceased.

Lutjens ordered a reduction of alert. He had been reluctant to run, but following orders was more important than anything else, and his orders had been to draw the enemy away from the Norwegian coast. The British Navy would be looking for them now, fearing a breakout into the Atlantic.

Other such successes, combined with some failure of Marschall's, would give him what he coveted most: fleet command of the most awesome battleships ever built, *Bismarck* and *Tirpitz*. With the support of *Scharnhorst* and *Gneisenau*, he would then direct the most powerful naval group in the world, vindicating the German Navy in the eyes of the *Fuehrer* and the German people, blotting out the shame of the meek surrender at Scapa Flow at the end of the Great War. Neither the victory at Jutland nor the heroic scuttling of the surrendered Navy vessels at Scapa Flow could erase that shame.

Forster came up beside him at the railing. "We could have beaten *Renown*," he repeated stubbornly.

Lutjens nodded, barely glancing at him. "I know. That's not our mission." Another man might have said something to soften the Forster's disappointment, but Lutjens turned and walked off the bridge without another word.

Kaiser Wilhelm Institute, Berlin, May 9, 1940

The metal sphere was one meter in diameter, held together by thirty-eight one-centimeter bolts. It was immersed in a bath of heavy water, which moderated the neutrons, slowing them down and reflecting them so they might more readily split the atoms of uranium. A nearby Geiger counter chattered steadily.

Heisenberg, Meier, and two students, dressed in white lab jackets and wearing protective glasses, stood around the primitive reactor, a large glass cylinder holding the heavy water and the sphere that contained an array of tiny cubes of uranium. The students, both of them young men in the graduate program, were too brash and confident, oblivious to danger. Heisenberg's worry lines were showing on his brow, and Lieserl, although outwardly cool, was tense inside, tightly coiled like a spring.

Heisenberg stepped over to the tank, peering cautiously at the suspended sphere. "How's the temperature, Jens?"

The strapping blond young man checked the thermometer. "Forty-five degrees centigrade and rising steadily, Doctor."

"That's good," Heisenberg murmured. He made a slight adjustment, removing a small graphite control rod. "I believe we're getting some enhanced multiplication."

The water surrounding the sphere began boiling, bubbles streaming up to the surface. The Geiger counter began to chatter faster, the sound approaching a continuum of white noise. Heisenberg, sweat glistening on his noble brow, squinted through the swarming bubbles of steam. "Neutron activity is considerably higher than before."

"Werner, it's going up too fast," said Lieserl, her breath catching.

Suddenly the steel sphere bulged, straining against its bolts, visibly stretching in an impossible and unearthly way.

"Out!" shouted Heisenberg. "Everybody out, now!"

Everyone raced for the door. The students were there first, throwing themselves through the doorway. Lieserl was right behind Heisenberg, and as she passed the threshold a violent explosion ripped the lab apart, sending her tumbling forward. She caught Heisenberg's coat, and they both went down in a heap in the hallway. Smoke poured out of the lab.

Heisenberg helped Lieserl to her feet and together they ran on down a short hall and went outside. The alarms were ringing, and already the fire brigade was on the scene, men running hoses into the lab, combating the flames.

Heisenberg looked at Lieserl and smiled ruefully. "Successful test, I think."

She frowned, thinking of the months of work that had gone into the reactor. "More like wasted effort. The sphere self-destructed. Not a good way to get power."

"But perhaps the precursor of a bomb."

She shook her head. "No, Werner. I don't think so. Not yet, at least. It blew itself apart before there could be any significant chain reaction, so it was more like a very expensive conventional weapon, and not a very strong one, at that. Just as well, at least we're still here."

He nodded, his lips pursed. "True enough. But this is cause for celebration, don't you think? We've generated a terrific amount of heat. It's just a matter of adjusting the moderator."

She sighed and took his hand in hers. "And after we find that adjustment?"

Heisenberg looked slightly puzzled. He stole a quick glance around, then turned back to her. "Our allegiance is to Germany," he murmured. "Not Hitler. Some day he'll be gone and society will go back to normal."

She smiled with brittle irony and released his hand. "Why are you talking so quietly? Are you afraid you might be shot?"

He looked around again, eyeing the students sitting nearby, then pressed his lips together and stared at her hard for a moment. Turning away again, he said, "We'd best start looking over the mess. I think the firemen are nearly finished. Gas masks and lead aprons are in order."

They donned the safety equipment and went back into the laboratory, which was still filled with acrid smoke. Lieserl nudged a twisted piece of casing with her foot. "If anything," she said, her voice somewhat muffled by the mask, "this shows that the heating of the uranium will cause the mass to fly apart, effectively curtailing any further fissioning. Not the stuff of a bomb."

"I think you're viewing the matter rather negatively. We have plenty of other experiments to do before reaching conclusions. Haberditz will be pleased."

"He's pleased by anything that blows up."

As they picked through the wreckage, carefully examining the fragments of the reactor, Haberditz himself knocked on one of the outer doors of the lab and partly opened the door. "I see you've been making progress," he called as he surveyed the damage, one hand on the doorframe. "Is it safe to come in?"

"No," Lieserl told him. "Not unless you want to go the way of Madame Curie."

Heisenberg glanced meaningfully at Lieserl as he put a reactor fragment down on the lab bench. He nodded toward Haberditz, and he and Lieserl stepped out of the laboratory to join him in the hall. "We've had a good test, Admiral. There was a significant amount of neutron multiplication, with enough thermal energy generated to cause this explosion."

Haberditz nodded. "Any chance of a stable reactor in the next few months?"

Heisenberg shook his head. "It's too soon to say. We may need a different geometry for the reactor vessel. Or a much better moderator."

"Keep up the good work. I've talked to Speer and arranged a further increase in funding, so money won't be a problem." He leaned in through the doorway, surveying the room. "We could put some uranium in the warhead of one of those rockets Von Braun is working on. Even if it didn't explode, it could poison their water supply, say."

"We'll do better than that," Heisenberg assured him. "In two years we'll have the prototype of a working uranium bomb that will be capable of annihilating entire cities."

Haberditz smiled wistfully. "In two years the war will be long over. In fact, it may already be over. Neither Britain nor France has made any serious attempt to challenge our control of Central Europe, and their resistance last month in the Norwegian campaign was simply anemic."

Lieserl snorted. "You've forgotten about America, Admiral."

Haberditz turned and smirked at her. "They're all the way across the Atlantic Ocean. I doubt they'll have much interest in us, especially with all the worry about Japan. They're isolationists. Lindberg is leading the way; he's with us, and has a great deal of influence. Why should America sacrifice their young men in a European war?"

"Wishful thinking is so reassuring," she replied acidly. "The States have no cultural ties with Britain, I suppose."

Haberditz mockingly saluted her. "Touché, Doctor. Your tongue, as always, is sharper than a sword." He straightened. "Be that as it may, that's all the more reason we need you to accelerate the pace of your work, in case the unthinkable starts to happen."

"You mean, in the event Germany starts to lose the war," supplied Heisenberg.

"Yes, of course. That won't happen if the war is left to the experts. Of course, that's not guaranteed." He cleared his throat and assumed a knowing look. "There may be a major escalation in the near future. The very near future."

"They're going to attack the French, I'd wager," stated Heisenberg flatly.

Haberditz put a finger to his lips. "The low countries, first, but yes. And please keep it under your hats. At any rate, there is at least a possibility that uranium research could eventually turn out to be pivotal. You never know."

"We've got work to do, here," Lieserl said. "Is there a purpose behind your visit, or are you just at loose ends?"

He smiled slightly, like an adult tolerating the antics of a child. "Now that you mention it, yes, I'm here on an urgent mission that concerns you." He glanced at Heisenberg. "Would you excuse us for a moment, please?"

"Certainly." Heisenberg turned away, lowering his mask again and striding back into the laboratory. Haberditz put a hand on Lieserl's shoulder and eased her outside into the courtyard, out of earshot. "I have bad news, I'm afraid."

Lieserl stiffened. "What's that?"

"The Gestapo is investigating your mother."

"How do you know?"

He waved a hand vaguely. "I met with Himmler the other day. I mentioned your fine work on the project, and he said he'd just signed an order on someone of the same name, someone from Hamburg. I inquired further, finding out the person in question was your mother. I can't stop the investigation, but I'll do my best to keep you informed."

Lieserl brought the back of one hand to her lips, her face pale. She felt as if a knife had been thrust into her belly.

"I must leave for Hamburg at once."

Haberditz frowned. "You can't do that. Your work here is quite important. I assure you..."

"No, what are you saying? I must go. Immediately."

She turned, but Haberditz caught her by the shoulder. "I'll drive you to the train station. It's the least I can do."

"Thank you. I have to tell Werner where I'm going. Excuse me a moment, please."

She found Heisenberg standing over the shambles of the reactor, papers in one hand, studying sketches of his spherical reactor design. He looked up. "Well?"

"I must leave for Hamburg at once. The Gestapo is investigating my mother."

He raised his eyebrows. "Has she been detained?"

"No, I don't think so, but I have to go warn her. She'll need my support."

"Of course, I understand perfectly. What will you do when you get there?"

"I don't know. I'll cross that bridge when I come to it."

He tossed the papers down on a nearby desk. "If necessary, I can contact Himmler directly. My mother and his mother, you know, are on very friendly terms."

She took a deep breath, remembering when Heisenberg himself had been investigated. "Yes, please. Between you and Admiral Haberditz perhaps something can be done."

"These things take time. It took several months to clear the air in my case." He reached into the inside pocket of his coat and drew out his wallet, removing a sizeable sheaf of bank notes and handing them to her. "Here, take this. That will save you the time of going to the bank."

She accepted the money gratefully. "I'll pay you back as soon as I return."

He shook his head and waved her offer away. "That won't be necessary."

"I'll come back as soon as I can."

"Don't worry about that, either. You'd best be going."

She hesitated, standing there before him with a wad of Reichsmarks in her hand, her oval, beautiful face turned up to him, lined with worry. "Werner, we need to talk about the project. About what you said."

He looked puzzled. "What I said?"

"About annihilating entire cities."

He shook his head. "That's a long way off. Let's not worry about it. You heard the admiral: the war will be long over before it comes to that. And you forget, we don't know how to do it, yet."

"But if we did..."

He sighed and leaned against the edge of the desk, as if tired. "Let's just take one day at a time, shall we? Our allegiance is to Germany."

She turned without another word and hurried back outside, shrugging off her protective gear and leaving it carelessly on the ground near the door. "I'm ready to go," she told Haberditz.

He smiled. "Let's go, then."

They walked briskly away from the Institute and got into the back seat of a waiting staff car. Haberditz gave an abrupt command and the driver pulled out into the busy street, tires squealing.

"Don't you need to stop by your apartment? Pack your bags?"

"That won't be necessary. I have plenty of clothes in Hamburg."

Haberditz regarded her shrewdly. "What's your opinion of Heisenberg? How would you rank him, as a manager of a major weapons initiative?"

She found his change of subject distracting, but said, "He's one of the most brilliant men in the world."

"That wasn't the question."

"I know."

"So what's the answer?"

She thought carefully before replying, then said, "He's very competent."

"Harteck says otherwise. He says he has absolutely no feel for experimental work. He's not practical."

"Harteck wants the job for himself."

Haberditz nodded. "Yes, you have a point. He sounded rather annoyed about the whole situation." He sighed. "I trust Heisenberg. Not many do. He wants to win the war for Germany, if not Hitler, and that's enough for me."

"You don't need a bomb. You've overrun every country you've attacked."

"We all have to do our duty, and we all have to survive. It's that simple. I don't like this war any more than you do."

"Then you should make a statement. Resign your position."

Haberditz laughed ironically. "They'd call me an enemy of the state and shoot me."

That made her think of her mother again. "Are you sure you don't know what they're going to do to her? Please, if you do know, you must tell me."

Haberditz lit a cigarette, then rolled down his window an inch. "I imagine they plan to interrogate her at length, at the time and place of their choosing."

"Does she need an attorney?"

"That wouldn't do her much good, I shouldn't think."

"If they send her to prison, do you think you'd be able to help get her out?"

He blew a stream of smoke at the open gap in the window. "I couldn't guarantee anything. Naturally, I'd do my best." He reached over and took her hand in his. "I won't rest until I've cleared this regrettable situation up. You may be assured of that."

He released her hand, and she breathed a sigh of relief. Sitting back, she closed her eyes, trying to relax. It had all happened so suddenly. What could her mother possibly have done? There were shortages all over Germany. Had she stolen some food? Said the wrong thing in front of an informer? Her mother's tongue could me nearly as sharp as her own.

They arrived at the train station. As usual the SS were all around, watching the crowd, checking the credentials of suspicious travelers. Whenever they saw Haberditz, however, they nodded tightly and turned away. Lieserl bought a ticket for Hamburg, and Haberditz accompanied her to the platform.

"Good luck to you. Please call me if I can be of service."

"I will. Thank you, Admiral."

He smiled broadly, offering his hand, which she took. "You're welcome, Doctor. Have a safe trip." He squeezed her hand briefly and then turned and left, heading back to the waiting staff car. The steam engine blew its whistle, and Lieserl climbed up into the passenger car without looking back.

* * * * *

From the back seat of his car Haberditz sat and smoked, still thinking about Meier, the feeling in his hand aroused by her touch still with him. She was a pearl of a woman, a pearl he had coveted since first meeting her at the conference months before. And he intended to have her, if the price weren't too high.

The interlude with Meier had whetted his appetite, and he leaned forward, giving orders to the driver. Ten minutes later the car pulled up to a luxurious apartment building. Haberditz got out, instructing the driver to wait for him. Stepping up to the front door, he rang the bell. A pretty chambermaid answered the door and let him in. He went upstairs to the third floor and knocked on number three hundred five.

A woman with flaming red hair answered the door. She had blue eyes, sensuous lips, a beautiful German nose. Freshly made up and in a fine silk Japanese kimono with a floral motif, she smiled and softly beckoned him inside.

"I haven't seen you for a quite a while, Admiral," she said as he strode into the living room.

"Hello, Marjot. I can't stay long, I'm needed back at the War Ministry." He walked restlessly over to the window, hardly looking at her. "What are you wearing under that kimono?" he murmured with a distracted air.

She dimpled. "What do you think?" She came up behind him and wrapped her arms around him, pressing her body into his back, one hand sliding downwards, questing. She paused. "What's the matter, aren't you happy to see me?"

He took out a cigarette and lit it. "I've got a lot on my mind, that's all."

"The war?"

He puffed thoughtfully. "Among other things."

"That's what I'm here for. To help you forget all those unimportant little details." She released him and took his hand. "Come with me. I know what's good for you."

She led him into the bedroom. Undoing her sash, she slipped the kimono off, letting it rustle softly to the floor. The skin of her back was white, the texture of cream. She turned slowly. Her breasts were large and proud, the dark nipples like eyes, watching him, inviting him. "Will you be undressing, Admiral?"

When he didn't reply she stepped over next to him, boldly placing her hand, feeling that he was still unready. She knelt before him and began undoing his belt and pants.

Haberditz stood impassively, smoking as she ministered to him, his mind miles away. "It's no goddamned use," he finally growled at her.

She momentarily ceased her activities and looked up at his face, a warm smile on her thick red lips. "Relax. It doesn't matter. I'm enjoying you. It's rather pleasant, having it in my mouth, all soft and warm. So pure, like a little boy."

"When was the last time you had a little boy?"

Her smile broadened, and she bent her head down again, nuzzling and kissing him.

He grabbed her by the shoulders and jerked her to her feet. Holding her upper arms in a painful grip, he shouted, "I said it's no goddamned use!"

"Let me go!" she commanded angrily. "You're hurting me!"

"You're not giving the orders, here."

She brought her knee up sharply into his groin and he howled in pain, grabbing her by the shoulders and hurling her violently across the room onto the bed. He followed her, clutching his pants so they wouldn't fall lower and trip him, feeling a hollowness in his stomach from the blow she'd dealt him, and paradoxically, a tightening between his legs, an incipient erection. She flipped onto her stomach and tried to scramble away, but he caught her, striking her so hard across the bottom with his bare hand that it left a flushed pink imprint. She yelped, twisting and struggling, but he turned her over and pinned her down on the bed. Pushing her legs apart with his knees, he wriggled down on top of her, entering her. She bit his ear hard, and he roared in anger and pain, driving savagely into her.

After he was finished he rolled off of her and lay back on the bed, staring at the ceiling. A moment later she got quietly up and went to the bathroom to clean herself off, coming back with a damp washcloth. She cleaned him, then put her kimono back on.

"Was it good?"

"Yeah, sure." Marjot was the best, but this time she wasn't good enough. He was smoking again, lying there in the bed, staring at the ceiling and thinking about Lieserl.

Chapter Four

Hamburg, May 10, 1940

An air raid in Hamburg delayed Lieserl's arrival: it forced the train to put over for several hours at a small burg while everyone waited for the all-clear signal. Everyone was talking about the attack on the Netherlands and Belgium that had just begun at dawn. Lieserl listened to the chatter with half an ear, too worried about her mother to get caught up in the speculation.

It was nine o'clock in the morning when she finally arrived at her house in suburban Hamburg. The maple trees out in front of the house were green with new growth. She was relieved to find her block had been spared. The gabled, three-story home she had grown up in was undamaged.

Her mother, Anna Meier, was surprised and delighted to see her at the door, and embraced her tightly. "Lieserl! How wonderful to see you!"

"It's wonderful seeing you, Mama."

"Come in and have some breakfast. I just finished making it." She ushered her into the kitchen, full of warm aromas, and served her a sumptuous breakfast of sausage, fresh bread, and porridge. Frau Meier was in her late middle age, her hair gray without a hint of the blond of her youth, but she was still lovely, willowy and graceful, with a noble chin and fine profile.

"I came as soon as I heard, " Lieserl said between gulps of hot coffee.

"I'm so glad you're here, Lieserl. Without your father..."

"Have you heard from Wilfred?"

Her eyes lit up and she softly swatted the tabletop with her fingers. "Yes! He's coming tonight!"

"Here?" Lieserl said, her eyebrows arching. "What wonderful news! I thought he was in Poland. Why did they give him leave?"

"I don't know. I'm just thankful he's coming. I received a telegram from him two days ago."

"I can't wait to see him!" Her face changed abruptly, brows furrowing. "Is he all right? Has he been hurt?"

"No, no, he's fine. He's in perfect health, and probably ready to challenge you at chess."

Lieserl grinned. "I'll let him win a game or two. But what about the summons from the Gestapo? Can you tell me anything about that?"

Anna shrugged nonchalantly and shook her head. "I confess I know nothing about it. I'm to report tomorrow to Gestapo headquarters downtown. I'm sure it's only a routine matter."

"Show me the orders."

Her mother went over to the silver chest and picked up an official-looking yellow sheet of paper. "There's nothing on it, no charges, nothing. They just want to talk to me, that's all." She handed the paper to Lieserl. "I am to appear at eleven o'clock."

"I'll go with you."

Anna shook her head. "That's not a good idea. You shouldn't get involved. You'd better wait for me here. There's nothing you can do."

"Don't be ridiculous. You need a representative. I have highly-placed friends. The Gestapo fear things like that."

"No, I can't let you go. I've always been a law-abiding citizen, and because I've done nothing wrong, I have nothing to fear."

Lieserl shook her head. "You know that isn't true. It doesn't matter what you have or haven't done. They'll find something to charge you with and you'll go to prison. The only weapon you have is influence, and then only if it's good enough to make them fear you more than you fear them. I'm going with you and that's final."

Anna bit her lip, her eyebrows knitting. "I'm not so old I can't take care of myself, Lieserl."

"Of course not, but does that mean a daughter can't help her mother?"

Anna gave Lieserl a long, guarded look. "You've got your father's temper, you know, at least on occasion. And it's usually on the wrong occasion. Promise me you won't say anything rash."

"Don't worry, Mother. Everything will be all right."

A dark little man with beady rat's eyes and a ridiculous parody of Hitler's moustache came suddenly into the kitchen. His hair was black and shaggy, and pasted on his sallow face was a nervous, suspicious expression.

"Good morning," he muttered, casting a furtive glance toward Lieserl and then looking quickly away. "Heil Hitler."

Anna rose to her feet. "This is Max Ritter, one of my new boarders. Herr Ritter, I'd like you to meet my daughter, Lieserl".

Ritter nodded tightly. "Yes, of course. Is there any more coffee?"

"I'll make you some," Anna said immediately.

Ritter took a muffin from the tray on the kitchen counter and sat down at the table, nibbling on it like a rodent while Anna busied herself with the gas stove, making more hot water for the coffee.

"Are you a student, Herr Ritter?" Lieserl asked politely.

"No."

He went back to nibbling his bread, as if he were alone in the room. "What do you do?" Lieserl pursued.

Ritter stopped eating and glanced her way. "I'm not at liberty to say."

"Secret work, then? War work."

He made a dismissing gesture with his hand. "It's technical. Nothing you'd understand."

Anna came over with the pot of hot coffee. "My daughter is a physicist of the first rank," she said, pride and reproof in her voice. "She works with Professor Heisenberg, the Nobel laureate."

"Ah, so?" Ritter turned and studied Lieserl's face with a rude intensity. "A woman in science?"

"I don't see what my gender has to do with it," Lieserl replied.

"Nothing, I'm sure." He drank a long drought of coffee, then smacked his lips in satisfaction. "Where is your husband? Your children?"

"I'm not married," Lieserl replied, annoyed. "Not that it's any of your business."

Ritter raised his bushy eyebrows. "Not married at a time like this, when the Fatherland needs more boys! Racial laws are one thing, but there should also be laws requiring women to do their duty. Don't you agree, Frau Meier?"

"That depends on how you define duty," replied Anna.

"Marriage, family, home, and hearth! Producing new workers and soldiers for the Fatherland! What else?"

Lieserl rose from her seat. "Excuse me, Mother, but I was wondering if we could go into the conservatory?"

Anna nodded, glancing at Ritter. "If you'll excuse us, Herr Ritter..."

He waved a hand, the fingernails dirty. "Don't mind me."

Anna arranged the dirty dishes in the sink, took off her apron, and then walked with Lieserl through the living room to the conservatory, an airy room attached to the back of the house. Six great windows were set in the walls of the odd, hexagonal room. On one side was a bookcase, and next to it, a quarter grand piano of reddish brown mahogany. A cello in its case lay beneath the piano. Outside the windows were several maples, budding with fresh new green leaves, and a couple of very tall firs, planted after Christmas years before.

"Why did you rent a room to that horrible little man?" Lieserl said in a low voice.

"He just showed up one day with papers saying he had a right to live here," Anna murmured as she sat down on one side of the old maroon love seat. "He had an order from the local party officials informing me I had no choice in the matter."

"I think it's outrageous they force you to put up with such a person."

Anna shook her head. "It could have been worse. With your father gone and Wilfred at the front, there isn't anyone to talk to, and my other forced border, Frau Witte, is a good conversationalist, at least. She's a school teacher." She took a deep breath. "Lieserl, I have something to tell you."

Lieserl touched her hand. "What is it, Mama?"

Anna bit her lip, looking a little flustered, then quickly stood up and strode over to the bookcase. Between two of the bookends—owls carved in ebony—was a small ornately carved mahogany box. As Lieserl watched her withdraw something, a curious sense of foreboding came over her. Her mother seemed nervous, fragile like a frightened bird, her face pale, and that scared her.

Anna turned, clutching something in her hand, a brittle smile on her face. She came quickly back across the room and sat down next to Lieserl, in something of a rush, as if she might change her mind and wanted to get the inevitable over with once and for all. "I thought I should tell you something important, now that everything is so uncertain."

She opened her hand, revealing a heart-shaped golden locket. She gave it to Lieserl. "Open it."

Lieserl moved aside the tiny clasp with her thumbnail and opened the locket. A picture of a handsome, dark-haired woman with a round face and Slavic features was set inside. Her eyes were a little hard, but her expression was soft and sad.

"Who is that?" Lieserl asked.

"That," said Anna, "is your birth mother."

Lieserl's eyes widened and she looked at her mother in shock. "You mean I was *adopted*? And you've waited all this time to tell me?"

"I didn't think you ever needed to know. Now I'm not so sure."

Lieserl stared at the picture. "What's her name? Where does she live?"

"I don't know. When we came for you at the orphanage, this locket was among your personal effects. They had no record of who your mother was. There are initials on the front cover."

Lieserl closed the locket, seeing two script *M*'s on the front. "Well, it doesn't matter. You're my mother, and you always will be. This person gave up her rights to me when she put me in the orphanage."

"The orphanage was in Vienna, where your father and I were vacationing back in 1903. Perhaps if you went there you could find some clues. They probably have records, but of course they don't open them without very good reason. All they would tell us was that you'd been born out of wedlock, that your name was Lieserl, and that you'd barely survived scarlet fever."

Lieserl shook her head. "This doesn't mean anything to me." She tried to give the locket back to her mother, but Anna took her hand and closed her fingers over it.

"I want you to keep it. It may be true that I'm your mother now, not her. I raised you, loved you, I took care of you. But the woman in that picture suffered for nine months carrying you and might have died in childbirth, for all we know. She's important, whether or not you ever know who she is, whether or not you ever meet her. And she probably loved you desperately."

Lieserl nodded quietly. "Yes, I guess you're right, Mother. She was probably desperate, and it likely saddened her enormously to give me up. I'll keep the locket."

"Somewhere out there might be a woman who dreams about you every night, wondering what became of you, wondering if you're happy. For all you know, you might have other brothers and sisters. And after the end of the war, that might be important. Wilfred ... "

Lieserl closed her eyes. "Don't say it, Mother."

"It's just that he..."

Lieserl opened her eyes and glared at her. "Please, Mother!"

Tears came to Anna's eyes, and Lieserl felt her own eyes moisten, regretting she'd been so harsh. "I just don't want to think about him that way, not when he's out there fighting."

"The war will be over soon, Lieserl. Maybe he's even coming home to stay."

"No. They'll need him in the new campaign. He's an engineer and he speaks seven languages."

"Yes, I suppose you're right." She looked into Lieserl's eyes. "Still, it's important to me that you keep the locket. Always."

"I know. I shall." Lieserl held the locket in her hand, feeling its smooth curves, the warmth of it, as if it were alive, although she knew it was only her own body heat.

"You might have a larger family, an extended family. What could be more important than that?"

Lieserl smiled wryly. "I think I'm old enough to take care of myself, now, Mother."

Anna shook her head, exasperated, and kissed her briskly on the cheek. "You've always been far too independent for your own good." She looked vexed. "You should have married Hans Bauer. He was a fine lad."

She blushed slightly. "Mother! He became a locksmith."

"You spent one entire summer with him, don't you remember?"

"I was just a girl."

"He's a good man and a good provider. I ran into him just a few months ago, at Christmas, at the butcher shop. He and Brigitte have three healthy boys, all but one of them grown. He asked me to remember him to you."

Lieserl recalled her sixteenth summer, when for a few months she'd forgotten her books and spent all of her free time roaming the streets of Hamburg and the outlying countryside with Hans Bauer. They'd bicycle far out of town, find a deserted wood, hike to a spot overlooking the sea, or seek out a secluded glen. Then, after a picnic lunch, they'd explore each other's bodies, languid in the summer sun, the rich smells all around them, bathed in the warmth and light.

She closed her eyes briefly, her breath going out of her at the thought. "He wasn't right for me. A very nice boy, but only right for a summer, not forever."

"Of course. No one was ever good enough for you."

She shook her head sadly. "Except for the man in Gottingen."

Anna nodded sympathetically. "Unfortunately, that's true. No one else would have been right for you except him. But he slipped away."

"I can't blame him. He wanted a wife, not a co-worker."

"Of course he wanted a wife! Why wouldn't he want someone to take care of his home and raise his children? For all you mean to him, you couldn't provide that."

Lieserl stood up and walked over the quarter grand piano at the far side of the conservatory. Idly she ran her fingers over the keys, playing part of a run from Chopin's *Fantaisie Impromptu* with her right hand. Chopin died at thirty-eight of consumption, and she was already a couple years older, and somehow still alive.

"Are you and Professor Heisenberg playing much together?"

She turned slightly. "We played at his home a couple Christmases ago, but we don't play regularly, not anymore. Not since Gottingen, really."

"That's a shame. I loved that Concerto of Grieg's you played together, you know, the A-minor with the two-piano score."

"I loved it, too." She looked down at the locket again in the palm of her left hand, and with her right she played several more notes of Chopin, her finger slipping on the last one, going flat.

* * * * *

Shortly after eleven that night a loud knock sounded at the door.

Lieserl and her mother were in the kitchen, drinking tea, talking about times long past. As one they jumped out of their chairs and rushed for the door. Lieserl got there first, slamming the bolt out of the hasp and opening the door.

"Willy!" she cried, throwing herself into his arms.

"Lissy!" He shouted joyfully in return, hugging her so hard she could scarcely breathe. "What a wonderful surprise!"

Then he hugged his laughing, relieved mother, and together they went to the kitchen, where he drank tea and wolfed down biscuits. He was a tall, rangy man in his mid-thirties, with blond hair and moustache, his blue eyes intelligent, his long face quizzical, plastic and animated, full of spontaneous good humor.

"We didn't expect you to visit so soon," Anna exclaimed. "I thought you'd be stuck in Poland for another year, at least."

He grinned, boyish and mischievous. "I'm afraid they can't do without a good engineer. I'd already messed up all the construction projects in Poland, so they transferred me."

Lieserl gave him a playful shove. "You've never messed up anything in your life, least of all a construction project."

"Well, I used some of that funny stuff you taught me—what was it? Physics?"

"How long will you be staying?" asked Anna. "Your room, I'm afraid, is taken by a boarder, but we can arrange something in the meantime."

His face fell slightly. "I'm just staying tonight. I'll be shipping out again tomorrow morning."

"Wilfred, no!" cried Lieserl. "Not again!"

"They need me. More construction."

"Where, back in Poland?"

He cleared his throat. "I'm not at liberty to say. But as you know, there has been new action in the lowlands, and you can draw your own conclusions from that."

"Well, that doesn't matter," Lieserl said quickly, reaching forward and squeezing his forearm. "What's important is that you're here, with us, that we're a family again, if only for the night."

"Hear, hear!" said Wilfred, raising his cup of tea. "To the Meiers of Hamburg!"

They all drank their tea in a single gulp and Anna refilled the cups. "Gertie was asking about you the other day," Anna said, a smile playing about her lips.

"Gertrude?" Wilfred said innocently, motioning whimsically with his teacup and raising his blond eyebrows.

"You know very well whom I mean. In fact, I'm surprised you didn't stop at her house before coming over here."

"How do you know I didn't?"

"Because you wouldn't have shown up here until morning if you had," said Lieserl.

Wilfred laughed. "You know me too well!"

They spent an hour catching up on news, discussing the war, the terrible air raid. Wilfred didn't think much of the summons and assured his mother that it meant nothing. "They're just getting bored. When they get bored, they call everybody in just for the practice."

"What time do you leave in the morning?" Lieserl asked him.

"The train leaves at nine thirty-three. We have plenty of time. Can't walk you downtown, of course, I've got to report an hour earlier."

Anna reached out and touched his hand. "You'll be coming back soon, won't you?"

"Soon, I'm sure." He paused a moment, as if not sure he should say anything more. "I won't be all that far away," he said in a low voice.

Lieserl and Anna exchanged a glance, silently agreeing not to ask anything further. The walls had ears, and it was treason to divulge anything that might be considered a war secret

"We'd better all get some sleep," Anna said. "I'll make you a bed on the floor in my room."

He smiled. "That sounds wonderful, after what I've been through."

"Sleeping on the ground, I imagine," Anna said.

"If I was lucky. Sometimes I had to sleep standing up, or behind the wheel of a jeep!"

* * * * *

They slept only two hours before the air raid siren went off.

Lieserl and Anna rushed downstairs, still buttoning their clothes. Wilfred was already there.

"Just the usual routine," he reassured them. "The British are probably hitting the docks. We'll be safe on this side of town."

They went out onto the street together. Other people in the neighborhood were stumbling out of their houses, buttoning their clothes, heading for the underground shelter a couple blocks away. It was brand new, a concrete bunker three meters underground with a narrow staircase leading into a claustrophobic little room with lines of narrow benches. People packed the shelter like sardines, ordered about by a pompous old man barking orders and sporting a

Einstein's Daughter: The Story of Lieserl

Nazi armband. Ventilation fans whirred, children and babies cried.

"Who are they? What kind of planes do they have?" Lieserl asked Wilfred. But her brother didn't answer; he was dozing, sitting up, beside her on the uncomfortable bench.

"I hope it won't be like last night," Anna said.

They sat for an hour, the air slowly growing stale. Lieserl was beginning to think they were all going to suffocate. The tension had given her a splitting headache.

Suddenly there was a series of distant thumps, then the sound of antiaircraft batteries opening up and more sirens. Bombs whistled through the air, each explosion seeming to come nearer their little shelter. The ground shook with each blast. Lieserl clung tightly to her mother and brother.

At last the world grew silent once again. Another half hour passed, then the all-clear signal was given. Lieserl nudged her brother in the ribs. "You can wake up now, sleeping beauty."

"Did I miss anything?" he said groggily, managing a wink.

"Don't tell me you slept through all that!" exclaimed Lieserl.

He shrugged. "In the army, you take a nap wherever you can get one."

They trudged back to their home, crossing paths with Ritter, who acknowledged them with a dark, tight smile and a nod. Yet something in his eyes was accusing, as if he suspected them of some infraction, as if the fact that their house was still standing, unharmed, was proof of their guilt.

* * * * *

The next morning Lieserl woke to the smell of coffee. For a brief moment she felt like a schoolgirl again, waking up early with the rich breakfast smells, and if she let her imagination wander she could nearly hear the sound of her father's quiet voice, gently discussing literature with her mother at the breakfast table. He had been a schoolmaster before the Great War, and a great admirer of Goethe. Reluctantly getting out of bed, Lieserl washed her face and dressed, then went downstairs to breakfast.

Max Ritter was at the kitchen table opposite Wilfred, drinking a mug of coffee and eating a muffin. He smiled crookedly when Lieserl came into the room.

"How wonderful to have someone younger around the house," Ritter said. "I'm tired of all the old people." Although he was in his twenties, he had facial expressions that made him look like a teenager, which wasn't helped by his toothbrush moustache. "How long are you staying?"

"I don't think that's any of your business," Lieserl replied.

"Just trying to be friendly. Is there anything wrong with that?"

Wilfred gave him a hard look. Ritter, self-conscious, looked back down at his muffin. Lieserl resented having to share the breakfast table with him, especially with Wilfred at home.

Anna came back in the house from the garden. She seemed embarrassed about something. "Here are some fresh tomatoes," she said. "I'll cut them up for you."

"That's all right, I'll just have some bread and milk," Lieserl replied quickly.

"I don't have any milk, I'm afraid. But you can have tea or coffee."

"She must have friends in the black market," Max commented, his voice low and rasping. "Nobody on this block has any coffee left."

Anna gave him a measured look. "For your information, Mr. Ritter, I put in a good store of coffee before the rationing began."

He smirked. "Whatever you say. Hoarding essential supplies is questionable in itself."

Lieserl frowned at him, her eyebrows drawing together. "We happen to be good Germans, Mr. Ritter."

"You're not a good German, frau, unless you're in the party. And I happen to know that not one of you is a party member."

Wilfred, sitting at the table in his dusty green army uniform, said quietly, "I suggest that you finish you meal and leave the table before I stuff the rest of your muffin down your throat, along with my fist."

Ritter cast a resentful look Wilfred's way. "I must respect a man in uniform. You, at least, are doing your duty." Bolting the rest of his food and taking a swig of coffee, he got up and quickly left the kitchen.

Lieserl and Anna exchanged a glance, but said nothing further. Somehow there didn't seem to be much of anything to say. The clock on the wall ticked away the precious time they had left together, and nothing they could do or say would stop it. Still, it was pleasant, cherishing that small measure of time, quietly breakfasting together, as soft light came in through the kitchen windows.

All too soon they were on the porch, hugging each other and saying their goodbyes, and finally waving as Wilfred strode away down the street, occasionally turning to wave again until he was finally out of sight.

"Do you think we'll see him again?" Lieserl murmured, putting a hand close to her heart.

"We were fortunate to have him with us for a few hours. Let's leave it at that."

An hour later Lieserl and Anna left the house, headed for Anna's appointment. Gestapo Headquarters was about a mile and a half away, and they walked briskly, not saying much, keeping the conversation on safe topics like the weather and music. The air was cool and the sun bright. Every few blocks they passed through an area that had been bombed. Lieserl saw a boy of about six sitting on the brick steps of a demolished apartment house, and briefly wondered if she should help him. His blond hair was singed, in disarray, and he had a lost look on his face, frightened and alone. She nudged her mother.

"Shouldn't we do something about that boy?"

"Probably. I don't see his parents around."

They went over to him, stepping over the shambling remains of a front porch that had fallen into the yard. Lieserl crouched down next to him. "Where are your parents?"

"Papa told me to stay here."

"How long ago?"

The boy shrugged. "I don't know."

"Where's your mother?"

The boy burst into tears. "She went away."

Lieserl straightened, exchanging a glance with her mother, just as a heavyset woman suddenly bustled up. "Heinrich! Come here this instant! Stop your crying."

"You're his mother?" Anna asked.

The woman stopped short, as if she'd just noticed the two women. "His mother...ah, well, let's not talk about that. I'm his Auntie Giesela. Thank you for stopping for him, I came just as soon as I could."

"If everything is all right, we'll go now," said Lieserl.

"All right?" repeated the woman, her eyes wide, looking at Lieserl as if she had lost her mind. "As if anything could be all right!"

"We're sorry, Madame," Anna said formally, and she and Lieserl left her there in the ruins with the little boy, who was still crying.

Gestapo Headquarters was in a stone mansion near the University of Hamburg. Nazi flags bracketed the steps, but otherwise the mansion looked strangely empty, abandoned, nearly hidden from view by all the trees and shrubs. Anna trotted up the granite steps briskly, not a trace of fear on her face. Lieserl admired her courage, feeling considerable trepidation, herself.

At the top of the steps was a row of great pillars, an imposing double door of oak a few meters beyond them. As Anna gripped the iron door handle, a buzzer sounded and the doors swung open automatically. She and Lieserl glanced at each other, then entered.

Inside was an empty hall with a hardwood floor. Their footsteps echoed in the hallway as they walked slowly along, wondering which of the closed doorways they were to enter. Old copper engravings and elegant paintings hung on the walls, remnants of the days when the mansion had been alive, vibrant with the life of one of Hamburg's finest families.

"Where are they?" Lieserl said in a whisper. "Where are the secretaries, the typists?"

"We'll simply have to knock on some doors," Anna said firmly. She proceeded over to the nearest one and rapped smartly. The sound echoed, accentuating the emptiness of the building.

"The next one," Anna said.

They found that the next door was very slightly ajar. Again Anna knocked, and as there was again no reply, she quietly pushed the door open. Another door lay inside, just three or four feet away, in a curious, truncated hall. The inner door was padded with brown leather. Anna marched up to it and knocked again, the sound of her fist hollow against the leather.

"Come in!" came a muffled voice from inside.

Anna cautiously opened the door. Lieserl followed her into a large, airy room with high ceilings and chandeliers. Three large windows gave a view of neglected gardens and a ruined, smoldering house beyond. A bland, nondescript bespectacled middle-aged man in a neat gray suit waited for them behind an enormous desk. His face was fleshy and blank. He looked up from the orderly stacks of reports before him, but somehow didn't seem to really focus on them. He could have been any clerk or bureaucrat, methodically attending to his paperwork, distracted by an unexpected visitor.

No one else was in the room. He said nothing, and after a moment readjusted his thick-rimmed glasses and went back to reading his reports while Lieserl and Anna stood before him. Lieserl started to speak, but Anna placed a hand on her arm, silencing her.

Behind him was an unmarked door painted glossy white. Lieserl wondered what lay behind it, and if those passing through it ever returned.

Finally, when he'd decided they'd waited long enough, he looked up from his work. "Heil Hitler," he said in a conversational tone.

They echoed the salutation back to him, Lieserl mumbling it. The Gestapo then leaned back in his chair and stared at them for a long time. The minutes passed agonizingly, but Lieserl did her best not to show the strain. She knew they fed on fear.

"I have an appointment for only one person," he said finally. He consulted his schedule. "Mrs. Anna Meier." He looked pointedly at Lieserl. "Who are you?"

"I'm her daughter, Dr. Meier, from Berlin. May I ask your name, sir?"

He paused a long moment, as if deciding whether it was wise to reveal the information, or perhaps astonished at Lieserl's effrontery.

"Dorfman," he said finally. The corners of his lips curled slightly downward. "So what are you doing here, Dr. Meier?"

"I'm representing my mother."

"You admit she has violated the law?"

"We're admitting nothing. My mother is innocent."

He pulled at a file and made a show of flipping through the pages. "According to information I have here, there is some question of Frau Meier's loyalty."

"Where did you obtain your information?"

He glanced at her. "The Gestapo isn't on trial, here."

"Neither is my mother!"

Anna leaned over and touched Lieserl on the shoulder. "Please, Lieserl." She turned her attention to Dorfman. "You'll have to forgive my daughter. She's too outspoken."

"She's a doctor, which is unusual in itself. It may be open to question why she isn't at home taking care of her children." He looked speculatively at Lieserl. "You *do* have children, Dr. Meier, don't you? As you know, it's your duty to the Reich."

"Sir," said Anna, stepping forward, "if you have any charges to discuss, please do so. I'm ready to answer all your questions as honestly and as completely as I can."

Dorfman nodded approvingly. "Excellent. Your cooperation will be taken into consideration. Now," he flipped through the papers again, "there is the charge that you have been stealing ration cards." He looked up. "How do you plead?"

"Not guilty," said Anna. "I have only purchased what is legally allowed."

"Another report says that you listen to British broadcasts. Is that true?"

"Absolutely false."

"You know we have agents everywhere, Frau Meier. They listen at windows, they even enter the homes of citizens. Would you like to change your response?"

Anna shook her head. The Gestapo chief flipped a few pages and then threw the stack on his desk in disgust. "My sources tell me they have heard you practicing English in the privacy of your room. This indicates, by itself, that you are insufficiently dedicated to the ideals put forth by the Fuehrer. In fact, I believe you are a British agent. Is that true, Frau Meier?"

Anna pressed her lips into a tight line. "No, sir."

"Workers will be needed to give direction to the British after they concede defeat," said Lieserl reasonably. "Surely knowledge of English can only help the war effort."

He stared at her, squinting slightly, pondering the logic. "There is some truth to what you say." Sitting back in his chair, he pushed a button on his desk, sounding a buzzer. The glossy white door opened and two other Gestapo agents stepped briskly into the room. They were young, as if they had been recruited a year or two after graduating from high school.

"Take her downstairs," Dorfman ordered.

Lieserl shot to her feet. "You're not laying a hand on my mother!"

Anna took Lieserl firmly by the arm. "Lieserl, there's nothing you can do..."

Lieserl angrily shook her mother's hand off. "I happen to be associated with one of the highest priority projects in Germany," she declared. "I have the support of Albert Speer and Hermann Goering. And I suggest that if you don't wish to be taken away for questioning yourselves, you'd better let my mother go."

Dorfman stared at her blankly.

"You won't get away with this," Lieserl said tightly. "One telephone call and they'll be demanding your head."

That seemed to get through to him. "If Himmler should call me," he said carefully, "I'll follow his instructions. For the moment, your mother must be detained. I assure you, it's a routine matter. If she's innocent she won't be harmed."

Anna took Lieserl by the hand again. "Go on home, dear. I'll be all right. They'll ask their questions and let me go."

The Gestapo chief nodded. "Your mother is correct. It's a routine investigation, that's all. Patriots have nothing to fear."

"Mother, you don't know these people."

"It's all right, Lieserl. I'm in God's hands."

"Get along with you now," Dorfman said gruffly. "I don't have all day."

"I expect my mother to be treated with respect."

Dorfman held one hand out, palm up. "Come now, Doctor. Be reasonable. We're all just doing our duty as Germans."

"We'll just see about that!" Lieserl said hotly. She defiantly ignored the guards and kissed her mother on the cheek, then strode angrily out of the office.

By the time she'd gone down the stairs outside hot, angry tears were coursing down her cheeks. She walked briskly home as fast as she could, slamming the front door as she entered the living room. Going straight to the telephone, she began making calls.

Heisenberg wasn't in his lab, nor at home. She spoke to his wife, Elizabeth, for some time, telling her everything that had transpired. She couldn't hate the woman, although she felt she was far beneath her husband. Mrs. Heisenberg agreed to pass the news on to him as soon as possible.

Desperately Lieserl wracked her mind for other people who might help leverage her mother free, finally thinking of the Reichsfuehrer for Aircraft Procurement, Udet. Luck with was her this time: he was in his office.

"Reichsfuehrer Udet, this is Lieserl Meier. Do you remember me?"

"Of course I remember you." His voice was warm and congenial, even over the telephone line. "What can I do for you, Dr. Meier?"

"My mother has been detained by the Gestapo here in Hamburg. I need help getting her released."

"The Gestapo? I don't know if I can help you with that. That's not my department."

"Surely you know someone? Could you speak to Field Marshal Goering? I wasn't able to reach him."

"The Field Marshal is quite busy these days, and in any case would be unlikely to help you. These are routine matters, best left to the local officials."

Lieserl's heart fell, but she plunged onwards. "Please, you must help me. She's innocent; they haven't a shred of evidence against her."

Udet grunted in disgust. "Since when have they needed any! I'm sorry, Doctor, but these matters are beyond my power. I am a mere pilot and mechanic, responsible for creating aircraft, not for setting political policy. But I'm very sorry your mother has fallen onto difficult times and will mention her plight to Hermann at my first opportunity. As you know, he retains influence with the Gestapo, although Himmler now commands them." He laughed shortly. "They probably spy on each other."

As she hung up the phone, she noticed movement out of the corner of her eye. She whirled, catching sight of Max Ritter as he quickly ducked out of the doorway of the bedroom.

"Mr. Ritter!" she bellowed, running to the door.

He was already bounding clumsily downstairs. "Spies are not welcome in this house, Mr. Ritter!" she cried angrily at his retreating back. "Pack up and get out!"

He paused at the bottom, huffing and puffing, and glared back up at her. "I have an order! I can stay as long as I want!"

He had authorization to stay with them, and technically there was little Lieserl could do about it without causing further trouble with the authorities. She didn't care. "If I catch you spying on me or anyone else again, I'll knock your weasel's teeth out!"

"Your mother is an enemy of the state," he shouted back at her, his face reddening. "I've heard her listening to the BBC on her radio almost every night. Wait until doomsday, she'll never come back!"

Lieserl pointed imperiously at the door. "Get out!"

Ritter hesitated, then turned and sullenly headed for the door. "I'll be back," he tossed over his shoulder. He left the house and slammed the door.

* * * * *

The next day Lieserl went back to Gestapo Headquarters downtown and once again spoke to Chief Inspector Dorfman. Again, he was alone in the spacious room, sitting at his desk before the white door.

"I've come to see about my mother," Lieserl said, standing before his large, polished mahogany desk.

He looked up from a report, moderately annoyed. "She has been transferred to a camp outside of town."

"Where?"

He waved his hand. "It isn't important. You shall be notified in a few days."

"What is she charged with?"

Dorfman cleared his throat. "The charge is treason. She is an enemy of the state."

"Treason! Are you mad? She's a patriot! My father fought in the Great War!"

"That's your father, not her," he said flatly. "And I must ask you to control yourself."

Lieserl took a deep breath. "What are you going to do with her?"

He shrugged. "I personally believe she can be rehabilitated. The war will be over soon, and I imagine she will be released at that time."

"You *imagine*! You're in charge, here. Can't you be more specific?"

"It's a routine matter. If not for the war, I'm sure I could overlook an aging woman from an otherwise good German family. But she listens to foreign propaganda nightly on her radio and has been overheard making statements that can be interpreted as contrary to the spirit of the National Socialist movement. She admitted as much last night during questioning."

He fished around on the top of his desk and pulled out a document. "Here is her confession."

Lieserl glanced at it, and could barely restrain herself from snatching it up and tearing it to pieces.

"Your superiors will hear about this. I have spoken to Reichsmarschall Udet, a confidant of Goering. You shall be disciplined."

At the mention of Goering's name Dorfman flinched, hunching down like a startled turtle retreating into his shell. Influence was everything in Nazi Germany, and he had a healthy respect for anyone with connections. Yet he straightened, again, marshaling himself, directing a stern look at Meier that was full of measured reproach.

"We all have our orders to follow. I'm following mine. This discussion is terminated."

"That's not acceptable."

He rose from his desk. "I'm sorry: you will have to accept it."

"You'll release her immediately!"

"If you insist on making a nuisance of yourself, I will have you arrested. Shall I call the guards?"

For a long moment they stared at each other. Then Lieserl turned and walked briskly out of the room, slamming the leather padded door on her way out, angry that it didn't make the loud noise she'd intended. She was furious, frustrated at her impotence, her inability to break through Dorfman's arrogant facade. In that moment she hated him so intensely she wanted to destroy him completely, using any means at her disposal.

She went home and packed her bag and headed for the train station. She knew she had to get back to Berlin. Influence was indeed everything, and only in Berlin could she rally the support she needed to free her mother.

Einstein's Daughter: The Story of Lieserl

Chapter Five

May 11, 1940, on the Meuse River

At this location the Meuse River flowed north and then turned sharply south, creating a narrow hairpin turn. The high ground and wooded hills on the north bank made for both excellent viewing of the opposite side of the river as well as cover for the tanks and artillery. The big guns spat fire at regular intervals, keeping the French at bay while the engineers built the pontoon bridge.

Wilfred sweated despite being soaked to the skin. As a chief Panzer engineer he could have remained high and dry, directing the operation in comfort, but he preferred to join hands with the workmen. They always worked harder when he worked with them, and it helped keep morale up. He struggled with one of the fittings linking one section of the pontoon bridge to the next, standing chest deep in water, applying all the torque he could muster to a massive wrench.

Shouts brought his head up. French aircraft were dropping out of the clouds, bearing down on them. Antiaircraft emplacements opened up, filling the air with a hail of flak. Wilfred ducked down behind a completed section of the bridge, going underwater and coming up underneath, safe from the strafing although a direct hit by a bomb would still finish him.

A sharp whistling sound had him instinctively hunching over, then the explosion and blast wave hit him, tearing loose his grip on the struts underneath the bridge. Spluttering, he came up for air in time to see one of the French planes hurtling to the ground in flames, the pilot bailing out too low, parachute flapping uselessly as it trailed out too slowly above him. Wilfred shut his eyes against the sight, then, sensing the threat was abating with the diminishing chatter of the guns, went back to the fittings.

By the end of the afternoon the bridge was complete and the panzers were lumbering across, one after another, entering France. Wilfred stayed back, his job finished. He saw General Guderian cross the bridge in his armored staff car, followed by more tanks, infantry, and armored cars.

Later there would be minefields to clear. That very dangerous job he'd always kept hidden from his mother. Exhausted, he closed his eyes. In his imagination he could still taste the breakfast he'd eaten three days before, back in his mother's kitchen in Hamburg.

Berlin

Heisenberg was in his office at the Kaiser Wilhelm Institute, buried under a mountain of papers, his door open. When he saw Lieserl walking resolutely towards him through the hallway, he jumped to his feet and trotted out to greet her.

"What's the latest word?" he said as he took her hand. "How's your mother?"

"My mother is in a camp outside of Hamburg. They won't let me see her. I need your help, Werner."

A shadow flickered across his face. "Come into my office."

He guided her to a seat in front of his large oak desk, then turned and quietly shut the door, locking it. Pulling up another chair, he sat next to her. "My wife told me a few details."

Tears came to her eyes, and she looked around desperately for a handkerchief. Heisenberg quickly produced one and gave it to her. She dabbed at her eyes, taking a deep breath and composing herself.

"Udet came and discussed the problem with me," Heisenberg said. "He thought I'd have better influence with Goering, but of course I'm not much more than a pawn, myself."

"I'm touched that he came by on my behalf."

"Yes, that was kind of him." He shook his head and exhaled sharply in exasperation. "If only I could give them their damned *wunderwaffen*..."

"You must *never* give it to them. No matter what happens."

"Well, of course not, unless things start getting much worse than they are."

"Things are already much worse. They're sending all kinds of people to the camps: Jews, gypsies, even high Germans who don't happen to be members of the party."

"I know how they operate."

"I know you do. You're lucky they didn't execute you."

Heisenberg, frowning, shook his boyish head resolutely. "They couldn't do that. Throw me in prison for a while, maybe. But that business with Stark was dangerous."

"You mean when he wrote that article calling you a white Jew?"

"Yes."

Lieserl's face darkened. "Stark may have a Nobel, but he's not fit to wash your feet."

"He's a good physicist, just misguided."

She looked up at him in astonishment. "How can you say such a thing?" She put her hand out as if gesturing at something disgusting on the floor, grimacing incredulously. "How can you be so fair-minded of...of that *creature*! And all the others, the party leaders, are even worse!"

He held up one hand, cautioning her. "Please, not so loud. My secretary might hear you."

She was instantly contrite. "Sorry." In a lower voice, she said, "My mother's boarder turned her in for listening to the BBC."

"Yes, Elizabeth told me all about it. Don't worry, we'll think of something. I'm sure they'll take good care of her. They wouldn't want to risk alienating us."

"She gave me this the night before she was detained." Lieserl handed him the locket. "She told me it was my birth mother, holding me in her arms."

His eyebrows went up in surprise. "You were adopted?"

"Apparently. My mother wanted me to know, in case..."

He made a slight dismissing motion of his hand, not wanting her to finish. "Yes, of course. I would have done the same." He handed the locket back to her without opening it. "Did she know the woman's name?"

"No. There was something familiar about her face. I felt almost as if I knew her, in my heart."

Heisenberg nodded reasonably. "Of course she would obviously resemble you in certain ways because she's your biological mother. Are you going to look for her?"

"I wouldn't know where to start. Maybe after the war, after I get my mother—I mean my adoptive mother—out of the camp."

"Yes, well, you know that Haberditz has a certain amount of influence with Goering and Himmler. I took the liberty of talking with Franz, and he indicated that you should go speak to him personally about the matter. I didn't have the impression you thought much of him, though, so didn't make any commitments."

She glanced away and made a dismissing motion with her hand. "Haberditz isn't all bad, I don't think. He's an opportunist, but he seems to recognize that the Nazis are dangerous reactionaries. If you think it's wise, I'll speak to him at once."

"That's up to you. Influence is the key commodity these days, and he has influence in several quarters. I imagine that answers your question." He gestured at his desk. "You may use my telephone, if you can find it among all those papers."

"Yes, thank you very much."

She managed to reach Haberditz's secretary at the Institute of Naval Research. At first the woman tried to brush her off, but when she mentioned she was a member of the *Uranvein* she suddenly became much more cooperative. A few minutes later Lieserl had an appointment for four o'clock in the afternoon.

Heisenberg looked pleased. "Once we get this little matter straightened out we can proceed with earnest on our reactor models. I'm certain we'll have significantly more neutron multiplication by the end of the year." He rose and strode over to the blackboard, which was littered with arcane equations and diagrams. "I've been playing with a layered model, with sheets of uranium metal alternating with paraffin and heavy water."

She wasn't much in the mood for talking about science, but couldn't resist commenting. "That looks a little unnatural for what we're trying to achieve. Spherical symmetry, or perhaps an array of cubes..."

"Well, these flat layers make the calculations much easier. You see..."

She sighed. "Werner, do you want it to work or do you just want an easy calculation?"

"Both, of course. The layers should work just as well, and..."

She interrupted him. "If you don't mind, Werner," she said, rising from her seat, "I think I'll go home, now. I want to rest alone in my apartment for a while before going to the Naval Institute."

He nodded and smiled. "Of course. Silly of me to start in like that. Can I escort you to lunch somewhere, perhaps? I could also have my secretary deliver something to your rooms, if you'd prefer."

"No, thank you. I'll be fine."

As she closed the door, she saw that he was already back at his blackboard, chalk in hand, studying his diagrams.

* * * * *

The Institute of Naval Research was a relatively modest building in the Navy block between the Landswehr canal and Bendler Street, near the center of Berlin, not far from the stupendous Air Ministry, a building of four hundred thousand square feet off the Leipziger Strasse. Men in military uniform were everywhere, walking briskly along the sidewalks, stepping decisively up and down the granite staircases.

Lieserl took the elevator to the fifth floor, where Admiral Haberditz' office was located. A beautiful blond secretary greeted her and offered her a seat near a window. Lieserl waited only five minutes in the outer office before being admitted.

Haberditz sat behind a grand desk of polished mahogany, a gold-plated pen set at one hand and virtually empty in and out trays. Blood red Nazi flags flanked him, and a broad paned window behind him gave a beautiful view of the city. On the wall was the obligatory framed photograph of Hitler, this one signed personally.

"Please sit down, Doctor," he said, indicating a plush leather chair. "What can I do for you?"

Lieserl sat uncomfortably down on the edge of the chair. "My mother is incarcerated outside of Hamburg. I wish to obtain her release."

"Yes, I'm familiar with your concern. Udet said something to me about it, as did Heisenberg."

She expected him to go on, but he sat there staring at her strangely for a moment, and Lieserl became impatient. "Well, Admiral? Can you help me?"

Haberditz shook his head and rose, pacing slowly over to one of the flags. "This is a rather difficult problem. Once you're in the system, there are all kinds of rules and regulations."

"That's where you come in. I understand the incredible lethargy of bureaucrats. I need you to cut through the red tape."

"I realize that. The problem is, it's not so easy, particularly when it's a question of patriotism."

Lieserl's eyes flashed with anger. "My father served in the Great War while my mother nursed the victims of mustard gas at a hospital near Hamburg, Both my parents are German through and through. My mother has never given any evidence of being a spy, or of being unpatriotic, but in the current political climate, who could blame her for questioning authority, for trying to get some unslanted news from the BBC? You yourself have indicated some reservations about your own party."

Haberditz raised a finger. "Careful, Dr. Meier. As you know, we've discussed your opinions before, and while I respect them, it's better to keep them to yourself."

"All right, so I'll keep them to myself. What are you going to do about my mother?"

He put his hands behind his back. "Well, I might be able to get her transferred here to Berlin, as a first step. Would that be helpful?"

Lieserl's forehead wrinkled. "What do you mean? Put her in a local prison?"

"Yes. That would allow us to keep a better eye on her while we maneuvered for her release."

"You mean to say you don't think you can get her out immediately."

Haberditz glanced away briefly, as if slightly nervous. "No, probably not. We could manage it in a few weeks, almost certainly, especially if she's here in Berlin. I can work through the local SS, who will surely see fit to be lenient with the mother of Heisenberg's assistant."

"You're sure that's the best you can do?"

Haberditz shrugged. "Who knows? Let me say that it's the least that I'm confident I can do."

Lieserl nodded stoically. "All right. How soon can you get it done?"

He stroked his chin, gazing at the ceiling. "Maybe a week, with luck."

"Do it."

"Consider it done." He turned and went back to his chair, sitting down. After scribbling a note to himself on a piece of paper, he looked up again at Lieserl. "If you'll give me a few minutes alone, I can make the necessary telephone calls."

"Of course, Admiral. I'll wait outside."

"Thank you."

Lieserl went back out to the reception room. The secretary eyed her suspiciously. Lieserl sat down and began sketching a few calculations on a pad of paper to ease her nerves and pass the time. Half an hour went by, then an hour. She was just about to get up and ask the secretary to call Haberditz on the intercom when the door opened and he stepped out, coat on and briefcase in hand.

Lieserl stood up. "Well?"

"There have been some positive developments. I suggest we discuss them over dinner, if you haven't eaten."

"No, I haven't." She took a breath, hesitating. She didn't want to go out to dinner with him, but didn't feel comfortable refusing, either. "All right. Where do you suggest we eat?"

"The officer's club is a little stuffy. I thought we might walk to a local restaurant."

"That will be fine."

A few minutes later they were in a private club, seated at a table looking out onto a small indoor garden. Haberditz ordered for the both of them and then lit up a cigarette. Their drinks came, the waiter popping the cork and pouring two glasses at their table, putting the rest of the bottle on ice.

Lieserl took a sip and put her glass carefully back down in front of her. "I note that our champagne derives from your hated enemy, the French."

"Yes, that's ironic, isn't it? They'll soon be our new subjects, if the campaign in France goes our way. I don't think much of their General Petain."

"And why not?"

"He doesn't have the guts of someone like De Gaulle. I don't know how Petain can call himself a military man. According to reports, his forces aren't putting up much resistance."

Lieserl took another sip of her wine. "De Gaulle can afford to rattle his saber. It's a little safer across the channel."

Haberditz snorted. "True enough, for the moment. Goering needs some long-range bombers. He and that pathetic clown Udet have been enamored with *Stuka* for years. A four-engine plane, on the other hand, could carry the *wunderwaffen* to the British homelands. He and Goering just don't see it."

"I think Udet is a charming gentleman."

Haberditz grunted and downed his wine in a gulp. "Sometimes I think he's just blundering around in the way. No matter. The war will be over by the end of the year."

Their food came, roasted duck with baked potatoes and lima beans, a salad on the side. They ate quietly for a few moments as a small ensemble consisting of a violin, cello, and flute played chamber music in the background.

Finally Haberditz dabbed at his mouth with a napkin and cleared his throat. "Arranging your mother's transfer to Berlin will involve considerable personal risk."

"I know. I appreciate your willingness to help."

He let his eyes travel over her face, and downwards, lingering on her low neckline, on the fine skin, the slight rise of her flesh before it disappeared behind the white cloth of her blouse. "I wouldn't do this for just anybody."

"I'm sure you wouldn't. I understand it's a big favor, and I appreciate anything you can do."

He signaled the waiter, who glided over and refilled their glasses, smoothly withdrawing. "You might say I'm rather taken by you. You have some very rare qualities for a woman."

"No more, I'm sure, than your beautiful wife."

"You mean Bertha?" He smiled sadly and shook his head. "For several years we've had a marriage in name only. We have separate bedrooms, you know."

Lieserl looked down, embarrassed, and then covered it by reaching for her wine and taking a sip. "Please, Admiral. You needn't hang your dirty laundry out on a line for my inspection."

"Bertha doesn't have your intelligence, your wit. She's attractive enough, I suppose, but she's turned into something of an old frau, if you know what I mean, long before her time."

"Five children will do that to you. How are they, by the way?"

He squirmed a little in his seat. "Hans is in the Kriegsmarine, of course, an engineer in the submarine corps. All the others are still in school."

"You have daughters, don't you?"

"Three of them." His face lit up briefly. "Kristin is just starting school. She's been reading since she was two years old."

"You must be very proud of them."

"Yes, of course." He shifted in his seat and cleared his throat. "Tell me more about your experiments with Heisenberg."

Lieserl relaxed slightly, glad to have deflected him from his intimate revelations. "It's fairly simple. It's mainly a question of finding the right geometry and proper moderator so as to reach a sustained and controlled level of neutron production."

"That doesn't sound so hard."

"Well, I'm sure it won't be, after we figure it out. That's the way science works. It always seems obvious after you understand it, but impossible before you don't."

"If you could make some significant progress, you know, everything would be easier for you."

"You know my stand on that, I'm sure."

"But don't you see?" he said, leaning forward eagerly. "If you and the *Uranvein* come up with a powerful new weapon, something that can minimize the loss of German life by ending the war, you'll be the greatest heroes of the Reich! And with Von Braun working on the A-3 in Peenemunde, it may even be possible to strike deep targets in Russia, even America! Hitler himself would be in the palm of your hand!"

She frowned and looked away. "Hitler is in no one's hands but his own. He's a lunatic."

"That's all the more reason for intelligent Germans such as yourself to assert your superiority." He spread his hands before him, palms up. "Look, even a working reactor will win you laurels you've never dreamed of. You'd be famous enough to call the Gestapo yourself and win your mother's release."

"Heisenberg will likely get most of the credit."

Haberditz frowned, pursing his lips. "Well, that doesn't really matter. He'll use his influence to help you, surely."

"Yes, quite possibly." She took a deep breath. "So you'll arrange for my mother's transfer?"

He sat back and drew out a cigarette, lighting it. "I'll do what I can. Why don't we leave it at that?"

When they'd finished and left the restaurant he offered his arm, and she accepted it despite her misgivings. She had no desire to insult someone who might hold the keys to her mother's prison cell.

CHRIS VUILLE

* * * * *

Wolfgang Weisz stood leaning against a lamppost at a bus stop not far from the restaurant. He'd gone out of the restaurant a few minutes ahead of Haberditz and Meier and then waited for them outside. He had little interest in the Admiral, but the woman was another matter. She was part of the *Uranvein*, the Uranium Club, and a primary target. Weisz wasn't sure where the Admiral fit in, although if he were weak he could turn out to be useful.

The woman was grasping Haberditz's arm as they walked north along the sidewalk, but she didn't seem too happy about it. If she were his lover she'd be hanging on him, maybe smiling or laughing. Maybe they'd just had a fight and she was stewing. Weisz casually followed them for a block, watching them get in a staff car and roar off down the street.

Meier was an attractive woman. He hoped he wouldn't have to kill her.

Chapter Six

Fritz Houtermans stood outside prison walls on the Alexanderplatz in Berlin, free for the first time in several years. A fine rain was falling, and it was cold, but to Houtermans, gaunt and haggard in his tattered trench coat, it felt wonderful.

Two and a half years he'd spent in a prison in the Soviet Union on trumped up charges of plotting to kill Stalin. He still remembered the friendly KGB officers who had questioned him, laughingly assuring him that he would confess to political intrigues, although he had in fact never been interested in anything other than physics. His inquisitors needed a confession, and that's all that mattered. That was their job.

Leaning against a wall supported by his fingertips for several hours, day after day, was their method of choice for eliciting those confessions. It was simple and effective, and didn't require any active torture, hence the accused and his interrogators remained on better terms.

Houtermans finally broke, naming fictitious co-conspirators who all lived far beyond the arm of the Soviet Secret Police. His inquisitors seemed quite satisfied just to get his signatures on the confessions and put him back in prison.

After the accord with Germany, the Soviets transferred him back to Berlin, where he spent several more months in prison waiting for Heisenberg to arrange his release.

"Where's Charlotte?" was the first thing he said.

"She's waiting for you in America," Heisenberg said. "I'm afraid you may not be able to see her until the war is over."

"That's just as well: one look at her and they might have wanted to keep her around to beautify the cells."

Heisenberg and Meier ushered him to the car, fussing over him, making sure he was comfortable. Then they were dashing through the streets of Berlin.

"Oh, Fritz," Lieserl said, her voice nearly breaking. She was in the back seat next to him, and she put a hand over one of his. "What did they do to you?"

Houtermans grinned toothlessly and smoothed his thinning gray hair back, his hand shaking slightly. "I'll need a good dentist, obviously. The GPU specializes in tooth and toenail removal, and of course life truncation."

"How did you survive?"

"Physically?" He shrugged, wide-eyed, and waggled his head comically. "I don't know. Dumb luck surely played an important role. Mentally, well, believe it or not, I kept my sanity by doing calculations in my head, hours every day. Now, if I can just remember a few of them, I'll win some Nobel Prizes and show our friend here a thing or two."

"It's nice to have you back, Fritz," said Heisenberg, smiling slightly at the friendly jibe. "Things have changed a bit since you were last in Germany."

"I noticed," Houtermans replied, chuckling. "For one thing, it's harder to find good cigarettes. Do you have any?"

Heisenberg took a pack out of his coat pocket and gave them to him, along with a box of matches. "Keep them, I bought them for you."

Houtermans put the pack to his lips and kissed it. "Thank you very, very much, Werner." He immediately began stripping open the cellophane.

"Max Von Laue has arranged a position for you in industry," Heisenberg went on, "working in Manfred Von Ardenne's lab in Lichterfeld. All that terrible business is behind you, now."

Houtermans lit a cigarette and took a deep drag, blowing smoke blissfully through his nostrils. "What project are you working on?"

"Neutron multiplication, with the aim of creating a reactor, and possibly an atomic weapon. You know, applications of nuclear fission."

"I'm afraid that during my sabbatical in Russia I wasn't able to keep up with the journals."

"Fission simply means the splitting of atoms, yielding various daughter particles plus energy," Heisenberg went on. "Hahn did the experiments, but didn't understand them. Lise Meitner and her nephew, Otto Frisch, worked out the theory. I imagine Von Ardenne will have you working along similar lines. The idea is to start a chain reaction using the extra neutrons, producing a tremendous amount of heat in a very short time. As it is, we need to enrich the isotope U-235, but so far don't have a good methodology for its separation. U-238 has too large a neutron cross section; it absorbs too many neutrons."

Houtermans' bushy gray eyebrows rose comically, and he grinned. "I'm sure Herr Hitler will appreciate our efforts on his behalf. An instrument of mass destruction is just what he needs to complete his life's work!"

"Not all of us are enthusiastic about the project," said Lieserl.

"Yes, I agree," said Heisenberg as he negotiated a left turn. "But on the other hand, faced with the destruction of Germany, we may have no other choice. We must preserve the Fatherland at all costs. The problem of Adolf Hitler's politics is secondary. He will eventually be replaced."

"If we wait long enough," said Houtermans, "he'll replace us first, with perfect, one hundred per cent Aryans. We'll be six feet under, helping the flowers bloom throughout our beloved Fatherland."

"I understand your feelings," Heisenberg said, glancing over his shoulder. "But it's best to be discreet when expressing them. Particularly with your background."

Houtermans waved a hand dismissingly, his face screwed up like someone who'd just sucked a lemon. "Of course, of course! They don't care for leftists. And now I don't care for them, either."

Heisenberg smiled and cleared his throat. "Your Jewish heritage is also viewed with suspicion, more so than your former sympathies for communism."

"One quarter Jewish!" He leaned forward and blew smoke at Heisenberg's face. "Well, let me tell you something, Dr. Heisenberg: when your ancestors were still swinging in trees, mine were already forging checks!"

Lieserl put a hand on his arm. "This is a serious matter, Fritz. Even I'm beginning to watch my tongue."

His eyes widened in mock lust. "And a very pretty tongue it is, too! Don't tell Charlotte I said that." He subsided, falling back helplessly against the car seat. "What a shame they march you to the wall for having a sense of humor! It used to be they only shot you when the jokes were bad."

They arrived at the apartment they'd rented for Houtermans, where von Laue was waiting to receive him. Standing next to the curb, Houtermans kissed Lieserl on the cheek and then turned to Heisenberg and shook his hand firmly. "I can't thank you enough."

Heisenberg smiled modestly. "Don't mention it. You'd do the same for me."

"We'll be in touch, won't we?"

"All the time. We have a lot of work to do."

Heisenberg got back behind the wheel of the car and pulled away, Lieserl in the passenger seat beside him. Turning to her, he said, "Well, that's one more top flight scientist on our roster."

"Yes, unfortunately."

He frowned and changed the subject. "How's your mother doing?"

"As well as might be expected, seeing as she's incarcerated in the collection camp at Grosse Hamburger Strasse."

"Yes, at the former Jewish Home for the Aged." He glanced at her apologetically. "Sorry, I haven't been much help. Haberditz hasn't been able to arrange anything?"

"Just the transfer to Berlin. That was helpful. Do we have time to go by? I haven't been to visit her as yet, today, and I've got a package for her."

"Of course, that won't be a problem."

The Jewish Home for the Aged at 26 Grosse Hamburger Strasse was a glum, anonymous building in the Mitte district, the city's center. Like the Jewish Hospital at Schulstrasse 79, it had been converted into a holding center for Jews. Heisenberg dropped her off in front and promised to return and wait for her after running some errands. Lieserl negotiated with the SS guards posted in the foyer, who checked her identification. One of them led her upstairs and, with deliberate motions bordering on ritual, unlocked the cell door with its tiny barred window, releasing her mother from her overcrowded cell. Other inmates called out to Lieserl desperately, some waving messages or currency.

Lieserl and her mother faced each other across a small desk in the hallway, an SS guard a few meters away. Her mother sat quietly in the chair with her head bowed. She was pale and thin.

"How are you, Mother?"

"I'm doing fine, Lieserl. I've made many Jewish friends since I came."

"I can't understand why they put you here. You're not even a quarter Jewish! I've been trying to get you transferred to an ordinary jail cell, but Admiral Haberditz says it's difficult to find facilities not already in use. Space is at a premium."

"Please don't endanger yourself for my sake."

Lieserl leveled a determined look at her. "I'll do whatever I have to do to get you free."

Anna reached over and gripped Lieserl's hand. "That's not what I want. Do what you can, but don't sacrifice yourself. Or your dignity and honor." She searched Lieserl's eyes. "Promise me."

Lieserl took her mother's hand in both of her own. "Without you I have nothing to live for, no one. Father's dead, and now Wilfred, at the front..."

"Your birth mother," Anna said in a whisper. "Perhaps she's still alive, somewhere. Maybe she has influence, maybe she can help you."

"That's ridiculous. She's probably a poor homeless wretch living in the slums of some south Austrian hamlet."

Anna smiled slightly. "In that case you could help *her*."

Lieserl nodded. "Well, of course I would, if I actually found her, and if she needed my help."

"You should have married. I warned you, when you came home and told me you wanted to be a scientist, that it would be difficult for you to find a husband."

"I know. You were right." She bit her lip. "If only Werner..."

Anna sighed. "He never saw you as anything but a colleague. You know that. And when he wanted to relax, he was always running off into the mountains with the members of his youth group. I always thought that was a little bit strange. The Gestapo did, too. Why would he or any normal man want to marry a scientist who sits around doing calculations all day long? He wanted a wife and children."

Lieserl gazed into her mother's face, her great luminous eyes liquid with regret and longing. "Don't you think I wanted that, too? Don't you think I wanted to have a husband, children, and a home of my own?" Tears began rolling down her cheeks. Embarrassed, she pulled a handkerchief out of her purse and dabbed her eyes and face. "It just didn't work out, that's all."

"Your standards have always been high. You deserved him, there's no question about that. Maybe he didn't deserve you."

Lieserl smiled through her tears. "Yes, he only had one Nobel Prize to his credit, after all. Fritz is already claiming he'll get two or more, if he can only remember what he was thinking in his Soviet prison cell. A better catch, potentially, but already taken."

Anna's lips turned up at the corners. "I've always liked Fritz. That's another one that got away. But it's not too late. Something will work out for you. The Great War made it so difficult to find a husband, so many of the young men died. That was during your prime marriage years."

"I was too young, then, actually. But you're right, afterwards there weren't as many men, and the economy was in a terrible turmoil. I'm too old, now, I'm afraid."

Anna reached out and put a hand on her daughter's cheek. "You're still beautiful, you look ten years younger than you are, and you're still young enough to have children, a whole family if you want. You'd have to work at it, of course, because it's harder as you approach middle age."

Lieserl straightened in her chair and took a deep breath. "Thank you, Mother. Here you are, locked up in this awful place, and I'm the one who's crying! But don't worry, I'll get you out, I swear I will."

"I know. But please, whatever you do, do it quickly. People are known to disappear with little notice. There are special trains that depart regularly, and lists of names. Every week they send people away from here."

"Where do they go?"

"Well, to various camps around the Reich. I understand some go to Ravensbruck, north of here. It isn't far. But there are many different camps. Some are sent to Theresienstadt, and just as many to Auschwitz. They tell me that if you have to go, it's better to go to Theresienstadt. They have an orchestra there, and if you can play an instrument you receive better rations."

"Surely you'd be a natural choice for their orchestra. No one plays cello better than you, and you could play the piano concertos, too."

"It sounds almost inviting. The commandant at Theresienstadt loves music, so I'm told."

Lieserl squeezed her hand. "I'll talk to Haberditz again and see if he can't intercede. Udet may also be helpful, he's an old flying ace, a friend of Goering. They were in the Ricthofen squadron together. One way or another I'll get you out of here."

The guard was looking meaningfully in their direction, and they rose from their chairs. Lieserl handed her mother the package. "There's food and some medicine."

"I'll share it with my cellmates."

"Make sure you take some for yourself. I'll bring more tomorrow."

"Thank you, Lieserl." Then, her voice breaking, she said, "I love you."

The two women, standing next to the little table, embraced each other tightly.

"I'll be back tomorrow, Mother," Lieserl called as the guard led Anna away. Her mother didn't answer, and Lieserl had a terrible feeling that everything was out of her hands.

She left the facility and stood out on the street. Traffic was light, and very few people were out and about. A handsome man across the street stood in front of a little pastry shop, looking at the display, his hands in the pockets of his jeans. He had a shock of blond hair, neatly combed, and when he turned he glanced past her, looking at the entrance of the temporary Gestapo headquarters. He had a strong chin and a relaxed handsome face. He glanced at her briefly and then strolled casually up the street.

Heisenberg's black Mercedes rolled quietly up before her, and she climbed into the front passenger side.

"Let's go to the office for a while and do some work," he suggested. "It'll get your mind off it."

Lieserl reluctantly agreed, and Heisenberg pulled out into traffic, headed for the Kaiser Wilhelm Institute.

In Heisenberg's cluttered office, Lieserl tried her best to follow as Heisenberg sketched his ideas rapidly on the blackboard, all the while talking about them in a calm, intense voice, questioning her sometimes to be sure she understood. He was the kind of theoretician who had to talk his ideas out while showing them to someone else, much like Bohr. As Heisenberg wrote Greek letters and mathematical symbols on the blackboard, Lieserl kept thinking about how badly Houtermans looked, and how much harder it would be for her mother if she were sent to the camps.

Suddenly she became aware a silence had descended over the room. Heisenberg was sitting on the edge of a student desk, holding a piece of chalk, leaning forward with an elbow on one knee.

"Your heart isn't in this."

She blinked. "No, sorry, go ahead. What were you saying?"

He shook his head and sighed. "I don't remember. Look, I'm tired too. Why don't we call it a day?"

"That's fine with me."

He tossed the chalk into the tray and together they gathered up their briefcases and left the suite of offices. On the steps outside the Institute, he asked, "Can I give you a lift?"

"No, thanks. I'd just as soon walk."

"Fine. Give me a call at home, later."

"Why?"

"I don't know. Just give me a call. Let me know how you are."

"Thanks, Werner."

He nodded, head tilted slightly to one side, then leaned over and kissed her on the cheek. "Take care of yourself."

He turned and walked briskly away toward his car, parked a short distance away. Lieserl, standing alone on the steps, slowly reached up and touched her cheek where he'd kissed her. It was the first time he'd ever done that: usually he just shook her hand or waved, as if she were one of his male colleagues.

She walked slowly back to her apartment, distracted, her mind flitting from one subject to the next, like leaves batted around by autumn winds. Occasionally she touched her cheek, which somehow still seemed warm from the kiss. It had meant nothing, he had only been trying to console her, but the gesture had been touching and strangely disturbing. Regret seeped into her, growing into a sense of bitterness that made her feel a vague revulsion for physics, for her life of science. Maybe she'd sacrificed too much on the altar of her own intellect just to satisfy her pride.

She climbed the stairs to her apartment, still distracted, not paying attention. When she reached her landing and looked up, she was so startled that she stumbled and nearly fell.

Haberditz was waiting at her apartment, a bouquet of flowers in hand.

Her mouth was hanging open, and she managed to close it. "Good evening, Admiral," she stammered out. "What a surprise."

"These are for you. Beautiful flowers for a beautiful woman."

She accepted the flowers, a mixed bouquet of zinnias, daffodils, and wild flowers. "Thank you very much."

"May I come in for a moment?"

She didn't want to let him inside her apartment. "Ordinarily, I'd say yes, but I'm afraid I'm rather tired. If you'll excuse me…"

"Please, I insist. We have important matters to discuss."

She thought it might have some bearing on her mother, so she said, "Well, for a few moments, then, if it's important."

He held her briefcase and flowers while she found her keys and opened the door. Her apartment, as usual, was immaculately clean and uncluttered, but spartan. A single bedroom led off the combination living and dining room, a small kitchen opposite it. The furnishings were modest: a small wooden table in the kitchen, an inexpensive but large desk in the living room. A massive bookcase crammed with science books and papers dominated one entire wall.

Haberditz looked around in amusement. "Where do your visitors sit down?"

"I'm sorry, I rarely entertain visitors. In fact, I don't believe I ever have, at least not here." She took the flowers and went to the kitchen and found a vase. She put the flowers in it and took her time arranging them, placing the vase in the middle of the table. Turning to Haberditz, she said, "And this business you wish to discuss?"

Haberditz strode over and seated himself at the table. Lieserl remained standing. "Why don't you sit down," he urged her.

She sat down slowly, as if fearing the chair wouldn't hold her. He smiled. "The fact is, I haven't been able to stop thinking about you."

She stared at him, and said carefully, "I'm very flattered."

He nodded briefly, pleased. "You should be. I'm a man of considerable means and influence. As you know, that's all that remains important in the Third Reich. It's more important than money."

"And I'm grateful for your help. Is there anything more you can tell me about negotiations to free my mother?"

"These things take time. I understand you have Houtermans back in the fold, and that he'll be working over at Von Ardennes' laboratory?"

"That's right."

"I want you to keep tabs on him. Von Ardennes tends to keep his people under wraps, and if we're going to finish this war off, we need to keep the lines of communications open. We're a team."

"I have no doubt of that, Admiral."

He cast her a puzzled look, as if he suspected sarcasm. "You can call me Franz, if you like. In fact, I'd prefer it."

"I'm not so sure that would be a good idea. We ought to maintain our professional discipline, after all. People might talk."

He stared at her, flushing, his eyebrows tightening. He made an angry, expansive throwaway gesture. "To hell with people and their talk. I've been burning the phone lines for weeks to save your mother, and you keep this brick wall built up between us like I'm some kind of miserable Jew."

"You have a wife, Admiral."

"Don't you understand?" he cried. "We don't live together as man and wife anymore. That's over with, finished!"

"Admiral, please, I'm not interested in your dirty laundry."

"Yes, you've said that, before." He pulled out a cigarette and lit it with a gold cigarette lighter. "Sorry," he said, puffing furiously, tapping his fingers restlessly on the table. "I shouldn't have gone off like that. I'm under a lot of pressure, that's all."

"That's perfectly understandable," she replied soothingly. She didn't want him upset at her, not with her mother's life in the balance.

"The least you can do is call me by my Christian name in private."

It was a small concession, she decided. "All right. Franz it is, then."

He sighed in relief. "That's much better. And you go by Lieserl, don't you? Or Lissy?"

"'Lieserl' will be fine."

"It's settled, then." He glanced around the kitchen critically. "If you have any wine glasses, I could use a drink."

She didn't have any, but was able to produce two tall, slender glasses that she placed on the table. Haberditz popped the cork off the wine and filled them each halfway. "Here's to your mother's continued health," he said, raising his glass.

Lieserl clinked her glass against his and then politely sipped, while to her consternation he downed his entire glass in one gulp. He then reached for the bottle and poured another glass.

"Excuse me, Franz, but are you quite sure you need a second drink?"

"Tough day." But he forced himself to take only a sip before replacing his glass on the table with some effort. "Part of the reason I came here today was to tell you your mother is in grave danger."

Lieserl felt a sinking sensation. "You mean they're going to send her to the camps?"

"Exactly. There's a man named Dobberke, he's the head of the SS at Grosse Hamburger Strasse. He makes up a list every week. An informant tells me your mother is on the list for Auschwitz."

A cold hand gripped Lieserl by the throat, and for a moment she couldn't speak. Haberditz, looking grim, went on. "It's very dangerous to intercede for identified criminals against the state like your mother. It would naturally be construed that anyone trying to help such a criminal must also be a criminal."

She frowned at him. "You know my mother isn't a criminal."

"What I'm trying to say is, I'm not sure how I can go about it without taking undue risks. As you have pointed out, I have a family, too. I can't rush in and help just anybody."

Lieserl felt a terrible crushing sensation, like someone had tied her down and put a concrete block on her chest. "What can we do?"

He took a long drink from his glass and then regarded her candidly. "This is a little difficult to express in words. If it were a question of one of my own family members, say, my wife, whom I love despite our separate lives, or my children, I wouldn't hesitate to step into the face of danger. Or, to give another hypothetical example, if the person in question were the mother of a lover, or mistress..."

She had seen it coming for some time, but even so she lapsed into a stunned silence. Haberditz peered at her quizzically, studying her face. "Well, you must admit we make a good-looking couple. You're unattached at the moment, with no emotional encumbrances. It makes a lot of sense, when you look at it logically."

"I...I'll have to think about it."

He softened. "Sorry to be so blunt about it, but I thought honesty was best under the circumstances, with time of the essence. That's just the way I am, that's all. I'm not a great hero, able to face danger for some casual acquaintance, or even a friend. There has to be more to it. I have feelings for you."

"What does it take to get her name off the list?" she asked carefully. "I mean, suppose I agree, in principle. How are you going to do it?"

"I'll go and face off with him in his office and either offer him a small pile of money, or if that doesn't work, start using implied threats. I have influence and he knows it, so I believe I can pull it off. But it could also go very badly, depending on how he takes it."

"Give me some time to think it over."

He shrugged and stood up. "I'll come back tomorrow night. Don't delay too long. On Friday morning the trains will be running."

Lieserl walked with him to the door, emotions heaving violently through her. In one instant, if she had a knife, she would have plunged it in his back. Then the next instant she was ready to give in, let him have what he wanted, just so she could be sure her of her mother's safety.

She opened the door for him but he paused on the threshold. "Thank you very much for having me in." And he bent over and kissed her on the cheek.

Somehow she managed not to flinch, although her revulsion was so great she had to suppress a shudder. After he was gone she locked the door behind him and ran to the kitchen to wash her face. Then she sagged down into a chair at the kitchen table. The pencil trembled in her left hand as she traced out spidery equations on the white tablecloth, seeking something familiar in them, something to take her mind away from the encroachment of reality.

26 Hamburgerstrasse

There were so many people crowded into the cell that Lieserl didn't know how they could breathe. The SS guard let her mother out of the cell, and again they faced each other across the small desk at the end of the hallway.

"You'll be on the train tomorrow," Lieserl said. "Admiral Haberditz…"

Anna held up a hand, silencing her. "Don't worry about me. I'll be all right."

Lieserl glanced at the guard. His eyes were closed, and he was leaning against the wall. She leaned forward and said, "You've got to fake an illness. Pass out and fall on the floor. They'll take you to the Jewish Hospital for treatment. That will give me another week, maybe longer if you can keep up the charade."

"What if they don't believe it?"

"Then I'll do what I have to do."

"What's that?"

"I can't tell you."

Anna stared at her for a long moment, then nodded. "All right. Just don't do anything you can't live with, Lieserl. And don't put yourself in danger."

"Pretend to have a seizure. Be sure to make a lot of noise. I'll come back later this afternoon and check on you." Then she kissed her mother and quickly left.

Heisenberg was waiting outside in his Mercedes, the engine running. When she got in, he asked, "How did it go?"

"We'll see." She slammed the car door shut.

"She's going to fake a seizure, as I'd suggested?"

"I don't know. I think Mother may be too honorable to do something like that."

He gave her a worried look. "Well, I hope she reconsiders. I tried to talk to Goering today. I told him I wouldn't work on the project any more if your mother wasn't released, that the whole situation was interfering with my concentration. I assured him you were fundamentally important to the effort."

"What did he say?"

"He laughed in my face and said if I didn't start getting results, he'd have me sent to the front."

She pursed her lips. "Don't take any more chances with him. I can handle this."

He glanced at her as he pulled out into traffic. "I'm not so sure."

Her lips tightened. "I have resources."

"I hope so, for your mother's sake. I confess that I don't understand this business at all. I can almost see them rounding up the gypsies, but when they start to take good Germans…"

She stared at him, amazed and startled. "Rounding up the gypsies! What a thing to say!"

He winced. "Sorry, I guess that was dense of me. But you know how some of them are, stealing, beating their children and so forth."

"They're people just like you and me. They're just more colorful, maybe, and generally poorer. Desperate people do desperate things to feed their children. Does that mean they should be 'rounded up', as you say?"

"Well, whatever." He changed the subject. "We need to get the project going. If we don't start getting better results there might be trouble. Our funding may dry up, as a minimal consequence."

"Yes, of course," Lieserl said sourly. "We have to be practical about these things, don't we?"

The conversation died, and they didn't speak until they reached the Institute, and then it was only half-hearted shoptalk. When, in the afternoon, she asked for a ride back to Grosse Hamburger Strasse, Heisenberg instead insisted on contacting the SS commandant, Dobberke, by telephone. He spoke with a secretary, and found that Anna Meier had taken ill and had been transferred to the Jewish Hospital.

He hung up the phone, smiling broadly. "Bravo! She did it! That's a piece of good news, I think."

Lieserl was slumped in her chair, one hand on her forehead, tears running down her cheeks.

"There, there!" Heisenberg said, getting up and giving her his handkerchief. "Everything's going to be all right!"

"It's just that I'm so relieved."

"Of course you are! So am I. Everything's going to be all right, didn't I tell you?"

She sniffed. "For the moment, maybe, until the next time."

"We have another week, at least. Maybe Haberditz can come through and get the orders changed."

She dried her tears and sat up in her chair again. "Werner, do you think I could stay at your house, tonight?"

He looked surprised. "Well, I suppose that could be arranged. What's the problem?"

"Admiral Haberditz was at my apartment last night."

"No!"

"I'm afraid so."

"What did he want?"

"He wants to sleep with me in exchange for helping protect my mother."

Heisenberg's brow furrowed, and a snarl came to his lips. "That unholy bastard! That's definitely a complication. You think he'll be coming again tonight?"

"I'm absolutely sure of it. He said he would."

"Well, certainly, under those circumstances you're welcome to stay with us. I'll give my wife a call so she'll be expecting you."

"Thanks, Werner."

"Please don't mention it."

They worked on reactor design another hour, then dropped by the machine shop to discuss their equipment needs with the shop foreman. Uranium was in short supply, and an additional fifty kilograms of the metal would have to be ordered. After further discussion they left the Institute in Heisenberg's car.

Half an hour later they pulled up in front of Heisenberg's Berlin residence. Elisabeth Heisenberg, nee Schumacher, greeted them at the door and led them into the living room. She was a tall, slender woman with an elfin chin and Gallic nose, a pleasant face to look at, modestly pretty. She wore her light brown hair short and had bright, frank blue eyes. She deferred to her husband, bowing her head to Lieserl, her youthful face coloring slightly. Children appeared out of nowhere, shouting, playing, bouncing off the furniture. Frau Heisenberg seemed graciously harried as she rebuked the children, running them off upstairs.

When she'd finally succeeded in restoring order, she turned to Lieserl and said, "You can stay here as long as you like. We have a guest room. You'll be quite comfortable."

"Thank you. I think just tonight will be sufficient. I can't face that man."

"I don't blame you. He's nice enough in some ways, I suppose, but when men get the wrong idea in their heads…"

"Yes, well, that's probably sufficient, thank you, Elisabeth," Heisenberg murmured.

Elisabeth hurried away. Heisenberg guided Lieserl to a comfortable leather armchair on one side of an elegant marble tea table, taking its twin on the other side. "It appears we have a little quiet for the moment," he said.

No sooner had he seated himself when three young boys came tearing back through the living room, shouting at the top of their lungs, tumbling onto the carpet, one of them throwing himself into Heisenberg's lap while another wormed his way in, trying to wedge himself in between brother and father. Heisenberg laughed and hugged them, and Lieserl couldn't help but feel a twinge of envy.

Hans, who was about six, came boldly over to her. "What's that?" he asked, pointing at the locket she wore around her neck.

"That? Oh, that's nothing. Just a locket."

"Can I hold it?"

"Hans, please don't bother Dr. Meier," Heisenberg said firmly as he struggled to disentangle himself from the other two boys, who were still laughing and poking at each other with Heisenberg between them.

"It's all right, I don't mind." She undid the clasp and handed the boy the locket.

He turned it over and over, looking at it from every angle. The other two boys slipped off Heisenberg's lap and went over to investigate for themselves. "Let me see it," said Wolf, and he grabbed for it.

Hans jerked his hand back, but Wolf caught hold of the chain. In the ensuing brief struggle, the locket went sailing through the air.

"Boys! Please leave the room at once!" commanded Heisenberg as he rose from his seat and pointed to the stairs.

The children scattered, Elisabeth coming back briefly and making sure they went to their rooms. Heisenberg stepped over and picked the locket up off the carpet.

"Sorry. I don't think it's damaged." He glanced at her, smiling ruefully. "That was a little embarrassing. I guess we spoil them."

Lieserl laughed. "Boys are like that. I think your children are charming, Werner."

She leaned forward to take the locket from him, but he stood there, staring at it. She realized that the little gold door of the locket was open, and he was looking intently at the photo inside it.

"That's supposedly a photo of my birth mother, holding me." Her eyebrows knitted and she looked in his face. "Is something wrong?"

He looked up and stared at her just as intently. "I'm not sure," he said in a soft voice. "It's just that I know that face," said Heisenberg.

Lieserl rose and bent over next to him, looking down on the tiny picture of mother and child in the open locket. "You can hardly see her face," she said. "The baby is in the way, and the picture's fuzzy."

"It's not possible," he muttered finally. "It just can't be."

"What are you talking about? Would you mind explaining yourself?"

Without replying, he took out a pocketknife and pulled the blade open. In a moment he'd pried the photo out of the setting and was holding it up to the light. He turned the photo over.

"My God!" he exclaimed. He tore his gaze away from the picture and stared up at Lieserl again in a mixture of pure astonishment and rapture.

"What is it?" demanded Lieserl. "Do you know who she is?"

"Of course, I see it now. It's so obvious, once you know."

"Know what? Explain yourself."

He showed her the back of the tiny photograph. Three words and a date were written there: *Mileva and Lieserl, 1902.*

"The woman in the photograph is Mileva Maric, Albert Einstein's first wife."

Lieserl shook her head in shock. "Maybe...maybe the baby in the picture isn't really me."

"It's you all right. It has your eyes, the same oval face."

"But it simply isn't possible." She slowly sat back down in her chair. He kept alternately looked at the photo and at her, shaking his head incredulously.

"This is some kind of joke, isn't it, Werner? A trick of some kind?"

"You know I don't do that. Besides, it's your locket. When could I have managed to pull such a stunt, even if I'd wanted to?"

"But it's impossible. You know that he and Mileva only had two children, and they were both sons."

Heisenberg's face assumed a slightly pained expression, as if he were struggling with some inner decision. "That's not quite true."

"You mean he had other children? By a mistress, perhaps?"

Heisenberg cleared his throat and leaned forward, a trifle uncomfortable, elbows on his knees, hands clasped. "Bohr once told me—in strictest confidence, you understand—that Einstein and Mileva had a daughter out of wedlock a couple of years before they married."

Lieserl smiled slightly. "That's just like Bohr. He couldn't keep a secret from anybody."

"They kept her for a few months," Heisenberg went on, "but finally put her up for adoption. It was just too difficult, with Einstein unemployed and the child carrying that terrible stigma. According to Bohr, Einstein bowed to family pressures and insisted Mileva give up the child. She fought him every step of the way. That's what eventually tore them apart, by the way—one of the things, anyway. She never forgave him."

For a while neither of them said anything. Heisenberg kept turning the picture over, looking first at the mother and child, then at the inscription on the back, then at Lieserl.

"Do you believe Bohr gave you a reliable account?" she said finally.

"We were very good friends at one time. I'm afraid that's no longer true."

"Because of the war."

"Of course. I can't say I blame him. I don't think any Danes cheered the occupation of their country, not like Austria."

"This changes everything."

Heisenberg nodded. "You're famous, for one thing. Can you imagine? Einstein's daughter and a physicist, to boot! You'll have influence."

Her eyes widened. "Haven't you seen the posters? The Nazis have a price on Einstein's head!"

"Well, yes, but if you can get out of the country…"

"It also means one thing more, I'm afraid."

"Yes? What's that?"

"I'm Jewish."

Heisenberg looked surprised. "Yes, I think I see your point. That could be a very serious problem." He sighed. "Well, no one would ever guess, with your blond hair and Germanic looks. And I certainly won't tell anybody." He slapped his knee enthusiastically. "Still, this is a fantastic find, it's unbelievable!"

"You mustn't tell anybody, do you understand me, Werner? Nobody, not even your wife."

He lifted one hand in a gesture of assurance. "No, of course not. Especially not my wife, for goodness sake." His eyebrows knitted. "We've got to get you out of the country as soon as possible."

"No. Absolutely not."

He looked at her in surprise. "But you said yourself that…"

"My mother."

"Yes, of course, your mother. I'd forgotten about her."

"If I can get her out, too, then I'll go. Otherwise I'm staying. In fact, I ought to go to the Jewish Hospital tonight and see how she's doing."

"Oh, I wouldn't recommend that. It's getting late, and the SS patrols will be looking for an excuse to harass someone. Let's have some dinner, maybe some conversation, then you can go first thing in the morning. I'll take you by."

She wanted to insist, but knew he was making good sense. "All right."

He stood up and offered his arm by way of escort, which she found to be a gallant gesture. But instead of going on, he regarded her with inhuman intensity.

"Yes, Werner?"

"Your eyes," he murmured. "Your eyes are just like his. Luminous and deep, like wellsprings of pure water at midnight."

She reddened slightly, the breath catching in her throat. She wanted to say something in return, compliment him or maybe make a joke of it, but before she could think of anything appropriate he turned and guided her to the dining room.

Elisabeth Heisenberg was putting food out on the table, her movements graceful and efficient. Lieserl still remembered the fateful January night a few years before, when she and Heisenberg had gone together to the home of Otto Mittelstadt, a Leipzig publisher. Heisenberg had performed brilliantly on the piano, and later begun talking with Elisabeth. Meanwhile Lieserl had become involved in a deep technical conversation with Weisacker, discussing a problem in scattering theory.

Heisenberg had never looked back.

Lieserl reluctantly sat down at the table with Heisenberg, his wife, and his children, painfully aware that Elisabeth offered him everything he'd ever wanted in a woman, including much that Lieserl, herself, could not.

* * * * *

Haberditz sat alone in his staff car outside Lieserl's apartment building, fuming. Where was she? He had fully expected her capitulation. After all, he was fairly sure she was attracted to him, so why not? It was obvious she wanted him and was only playing the usual female games.

He'd called Dobberke and found out about the transfer of her mother to the Jewish Hospital for treatment. Apparently she'd had some kind of seizure. While the Gestapo routinely stripped people of their rights and sent them off to camps, a few of the distinctly German policies of proper treatment of prisoners still prevailed in certain institutions, sometimes leading to bizarre and contradictory policies, such as doing dental work on criminals who were to be executed only days later.

No matter. Things were progressing well, and within a year or two Nazi leaders would eliminate such extravagances once and for all. And as far as Lieserl was concerned, he simply had to up the ante, that's all. She was a stubborn woman who didn't know who her real friends were.

He felt lost for a moment, and then pounded viciously on the wheel. He felt like getting drunk and maybe a little rough. Still angry and fuming, he turned the key in the ignition and drove off to see Marjot.

CHRIS VUILLE

Chapter Seven

Berlin

Wolfgang Weisz found an apartment directly across from the one occupied by Lieserl Meier and rented it from a shrunken old German lady. Her name was Pauline Bauer, and she spent all her time knitting and drinking brandy. She told him she had three sons, all of them in the army, and that she thought they were headed for training camps in the east, near the Russian border.

Weisz found his one bedroom apartment perfectly situated. She was on the third floor, as was he, so with his binoculars he could see right into her windows. Later he would stake out Heisenberg, but in many ways Meier was the ideal candidate. She lived alone and had no family, which meant there wouldn't be anybody in her apartment should he find it necessary to gain entry. She lived close to the Kaiser Wilhelm Institute. Finally, she wasn't nearly as conspicuous as Heisenberg, but had easy access to important secrets.

Not far away he found a small market where he could buy virtually anything he wanted for the right price. He had thousands of new German Reichsmarks hidden in his money belt and more stashed in his apartment, yet he knew it wouldn't do to flash it around. People remembered the rich and quickly forgot the poor.

One morning he crossed paths with Meier. She was at the baker's buying bread while he loitered in front of a bookshop next door, pretending to gaze in the window at the display. Meier popped out of the bakery with a basket under her arm, walking right by him without giving him so much as a glance. He followed her casually, watching as a young beggar with a prominent nose and dark hair accosted her, maybe a U-boat, the name the Gestapo gave to Jews in hiding. He expected her to brush the scruffy young man off, but she stopped and gave him a large portion of pumpernickel bread. The beggar bowed graciously and disappeared into a side alley, clutching his prize.

She walked several more blocks, crossing the street and dodging traffic, finally arriving at the Kaiser Wilhelm Institute. Weisz bought a newspaper from a vendor and leaned against a tree. The headlines, blaring military successes, repelled him. Goebbels was a target—not really his, but a target all the same. He wanted to take him out, eliminate him like a poisonous snake. Goebbels' control of the media had been instrumental in bringing about the moral destruction of Germany in the first place, and Weisz hated him for it.

A few minutes later Meier and Heisenberg came out of the institute. They climbed into Heisenberg's car and drove off down the road. Weisz made a mental note of the license plate. Then he crossed the road and walked casually around the outside of the institute, noting the doorways and office windows, developing a picture of all the entrances and exits. Professors tended to be a trusting lot; he was confident he'd have no difficulty breaking into their offices that night and going through their files.

*****

The Jewish Hospital was only a few blocks away from Grosse Hamburgerstrasse, and was much more lightly guarded than the Gestapo headquarters. Heisenberg and Meier checked in with an SS guard in the front lobby, but after that it appeared people could come and go as they pleased. A nurse led them to a small ward on the third floor. Beds were lined up against either wall with curtains for privacy hung between them.

"Frau Meier is somewhat quieter today," the nurse told them. She was a buxom blond, nearly bursting out of her nurses' uniform, with rosy cheeks and a brisk, confident manner. "Doctor Doctor Lustig will be making rounds in a few minutes. He'll be happy to discuss her progress."

"Doctor Doctor?" Heisenberg asked, puzzled.

"He is a doctor of philosophy as well as a doctor of medicine," the nurse informed them, beaming almost as if she had personally assisted in the making of the great man. "Therefore a single 'Doctor' would not be correct."

"I see," said Heisenberg, suppressing a smile.

The nurse peeked in through the curtain, then turned back to them. "I will leave you with the patient. Please, no more than fifteen minutes. You mustn't tire her."

Lieserl eased inside the curtains. Her mother appeared to be sleeping peacefully beneath the starched white sheets and covers. "Mother?"

Her eyes flickered open. "Lieserl," she said in a whisper. She took hold of her daughter's hand.

"How are you feeling? Better?"

Anna smiled slightly. "It comes and goes, the seizures and headaches. They're giving me tranquilizers to make me sleep." She looked at Heisenberg, who had joined them. "You must get her out of Germany, Professor Heisenberg. And you'd do well to do the same."

"Don't talk nonsense, Mother. We're perfectly fine at Kaiser-Wilhelm."

"I don't trust them. It's going to get worse."

Heisenberg cleared his throat. "All the more reason for her to stay. Germany needs good Germans now more than ever before."

Anna pushed herself up to a sitting position. "It's futile, don't you understand? I didn't know until I'd been put in the camp outside of Hamburg. Flee the country, like Einstein did! Save your family!"

Werner and Lieserl exchanged a glance, but said nothing. Lieserl reached down into her basket. "I brought you some bread and mineral water, and some apples."

Anna frowned, falling back against the pillows. "You don't understand, do you? Neither of you do."

"Please, Mama, eat a little. It will make you feel better."

Anna accepted the food, and once she began to eat, it was with gusto. "The food here isn't very good. Have you met Dr. Lustig?" When they shook their heads, she went on. "A very interesting man, and more than a little odd. I'm not sure he can be trusted."

"Are you in danger, here?" Heisenberg asked.

"Only of being sent back to Grosse Hamburgerstrasse."

Heisenberg set his lips in a thin, grim line. "I'll speak with the doctor on your behalf. Perhaps some suitable arrangements can be made."

Anna drank some more mineral water. "Please be careful. He's extremely sharp, and I'm not sure what side he's on."

"He's Jewish," Lieserl said. "And a doctor. Surely he's sensitive to people in need."

"One of the other patients told me he fills out a list every week, marking the ones who are ready for deportation. And the nurses compete for his affections. He sleeps with a different one almost every night."

Heisenberg grunted, uncomfortable with the turn the conversation was taking. "Surely those are only rumors. I can't imagine a man of his accomplishments indulging himself in such scandal."

Lieserl looked pointedly at Heisenberg. "You've forgotten Erwin."

"Ah, yes," said Heisenberg, a little smile coming to his lips when he contemplated the outrageous infidelities of his principal rival in quantum theory. "Schrodinger. But he's a special case, surely."

"Still," Anna said, "be careful with him. You'll see what I mean when you talk to him."

They chatted idly for a few more minutes, and then the nurse came back to inform them their time was up. Anna looked suitably exhausted for the nurse's benefit. Meier and Heisenberg made their way through the antiseptic halls to Dr. Lustig's office.

Dr. Dr. Lustig was a rotund man with a wide brow and a florid face. Heisenberg and Meier, ushered into his office by the nurse, found him bent over his desk, muttering to himself as he pored over a long list of names, completely ignoring his visitors as they seated themselves opposite him at his carved oak desk.

Heisenberg cleared his throat. Dr. Lustig, his thin eyebrows knitted, glanced up in annoyance. "Yes? What is it?"

"I'm Dr. Heisenberg. I take it you're Dr. Lustig."

Annoyance flitted across his face. "I also have a degree in natural philosophy."

"Yes, the nurse mentioned that."

His beady, dark eyes darted to Meier. "Your wife?"

"No, no, just my research associate. You've heard of my work?"

He waved a hand. "Uncertainty principle? Yes, of course I have. And quantum mechanics." He held up one finger imperiously. "Wait one moment, please, I must finish my checklist."

"Certainly," Heisenberg said. He glanced at Meier and shook his head slightly.

A few minutes later Dr. Lustig finished his checklist, signing it with a flourish. "There, that's done, thank God." He looked up. "What can I do for you? I'm a very busy man, you know."

"We wanted to ask you about my mother, Anna Meier," said Lieserl.

"Interesting case, interesting case," Dr. Lustig replied, settling back in his brown leather chair. "For the moment I'm keeping her in reserve." He gestured at the list. "Some, on the other hand, are healthy enough to help out in the work camps."

Heisenberg took a deep breath. Dr. Lustig seemed to think nothing of the fact he was talking to a Nobel Laureate. That was unfortunate. "We'd hoped to be able to ask for special consideration in the case of Anna Meier. Her daughter," he nodded at Lieserl, "is currently assigned to me on an important project funded by the Wehrmacht. Concern for her mother has disrupted her work."

Lustig sat straight up and looked at Heisenberg over his glasses. "What sort of project?"

"I'm afraid it's classified. However, it's essential to the war effort. Weapons research."

Lustig smiled slightly. "Well, now, I'm not sure you fully understand my position, here. I am counted upon to make accurate determinations about the health of my patients. In return, their families and friends show their gratitude by supporting me in the style to which I have become accustomed."

"We realize that, Doctor," said Heisenberg. "We're very concerned about Frau Meier. Her husband is dead—a hero in the Great War, by the way—and she's in poor health. We would appreciate it very much if she could be retained here as long as possible so that she could fully recover."

Lustig folded his fat-fingered hands on the desk in front of him. "Anything is possible, my dear Professor Heisenberg. Did you wish to discuss any specific arrangements?"

Meier glanced at Heisenberg, and he nodded and smiled briefly at her. Turning back to Lustig, he said, "I have good contacts in the War Ministry. I may be able to help assure a steady stream of certain supplies, perhaps some luxury items."

"We would appreciate that very much. Sometimes satisfying basic needs is quite difficult. How may I contact you?"

"Call my offices at the Kaiser Wilhelm Institute. They'll get a message to me." He took out one of his cards and handed it to him.

Dr. Dr. Lustig took the card, carefully placed in a small file box he had in one of his drawers, and stood up. "I believe we understand each other. I'll be sure to take good care of Frau Meier. Her condition is probably too unstable to warrant shipping her to the camps, after all."

"We quite agree," said Heisenberg, as both he and Meier rose from their seats.

Lustig came around the desk, bending over Lieserl as he gallantly offered his arm. He walked them to the door, sliding his arm around Lieserl's back as he guided her along. The hand at her waist was too warm, too familiar, and

Lieserl shuddered slightly.

"I shall be in contact with you concerning our requirements, Professor Heisenberg. In the meantime, do you think you could manage to find me a case of French champagne?"

Heisenberg nodded. "I'll look into it. I'm sure I can."

"Excellent. I imagine the War Ministry has a good supply of French wines, now that the war in France is going so well." He smiled slyly. "Please keep me well supplied. It's important, you know, to be able to gain favor with the local SS officials."

"I understand completely," Heisenberg replied.

"That's good." He turned back to his office. "You may go, now."

As Meier and Heisenberg descended the steps of the hospital, she said, "Can you get the champagne?"

"Of course. In fact, I can probably get Albert to give me a case or two from his private cellar."

"Do you really think you can get supplies for the hospital?"

"I don't really know about that. Maybe Udet can help. He's a good sort." He glanced at Lieserl. "Did you see the way he was staring at you?"

She made a face. "He was disgusting. When he touched me I nearly hit him. If not for my mother, I would have."

They reached Heisenberg's car. "Are you going back to the Institute?" he asked.

"Actually, I told Fritz I'd spend the afternoon with him. He's been working hard on some new ideas and wanted to discuss them with me."

"I'll drop you off. Can you make your way back on your own?"

"Yes, I'm sure that won't be a problem. Where are you going?"

"The family and I are going to our house in Leipzig for a few days. I've got some business at the university there."

They got in the car, and Heisenberg pulled out. "Do you think I might stay over at your Berlin residence while you're out of town?" Lieserl asked.

He glanced at her. "Yes, I don't see why not. Are you afraid Haberditz might come calling again?"

"Yes."

"He can always track you down in your office."

"I know, but I feel safer there."

"I'll tell the maid to expect you."

Twenty minutes later they pulled up in front of Manfred Von Ardennes' laboratories in Lichterfeld, where Houtermans was working. She got out and waved as Heisenberg drove off, but he seemed preoccupied and didn't wave back.

She turned and went into the laboratories, checking by security at the front foyer, then finding Houtermans in his lab toward the back. He was sitting at a lab bench, papers strewn everywhere. As she entered he jumped up as if he'd received an electric shock, then ran up to her, grabbing her hand and pumping it enthusiastically.

"Welcome, Dr. Meier! It's so very kind of you to visit me in my new cell," he said, grandly offering her the lab.

Lieserl smiled. "You love working and you know it."

He chuckled and shook his head. "There's love, and then there's obsession. But you're right, I have everything here I need: a bench to work at, books to consult, and even a bed, for nights of torrid passion."

She grinned. "Charlotte will be happy to find you've recovered so well. You don't really sleep here, do you?"

"Only when I'm obsessed with a new idea."

"You're probably here every night of the week, then."

"Well, I visit my apartment occasionally. Just to water the plants."

He guided her over to the lab bench and sat her down amid the clutter of papers, taking a seat next to her. "I've been working on the separation problem."

"Of the different isotopes of uranium, of course. Have you made any progress?"

He spread his hands and shrugged, frowning and shaking his head. "The answer to your question is no. At least the question about separation."

Lieserl looked at him keenly. He sat in profile, arms resting on the asbestos table in front of him, an ambivalent expression on his gaunt, handsome face. "What do you mean?"

"I'm making progress, but not on the separation."

She pulled back and gave him a pained, amused look. "Whatever are you talking about, Fritz? First you are, then you aren't. So which is it?"

He laughed. "Both. And neither. The separation process is difficult. Some kind of diffusion through filters would be needed, and I'm not sure anyone can do that, except maybe Hertz's little grandson, but he's a Jew and out of the country."

"You've got an alternate process."

"I haven't got a process at all. I've got a totally different fissionable material."

Lieserl sat back and touched her chin reflectively. "A new isotope?"

"A new element, one that doesn't exist in nature. According to my calculations, it should be possible to breed it in a nuclear pile. It would have an atomic number two greater than uranium."

"Then it would be chemically different and we could separate it quite easily."

He nodded, but he was still unhappy. "If we solve the nuclear reactor problem, we could get large quantities of this new element. Put together a critical mass, and," he paused, making a waving motion of his hand, "there goes London. Then Washington. One world under Hitler." He looked over at her. "Just think, no more war. Peace at the price of Nazi jackboots on our chests."

"We don't have a nuclear reactor. Not yet, anyway."

He looked at her and snorted. "Not yet. But I think you already know how to build one."

She shifted uncomfortably in her seat. "What makes you think that?"

"Because you've always been a hell of a lot smarter than that boy scout from Bavaria."

She colored slightly shook her head, a blond curl falling on her forehead. "He's the one with the Nobel prize."

"Don't change the subject. We've got a problem, here. Do you, or do you not, have a working reactor design?"

She bit her lip. "I can't answer that definitively. There are experiments to do."

He smiled ironically. "So what you're saying is, you think you've got one, you just haven't proved it, yet."

"Heisenberg doesn't agree. He prefers a layered symmetry just because it makes the calculations work out better. I think suspending cubes in a moderator lattice would work far better."

"What moderator?"

"Graphite. He's fixated on heavy water, and believes our graphite reactors didn't work, but I think the purity was a problem, a boron contaminant, perhaps. It wouldn't take much to reduce the neutron flux and put it below the critical value."

Houtermans nodded and drew out a cigarette and lit it with a match. "Next question." He took a long drag and exhaled a stream of smoke, looking her in the eye. "Whose side is Werner on?"

When she didn't answer immediately, he went on. "I've known Heisenberg for a long time, in England, in Denmark, here in Germany. He's a straight arrow all the way, always tromping around in the mountains with the old members of his youth group, most of whom have gone over to Hitler. What I want to know is, can we trust him to keep things under wraps even if the war starts going against us?"

"I can't answer that question for you, Fritz. We've discussed it on several occasions, but he's always evasive, turning the question away from Hitler and back on Germany, the Fatherland. And then he changes the subject."

Houtermans grunted, took a huge drag on his cigarette, then flipped it into a water glass where it sizzled briefly as it went out. "That's what bothers me."

"At a meeting with top brass not long ago he was similarly evasive. Speer pushed him for an answer, yes or no, and he wouldn't commit."

"He's very careful about things like that. Afraid to be wrong, but he's still moving ahead with the work at a steady pace. He probably knows more than he's letting on."

Her lips curled in a half smile, and she looked at him askance. "I haven't noticed you slowing down. That alternate element…"

"Are you kidding? I figured that out two weeks after I came to work here. I've just been dragging it out."

"Why do it at all?"

He shrugged. "Why do you keep working for Werner? I have to survive. It's either do the work or go to the front." He drew out another cigarette and lit it. "Besides, it's interesting. I enjoy it."

"It's dangerous."

"Yes, that I agree with. Now, what's your excuse?"

"Survival," she replied reluctantly, "just like you, and my mother's survival. She's still incarcerated at the Jewish Hospital."

"If you ask me, they're holding her to put the squeeze on you. They don't want you splitting town like Lise Meitner. Maybe even Werner's doing it, or this guy Haberditz, who keeps pretending he's trying to help you."

"Haberditz has a crush on me."

"Hey, I don't blame him, so do I. Of course, I'm not a goddamned Nazi, so maybe I'd have half a chance, if I weren't otherwise engaged."

She smiled. "I believe I'm flattered." Looking away, she said, "We've got to get word of this out, somehow. Somebody has to warn the Allies."

"I agree. Who can get out?"

"I don't know. We'll just have to wait for an opportunity, somebody with an exit visa that we trust. In the meantime, we have to keep careful watch on developments. When will you be publishing your work?"

"Oh, I think I can drag it out two or three more months. There are some calculations on the mean free path that I can show Manfred to keep him happy. Those calculations are pretty harmless by themselves. He's a bit proprietary: if I phrase things just right, he may not understand the implications. And he doesn't know about your work."

"What about falsifying your results?"

Houtermans finished his cigarette, shaking his head. "Von Ardennes is a rich, greedy bastard, but he isn't stupid. Even if he didn't notice, somebody else might, even Werner. Can you talk to him?"

"I'll try."

"Be discreet. I don't think he'd turn us over to the Gestapo, but you never know who else is listening."

"Right."

Shortly thereafter she left him, heading for the nearest subway station. On the platform waiting for the train she felt like guarding her thoughts, as if the SS standing around staring arrogantly at the commuters could read her mind. What if they guessed she knew a secret that could win the war? They had her mother, and if they suspected something, they'd use her for leverage.

And how much did Heisenberg know?

The subway ride was uneventful. Everyone on the train looked tired and beaten down. This new war wasn't anything like the other one. Before, mothers and girlfriends had cheered and thrown flowers as their men went off to war. This time no one particularly wanted it except for the zealots.

A few stops later she got off, mounted the stairs to street level, and walked to the Institute. It was already dark, but she wanted to check through her files before going home. The guard at the foyer checkpoint, a Gestapo agent, was slouched in his chair and smoking. He recognized her and tiredly waved her on.

She went down the darkened hall to her office and unlocked the door. Stepping inside, she felt along the wall for the light switch.

A dark shape loomed up in front of her. Powerful hands struck her in the chest, pushing her sprawling backwards. She slammed into the door, knocking it wide open, falling onto the floor in the hallway. The key flew out of her hand and skittered across the floor. She shouted in indignation and fright, holding her hands up to ward off a blow, but the man turned abruptly and went back into the office, slamming the door shut behind him.

The guard was running down the hall towards her. "Are you hurt?" he said as he ran up. He helped her back up on her feet.

"Quick," she cried, "he's getting away!"

He tried the door, finding it locked again. Rather than reach for his keys, he kicked the door open, shattering the rippled glass window. He entered the room, his gun drawn.

Cold air rushed through the hall. The guard flipped on the lights, finding the office empty and the window at the far end wide open. He and Lieserl ran over and looked outside just in time to see a tall, athletic man in a ski mask making good his escape across a courtyard. The policeman blew his whistle and shouted, and when the man didn't stop, he drew out his Luger and took careful aim. Three shots rang out before the man disappeared around the corner of a building.

The Gestapo agent turned, cursing, and grabbed Lieserl's office telephone, immediately calling for backup support.

Lieserl cast about the room, looking to see if anything had been taken. Her file drawers were ajar: ordinarily she was very neat, so the man must have rifled through them, looking for something. Could he have been searching for her work on the bomb project? Nothing else made sense. She also had some papers on energy production in stars, but that was only of academic interest.

Klaxons screamed in the distance. The Gestapo agent put down the phone and regarded her sternly. "I must take you to headquarters for questioning."

"Why not question me here?"

"I'm sorry, but I have my orders."

Fear clutched at her gut. "I want an attorney."

"You are not under arrest, so you may not have an attorney."

"If I'm not under arrest, then what am I?"

"You are under voluntary detainment."

The sound of boots against tile came from the hallway, and a moment later three Gestapo agents presented themselves and escorted her outside to a waiting staff car. Half a dozen other cars were in the area, agents fanning out in all directions, with a lot of shouting back and forth.

The back seat of the staff car smelled like three-day old vomit. Agents got in on either side of her, the third agent taking the drivers' seat. She was trembling. Everything seemed surreal, bright and dreamlike.

Half an hour later she was at 26 Grosse Hamburgerstrasse in the office of Captain Dobberke.

Dobberke was a short, stern-looking man, born and raised on a farm, formerly a police chief in a small outlying town not far from Berlin. His round, craggy face carried a permanent five o'clock shadow and thick moustache that he often stroked. His nose was bent as if it had once been broken, and his beady, deep-set eyes peered from beneath dark, thick eyebrows. He carried a short whip in one hand as he prowled back and forth across his office, staring at Lieserl, who sat in a straight-back chair. A beautiful young red-headed woman with a desultory look sat behind Dobberke's desk, and Lieserl wondered what she was doing there. Was she a secretary?

Dobberke flipped on a set of bright lights, aiming them into Lieserl's face.

"What were you doing in your office after hours," he said, spitting the words out like a machine gun.

"I was getting some work to take home with me."

He tapped the whip on his palm. "Classified documents?"

"I have clearance."

He brought the whip down with a loud crack, striking the table right next to her. "You were at the Institute earlier. Why didn't you take the papers with you, then? Why come back later under cover of darkness?"

"Your own agent admitted me to the building."

"For that he will be disciplined."

"Captain, I don't know what you think you're doing, but I happen to be associated with a high-level project subsidized by the Wehrmacht. I went to my office, surprised an intruder, and now you're treating me like the criminal."

"How do we know you weren't meeting this criminal at your office? Your file drawers were unlocked. Do you always leave your important papers unlocked?"

"He must have picked the lock."

"Speculation. It's easier for me to believe you're working with him."

"He pushed me down and locked me out of the office. Isn't that proof enough?"

"You collaborated with this enemy agent of the Reich. You feigned an attack, knowing full well your accomplice would escape through your window. You facilitated his theft of important government documents." He took a long drag on his cigarette and blew the smoke in her face. "Give us his name and where we can find him. Cooperate and we'll go easy on you."

"I demand an attorney. It's my right."

"You have no rights!" he shouted, a blue vein standing out in the side of his neck. "I'm the law, here."

"You will allow me to contact my attorney," Lieserl said firmly. "You're making a serious error if you think I will allow you to continue to interrogate me."

Dobberke raised the whip and brought it sharply down on the back of

Lieserl's hand, slicing open the flesh. She cried out, snatching her hand away. Blood oozed from the wound.

"You will answer my questions!" Dobberke shouted.

The redhead behind the desk got lazily to her feet. "Let me handle this," she said quietly. She went over and sat on the table next to Lieserl. She was amply endowed, her low cut dress designed to reveal that fact to maximum effect. She had green eyes and wore heavy eyeliner. "Cherie, my name's Pauline. I realize this is all very difficult for you. Captain Dobberke doesn't understand how a woman feels." She leaned over and said conspiratorially, "But I understand what a man can do, how he can cast a spell on you and take advantage of your feelings. You don't have to protect him. He used you."

"You're out your mind. I never saw that man before in my life."

Pauline frowned. "I don't think you're in any position to play games." She shifted and cast Lieserl a sympathetic look. "We're all doing what we have to do, just to survive. That's all. Maybe you got mixed up with the wrong crowd, maybe you fell in love. I don't know, but I understand what you're going through, and I'm telling you, it's not too late. The man that you're protecting isn't worth the sacrifice, believe me. I've been there."

"I'm sorry, I don't know the man, and I'm a victim of a crime, not a perpetrator. There will be serious consequences when Reichsmarschall Goering learns you're detaining me."

Dobberke flipped his whip in a dismissing gesture. "It's no use. I'll deal with the bitch." He barked an order, and two SS officers came into the room. "Take her down to the interrogation room."

"You can't do this!" Lieserl said, her voice breaking as they took her by the arms.

Dobberke let out a short bark of a laugh. "You'd be surprised at what I can do. And get away with it, too!"

The basement was wet and cold. The silent men, in their early twenties but strangely old and jaded, tied her to a wooden tabletop, her arms stretched out. They adjusted several bright lights so they were shining directly in her eyes. The light flooded out everything; she couldn't see anyone or anything. She heard Dobberke enter the room, giving orders. She heard the sound of a match, then smelled tobacco smoke. He began pacing the room, and she could feel him staring at her. She felt the hard looks of the young men: they were not totally without feeling, they were staring at her experiencing lust, excited by her helplessness, imagining her body beneath the thin veneer of her clothes.

"You can make this hard or easy," Dobberke said. "That's up to you. Once again, who was the man who met you at your office this evening?" When Lieserl didn't reply, he lifted his whip and brought it down on her midriff with a crack. A tortured cry erupted from her throat, and she twisted in her bonds, trying to shield her front from the whip as it whistled through the air again, striking her under her arm near her left breast.

Dobberke stepped over next to her and stuck his face in hers, his breath smoky and sour. "Whom are you working for? British intelligence? The

French?"

She spat in his face.

He jerked his head back with a sharp intake of breath. "That will cost you." He turned and beckoned one of his officers. "Horst, please convince the doctor we mean business."

Horst stepped over next to her. Lieserl tried to squirm as far away from him as possible, but she could only shift a few inches. Horst kept standing there at her side until she was shaking with fear, anticipating the blow to come, the blow he withheld from her.

"Damn you!" she shouted.

Horst threw a fast, hard punch solidly against her left kidney. She grunted, and he whipped a second punch into her solar plexus. She tried to double up, the breath whooshing out of her.

Dobberke blew smoke in her face as she choked, gasping for air. "It's easier to cooperate. We can make it worth your while."

"Go to hell," she managed to wheeze. "I don't know anything."

He took another drag on his cigarette and then placed the tip a centimeter from her cheek. She could feel the heat, and her skin crawled. "It would be a shame if we had to scar that pretty face." He moved the tip closer, close to her left eye. She turned her face away, shutting her eyes tightly.

Angry shouts suddenly came from upstairs, and the door on the landing banged against the wall, and there were more shouts and the sound of heavy boots on the wooden stairs. Dobberke turned, taking the cigarette away from Lieserl's eye.

"What's going on here? Release her at once!"

Lieserl recognized Haberditz's voice instantly.

"I could have your head for this," he stormed. "One word to Goering..."

"You know the prisoner?" Dobberke asked, interrupting him.

"Know her? Of course I know her. She works for me on secret military research. But you should have been able to figure that out for yourself, you idiot!"

"Sorry, Admiral, we were simply investigating..."

"Shut up." He stepped over and cut Lieserl's bonds with a pocketknife. "I'll take you home," he said gruffly. "As for you, Captain Dobberke..."

"My apologies, Admiral. I was only doing my duty."

Haberditz stared witheringly at the Gestapo captain. "We'll see what Goering has to say about that."

He led Lieserl outside to his waiting staff car, supporting her with his strong right arm, making sure she was comfortable in the back seat. Then he went around and got in on the other side with her and ordered the chauffeur to pull out.

"Thank you," she said weakly.

He waved a hand dismissingly. "Don't thank me. Dobberke should know better. I'll see him horsewhipped. Are you all right?"

"Some cuts and bruises. I'll be all right."

"I'll take you home and let Bertha clean you up. She was a nurse in the Great War."

"Thank you."

Half an hour later they were in a nice home in suburban Berlin. Frau Haberditz was an attractive woman in her early forties, with a beautiful head of light brown hair that she had coiled in a crown. She was a large woman, and Lieserl suspected she had been strikingly beautiful at one time but had softened with age.

"We'll have you fixed up in no time," she assured Lieserl as she washed her wounds in the bathroom.

Bertha was regarding her with more than a little interest, and Lieserl, remembering what Haberditz had tried to arrange with her, felt color coming to her face. "Your husband was quite gallant," she murmured, just to say something to fill the silence. "You must be proud of him."

Bertha looked at her sadly, secret pain in her cow's eyes. "He's always very gallant around beautiful women."

That told Lieserl volumes. "Like any other man. They can't stop being what they are."

Bertha smiled and relaxed. After she was finished with the bandages, she brought Lieserl some chicken soup, making sure she was comfortably warm in a reading room. Haberditz joined her there a few moments later.

"If you like you may spend the night here with me. Or I can have my driver take you home."

"I think I'd prefer to go back to my apartment."

"That's fine. Just let me know when you're ready." He shook his head. "This is a very serious matter. It's evident the British realize what we're working on and have agents in place. I'll order more security first thing in the morning. Was anything of importance missing?"

"I'm not sure. I'll have to go carefully through my files."

"Do that. Heisenberg has assured me that the project is moving forward at a steady pace. Speer is less certain, but wants to see it continue. I've ordered fresh supplies of heavy water from the Nordvask plant in Norway, which the Fuehrer's recent initiatives have secured. Is there anything else you need?"

"More radium, more uranium, and higher-quality graphite."

He nodded. "Those you shall have, and anything else you need. I can't emphasize to you how important it is to get a working reactor, and the sooner the better."

She thought of Houtermans and his theories about alternatives to uranium that could be created in a reactor. "Why is that?"

"*Bismarck* and *Tirpitz* are currently under construction at the Kiel shipyards. If there is any chance they could be run with atomic power, that in itself could win the war, even if it turned out a *wunderwaffen* wasn't feasible."

"Yes, of course," Lieserl said faintly. "You could destroy British shipping."

"They'd be far faster and more powerful than anything the British have, and that would tip the scales in our favor. And we could install the engines in submarines. Think of it! Never having to come to the surface, never having to run a snorkel. Inside of a month England would be starving."

"I suppose some would view that as a favorable consequence."

Haberditz shrugged. "We've been over this before. True, Hitler isn't the ideal man for the rulership of a united Europe, but someone has to provide a buffer against Stalin, if only as a lesser of two evils. And dominance on the seas would end the war rather quickly. I imagine Churchill would sue for peace, and from my conversations with the Fuehrer, he'd be more than happy to settle on good terms. Defeating England would be rather risky."

"Because of America."

"Of course. They're very much like us, of course, the English. And the last thing he wants is to bring the Americans into the war. No, he's looking to the east to get his *lebensraum*." He stood and stepped over to her, offering his hand. "If you've finished your soup, I'll escort you to the car. I imagine you're quite fatigued."

"Thank you," she said, rising and taking his arm.

Bertha reappeared, offering her a warm coat and fussing over her. Moments later Lieserl was in the back seat of Haberditz's car on her way back to her apartment. As she sat alone, the taciturn driver impassively conducting the car through the wet midnight streets of Berlin, she thought about Haberditz and how many facets he had. She was grateful for his kindness that night, the rescue, and was surprised he brought her home before his wife. Perhaps she had misjudged him. He was just a man, perhaps in the throes of some personal crisis, but it seemed there was good in him.

Yet he had freed her so easily. Why could he not have similarly freed her mother?

Her apartment building was dark when she arrived. The chauffeur graciously offered to escort her to the door, but she declined. She wearily climbed the three flights of stairs to her apartment, fumbling with the key in the lock. Once inside, she pushed the button for the lights in the living room and quickly shut the door behind her.

A cold wind came through the open door of her bedroom. She walked over to the door and peered inside, into the darkness. The bedroom window was ajar, although she was sure she had left it closed and locked when she left earlier in the day.

A shiver ran up her spine. Fighting down panic, she quickly searched the apartment, looking in closets, under the bed. No one was there, not anymore. In her small kitchen, however, near the refrigerator, she found the muddy outline of a man's boot.

* * * * *

Wolfgang Weisz sat at the window of his apartment, looking across the street into Dr. Meier's apartment with a small pair of binoculars. Her lights were on and she was in the kitchen. The drapes and blinds were still open, because she had been out all day and had only just returned, in the middle of the night. From her movements he could tell she was upset about something, probably about the fact he had violated her privacy. He watched as she made tea and sat at the table sipping it. She appeared to be sketching equations on the tablecloth. Wolfgang had photographed the others, and soon he would have to contact an agent and arrange the return of the microfilms to Britain for analysis. She knew something; she had to, since she had been talking to Fritz Houtermans that afternoon. Weisz had been watching him; he was much too close, with his element 239, and maybe she was, too.

Von Ardenne's lab was actually more worrisome than Heisenberg's facility at the Kaiser Wilhelm Institute. He made up his mind to go out in the country and see about contacting Britain by wireless. At some point they needed to hit the lab and knock it out of commission, and the RAF, with some of the new Lancasters, could do the job.

A little while later she got up from the table, put her teacup in the sink, and moved to the bedroom. He watched as she shrugged off her coat and then began unbuttoning her blouse. It surprised and excited him; he wondered why she didn't close the blinds, but maybe she was too upset, she wasn't thinking straight. She removed her blouse, walking over to the closet in her brassiere to hang up her clothes. She had a beautiful back.

He felt himself becoming aroused. Frowning, he forced himself to put down the binoculars and avert his gaze. Taking secret documents was one thing; gazing upon a woman's body, when the view was not freely offered to him, was another.

Not only did such voyeurism violate his sense of decency, it could also jeopardize his mission. He couldn't afford to become enamored with someone who was working for the enemy. That lovely, innocent-looking woman with the creamy skin might hold the key to a Hitler victory.

If so, like it or not, he would have to kill her.

26 Hamburgerstrasse

Haberditz disliked the short, violent little man. He didn't like his thick, drooping moustache that always seemed dirty, nor his rough, pock-marked skin or his sneering lips. Dobberke, in his eyes, was a country bumpkin, suited to farm work and little else. But he was the local captain of the Gestapo, and further was in charge of rounding up gypsies, Jews and other undesirables in the city, processing them for shipment to the camps. Haberditz needed him.

"Well, Admiral, what other service can I perform for you?" Dobberke asked as he got up from his desk.

"You've done well. The charade was convincing."

"I don't understand why you didn't let me finish questioning her. She's hiding something. I can tell."

"Perhaps. No, almost certainly. She's truly brilliant, a genius, really, but she isn't a patriot. We need her cooperation."

Dobberke lit a cigarette and took a long, slow drag, letting the smoke blow out of his cavernous nostrils. "In a quarter hour I could get her to piss on a crucifix."

"Please, Captain, this is a delicate situation. I believe we can gain her willing cooperation, but we'll have to use more subtle means. The main problem appears to be this man, Dr. Lustig, at the Jewish Hospital. Anna Meier has been undergoing treatment there for some time. I've talked to Lustig, even threatened him, but he refused to cooperate. He has powerful friends, apparently. I thought you might be able to persuade him."

Dobberke nodded casually. "I can persuade him."

"It might also be useful to interrogate Professor Heisenberg."

Dobberke shook his head. "No. I'm sorry, but that I cannot do. Herr Himmler would have my head on a platter."

"But that was several years ago. And surely Heisenberg would be easy to intimidate."

Dobberke grunted in agreement. "He's a pansy. I could break him without laying a finger on him. But Himmler is still Himmler, so you can forget it. I won't touch Heisenberg."

"You wouldn't have to do it yourself," Haberditz pressed, irritated. "Just get one of your men..."

"I repeat, Himmler has given me direct orders not to interfere with Professor Heisenberg. I suggest you speak to him directly about the matter."

Haberditz wanted to insist, thought better of it, and held his tongue. Nodding stiffly, he said, "No doubt you know best how to conduct your business."

Dobberke grinned. "I'll have your reluctant colleague working around the clock. I understand these backsliders."

"I'm sure you do," replied Haberditz. "The problem is, she mustn't be physically harmed, at least not seriously."

Dobberke snorted. "One of my best agents is a Jewess, did you know that? I can put her on the case." He put a hand on Haberditz's shoulder and guided him towards the door. "Leave it to me, Admiral. I'll take care of her."

The Jewish Hospital

Two days later Lieserl decided to visit the Jewish hospital again.

She awoke late, at nearly ten o'clock, when she was used to getting up at dawn. She dressed quickly and walked to the marketplace and bought some lunch to take to her mother, then caught the bus to the hospital.

After getting by the usual SS officers at the entrance, she went to the third floor wards where her mother was located. The same buxom nurse with blond hair was on station.

"I'm sorry," she told Lieserl, recognizing her immediately. "We released your mother earlier this morning."

Lieserl stiffened. "What do you mean, 'released'?"

"Doctor Doctor Lustig determined that she'd recovered. Gestapo agents took her back to 26 Hamburgerstrasse."

Lieserl felt rage boiling up in her, but she kept it in check. "Where can I find Doctor Lustig?"

"He's doing rounds this morning. He could be anywhere. In any case, you are forbidden to disturb him. He's a very busy man."

"I want to know where he is," Lieserl repeated, her voice rising.

"And I'm telling you, you have no business here. If you wish to see your mother, you must go to 26 Hamburgerstrasse."

Lieserl glared her. "I'll find him myself."

She started to brush by the woman, but the nurse reached out and took her by the arm. "I'm sorry, but you can't..."

Lieserl angrily tore her arm out of the nurse's grasp. "Let go of me, you whore!"

The nurse's face turned crimson, then her lips curled into a grimace. "Who are you calling a whore?"

Lieserl pushed past her and strode quickly away down the hallway, while the woman shouted threats at her back. She checked Lustig's office, barging past the surprised secretary, ignoring her protests. He wasn't behind his desk, so she left and charged down the hall looking for him. Finding a stairway, she went up to the next floor, asking orderlies whether they had seen him.

Finally she found him in a post-op ward, checking some of the patients who had recently undergone surgery. He looked up from his clipboard as she marched up to him.

"Dr. Meier," he said cordially. "A pleasure to see you."

"You released my mother."

"Of course I released her. She'd recovered from the seizures. That's a routine matter."

"We had an understanding."

Lustig frowned through his thick gray moustache. "I'm not sure I follow you."

"Professor Heisenberg bribed you to keep my mother safely in the hospital, as you well know," she said sarcastically. "And you haven't kept your side of the bargain."

"I'm not sure what you're talking about, but I find it offensive. Now, I'm very busy..."

"Where did you put the case of Bordeaux? Or have you drunk it already?"

He reddened and turned to the nurse, excusing her. Turning back to Lieserl, he said quietly, "I'm afraid there was nothing I could do. Orders came from the local Gestapo headquarters. I have a certain amount of latitude, but in this case I was not permitted to exercise it. I am very truly sorry about any inconvenience this incident may have caused you."

"Inconvenience? You talk about death in the camps like it's just an inconvenience!"

"I doubt they've shipped her out, yet. That will come at the end of the week. May I suggest you speak with Captain Dobberke? It's out of my hands, so you're just wasting your time and mine."

She turned and stalked out of the ward. It was absolutely true: she was wasting her time. Lustig was weak, a pawn working for the Nazis for his personal gain, and there was nothing he could have done in any case.

She hurried down the front steps and flagged down a taxi. All the way to 26 Hamburgerstrasse she planned her strategy, what to say, what to counter. She fretted, wondering whether she should call Haberditz or Heisenberg first, or maybe Udet, who had promised to help. She needed a good lawyer, one who wasn't a dyed-in-the-wool Nazi, which left her little choice other than a Jewish lawyer, all of whom had been disbarred.

The guards at 26 Hamburgerstrasse were used to seeing her and waved her on through. After a few minutes in a waiting room, another guard ushered her into Captain Dobberke's office. He was sitting behind his desk smoking a cigarette and studying a long list of names, making a show of ignoring her. Lieserl marched up to the front of his desk and stood glaring down at him.

"I've come to demand that my mother be returned to the hospital. She's seriously ill and needs treatment."

Dobberke looked up, his face slack with boredom. "Your mother," he stated matter-of-factly, "is an enemy of the state. She fakes illness so as to avoid doing her duty for the Reich."

She took a deep breath. "I have friends in high places, as you know, Captain. I suggest you cooperate and return my mother to the hospital where she belongs."

Dobberke cleared his throat. "Speaking of our duty to the fatherland, some may wonder why you aren't working to increase the population. As a woman, it's your patriotic duty. There are various experiments going on at the moment…"

Lieserl flushed angrily. "You dare to suggest I'd be a suitable guinea pig for Hitler's experimental breeding programs?"

"I could have you reassigned." He leered at her. "You'd get the best the German Army has to offer. Not all duty has to be unpleasant, eh, Doctor?"

Her right hand swept abruptly up and across his face in a resounding slap. The short man fell back in his chair and put a hand to his cheek, his face flushed. He stood up and faced her across the desk. "You dare to attack an officer of the Gestapo?" he shouted.

"It so happens I know the former head of the Gestapo, Reichsmarschall Goering. I'm sure he'd be very interested in what's transpiring here."

Dobberke regained his composure and straightened. "You aren't nearly as important as you think you are, Frau Meier." He drew his hand back and struck her across the face, staggering her. He walked around the desk as she straightened. "Strong discipline is important, Frau Meier." He struck her again, this time with the back of his hand.

She held her hands to her face, tears of pain and rage coursing down her cheeks. "Striking a woman! You're not a man, you're a creature, a filthy sadist."

He struck her again, and she fell back against the desk, her nose erupting in a stream of blood. "Haberditz will have you shot!" she cried.

Dobberke laughed. "First it's Goering, now only Haberditz. Who's next? Heisenberg?" He spat. "He's nothing but a faggot. A filthy, white Jew queer."

Getting up off the desk, Lieserl marched toward the door, handkerchief on her bleeding nose. Dobberke stepped quickly after her and grabbed her arm.

"Let go of me, you bastard," she said through clenched teeth.

He tightened his grip and jerked her close. "Listen to me, you pampered little Jew-loving bitch," he said, his face inches from her own. His breath was sour with smoke and sausage, and Lieserl tried to tug free, but he held her firm.

"I'm putting your mother on the list," he said. "She leaves for Auschwitz on the Friday train. And this time, we won't be paying attention to any of her tricks."

"She's innocent! Her husband—my father—died in the Great War!"

"I don't give a damn about that."

"I'll pay..."

"That's not what I need from you."

Fear gripped her, displacing her anger, and she felt weak, powerless in his hands. "What do you want from me?"

He released her, shoving her toward the door of his office. "Just do your German duty. That's all."

"What duty?"

"If you don't know your duty, then your mother might as well be dead already."

"And you'll release her if I do my duty? My war research?"

He took out a cigarette and lit it with a gold-plated lighter, complete with swastika engraved on the side. Puffing a large cloud of smoke, he looked like a sinister gargoyle in flesh, an agent of evil. "She'll be well-treated at the camp. If you do your duty."

"And if I don't?"

"Then you'll join her there. You'll work every day, all day, at hard manual labor. While the guards beat you into raw hamburger."

"Let me see her. Let me see my mother."

He smiled cruelly. "Visiting hours are over, and so is this interview. You are dismissed, *Doctor Meier*." He snapped to attention, his arm rocketing straight up from the shoulder. "*Heil Hitler!*"

Lieserl fled the office, slamming the door behind her.

She hurried past the guards. As she went down the front steps to the sidewalk, she ran into a passerby, tripping on the bottom step and sprawling forward.

The man caught her adroitly. "Are you all right?" he said, staring at the marks and blood on her face.

The man was young, in his late twenties or early thirties, handsome, blond and blue-eyed, but he had that look, too confident and self-assured; he was probably a Nazi, and Lieserl wanted nothing to do with him.

"Of *course* I'm all right, you *idiot*!" she shouted through her tears. "Watch where you're going!"

"Sorry. Just trying to help."

He steadied her, and she shook his hands off, clutching a handkerchief to her bleeding nose. "Let me go, God *damn* it!"

She turned and fled, desperately hailing a taxi.

* * * * *

Weisz watched her as she climbed into the taxi. He had been under Dobberke's office window during the interchange between them, managing to catch fragments of the conversation and the sound of violence. Weisz would have liked to kill him, but the Gestapo captain was basically a small fry, and putting a hit on him would jeopardize his mission.

It was beginning to seem that she knew something, and the Gestapo wanted to get it out of her. That might mean she wasn't cooperating, that she had doubts about handing the power of atomic energy to Hitler. And if the Gestapo thought she was holding something back, they would eventually get it out of her; probably sooner rather than later. Weisz needed to find out what she knew or, failing that, prevent the Nazis from finding out.

He remembered how she'd felt in his arms the moment he'd caught her. That had been an error, but he hadn't been able to help himself. Now she'd be sure to recognize him if she saw him again, and what had been just a happenstance on Grosse Hamburgerstrasse would turn into an incident. He'd have to be more careful.

Still, she'd been soft and warm, yet strong, in his arms. Her scent seemed to linger, although the breeze was cool and brisk. He liked the way she'd stood up to Dobberke.

Maybe he'd kill the bastard, after all.

Chapter Eight

Berlin

The next morning Lieserl took a taxi to an airfield outside of Berlin. All the way there she sat in the back seat, thinking furiously, wondering if she were doing the right thing. Her exchange with Dobberke had persuaded her that Haberditz wasn't powerful enough to protect her; Dobberke didn't seem to fear him at all. Hiring an attorney was a possibility—not to argue the case before the Nazi-ridden People's Court, but to insinuate the proper bribes. Dobberke seemed rather stupid, and stupid people could often be bought.

She wasn't sure where Dobberke had gotten the strange idea that she wasn't doing her war duty. He didn't know any science, and couldn't possibly have any idea of whether she were impeding progress or simply stumped on a difficult problem. Most likely he had simply dreamed up the charge as an excuse to harangue and threaten her.

The airfield security was tight, but her identification as a member of the Kaiser Wilhelm Institute and involvement in high priority war research got her inside the gate. She paid the cab driver, giving him a big tip, hesitating, not knowing whether she should have him wait. Finally she went ahead and dismissed him. Watching him drive away awoke a feeling of inevitability in her, as if she'd crossed a rope bridge and then turned and cut the cords.

She walked slowly across the tarmac towards a massive hangar. Aircraft of all kinds were lined up in rows: Messerschmitts, Heinkels, and Stukas. In the distance, out in front of the hangar, she could just make out the portly figure of Udet, decked out in test pilot gear, talking animatedly with a tall, gaunt gentleman, bald except for a thick fringe of hair around the sides of his craggy head.

Udet caught sight of her and motioned her over. "Dr. Meier! This is such an unexpected pleasure! Have you ever met Dr. Messerschmitt? He's one of your fellow scientists!"

Messerschmitt, one of the most famous names in German aviation, had the look of an academic, bookish and learned, combined with that of a mechanic; his hands large and skillful, his eyes clear and intelligent. He bowed slightly. "Pleased to meet you, Doctor. Reichsmarschall Udet has told me much of your work with the famous Professor Heisenberg."

Udet grinned. "I have informed him that you are the real brains behind the operation, and he eagerly awaits your new power plants. Airplanes the size of battleships! Think of it!"

"I suspect you're joking, Reichsmarschall," said Lieserl. "After all, you're most famous for your love of the dive bomber."

His face lit up, like a proud father at the mention of a precocious child. "*Der Stuka*! Yes, that's my baby." He gestured casually at the sleek plane behind him. "But I've got a new one, and you're just in time to observe the test flight."

The wings appeared to be rather stubby, and Lieserl noticed there were no propellers. "A new jet aircraft?"

Udet nodded, his face breaking into an irrepressible grin. "Not exactly. This one, unlike a normal jet, really works!"

Messerschmitt nodded sagely. "I believe it may be the fastest aircraft in the world."

"Surely you're not going to test it yourself."

Udet made a show of looking around, a roguish smile playing about the edges of his mouth. "I don't see anybody else in a flight suit." He laughed. "Don't worry. I used to walk on wings over in the States without even so much as a safety harness, no less!"

Lieserl took a step closer to him. "Reichsmarschall, I came here because I have a rather pressing concern." She glanced at Messerschmitt. "If you could excuse us a moment, Doctor?"

Messerschmitt nodded. "Most certainly."

He walked over to the jet and began studiously examining it. When he was out of earshot, Lieserl turned to Udet. "I desperately need your help. I don't know who else to turn to."

He frowned and his forehead wrinkled. "Let me guess. Your mother's condition is getting worse. I'm very sorry to hear it."

"Not her medical condition. She's going to be transferred to Auschwitz."

Udet drew in a sharp breath and began to splutter. "This...this is an outrage, the wife of a hero of the Great War sent to an internment camp, as if she were an enemy of the state! This must be protested in the strongest possible terms, all the way to the Chancellor if need be!"

"Admiral Haberditz tried to help me, and so did Professor Heisenberg. Captain Dobberke at the Gestapo headquarters on Hamburgerstrasse doesn't fear either of them."

Udet grunted. "If their names didn't work, I'm not sure I can help you. Nobody is afraid of me."

"But I understand you're a good friend of Reichsmarschall Goering."

Udet nodded. "Yes, of course, although lately it seems my influence is going down like a plane with a wing shot off." He laughed, then quickly sobered. "Goering used to be head of the Gestapo, and Dobberke would have to listen to him even now."

"Could you convince Goering to help me?"

"I don't know. The Reichsmarschall does only what pleases him. If you offered him a Monet, perhaps. He likes art."

"Please, Reischsmarschall, this is serious."

"I was being serious." He put a hand to his chin, stroking an invisible beard. "Our troops are outside of Paris. French capitulation is a matter of days away. Maybe one of my officers could arrange borrowing a painting from the Louvre."

"They've probably hidden all the art by now, and anyway there isn't time, she leaves Friday on the trains. Can you get me an interview with

Goering?"

"He's at the Berghof in the Bavarian mountains, conferring with Hitler." Udet studied her a moment. "I don't suppose you wish to speak with Herr Hitler."

She felt dizzy at the thought. "No, I don't think so. I mean..."

"He likes beautiful women, Doctor. You might be able to persuade him."

Lieserl looked off across the airfield to the southwest. "If you'll write a letter for me, I'll go hire a car immediately."

Udet thought a moment and then smiled congenially. "I have a better idea." He pointed at the jet aircraft. "I'll take you there, myself!"

Lieserl's mouth hung open for just an instant, and then she frowned. "I'm not about to get into an experimental aircraft."

"It's perfectly safe." He raised his voice. "Isn't that right, Willy?"

Messerschitt turned. "What's that, Ernst?"

"The plane, the plane, perfectly safe, wouldn't you say?"

"Only when you're not holding the stick!"

Udet laughed. "Right!" He turned to Lieserl. "If you find the prospect daunting, I'll be happy to take you in one of the other planes. A Dornier, perhaps. They're plodding and dull enough."

"I wouldn't want to interfere with your test."

He waved a hand dismissingly. "It's not going anywhere. Come on, let's go commandeer an aircraft."

She colored slightly. "Well, Reichsmarschall Udet, I might prefer, after all, to take a car. I admit I've never flown before."

His eyes widened in mock surprise. "Never *flown* before? You mean to say, never *lived* before!" He turned to Messerschmitt. "Unbelievable! Absolutely unbelievable! I must take this young lady for a ride!"

"That you must," Messerschmitt agreed.

He made apologies to Messerschmitt for the delay in the test and then took Lieserl's overnight bag, leading her across the field where dozens of different aircraft were lined up. Mechanics worked on some of them, in others pilots checked out the systems. Many of the pilots were young and in training, although their youth didn't seem to affect their brash self-confidence. They strutted around, as cocky and self-assured as if they'd already flown in dozens of raids.

He stopped in front of one of the airplanes and conferred with the pilot, who had nearly finished his check of the plane. A moment later he turned to Lieserl.

"Jan kindly offered me his airplane, an ME101. It's a fast and reliable aircraft. There should be a helmet and goggles on your seat, I suggest you use them." He helped her step up into the navigator's position and then climbed into the pilot's chair in front of her. An airman pulled away the chocks. Udet briefly checked the instrument panel and spoke quietly with the control tower over the radio. Then he exchanged a thumbs-up with the airman and displaced pilot and cranked up the engine.

The roar was incredible, and Lieserl found it thrilling. Udet maneuvered the aircraft out of the line and onto the main runway, and then they were dashing across the field, the air rushing past them like the winds of a hurricane. Lieserl was breathless with excitement, and cried out in terror and delight when, with a sudden bump, they were airborne. Udet spoke with the tower again, then rapidly gained altitude. Shortly thereafter he made a great loop of the field and headed south.

Lieserl leaned against the side of the open cockpit, transfixed by the amazing panorama beneath her: Berlin was to the east, the countryside beneath her, and mountains to the south. She could understand how people could become enamored with flight. With all the beautiful land that was Germany stretched out below her, she felt like a goddess with a view from Olympus, drunk with euphoria, invulnerable to harm.

In a few minutes she sobered and began to think about what she would say when Udet presented her to Reichsmarschall Goering. If she told them about Houtermans' work, about her reactor design, all of Nazi Germany would be at her feet and she could have anything she wanted: an enormous research budget, monetary rewards, her mother's freedom. She could probably even have Dobberke sent to the work camps.

She had to shut her eyes and clench her fists, fighting the temptation silently within the confines of her mind. How much could she afford to give them? How much would they require before giving her what she wanted?

Within an hour they were deep in the Bavarian Alps. Himmler had been born there, and Lieserl wondered how such a beautiful land could have birthed his meticulously dark spirit. Pastures rolled beneath them, and tall, deep forests. Udet started the descent, and before long they were coming down for a landing in a small airfield just outside of Salzburg.

The aircraft bumped softly twice before it settled down into a gentle roll. As the plane came to rest, Udet twisted in his seat and peered back at Lieserl.

Despite the thrill of the ride, Lieserl's stomach was tying itself in knots as Udet helped her down out of the aircraft. "Good ride, wasn't it?" he said to her jovially. He seemed oblivious to her inner tensions, and laughed as if they were a pair of students out on holiday. "Teach me something about physics and I'll teach you to fly!"

"Yes, I'd be happy to learn," she murmured. "Especially from you." She leaned over and gave him a kiss on his cheek. "Thank you, General. You've been most kind."

Udet blushed and grinned. "You're quite welcome, Doctor."

A black Mercedes waited on the road a short distance away, dour chauffeur standing by.

"We don't have an invitation, I'm afraid, but they sent the limousine instead of a hearse, so that's a good sign," Udet said as they walked over to the car. The chauffeur opened the back door for Udet, then trotted around to the opposite side and did the same for Lieserl. A moment later they were heading up a gravel road.

"It's only a ten minute ride up the Obersaltzberg," Udet commented as the driver negotiated the drive up the hill overlooking Saltzberg. He reached over and patted Lieserl's hand in a paternal gesture. "Don't worry, I'm sure we'll be able to work something out. At least, we'll do our best."

"I know."

The retreat was a spectacular mansion of stone perched on top of a hillside, the Bavarian mountains rearing up all around. Part of the mansion was older, having the appearance of a typical vacation home, but around this core were impressive wings of stone, massively amplifying the original structure's size.

Lieserl and Udet got out of the Mercedes at the foot of a flight of marble steps that led upwards to the house, Nazi flags on poles flanking either side of the staircase. Elite SS guards were posted everywhere, but Udet nodded his way easily past them without challenge. At the top of the staircase was a grand plaza that nearly encircled the mansion, a low, ornate wall running around the periphery. The air was cool and pure, and as Lieserl breathed deeply some of her tension seemed to evaporate away.

The architecture of the house wasn't pretentious; it was large and comfortable. Hitler had owned the property for many years, purchasing the original house and grounds at low price from a wealthy member of the Nazi party. Udet led Lieserl across a courtyard towards the main building, and as they approached the double doors opened and several SS men stepped out, followed by an enormous, rotund man, whom Lieserl recognized as Hitler's personal physician, Dr. Morell. He talked and smiled too much, more like a politician than a doctor. Hitler was right next to him, dressed in his faded green military uniform, listening intently as the doctor spoke. Goering's great bulk was on Hitler's other side, and several high-ranking members of the Wehrmacht were behind them.

"Whatever you do, don't get into a disagreement with the Fuehrer," Udet said quietly, his lips curled in irony. "Try to guess how he feels about something and agree in advance, but make him think his brilliant logic is convincing you."

"Don't worry, I'm not even going to talk to him."

Udet nodded. "That's a better idea. But he can be gallant sometimes around the fairer sex. He'll probably invite you to dinner. If he does, you would be wise to accept, although it means four or five hours of rather tedious conversation, including foreign films and a lot of staring at walls in one of his giant pieces of furniture."

"Giant furniture?"

"Well, for Goering they're almost normal size. They swallow everyone else up. The Fuehrer designed it all himself with help from Speer."

Hitler noticed them and strode over. "I understand production of warplanes is up for the month of October. That's very good."

"Only because the Reichsmarschall is sitting on me," Udet joked, pointing at Goering.

"Someone has to do it," Goering replied, and he laughed shortly. "We'll need every airplane we can make, especially for Barbarossa."

Hitler shot him a hard look, then turned his attention to Lieserl. "I haven't had the pleasure, Frau."

"Doctor," Lieserl said. "Doctor Meier."

Morell looked suspicious, but covered it with a grin. "A physician?"

"A physicist."

"A woman physicist!" Morell replied, raising his eyebrows. "You are a rare breed, indeed! Some say the female of the species is ill-suited for such intellectually intensive work."

"Madames Curie and Meitner put that curious idea to rest, I believe," Lieserl replied.

"Lise Meitner is a traitor," Goering said with a frown, "and if the Gestapo had caught her before her escape to Sweden, she would have hung from the highest tree!"

"Lise Meitner's only fault, if you can call it that, is the fact she was born in Austria."

At the mention of Austria, Hitler's eyes smoldered. "We will talk later, perhaps up at my tea house," he said carefully.

Udet nudged Lieserl in the ribs. "Dr. Meier is from Hamburg, from a very excellent family. Her father died defending the Fatherland in the Great War."

Hitler nodded judiciously. "That is meritorious, but of course it is her father's merit, not hers."

"I need not bathe in anyone's reflected glory," Lieserl replied. "My accomplishments speak for themselves."

"That's excellent," said Hitler, nodding again. "You're strong, and that's the kind of German I need to help me reach my goals. Will you join me for dinner?"

Lieserl felt positively sick at the prospect, but Udet was nudging her, and she accepted. "Good!" Hitler suddenly beamed with pleasure. "We will eat, and then perhaps retire for some entertainment, some discussion. I want to know all about your work. Goering has told me something about it, now that I recall. With Heisenberg, isn't it?"

"Yes, I work closely with Professor Heisenberg. I've been his assistant for several years."

"I'm very interested in German science, as you know."

Hitler turned abruptly and led his retinue away in the general direction of the lake. When they were well out of earshot, Udet said, "You handled that well, although you almost stopped my heart with that little exchange with Goering. Fortunately the Chancellor likes you, you came across as strong and brave. I think maybe he'll help your mother."

"Maybe."

Udet spread his hands. "Well, you know, there's nothing left for me to do, here. I've got to get back to Willy and help him with his toys."

Her eyes widened. "You're not leaving me, are you?"

"Sorry, Doctor, but I have my own work to attend to. Besides, I have no desire to spend an evening trying to make idle chatter in between long, awkward silences. And that furniture!"

Udet laughed, then turned and motioned to the chauffeur, who was standing nearby. Lieserl felt lost for a terrible moment, and said desperately, "You were going to talk to Goering for me, weren't you?"

He hesitated, and then waved his hand dismissingly. "He's not in a receptive mood, at least not towards me. Believe me, you're better off on your own. You could charm him; I'll just make him mad."

"Will you be coming back for me?"

He shrugged. "If I can, yes, of course. But there are trains, too, you know. Did you remember to bring your pocketbook? I can give you train fare back to Berlin, if you need it."

"Thank you, no, I have enough money." She walked with him back to the limousine. "Thank you again for your help."

"Don't mention it. Let me know how it turns out. Good-bye!"

He climbed into the back seat of the limousine, then rolled down the window and leaned out. "Remember, don't make him mad! Don't talk about the Jewish question, nor about Bolsheviks. Steer clear of the war, too, unless you are careful to praise its conduct and prospects. He doesn't like pessimists, they make him angry. Do you understand?"

Lieserl nodded, and Udet said, "Good!" He sat back in the car and ordered the driver to pull out.

Lieserl stood there in the dust, staring at the limousine until it disappeared from view down the hillside. She couldn't help feeling abandoned. She'd hoped Udet would stay and help guide her through the political minefield that awaited her back in the Berghof.

SS guards watched her carefully as she walked back up to the terrace. She studiously ignored them. Hitler's half sister, who also acted as housekeeper and cook, showed Lieserl to a small guest room on the second floor of the main house, informing her that dinner would be at six. Hitler and Goering were in meetings with various high-ranking members of the Wehrmacht, so there wouldn't be any chance of speaking with either of them until later.

After resting in her room a while, she left the Berghof and wandered through the fields. She found the pure air and the beauty of the hillsides and mountains rejuvenating, and it seemed strange to her that a man who was so filled with hate could appreciate the beauty and tranquility of such a place, even while planning fresh attacks on his neighbors in the privacy of his study.

She found a beautiful lake hidden among the hills. On the far end a majestic waterfall threw up an enormous spray. A path ran around the perimeter, and she began following it.

As she neared the opposite side of the lake she saw someone swimming near the falls. Clothing was neatly folded in a pile on a nearby rock, and Lieserl realized, to her embarrassment, that the person was naked. She very nearly turned back, but realized it was another woman. As Lieserl watched, the woman climbed out of the water and lay down on her back spread-eagled in the sun. Her body was not unattractive, but her hips were heavy and rear end too large. Despite the awkwardness of the situation, Lieserl walked over to her.

"Excuse me..."

The woman's eyes flashed open. "Oh!" she cried, jerking upright and grabbing for her clothes.

"I'm sorry, I didn't mean to startle you."

The woman smiled and relaxed, still holding her clothes up before her chest. She was blond and pretty in a vapid, salesgirl kind of way.

"No, that's all right, I'm just relieved it wasn't one of the men." She was still damp from her swim, but she went ahead and slipped a shift over her head, not bothering with her undergarments, which were still neatly arranged on the rock. "You gave me a start."

"Sorry."

"Are you one of the new secretaries?" the woman asked.

"No, I'm a scientist, Dr. Lieserl Meier, associated with the Kaiser Wilhelm Institute in Berlin."

"Oh! A scientist!" Her eyebrows rose. "That sounds very exciting. My name is Eva Braun."

"I take it you're one of the other secretaries?"

Eva laughed and blushed slightly. "No, not exactly, although sometimes it feels that way. I'm the Fuehrer's girlfriend. Haven't you read about me in the gossip columns?"

"I don't read newspapers."

Eva cocked her head. "How very strange. I think you're the first person I've met who doesn't. Why not?"

"I don't have that much time to waste."

Eva tilted her head in a facile, knowing nod. "Well, it's true you can't believe most of what you read. Did you come here for a meeting of some kind?"

"Yes. I'm hoping to talk to Reichsmarschall Goering about my mother, who has been unjustly detained by the Gestapo for the past several months."

"Goering." Eva shuddered. "What a horrible man. If a bull mated with a giant toad, he's what you'd end up with."

Lieserl laughed. "I'm sure of it!"

"He's always trying to curry favor. He'll tell the Fuehrer anything, no matter how untrue, just to get him around to his point of view. And he says one thing to his face, another behind his back. I don't trust him."

"Chancellor Hitler apparently does."

"The Fuehrer is very busy. He can't possibly keep an eye on what all his people are doing. That's why we're in the middle of this terrible war. I was afraid, when it broke out, that I'd never see him again, but it's worked out rather well, actually. He's here at the Berghof nearly all the time, meeting with his generals and with that two-faced Italian, Ciano." She made a face. "He's almost as bad as Goering."

Lieserl eased down on the rocks near Eva, realizing she had stumbled onto a golden opportunity. The woman didn't seem very intelligent, but she shared Hitler's bed and might have some influence. She thought of Haberditz's statement about influence being everything in the Reich, and smiled grimly.

Eva noticed, and said: "A pfennig for your thoughts, as the English say."

Lieserl shook her head. "Nothing. I was thinking of something else."

Eva took a brush out of a small backpack and began brushing her hair, regarding Lieserl thoughtfully. "What do you think of him?"

"Of the chancellor?"

"Who else?"

Lieserl saw the guarded look in Eva's eye, and realized she was worried about competition. "Well, I think he's done a great deal for Germany. He's a greater man even than Bismarck."

Eva nodded, but she looked a little anxious, unsure of how to pursue the question. "Yes, of course. But, as a woman, what do you think of him? Of him as a man?"

"You would know more about that than I would. Is he easy to get along with?"

She snorted and set her lips in a tight line. "He can be very difficult. Most people don't realize all I've gone through for him."

"I can't imagine."

"Of course you can't. Not unless you've had the man you loved more than anything in the world treat you like an old piece of furniture."

Lieserl rolled her eyes and said encouragingly, "Men! They're all alike."

Eva giggled and shifted closer. "They ignore you for days, and then when they finally notice you're there, they can only think of one thing."

"That sounds like every man I ever knew. Is he attentive when you're alone?"

"Sometimes his is. Well, come to think of it, almost never. He's always thinking, planning this or that. I guess he has a good excuse."

Lieserl nodded sympathetically. "Someone has to lead the country."

Eva had an apple that she shared with her, cutting off pieces with a Swiss army knife. They chatted for a while, Eva very interested in fashion, talking at length about all the clothes she'd obtained from the most expensive houses in Paris. Lieserl found her boring; Eva didn't seem like the kind of person who could ever wield any influence. She only barely had a will of her own.

Finally Eva suggested they walk back to the Berghof. "I've been in love with the Fuehrer ever since I first heard him speak," she said as they walked through the pastures next to the lake. "But he neglects me and he's still too embarrassed to even acknowledge his feelings for me. Did you know that I still have to address him as Fuehrer when anyone is around? It's silly."

"I'm surprised he doesn't make you address him like that in private."

She giggled. "Don't give him any ideas! Why do you think he's like that?"

Lieserl shrugged. "A lot of men are like that. They keep their feelings to themselves."

"Yes, I suppose so. Still, after all these years, you'd think he'd be ashamed to be carrying on, not making a decent woman out of me."

"Have you suggested marriage?"

"Are you kidding? He'd have me put away!"

"Surely not."

They reached the Berghof. Several black staff cars were lined up outside, the uniformed chauffeurs standing around smoking. "He must be having a meeting of the general staff. I think they're planning something important."

"When do you think I might be able to speak with Goering?"

"You'll have to wait until after dinner. Maybe after we see some of the movies. There's an American film about a man who lives with apes..."

"I'm not familiar with it."

"Well, it's rather funny. The Fuehrer says that it shows how low the Americans are, the way they make films about men consorting with apes, living like savages out in the jungle. But it's rather entertaining. 'Tarzan of the Apes', I think it's called. Do you go to the movies, or is that like reading newspapers?"

"Worse." Lieserl put a hand to her head. "If you'll excuse me, Eva, I'm rather tired, and it seems I have a headache."

"Oh, of course, I'm sorry. You have a room?"

"Yes, thank you."

"Well, it was nice meeting you." She held out her hand and Lieserl shook it. "I suppose I'll see you at dinner."

"Of course. See you then!"

Lieserl left quickly and went upstairs to her room, glad that her feigned indisposition had enabled her to escape the woman so quickly. The room was simple but tastefully furnished, with a comfortable bed and a writing table and chair. Someone had put a box of chocolates on the night table beside her bed. She sat down on the bed and ate one, the rich taste soothing her nerves. How could she take advantage of the situation? Could she manipulate Eva and get some concession from Hitler through her? Yet it seemed he didn't treat her very well to begin with, so maybe her suggestions would only prejudice or enrage him.

She rested on the bed, dropping off to sleep for a few minutes but soon awakening too soon. She stared at the ceiling, thinking, still tense. She felt as if she were a traitor, hiding right in the middle of an enemy camp, on the verge discovery.

At six o'clock an aide knocked quietly on her door, informing her that it was time for dinner. Lieserl freshened herself at a small sink in the corner and went downstairs.

The dining room was spacious and well appointed, with wood paneling on the interior walls and a line of windows facing out on the slopes of the Obersalzburg. Goering and the Wehrmacht staff were already seated at the table, as was the obese Dr. Morell and a thin, reedy-looking man with a narrow, hatchet face and something of the appearance of a large rat. Yet his eyes were highly intelligent, bright and probing behind thick glasses, and he had a congenial, relaxed air that belied his appearance. Lieserl recognized him: Goebbels, the minister of propaganda.

"Well, well!" exclaimed Goebbels, mouth stretching wide into a grin. "We have a new guest!"

He rose and went directly over to her, extending his hand. "I am Dr. Goebbels," he said cordially. "Welcome to our small gathering of friends. May I ask your name?"

"Dr. Lieserl Meier, of the Kaiser Wilhelm Institute in Berlin."

"Yes, of course, Heisenberg's protégé!" His thin fingers gripped her hand tightly as he enthusiastically pumped her hand. "I've heard much about you!"

"Complimentary, I hope."

"Yes, of course!" He took her by the arm and led her to the chair next to his. "We've all heard of your work in your Uranium Club and the fascinating possibility of new sources of power, of a *wunderwaffen*, and I don't mind telling you that whether or not your research is successful, the propaganda value alone is worth the cost!"

"I assure you, Dr. Goebbels," said Lieserl, with an air of complete self-assurance, "if a controlled nuclear reaction is possible, then German science will achieve it."

"Bravely said, bravely said." Goebbels reached for his wine glass and stood up. "Let's drink a toast to German science!"

A clinking of glasses all around was followed by a general bending of arms. Waiters went around the table, refilling the glasses as everyone sat down again. Lieserl found herself between Goebbels and Morell.

"Of course, we shall not be needing your help to win this war," Goebbels said. "But imagine, a woman of your charm who is also highly trained and intelligent!"

Dr. Morell leaned his great toad-like bulk over toward Goebbels, crowding Lieserl and making her uncomfortable. "She is most certainly a forerunner of the next stage of Aryan evolution," he said thickly. He began pointing at her face, his fingers lightly touching her hair. "Note the lovely blond hair and eyes, which are dark but highly intelligent. Note the structure of the cranium, the noble forehead. I estimate her to be eighty per cent pure-blooded Aryan for the last five generations, at the very least."

Goering, sitting across from them, said, "We need more like her on the farms, pushing out a new *ubermensch* every year."

"You have children?" Morell asked.

Lieserl shook her head. "No, not yet."

"What, no children?" he exclaimed. With a sly look he said, "Your husband doesn't pay you proper attention, does he?"

Lieserl colored slightly. "I have no husband. The demands of a life of science, you understand, are considerable."

"I'm surprised at you gentlemen," said Goebbels. "You are treating the lady as if she were a prize cow. I, for one, am pleased that she has answered a higher calling. Too many fraulein are discouraged from using their minds, and now that you've found one you're making her feel abnormal."

Morell raised his thick, bushy eyebrows. "I believe the exceptional may be properly considered abnormal."

"In which case," Goebbels proclaimed, "everyone in this room must be considered abnormal!"

Everyone laughed except for Lieserl. Goebbels noticed, and said, "Don't pay any attention, Dr. Meier. I assure you there isn't a man in this room who wouldn't give anything to possess your scientific acumen."

"Each person possesses different talents and abilities," Lieserl replied. "My personal ability happens to lie in the sciences, but a master carpenter or a brilliant military strategist are of equal value to the Reich."

"Well said, well said," Goebbels said, beaming. "You know, I could use someone like you in my department if you weren't already better employed at Kaiser Wilhelm."

"Don't be fooled by his smooth tongue, Dr. Meier," Goering said with a sly smile. "His head turns one hundred eighty degrees when a skirt walks by. And I'd wager he's already set his eyes on you."

Lieserl turned to Goering. "Thank you for the good advice, Reichsmarschall Goering. You're most gracious."

Goering reached for his wineglass, still grinning. "Somebody has to keep Goebbels from making a damned fool of himself."

"He specializes in protecting me from myself," Goebbels told Lieserl. "But I assure you, Doctor, nothing you've heard about me is true."

"The real truth is worse, no doubt."

Goering laughed hugely, joined by Goebbels and the rest of the entourage. "She has a great sense of humor, that one!" Goering said. "At Carinhall I was speaking of protecting endangered species, moose and the like. She speaks up and says, 'And the Jews, too?'"

The men broke out laughing again, but quieted quickly as Hitler came into the dining room, accompanied by Eva Braun. Everyone rose, right arms shooting out straight from the shoulder with a chorus of heil Hitlers. Lieserl stood but did not salute.

Hitler walked over to her and bowed, taking her hand and kissing it. "I'm pleased to see you. Fraulein Effie has informed me you and she have already met. She has spoken highly of you."

Lieserl felt intense revulsion at the touch of Hitler's lips on her hand, but masked the reaction. "Thank you very much, Chancellor."

"You will join me at the head of the table, please."

"Of course, sir."

Hitler strode over to the head of the great table, indicating that Lieserl should sit at his right hand. The first course came out, a thin vegetable gruel that was warm but tasteless. A vegetable pasta followed.

"You note the absence of meat," Hitler said between mouthfuls.

"Yes. I take it you're a vegetarian."

"The butchering process is barbaric. I hold that anyone with too weak a stomach to slaughter the beasts himself has no business eating meat. Furthermore, meat is bad for the health."

"That's very interesting. I wasn't aware of that."

"Smoking is just as bad, or worse. Do you smoke, Dr. Meier?"

Lieserl shook her head. "I have never smoked."

Hitler looked up and smiled, gesturing at her, offering her to the others around the table. "You see, you should all take lessons from the scientist. She knows better than all my advisors."

"Hear, hear!" cried Goebbels.

"Especially you, Effie," Hitler said, frowning at his mistress. She merely smiled and looked back down at her plate.

"Smoking will kill you," said Goering. "So maybe we should air drop cigarettes to the enemy!"

"Sadly enough, no tobacco is grown in Germany," Goebbels pointed out.

"So I'll send my Luftwaffe against Turkey!"

"When the time is right, yes, of course," Hitler said, self-assured when discussing military tactics. "But there are far more important objectives."

"Such as finishing the British," declared Goering. "Give me the authority, my Fuehrer, and in three days the skies over England will be black with Stuka. In two weeks the British will be begging to surrender unconditionally."

A resonant voice came suddenly from behind them. "The English pilots might have something to say about that."

Everyone turned in their chairs. "Speak of the devil!" Goering exclaimed.

Haberditz strode confidently over from the outside entrance. "The Kriegsmarine has sunk four hundred thousand tons of shipping in the last month. You have Donitz and Lutjens to thank for that."

"U-boats!" sneered Goering. "They're much too vulnerable to destroyers." He looked around the table, gesturing with open arms. I assure you all, once the United States enters the war they'll be finished."

"Not U-boats alone," Haberditz said, lifting a cautionary finger. "I remind you that *Bismarck* and *Tirpitz* will soon be operating in the North Atlantic. They will decisively shift the balance of power on the high seas."

Hitler stroked his chin, his face shadowed with worry. "Capital ships are quite vulnerable to torpedoes, aren't they, Admiral?"

Haberditz frowned and made a dismissing gesture. "They're like mosquito bites on a cow's hide. I assure you, the British may have a larger navy, but they won't be able to match our firepower."

"Still, you are highly limited," Goering spoke up, his great brow wrinkling in annoyance. "Unlike the British you have no ports, no bases at which to get supplies and do routine repairs and maintenance. And the River Plat affair cast some doubt on the courage of your naval commanders."

Haberditz interrupted him. "You refer to the *Graf Spee* and its cowardly captain. Alas, we have our defectives, although in our case it is the exception and not the rule."

Goering reddened and shot to his feet, knocking his chair over. "What are you implying, Admiral?"

"Only that cowardice is found everywhere, and must be rooted out if we are to continue our successes on all fronts."

"German pilots aren't cowards! There isn't a one among them who wouldn't gladly die for the Fatherland! I myself would pay the ultimate sacrifice, even in the face of hopeless odds!"

"You are an exception, Reichsmarschall. That clown Udet, on the other hand..."

Goering snorted like a great bull. "Even the so-called clown Udet has more guts than a hundred sailors!"

Hitler suddenly pounded the table with his fist and stood up. "Enough of this bickering! You are both right. German pilots have great courage, but Admiral Haberditz is also correct in saying that there are Jews and other degenerates who are undermining our country." Throwing an arm dramatically up, he pointed skyward and thundered: "The Jews and Bolsheviks betrayed us at Versailles! They shall not betray us again!"

Goering, mollified by Hitler's remarks, grinned. "Hear, hear! I should hate to be a Jewish traitor in Germany at this moment in time."

Hitler waved the issue away with an abrupt gesture. "I have charged Himmler with implementing a final solution to the problem, but we must be eternally vigilant." He sat back down and waved at the food on the table. "Eat, it will settle all your nerves."

For a few minutes everyone was silent, attending their dinners. Then Hitler started into one of his monologues, talking in between bites with his mouth half full, lecturing interminably on the state of Europe before the outbreak of the war and on the imminent collapse of England.

"It's only a matter of time," he said at last. "In a few days, a few months, they'll sue for peace. Then we'll carve up their empire between us."

Lieserl cleared her throat. "Who shall benefit?"

Hitler made an expansive gesture. "Japan, Italy, our other allies."

"And Russia," said Goering.

"Russia!" spat Hitler. "Yes, of course, I suppose so."

"It surprised me when you made a treaty with them, my Fuehrer," said Lieserl carefully. "After all, you fought them for years in Munich and even in Parliament."

Hitler nodded. "I fought the communists on the streets, yes, and then made a deal with the devil, himself. And when I offered to share the world with him, do you know what that cold-blooded blackmailer did? He sent me an endless list of petty demands! Get out of Finland, he said, stay away from the Middle East, give me a seaport on the Bosphorus. *Ach!*" He threw his hands up. "No matter. The important thing is that England has nearly collapsed."

At that moment the air raid sirens went off, wailing like banshees. Eva Braun jumped up excitedly, eager to be off to the bomb shelters. Goering made a show of smiling confidently, as if he had some special immunity to English ordnance. Bormann took charge of organizing everyone, ushering them in the direction of the underground bunkers.

Lieserl felt someone brush up beside her, and found Haberditz at her arm. "If England has collapsed," she said to him with quiet irony, "why are we rushing down into the bomb shelters?"

Haberditz smiled grimly. "An excellent question. I imagine there's still a little cleaning up to do. Actually, the real problem is that bastard Churchill. He doesn't know when to quit."

The bunker was only dimly lit. Lieserl found herself ensconced between Haberditz and Eva Braun. Everyone sat silently on the benches with bated breath, as if the English pilots might hear them if they talked or breathed too loudly.

Minutes dragged by slowly. Eva let out a sigh and whispered throatily, "God, for a cigarette!" Goering muttered something to Goebbels, who laughed softly. Lieserl closed her eyes and gritted her teeth. The closeness of Haberditz, his warm body right next to hers, was oppressive.

Finally the all clear signal came and everyone relaxed. "What did I tell you?" announced Goering with satisfaction. "My night flyers took them all out before they could get anywhere near the Berghof!"

Hitler led them all upstairs and guided the group towards the movie room where he promised the latest films from America. Haberditz took Lieserl aside.

"Let's get away from here."

She bristled, shrugging off his hand. "I'm here on business."

"You don't know what you're in for. We'll be watching films until midnight, then we'll sit around in those overgrown chairs and listen to a monologue for the next three hours, punctuated by bored silence."

Lieserl shook her head. "Maybe so, but I've got to get one of them to help my mother."

"I know all about your mother, and I'm the man who can take care of her. Do you really think they give a damn?"

"Eva might."

He grimaced in disgust. "Eva is a pathetic toy, the Fuehrer's bauble. Trust me, she won't help you, most especially because you're competition." He gestured toward the door leading out onto the spacious courtyard. "Come on. I'll show you the eighth wonder of the world and give you the latest news on Anna Meier."

Reluctantly Lieserl followed him outside past the SS sentries, who stolidly ignored them. She didn't have any idea where they were going, but the evening had left her drained. She felt she had almost no will power left.

Haberditz led her to his shiny black Mercedes out in front of the Berghof, looking like a chariot to the underworld. He opened the passenger side and seated her. Going around and getting in behind the wheel, he turned on the engine and pulled out onto the main road. But instead of going back towards Berchestaden, as she had expected, he turned up the hill.

The one lane road wound up and around the Kehlstein, leading several kilometers through forest and then beyond, above the tree line, through tunnels and along cliffs. The moon cast a mystic light over the Bavarian mountains. They passed no one on the lonely road, which despite leading up into the upper reaches of the Kehlstein, was very new, in perfect condition.

The pavement ended at a short tunnel with an elevator at the end, guarded by a single SS, a member of the Death's Head regiment.

Haberditz pulled out a golden key. "This is our ticket to a very interesting evening."

"Where is that?"

"You'll see soon enough."

They got out of the car. Haberditz exchanged a few words with the sentry and then used his key on the elevator, opening the doors.

The inside of the elevator was gold-plated. The seats were plush leather, and there was even a telephone. "Nothing but the best for the Fuehrer and his retinue," cracked Haberditz.

"I can see that."

Haberditz punched a button, and the elevator started up at high speed. Moments later it slowed to a stop and the doors opened.

Lieserl stepped out into a fantasy. A semi-circle of enormous marble columns braced the sky, with the snow-capped Bavarian mountaintops all around, gleaming in the moonlight. Grand staircases carved of stone led to terraces overlooking the valley. The air was cold and pure, and as Lieserl breathed it in she felt invigorated and powerful. A giant fireplace burned brightly, and there were a few pieces of oversized chairs set near low marble coffee tables and a great table of oak surrounded by luxurious leather-upholstered executive chairs. The marble pillars supported a dome overhead.

"Hitler's private teahouse," Haberditz said, a touch of sarcasm in his voice. "A most ambitious undertaking led by Bormann, and built at a cost of thirty million marks."

Lieserl walked around the room, taking it all in, gazing at the amazing vistas. "It's fantastic, I must admit. He must be very proud of it."

"He's used it a total of three times, and that was all shortly after it was built. He actually doesn't care for it, for some reason."

"I can understand why. It makes you feel small. That would be repulsive to him."

Haberditz nodded. "Yes. I think you've hit on it."

He led her over to the fireplace and pointed at the mantle above it. "Do you see that spearhead mounted on the wall?"

"Is it valuable?"

"It is the most valuable artifact in the entire world. Do you know what it is?"

"It looks very old. Roman?"

"We obtained it from the museum in Vienna. It's German by right, because it was stolen from us. Frederick the Great owned it during his conquests throughout Europe, winning his campaigns against overwhelming odds. Legend has it that whoever possesses it cannot be defeated in war."

"Frederick the Great was finally defeated, I think."

"Yes, but that was after he lost the spearhead."

"And what's so special about it?"

Haberditz turned to her, his eyes a smoldering fire. "That is the spearhead that pierced the side of Christ."

A shiver went up Lieserl's spine. "Surely no one knows…"

He waved his hand. "It doesn't matter whether it's authentic or not. Yes, it may be a copy, but Hitler believes in legends. The spearhead is the first thing he wanted when Vienna capitulated."

As Lieserl stared at the spearhead, fascinated, Haberditz moved up beside her. "Your mother is safe. No harm will come to her."

She turned to him, her eyes widening. "She's no longer at 26 Hamburgerstrasse, then?"

"No."

"Well, where is she?" she demanded impatiently. "Back home in Hamburg?"

"She was to go to Auschwitz. At the last possible moment I arranged a transfer to Theresienstadt."

"Theresienstadt! But that's hardly better than Auschwitz!"

"She's a musician, and Theresienstadt has an orchestra. It's irregular, but the commandant likes music, and thinks it helps keep his charges in line. As long as she pleases him she'll be well-treated."

Lieserl's face darkened with fury. "That's the best you could do? Send her to a concentration camp?" She turned abruptly and started walking swiftly for the elevator.

"Where are you going?"

"I must go speak with the Fuehrer immediately."

Haberditz moved quickly, catching up with her and taking her arm. "It's no use talking to Hitler. He won't do anything. Himmler, perhaps, that's his sphere of influence."

She shook his hand off. "Hitler is the supreme authority."

"But he won't exercise it, here. You could jeopardize your mother's future, don't you understand? Even your own future is at stake. I can help you, but you must learn to trust me."

"Trust you?" she said, her face incredulous. "You expect me to trust you? I'm sorry, you haven't earned it."

She turned again to leave but this time Haberditz caught her by the wrist, his grip firm.

"Let go of me!"

"I can't allow you to storm back to the Berghof in your present state of mind. That wouldn't be responsible."

"You can't stop me!"

"I will protect your mother, and I will protect you." He pulled her close, staring down into her eyes. "I swear it."

"I told you to let me go. Do you understand me? You are not to touch me."

"I'm a powerful man, Lieserl, far more powerful than you realize."

"If you're so powerful, why is my mother in a camp?"

He grinned slyly. "Knowledge is power. You of all people should understand that."

The tone of his voice caught her unaware, and she spluttered, "How...what are you talking about?"

He brought his face close to hers, so close she could smell his sour sweat and Turkish cigarette smoke. "I know who you are."

The words chilled her to the bone, and for an instant she didn't know what to do. Did he really know? And, if so, how had he found out? Had Heisenberg told him?

"I can help you," he said again, his voice calm and soothing. "Together, we can get anything we want, anything!"

Fury rose in her like a juggernaut. "I don't give a damn! Not about you, not about anyone!"

She brought her knee up sharply, striking him in the groin. He grunted in pain, but his grip on her wrist grew tighter. Bringing her hand around, she slapped him hard on the face. Before she could strike him again he caught her hand, then held both of her hands in one of his.

"I'll scream!"

He grinned. "Here's a little of your own medicine." Lifting his free hand, he slapped her across the face. Her cry of pain echoed off the cold marble walls. He slapped her again, and she twisted and began screaming for help at the top of her lungs. He cuffed her on the side of the head.

"Help!" she cried. "Please, somebody help me!"

Lifting her up, Haberditz threw her over his shoulders. For a terrible instant she feared he might hurl her over a nearby railing into an abyss, but he carried her back up the steps close to the fireplace.

He carelessly tossed her down on the oak table and climbed up on top of her. Flipping over onto her stomach, she tried to crawl away, but he caught hold of her shoulder and forced her onto her back again. Reaching under her dress, he tore down her panties, holding her legs as she struggled and kicked. With a second jerk, he got them clear of her right foot so they gathered around her left ankle.

Then he was on top of her, crushing her. He was heavy, his breath smelling of tobacco and alcohol. He pawed her breasts, nuzzling her neck while she tried to bite his ear and dug her nails into his back. He fumbled with his trousers, and then she felt him forcing his erection against her. Managing to get a breath, she screamed with every ounce of her strength as he penetrated her, tearing into her, hurting her. She beat at his back, clawed at his eyes, tried to bite his neck, but he only bore down on her all the more, all of her struggles seeming only to add to his excitement as he thrust deeply into her.

In two minutes he came to a great, shuddering orgasm, then lay atop her, a dead weight, spent.

Lieserl lay coldly beneath him. She felt utterly defiled, like a leper. All she wanted was for him to get up off her and leave her alone so she could go away, anywhere, somewhere she could bathe.

"What a delightful Jewish bitch you are," he said without malice.

Pushing up off her, he eased off the table and rearranged his clothing. "You might as well get up and put yourself together. I'll give you a ride back to the Berghof."

He offered his hand. She took it, and as he helped her down off the table she spat in his face.

He smiled casually, and calmly wiped the spit away with a handkerchief. "That would cost you, but I understand you're going through some difficult feelings at the moment, knowing that your mother is in a camp. I assure you I'll protect her as long as we have an understanding."

"You've got what you wanted. Let her go."

He stared at her, the fire flickering in his blue eyes making him look like a devil. "First of all, I'm not done with you, not by a long shot. I value you highly on a personal level, and of course as a servant of the Reich. Second, releasing your mother is not within my power."

"You're lying." Tears welled up in her eyes, and her voice grew husky. "You're a God damned lying son of a bitch."

"You're lucky I was the one who did it and not somebody like Bormann. And you don't need to pretend that you didn't enjoy it. You've been toying with me a little too long."

"You are despicable."

"Here." He offered his handkerchief. She tore it out of his hands and threw it on the ground.

"You'll learn to appreciate me. You'll get privileges. I've arranged extra rations for your mother, you know."

"If you're finished, I'm ready to go back, now."

"Certainly."

They went to the elevator, and in a few minutes went out past the lone sentry, who didn't as much as look at them. Haberditz opened her door for her, then got into the driver's side and started the engine. As they descended the Kehlstein, Lieserl stared out the window, half hoping that somehow Haberditz would lose his way and run off the side of a cliff. She didn't want to live any longer.

Twenty minutes later they pulled up in front of the SS who stood guard over the grand stairway leading up to the Berghof.

"I won't be staying," he said. "Too much important business. But I'll come see you from time to time when you get back to Berlin."

Lieserl muttered something low and guttural in her throat. Haberditz leaned over. "What did you say?"

"I said I will kill you if I see you again. Stay away from me."

"I'm afraid I can't do that. You see, I'm rather taken by you. And you could be of enormous value to me in other, completely unexpected ways. You understand, don't you?"

Lieserl said nothing. After a long moment, Haberditz said, "You're an intelligent woman, so I will expect you to behave intelligently. In return, I will keep my word, and protect you and your loved ones to the best of my ability. As long as we have an understanding, your secret is safe with me. You can't ask for more than that."

"You're mad."

He shrugged and shook his head. "No more than any other man in my position. I admire you. And I admire your father—your real father, that is. He's wanted, you know. There are posters all over Europe: Wanted, Einstein, Dead or Alive." He chuckled. "I have a hard time understanding that. Any fool would want him alive."

Lieserl gave him a withering glare that made him smile. She opened the door and stepped out of the black Mercedes. Shutting the door, she turned and began to slowly mount the stone steps, walking unchallenged between the two SS guards.

Back in her room she knelt down beside her bed and clasped her hands together and wept. Only a moment passed before she realized she had to clean. She went to the bathroom, with its gold-plated fixtures, and washed herself over and over again. She thoroughly douched, praying the bastard hadn't impregnated her.

She lay down in her bed in the dark but couldn't sleep. For hours her mind spun countless scenarios, things she could have done to prevent the rape, things she should have said. Had he done it because she had struck him? Whom could she appeal to? Would Udet help her? He seemed to be nothing more than a well-meaning, powerless buffoon. And Heisenberg had been of no help whatsoever. Nazi authorities pushed him around like a pawn.

A vague, irrational idea gradually formed itself out of the shadows of her past, product of the anxieties of her present and future. All her problems stemmed from her parents abandoning her when she was only a child. It was their fault: everything would have been different if only he and her mother had not given her up for adoption. That was why she had always felt lost; why she had never married.

A small clock chimed four times. She heard muted voices in the room next door, Eva's room. She and her lover had returned from a tedious evening of American movies, followed by long sessions of turgid silence, occasionally relieved by one of Hitler's obsessive diatribes.

A short while later she heard a distant moan, Eva's moan, moans that gradually intensified. A vision of Hitler crouching down between Eva's thighs leapt unbidden to her mind, and she saw the horrid little man, his pale blue eyes beady with lust, greedily mouthing her pubic mound as if it were a juicy piece of steak.

She smiled weakly when she remembered Hitler was a vegetarian, but then felt sick to her stomach again. She groaned, sick with disgust and horror, burying her head in her pillow. Still, she couldn't help but hear the creaking of the bedstead nor, a few minutes later, the sound of animal grunting.

* * * * *

Haberditz drove down the winding road, through the checkpoints, past the large encampment of fanatics that populated the fields on the lower hills. Many of them were the scum of the Earth, their only saving grace being they believed in the cause. They lingered on the Obersalzburg, hoping to catch a glimpse of the Fuehrer, desperately seeking favors of one kind or another, favors they would never receive. They were pathetic; he half hoped an Allied attack would remove them from the landscape they sullied.

Haberditz rolled the window of his Mercedes down halfway, delighting in the cold wind against his cheek. He hadn't intended to take her like that; but when she struggled, and struck him, he had become painfully aroused. Regardless, she had provoked him. He felt powerful, exhilarated by his own strength and daring. Taking a woman he wanted in the tabernacle of Nazi destiny had always been one of his fondest dreams. Months had passed since he'd experienced such exquisite sexual pleasure.

He wasn't afraid of being reported. She wouldn't dare, and in any case he could easily deny everything. Close to forty and unmarried, he had done her a favor. Some women were naturally frigid, and it took the right kind of man, a strong man, to show them the way. Meier had always been too wrapped up in herself and her stupid calculations.

No matter if she hadn't completely enjoyed the tryst atop the Kehlstein. In time she'd become more aware of her womanhood, her intrinsic sensuality. Some women resisted that important awakening; that was why she had spent her life in laboratories and libraries, never marrying. Thanks to his decisive action, she could move on, and grow. All she had ever needed was a good German cock deep inside her, as far as it would go.

Besides, she was the daughter of the most famous man of the century, a man marked for death, a lying manipulator, a perpetrator of Jewish pseudo-science. And she, herself, was a Jew; by all rights he could have reported her to the Gestapo, so she'd gotten off easy. Lieserl's secret still amazed him, and it was even more incredible that Heisenberg, aptly accused of being a white Jew, could have been stupid enough to mention the fact in his personal journal. How could he not have known that Haberditz had spies that regularly read everything he wrote?

Einstein was another matter, a possibility that Haberditz relished. What would the famous man do if he learned his long lost daughter was under a Nazi boot? Would he return to Germany and face the gallows, and trade his life for hers? Or would he hide out in his Princeton offices and deny the truth?

Haberditz grinned tightly. He had a high card, and when the time was right, he'd play it. At the very least, he could win Hitler's favor by turning her over to him. There was even the possibility that he could ransom her to Jewish bankers and make a fortune. How much would they pay for the daughter of the greatest Jewish genius of all time?

Money, of course, was an important but secondary matter. While he contemplated her fate, he'd go ahead and enjoy her. There was something about fucking a scientist—a beautiful, intelligent, female scientist—that put real fire in his blood. Marjot just couldn't compare.

Chapter Nine

Theresienstadt

Lieserl sat in the crowded passenger car, filled with dread, worried sick about her mother. The train ride back to Berlin had been lonely and bleak, but the trip to Theresienstadt was even worse. Heisenberg would have driven her there, but after the utter humiliation she'd suffered at the hands of Haberditz, she had no desire to see him or ask for favors.

She was still angry with Heisenberg. He was the only one who knew her secret, and had therefore been Haberditz's source of the information. Maybe he'd let on to his wife or inadvertently shared the knowledge with a Nazi sympathizer. However it had happened, it was his responsibility.

She still reddened with shame and fury when she thought of what Haberditz had done to her. Even in Nazi Germany there were still laws, although often they were only capriciously applied. She didn't dare go to the police. Haberditz had only to declare her Jewishness and her case would be thrown out of court. Haberditz, himself, might face charges, because consorting with lesser races was against the law, but she had no desire to go down herself just to get back at him.

Influence in high places was the only possible way of freeing her mother, and so far she hadn't had any luck cultivating the right people. Udet seemed to be the most sympathetic of them all, but that very quality made him ineffectual.

Theresienstadt was an old town with ancient buildings and narrow, cobbled streets. A rundown section of the town had been declared a Jewish ghetto. Nearly every building had been converted into prison barracks. There was no barbed wire; escape was punishable by death, and the Jewish police were held responsible with their lives for any escape attempt.

Lieserl got off the train and, getting directions from an SS officer at the train station, found her way to the ghetto. She identified herself to a clerk in the administrative office, showing her papers. The clerk was a bookish man in his mid-fifties, his darting gray eyes suspicious and hard.

"Visitation is not normally allowed," he said.

Except for his eyes, he had the bland look of a sleepy dachshund, performing function without any feeling of purpose. Lieserl despised him. "My mother has a serious medical condition. It's important I speak to her and arrange to examine her."

"You're not a medical doctor."

"I'm familiar with her case and have had extensive training. Would you prefer to call Reichsmarschall Goering concerning this matter?"

The clerk raised his eyebrows. "And what is your relation to him?"

"He's my immediate supervisor," she replied icily. "And I assure you he won't be pleased, having his important business interrupted by such a trivial matter."

The clerk blanched, the first real reaction she'd gotten out of him. "That's

Einstein's Daughter: The Story of Lieserl

a different matter. Yes, I'm sure a brief visit can be arranged."

He disappeared into a back room for a few minutes. Lieserl pressed her lips into a tight line, hoping he wasn't trying to verify her story, which was mostly a bluff. It was true she worked indirectly for Goering, who had an interest in the uranium project, but Haberditz was the official directly responsible for the project, and it was he to whom Heisenberg made regular reports. Further, Goering was not terribly concerned about the fate of her mother.

The clerk returned. "The inmate you seek is working on a railroad line a kilometer outside of town. You may visit her there, but must not interfere with the work." He produced a short script, stamped in red. "If you are questioned, this is your authorization."

Lieserl accepted the paper. "Thank you."

"Don't mention it." The clerk gave her brief directions and turned away.

She walked out of the ghetto and headed in the direction indicated by the clerk. A feeling of unreality consumed her as she observed the bleakness of the town, the people that went listlessly about their duties as if already condemned. She walked to the outskirts of town, and a quarter hour march later she saw the railway branch line in the distance, the prisoners moving slowly over the embankments like sluggish insects. Her mother was among them, a concert pianist, cellist, and linguist reduced to a common laborer.

A jeep carrying SS officers passed and one of them briefly raised a hand, waving to her. She choked on the dust. It only briefly crossed her mind to try flagging them down. She had no desire to accept unnecessary favors from such men.

As she approached the work detail, she finally spotted her mother. She was shoveling gravel into a wheelbarrow, helping build the railroad drainage ditches and embankment. Another inmate stood ready to push the wheelbarrow over to the railroad line. Half a dozen armed guards stood supervising, rifles pointing at the ground but ready, while kapos—inmates themselves who organized the blocks in return for extra rations—shouted out orders and threats, wielding short whips.

Lieserl went to the nearest SS officer and showed him her papers. He took the papers from her, glanced at them, and then nodded. "Be quick. I will give you five minutes, no more. Is that understood?" He looked at his watch. "They have a short break in twenty minutes. At that time you may approach the inmate in question."

"Yes, sir."

Lieserl turned and watched as her mother shoveled gravel. She desperately wanted to shout out her name, but feared any deviation from the instructions might be severely punished.

Finally Anna finished shoveling, straightening as her partner rolled the load away. She rubbed her back, grimacing, and looked around. Her gaze met Lieserl's, and their eyes locked. Anna's lips moved, but Lieserl couldn't make out what she was trying to say.

The wheelbarrow came back and Anna bent to her labor, again, painstakingly loading the shovel and placing the gravel in the wheelbarrow. A wiry kapo, unhappy with her work, strode over to her and began shouting abuse at her. When she protested, he raised his whip and struck her across her arms and face. She cried out, and the kapo struck her again. Anna fell to her knees as he delivered another blow across the back, tearing her striped uniform..

Lieserl, overcoming her initial shock, ran forward, throwing up her arms. "Stop at once!"

Anna raised her head and screamed, "No, Lieserl!"

The SS storm trooper, watching the proceedings from a few meters away, swiveled like a machine, training his gun on Lieserl, his finger tightening around the trigger.

"She's going as fast as she can, can't you see that?" Lieserl shouted at the kapo.

"Maybe you'd like to take her place?" He was hardly more than a teenager, scrawny and dull, his face set in a cruel leer.

"Listen to me, Lieserl," Anna said, on her knees before her tormentor. "You're not helping me. Leave quickly!"

The kapo turned. "No one said you could talk." He raised his whip again.

Lieserl launched herself at him, diving through the air like a she-cat, grabbing the young man's arm and knocking him to the ground. He grunted in surprise but easily fended off her blows, pushing her off and forcing her down on her back. He put a knee down on her chest between her breasts and put his full weight on her. She fought, trying to hit him in the groin, but he just laughed at her. She couldn't breathe.

Anna hit him on the back of the head with a shovel, and he fell forward on his face. At the same time the storm trooper fired his rifle. Anna let out a cry and dropped the shovel, clutching her shoulder as she dropped to her knees.

The storm trooper shouldered his rifle and took a Luger out of his belt holster, striding over to the unconscious kapo and Anna just as Lieserl was getting to her feet.

"Stupid ass," he said without particular malice. Aiming his pistol, he shot the kapo in the back three times, the man jerking with each impact, dollops of his blood spurting into the air. The storm trooper turned to Anna, who was holding her shoulder and sobbing. "As for you, cunt..."

"Shoot her and the Fuehrer will have you executed," Lieserl cried with all the conviction she could muster.

The storm trooper hesitated, then turned the pistol on her, leveling it straight at her head. "What are you talking about? You don't have that kind of influence."

"On the other hand, maybe you'd prefer they hung you on a meat hook in the town square."

He stared at Lieserl ferociously, still holding the gun inches from her face as Anna wept softly.

Finally the storm trooper holstered his gun and gestured brusquely to the guards, pointing at the two women. "Take them back to the camp and put them in a holding cell. I'll speak with the kommandant."

One of the guards flagged down a passing jeep. Anna and Lieserl got into the back seat, guards on either side of them, while the SS man climbed into the passenger side of the front seat.

"You shouldn't have come," Anna whispered fiercely as the jeep pulled out, kicking up dirt and dust.

"You're my mother. I had to come."

"Yes, it's true, I'm your mother, and it's also true I never would have wanted you to get into this kind of trouble!"

"It's done, Mother."

"You will listen to me next time."

Lieserl sighed and didn't respond. The jeep kicked up dust and gravel.

Back at the ghetto, the guards led them to a holding cell in the administrative building. The room was bare, without furniture or carpeting of any kind, and having only one small window with bars on it. The two women sat down on the wooden floor near a patch of sunlight.

Three hours later the kommandant came into the room alone. They stood and faced him. He was a thick-necked man, overweight with a torso like a barrel, with squinting pig's eyes and thin lips. He looked them up and down shrewdly, lingering on Lieserl.

"Insubordination of any kind is punishable by death," he said without preamble. "You shall both be hung at dawn."

Lieserl's lower lip began to quiver, but she threw her chin up and said, "I happen to be a very important member of a research team working on a *wunderwaffen* for the army. I demand that you release my mother and I immediately."

He smiled and nodded his head. "Perhaps what you say is true, but unfortunately there can be no exceptions. Discipline, you understand."

"Let me make one call to Admiral Haberditz. He has oversight of the program. He'll clear this up."

"I don't give a damn about armchair admirals, and I haven't time for the games of the condemned." He swiveled on his heel as Lieserl shouted further protests. The door slammed in her face, and, finding it locked, she began banging on it.

"God damn you, you filthy pig!"

Her mother grabbed her by the shoulders. "Stop it! You're just making it worse!"

"They don't know what they're doing!" Lieserl raged, turning toward her. "When Hitler hears about this..."

"Hitler? You're on speaking terms with that man?"

Lieserl stopped to take a breath. "No, no, of course not."

Her mother eyed her. "But you're working on something for him, aren't you? Some kind of weapon?"

Although the words were spoken softly, they brought Lieserl up short.

She closed her mouth, then turned slightly, saying nothing.

"It's true, isn't it? You're working for him? For the Nazis?"

"Yes," she whispered. She glanced at her mother, then looked down and away. "Not by choice."

Anna's shoulders sagged. "Then my life is over. I have failed: I have raised a daughter without a moral conscience."

Lieserl raised her head again. "No, Mother, you don't understand. I'm doing as little as I can, just enough to remain valuable to them. For you, Mother."

Anger flashed in Anna's eyes. "Don't be a fool. You might as well shoot me, that's how I feel."

"It's only a small compromise. I'm giving them just enough to keep them happy. It's under control."

Anna's arm swept out. "You call this control? Here, locked up in a camp, condemned to death? And you talk of compromise, well, you don't compromise with the devil, you sell your soul and then he owns you forever!"

"If...if I remain involved..."

"You don't involve yourself with such people, you simply don't!"

"Mama, you don't understand, what I'm doing is pure science, I'm not giving them enough to get what they want."

"They'll get it from you, whatever it is, they'll get it from you. And then what? Better to have never been born, I say."

"Mother, you're not being reasonable."

Anna threw her arms up in the air. "Do whatever you want, but you're no daughter of mine."

Lieserl turned away, a retort frozen on her lips. Walking over to the barred window, she looked out on the dirt yard where the prisoners assembled every morning for roll call. She thought of Houtermans and his calculations, his new element, which together with her own insights could produce a breakthrough, give Hitler reactors and a bomb far more powerful than any the world had ever seen. If anyone else had similar thoughts, she'd find out, and maybe she could misdirect them. Her mother didn't understand that, and there was no way to explain it to her.

She could trade the knowledge for her life, and for her mother's life. That was the temptation, and it gnawed at her insides like worms, making her feel sick and ill at ease. How long would she have lasted in Dobberke's basement if Haberditz hadn't rescued her? At what threshold would she tell all, no matter what happened to the rest of the world?

She felt her mother come up behind her. "I'm sorry. I didn't mean it. The last part, anyway."

Lieserl turned, and the Anna kissed her on the cheek. Lieserl hugged her and kissed her back. "Mother, you may be right."

Anna shook her head. "I'm an old woman and there's not a lot I understand about the new world we've fallen into. God only knows what's right anymore."

Everyone seemed to have forgotten about them. They passed the rest of the day alone in the holding cell, receiving no water or food. At dusk a guard came and led them to an open latrine, just a ditch dug in the ground behind one of the barracks. On return to their cell, their requests for bedding were ignored and they spent the night on the wooden floor, lying next to each other, unable to sleep due to the cold and the pounding of hammers outside. Lieserl strained to glimpse what they were building, but it was out of her direct view.

In the morning two guards came for them at dawn, marching them to the latrine. It was humiliating attending to their needs in front of the men, who hadn't the decency to turn away. A bugle sounded the call for general assembly out in the square, and the kapos were busy shouting at the inmates, striking those slow to respond. The inmates assembled on the field of inspection, five abreast, standing at attention in their rags before a broad platform with overhead beam: a gallows.

The guards ushered Anna and Lieserl over next to the platform, ordering them to stand at attention.

"Be brave, Lieserl," Anna said, her voice shaking.

Lieserl tightened her lips. "I'll try, Mother."

As the sun pushed up in the east, the inmates stood out in the chill as the kapos—many of them Jewish—hurled verbal abuse and swung their clubs, inflicting discipline on those weakened inmates who wilted under the physical effort of standing at attention for so long a time in the cold. Minutes stretched to over an hour in a Kafkian scene of dominance and sadism.

Finally the Kommandant came swaggering confidently out of his offices and strode over to the assembled rows of five. He marched up the line, inspecting the men and women.

Suddenly he stopped and pointed at an old man. "That one," he said, and the guards stepped over and hustled the trembling, feebly protesting man out of the ranks.

He continued his inspection. All the inmates stood as erect as they possibly could, chins thrust upwards, a show of good health, of their value as worker-slaves to the Third Reich. Minutes passed with excruciating slowness, as if time had entered a shell and was twisting slowly through the inner passages.

A boy of about fourteen was shivering from the cold and the strain of standing for so long a time, and the Kommandant pointed his swagger stick at him. "That one." The guards hesitated, and he angered. "Yes, the boy! Take him!"

An older man stepped out of line. "Wait! Take me instead."

The Kommandant strode over to him. "And who are you?"

"I'm his father."

"Who gave you permission to speak?"

"He's just a boy. I'll take his place."

The Kommandant turned, and with a nonchalant gesture to his guards, said, "Take them both. We don't need a hero. That's bad for discipline."

The boy struggled and cried out, but his father went with quiet dignity. They took their places on either side of the elderly man, already standing on the chair on the scaffolding platform with his hands tied behind his back and noose around his neck. He was reciting scripture, mouthing the words. One of the guards struck him across the face with the butt of his rifle.

The Kommandant mounted the platform. "Someone has left the camp without proper permission. One or more of you could have prevented this error if you had brought it to our attention. As retribution, these men," he hesitated only briefly, "and the boy, will be hung by the neck until dead."

The Kommandant climbed down from the platform and gave the signal to proceed. One of the guards stepped up and kicked the chairs out from underneath the father, then the old man, then the boy, one at a time. Anna closed her eyes and muttered a prayer, but Lieserl watched every minute, a fierce hatred burning inside her as the two men and the boy choked and struggled, turned purple and strangling to death.

The kapos then began taking roll call, dividing the inmates up into different work details. Anna's name was called for orchestral practice, but the Kommandant gave a word to one of the guards who hastily countermanded the order.

The Kommandant walked over to them. "I trust you slept well, ladies?" When they didn't reply, he went on. "That could have been you, today, but father and son took the place of mother and daughter." He smiled. "A certain irony, there." He lifted his swagger stick and adroitly touched the handle to his shoulder with a practiced flick of his wrist.

"What are you going to do with us?" asked Lieserl.

He put his hands behind his back, still clutching the stick. "I hope to retain your mother on the orchestra. I understand they'll be performing a symphony by Beethoven, and we can always use another fine cellist. In your case, however, I've decided you may indeed be more trouble than you're worth, so I'm arranging your transfer."

"Back to Berlin?"

"No, I'm afraid not. You'll be going to another camp."

He gestured at the guards, and turned and walked briskly away.

"You can't do this," Lieserl shouted after him. "You have no right!"

"Shut up," ordered one of the guards.

Lieserl bristled. "If Reichsmarschall Goering hears of this…"

The guard slapped her across the mouth with the back of his gloved hand, a buckle catching her lip. She tasted blood. Another guard lowered a rifle, separating Lieserl from her mother. Lieserl flung out an arm, straining to touch her, missing by a scant centimeter as the guard pushed her along.

Tears sprang to her eyes, as she realized she might never see her mother again. "I love you, Mama!" she called.

Anna strained back, vainly reaching for her daughter. "I love you, Lieserl!"

Lieserl's guard hit her in the rear with the butt of his carbine and the

Einstein's Daughter: The Story of Lieserl

other guard hustled her mother away.

Lieserl was put with a group of about two dozen others prisoners. The guards marched them out the gate of the camp. She worried they were just going to lead them to a ditch and shoot them, but soon they reached the train station, where the guards herded them into one of several waiting cattle cars. The heavy door slammed shut, locking them inside.

The cattle car had the sweet, heady odor of hay and cow excrement. Lieserl found herself on the far side next to a short woman with angular features who was about her mother's age. She'd once been plump, but now her skin hung loosely on her.

"Do you know where we're going?" Lieserl asked her.

"I don't know," croaked the woman. "But it has to be better than this place."

Her name was Sigfried, and she'd worked in a grocery with her husband in Leipzig until the night of long knives, when brown shirts had wrecked the store and beaten her husband to death in the street.

"If my son had been there, he would have taken them, you can bet your life on that."

"Where is he?"

Sigfried glanced dourly at her. "Even if I knew, I wouldn't tell you."

Lieserl nodded. He was probably a submarine, which meant he was Jewish and living under cover. They stood there, she and the other inmates, for nearly an hour before the train finally blew its whistle, signaling imminent departure. Lieserl clutched at the slats of the car, praying for some miracle. Even Haberditz would be a welcome sight.

The whistle blew again, but the train still didn't begin moving forward. Lieserl wondered what the problem was, and began to cherish the hope that a mechanical failure might strand the train in Theresienstadt for the night, giving Heisenberg or Udet time to act on her behalf.

Then she heard some commotion, and one of the other inmates shouted out, "Look! It's one of the strings!"

The door crashed open, and two SS officers thrust Anna bodily into the car. Beating back the clamoring inmates with clubs, they slammed the door shut again, catching one man's finger in the door. He howled in pain.

"Mother!"

"Lieserl!"

They pushed and shoved through the crowded car until they reached one another, embracing each other fiercely.

"It's a miracle, Mama," Lieserl said breathlessly, "a miracle we're together again."

Anna smiled, the happiest smile Lieserl had seen on her face in months. "I'm afraid I put up a terrible fuss and called the Kommandant a few names he didn't care for. I just wasn't myself."

"Thank God for that, Mama, thank God for that. Where are they sending us?"

The whistle blew again, and this time the train lurched forward. Anna sobered, physically subsiding in Lieserl's arms. "I don't know."

Lieserl tightened her hold, pressing her cheek close to her mother's. "It doesn't matter where we're going, she murmured into her mother's ear. "We're together again, Mama, at least we have that. We just have to wait it out. Someday it will be over."

"We can always hope."

The exhilaration of the previous moment had already vanished. As Lieserl held her mother, she felt her begin to tremble and shake.

"We're in God's hands, Mama. That's what you always told me when I was little, when I was afraid of the dark. Remember?"

"I remember. But sometimes I wonder."

* * * * *

For several hours the train rolled forward. Those in the car who had food or drink shared it, but there wasn't enough to go around. Lieserl and Anna managed to squeeze into a spot where the sun shone through the slats of the car, creating a small pocket of warmth. They sat holding hands, not talking much.

At the first stop SS guards thrust a young man and woman in full wedding dress into the car with them. The bride, still clutching a bedraggled bouquet of flowers, was not more than nineteen, darkly Jewish and beautiful, her white dress covered with mud, her eyes bloodshot and defeated. The groom, one lens missing from his glasses, held his hand gingerly over his mouth and nose, blood on his fingers and his tuxedo.

The train rolled onwards. As the hours passed, people began relieving themselves any way they could, and the stench of human waste in the crowded quarters and heat became almost intolerable.

At one stop, in the middle of the second day when the heat was most oppressive, an SS officer threw open the doors and sprayed water on them all, hosing them down, washing away some of the smell. A tall, handsome German man in a fine business suit and hat supervised the operation, and Lieserl marveled at the way he seemed to be able to give orders to the SS when he himself was only a civilian. She had never realized how much she took fresh water for granted, and held her arms up as the businessman came to her car, personally taking the hose and spraying her and the others down. She was so grateful for the soaking she felt her heart would burst.

A superior officer suddenly shouted out orders, and a brief argument ensued between him and the businessman, the officer livid and shouting, the businessman speaking in a calm, soothing tone. Someone shut the water shut off. SS men stood around looking confused, then in response to barked orders walked quickly away, taking the life-giving water hoses with them.

"No heart allowed," Anna muttered darkly. "They'll probably shoot that man in the head."

Once again the doors slammed shut and the train lurched forward, the rhythmic clacking beginning anew. Day turned into night, with more cattle cars added to the train. Lieserl crouched in a corner next to her mother, trapped in a netherworld that was neither wakefulness nor sleep.

During the second night an old man died, and although people shouted for the guards to come take away the body, no one answered the call. The body ended up facing the back of the car next to the wall, and despite the cramped quarters everyone managed to stay clear of it.

Some considerable time later, at the end of a nightmare of tortured dreams, Lieserl awakened to a squeal of brakes as the train pulled up to a great cement slab. Peering blearily out between the slats, Lieserl saw a camp surrounded by barbed wire, men and women in striped prison clothes walking here and there in groups, herded by shouts and threats and blows. A placard hung above the platform: *Auschwitz*.

The single word, like a curse, seemed to change the quality of the air around them, making it thicker and suffocating. She took her mother by the arm. "Mother," she said, her voice shaking slightly, "wake up, I think we've arrived."

Her mother stirred. "Thank God. Where are we?"

"Auschwitz."

Guards were throwing the doors open, one loud crash after another. "*Raus, raus, alles raus!*"

Lieserl and Anna moved slowly along a line towards a nexus, where a doctor, as signified by the pin in his lapel depicting a serpent coiling around a tiny sword, stood examining the prisoners as they passed. The examinations lasted only seconds, and consisted of shining a flashlight in the prisoner's eyes, sometimes asking a question or two. He made arcane gestures, blinks and nods, curious motions of his fingers that the guards seemed to understand. Many prisoners, the old and weak, or the very young, were going to the left, the others to the right. Mothers were separated from their children, fathers from their sons, husbands from wives, all divided by one man and a few gestures.

When their turn came, the doctor barely glanced at them. Again the gestures, and a guard indicated with his rifle that Lieserl should go to the right, her mother to the left.

"You don't understand," protested Lieserl, "this is my mother, she's going with me."

"She's old, she won't be much use to us," said the doctor matter-of-factly, shaking his head. "You, on the other hand, could serve well." The doctor, overweight with a cherubic face not unlike Goering's, looked at her speculatively.

Before he could go on, however, a commotion broke out. A prisoner was making a break for freedom. The effort was doomed from the start, but all heads swiveled to watch the drama as a young bearded man in colorful gypsy garb broke ranks and ran with amazing speed back toward the tracks, toward the fields beyond. There was no cover for hundreds of yards, yet he ran with strength and confidence, dodging to the left and right to make a harder target.

Several shots rang out, all of them missing. The chief SS officer, apoplectic, shouted obscenities at his men. Another volley followed, but still the gypsy ran on, dodging back and forth like an American football hero, putting distance between himself and the guards. Some of the prisoners cheered, shouting encouragement, and the crowd swayed and milled about indecisively, as if others, inspired by the gypsy's courage, gauged their own chances.

There was a brief lull in the shooting, followed by a lone gunshot. The gypsy stumbled and spun around, falling spread-eagled in the dirt.

The guard who had fired the last bullet grinned, and his fellows congratulated him. The commanding officer, however, barked orders, and quickly restored discipline; the guards closely trained their guns on the restless inmates to discourage any similar attempt.

Lieserl had taken advantage of the distraction to grab her mother's hand and pull her over to the line on the right. The doctor and guards, still distracted by the disorder, didn't notice, allowing them both to pass.

"We'll stay together, Mother," Lieserl said, squeezing her hand. "Heisenberg will come for us if we can just hold on a couple more days."

"Professor Heisenberg, it seems, has enough problems of his own."

Lieserl pressed her lips together in a thin line. "He'll come. He's got to come."

The guards herded them into trucks, cramming them together like sardines. The trucks rumbled to life, carried them along the barbed wire enclosure. Waffen SS in their green uniforms stood in sentry towers, guns pointed inside the camp.

A moment later they passed a large three-story brick building, and then the truck turned and headed toward a gate. Above the gate was a sign upon which was written 'Auschwitz'. Below it was another placard, paradoxically proclaiming that 'work makes you free'.

The truck stopped in front of large brick building. An SS Scharfuehrer ordered everyone down out of the truck, arranging them in the usual ranks of five. Then they were ordered to strip off all their clothes and leave them at their feet.

Everyone did as they were told. Men and women, old and young, stood stark naked in the morning chill, embarrassed, not knowing which way to look. Lieserl felt thin and small, gooseflesh all over her white skin, but she especially felt acute embarrassment for her mother, standing naked beside her.

The guards marched them into the building down a narrow corridor, where other SS examined them again. Lieserl nearly spit in fury when ordered to spread her legs and bend over. Further down the corridor she and her mother waded through a brackish fluid smelling like kerosene, then through horrible showers of the same fluid.

The guards led them all out into the yard, again, where the sun had finally burned off the mists, warming the air. The small cuts and scrapes on Lieserl's body itched and burned from the delousing fluid. Moments later they reached a separate facility nearby. The sign over the door said *brause*—shower.

Inside, Lieserl stood under a shower head with her mother, not a trickle of water coming out, naked, white skin all around, some of it young and smooth, some of it older and wrinkled, men and women, young and old, not knowing what to do with her hands as the prisoners packed in and everyone was much too close, softly jostling each other.

The lights failed, and in the sudden darkness erupted a spontaneous outcry of nervous fear. Lieserl felt her mother grab hold of her and hold her close, kissing her on the cheek.

Then the lights went back on, and warm water began trickling down out of the showerheads. The streams gradually increased in strength, and Lieserl thought she'd never felt anything so wonderful as that water coursing over her body. People laughed and wept, talking in a quiet explosion of relief.

The shower lasted only a few minutes, and the guards then ushered them through doors opening into a makeshift barbershop. Naked inmates sat passively on benches, waiting as inmate barbers, wearing stripes, worked steadily, clipping everyone's hair off, men and women alike.

Anna ran a hand through Lieserl's long, blond hair. "What a shame to lose your beautiful hair."

"It's nothing," she said, her voice trembling.

Lieserl's turn came. Still unclothed, she sat down on a stool before the male barber. He went professionally about his business, ignoring her nakedness, cutting her long tresses. "You are helping the Reich with your hair," he said, almost as if he were proud to be a part of the war effort. "They weave special cloth from it, you know."

"What happens next?"

"Nothing, you'll get tattooed, that's all, so you'll have a number. I don't know why they're leaving so many alive. Dr. Mengele must need workers or he would have sent you up a chimney."

"How did you survive?"

He smiled ironically. "I'm a barber, I'm useful. If it gets bad, just go to the fence and grab hold. Either the electricity or a bullet will kill you. But if you want to survive, make yourself useful." He looked over at Anna. "Next, please."

In the next barracks other inmates behind counters threw pants, clogs, and shirts at them, all stinking of kerosene. Nothing fit, and when Anna complained they told her to trade with someone. Casting about, she found a woman with a smaller set of clothes, and managed an exchange. Still, the fit was poor, and she had to keep hiking the pants up so they wouldn't fall off.

At the next station a female inmate with a tool that looked like a fountain pen inked numbers into Lieserl's lower left arm. Lieserl sat perfectly still, humiliated, reduced to a series of digits. She reflected that perhaps that was the whole point, to reduce everyone to ciphers so they weren't people anymore.

"You're lucky," the tattooer told her. "You're a very healthy specimen. Maybe they'll use you in the fields for a while, or the factories. As for everybody else..."

She rolled her eyes and made a twirling motion of her finger.
"What do you mean?" asked Lieserl.
"Up the chimneys. Didn't you smell it on your way in?"
"That was the friction of the train wheels against the rails."
The inmate laughed at her. "Stay useful. It's the only way to stay alive."

Once again their Scharfuehrer ordered them in trucks. Lieserl held her mother's hand, thankful to be with her, to have a small island of security in the midst of uncertainty. The engine started up, coughing a lot, the fumes filling the confined space.

"They're gassing us!" a woman screeched in panic.

Several others cried out in horror. Lieserl, speaking firmly, said, "If they were going to gas us, they wouldn't have bothered cutting our hair." She was only half-convinced of her own words; the same thought had occurred to her, and she had quickly suppressed it.

They rumbled through the camp and out another gate. Workers in striped prison clothes worked fields outside, harvesting potatoes. In the distance, Lieserl could see more barbed wire and more enclosures, the satellite camps.

Anna sighed. "I just hope next time you'll do as I tell you. You were always such a headstrong child."

"It'll be all right. Someone will come for us."
"Do you really think so?"

Lieserl bit her lip, already not as confident as she was a few hours before. Now, after what they'd gone through at the camp, she found her shreds of hope beginning to weaken.

"We'll see," she said. "We'll see."

Berlin

Haberditz paced the floor of his office, chain-smoking, beside himself with fury and frustration. He had spies watching Meier's apartment around the clock, but she'd never returned. Was it possible she had gone underground? Maybe found a way to escape Germany?

That was unacceptable on several counts. For one thing, she knew secrets of the German bomb project, and for another, he wasn't done with her, yet. She was of enormous value, not only as a scientist but also as a hostage. Her propaganda potential was virtually unlimited. If she could be won over, it would be a great coup for Germany, and a boost to his personal career. When he'd finished awakening her womanhood she'd fall in line like a good German frau and be of great service to the Third Reich.

He had arranged her mother's transfer to Theresienstadt, calculating that she was the obvious lever to get what he wanted. Picking up the phone, he dialed an operator, standing next to his desk, smoking and drumming his fingers on the ink blotter, waiting for the call to go through.

After going through three different idiotic clerks, he finally got through to the kommandant. "A few days ago a Frau Meier, an excellent cellist, was transferred to your facility," he began.

"Meier? She's no longer here. She was a troublemaker. I sent her to Auschwitz."

"You what?" Haberditz exploded.

"I transferred her to Auschwitz, her and that meddling daughter of hers."

The breath caught in Haberditz's throat. "Her daughter, too? When?"

"Just two days ago."

"You idiot!" he shouted into the mouthpiece. "I could have you shot for that!"

"I thought it prudent…"

"You're an utter and complete fool! If I have anything to say about it, you'll be sent to the front!" Haberditz slammed down the receiver and stood by his desk, sucking smoke, angry that the kommandant had acted without orders and not sure what to do next.

Then he shrugged. "What the devil," he said aloud, blowing out a large cloud of smoke. "A few days in that camp and she'll appreciate me all the more."

* * * * *

Wolfgang Weisz watched Lieserl's apartment for several days but never saw her.

He decided Dobberke had done something with her. He went to a beer hall a few blocks away from 26 Hamburgerstrasse, waiting for his prearranged contact, nursing a beer in a dark corner table.

A young, buxom redhead with green eyes showed up at around 10:30 in the evening. She was thickly made up, with a friendly, intimate manner that made her look like any other hooker. She bought a cheap glass of wine at the bar, then walked casually over to Weisz's table.

"Hi, handsome. May I join you?"

Weisz nodded, and the girl sat down. She was a dangerous contact; Weisz knew she worked for the Gestapo, but was also in the pay of the British Secret Service. "I'm looking for Lieserl Meier."

The woman nodded. "She was here a couple months ago; interrogated and released."

"Where is she now?"

"I don't know. She hasn't been back."

"Do you think Dobberke knows?"

She made a sour face. "That bastard knows everything. Thinks he can manhandle me just because I work for him."

"Where does he live?"

"He has an apartment east of here, about ten blocks away. Fifth floor, northwest corner, number 506."

"Does he live alone?"

"Sometimes his wife visits him. Most of the time she stays on the family farm in Bohemia. I'm sure she can't stand him any more than I can."

"Keep an eye out for Meier. What's Dobberke's address?"

She told him, and he committed it to memory. Reaching under the table, he slipped an envelope into her lap, his hand inadvertently brushing her leg.

"You really know how to please a girl." She looked at him askance, eyes narrowing, a teasing smile on her lips. "Walk me home?"

He shook his head. It was a tempting but dangerous invitation. "Thanks for the offer. Some other time." He winked as he rose from the table.

Dobberke lived on the fifth floor of a rundown apartment building. It was a seedy neighborhood: broken windows, trash that hadn't been picked up, a few vagrants in the alleys. Weisz watched the window for a while, looking for telltale shadows, evidence that would tell him Dobberke was alone. It was a tricky business, but Weisz wanted to know what was going on. He was convinced Dobberke knew the answer.

Rather than try to go through the front door, Weisz found a fire escape on the side of the building and climbed up to the roof. There he picked the lock of a door leading into the main stairwell inside. Making his way down to the fifth floor landing, he entered the hallway and soon was in front of Dobberke's door.

No light leaked out from under the door. Taking out his pocket toolkit, he went to work on the lock. A moment later he slowly eased the door open, holding his breath as it creaked. Moving into the apartment, he closed the door behind him.

Near total darkness pervaded the room, just a little light leaking in from the hallway outside and from the edges of the curtains. He moved silently through a small living room filled with furniture, placing his feet and slowly shifting his weight as he walked, dimly aware of the shapes of furniture and personal effects.

There was a single bedroom. Dobberke was a lump in the bed, sleeping on his stomach, snoring loudly, alone. Weisz breathed a quiet sigh of relief. That made his job easier. At least he wouldn't have to kill an innocent.

He slid his hand under Dobberke's pillow, finding and removing a gun and ditching it under the bed. Then he quickly got up on the bed and put a knee in Dobberke's back, forcing his face down into the pillow.

The Gestapo captain made a few muffled noises of protest, struggling to turn his head. Weisz pressed the muzzle of the Walther against Dobberke's temple. "If you call out you're a dead man. If you look at me, you're a dead man. If you struggle, you're a dead man. Do you understand?"

Dobberke stopped bleating and became very still. "What do you want?"

"What have you done with Dr. Lieserl Meier?"

"Who are you? What do you want with her?"

Weisz struck Dobberke across the back of his head with the muzzle of his gun. He cried out but quickly stifled himself when he felt the end of the barrel against his right temple. "I'm asking the questions, not you. Where is Dr. Meier?"

"The hell with you. I'm not talking."

Weisz threw his full weight onto Dobberke's back. The wind exploded out of him. Weisz grabbed his hair and jerked his head back, jamming the gun muzzle into Dobberke's mouth. "You bastard, you're better off dead."

Dobberke stammered fearfully, unable to talk with the gun in his mouth. Weisz eased up on him. "Talk to me."

"I haven't seen her in two months, I swear."

"Who knows where to find her?"

"Haberditz would know, or that white Jew, Heisenberg. I don't know anything, I swear."

"What do you know about her? Who is she, what does she do?"

"She's a scientist at the Kaiser Wilhelm. They wanted me to scare her, make her cooperate."

"Cooperate in what way?"

"The hell with you!"

Weisz shoved his face in the pillow struck him again with the gun. His scream was muffled. He started bleeding from a gash in the back of his head. "Last chance."

"Haberditz was fucking with her. Said she knew something. I was supposed to soften her up."

"What does she know? Why is she so important?"

"I don't know. I swear I don't know."

Weisz believed him. He flipped the gun, catching it by the muzzle. "Listen to me, Dobberke. We're watching you. Don't forget that. Make a mistake, and you're finished."

"Who the hell are you? Who sent you?"

Weisz smiled slyly, and said, "I think you already know that. And if you don't, call the Naval Institute. He doesn't think you're playing straight with him and he's pissed off about it. Fuck with him, and next time I'll really hurt you." He took the gun back and slammed the butt down on Dobberke's skull with a solid thwack. Dobberke went limp face down into his pillow. Weisz didn't even check to see whether or not he was dead. He didn't care.

He left the same way he'd come in, then quickly put several blocks between him and the scene of the crime. Haberditz was next on his list, then maybe Heisenberg. And he still needed to break into Von Ardennes' laboratory and check Houtermans' notes. If Dobberke didn't know where Meier was, it was possible she was at a secret industrial site working on the bomb.

Soon he was lost in the shadows of the city, so he headed back for his apartment. It had been risky breaking into Dobberke's apartment, and he hadn't found out anything useful, except for the fact that Meier definitely knew something the Nazis were interested in.

He'd taken a big chance and could have lost everything, but he had to admit to himself, after what Dobberke had done to Meier, that he'd enjoyed cracking the bastard's skull.

Auschwitz

Roll call, at Auschwitz, began at 3:30 in the morning.

Lieserl became aware of shouting and the whistling sound of the blockhova's whip. She opened her eyes, returning from tortured dreams, wedged between her mother and someone she'd never seen before on the hard boards of the top bunk. Four other women were in the narrow bed with her.

"Fifteen minutes! Roll call in fifteen minutes!"

Lieserl shook her mother and together they climbed down and hurriedly went to the toilets, a long trench in the ground not far from their block. The stench was overwhelming, and she urinated in full view, oddly embarrassed that her own body was so much healthier and robust than most of the others.

"*Schnell, Schnell!*" shouted a kapo, well dressed in an angora sweater and cap.

They ran back to the yards in front of their block and quickly joined the ranks of five that were forming, five inmates abreast, five rows to a group to make twenty-five, everyone holding their arms out, making sure the spacing was even to please their masters.

When everyone was in rank, the scharfuehrer began calling out the numbers. Lieserl stood at attention during the roll call, the minutes turning into hours as the SS guards stood watching them, their ferocious German shepherds on a tight leash. The dogs regarded them with hard, hungry eyes, sometimes growling deep in their throats.

By the end of the second hour an elderly man to Lieserl's left passed out, dropping to the ground. The Scharfuehrer abruptly stopped calling roll and gestured to a guard. He ran over to the old man, holding his dog on a short leash. He kicked the scrawny inmate in the ribs. The exhausted man stirred slightly but didn't get up, earning another hard kick.

"You there!" the scharfuehrer shouted, pointing at Lieserl and the inmate in front of her. "Take him away!".

Lieserl turned to comply, but the man on the ground suddenly scrambled to his feet and began stumbling away. The guard released his dog. With a growl, the German shepherd leaped powerfully through the air and landed on the inmate's back, knocking him back down to the ground. The old man screamed and threw his arms up, trying to defend himself, but already the dog's mighty jaws were tearing at his throat. He had time for a single tortured cry of pain and fear before the dog ripped into his voice box.

Blood jetted onto the ground from the inmate's torn throat, and he choked and gasped for air. The guard shouted an order to the dog, which obediently returned to his side. He turned to Lieserl. "Don't just stand there gawking, go take him to the dentist."

"Dentist?"

"He's dead," the guard said impatiently, "or he will be in another minute. He goes to the dentist."

Lieserl, trembling all over and still confused about the bizarre request, took the dead man's hands, thinking he'd be heavy, but finding it was easy to lift him. He was still twitching and jerking in his death throes. She dropped him.

The guard struck her in back with the butt of his rifle. "Pick him up! Or you'll be next!"

The man's body was calming; he was dead. Lieserl reached down and took his hands again. The other inmate took the feet, and together they started carrying the twitching, still-warm body to the dentist's office, down the Lagerstrasse towards the front gate. She stumbled and had to stop, emptying her stomach in the dirt of the street.

"Hurry, they'll get angry," said the inmate helping her, anxiously peering across their burden at her.

Lieserl grabbed the dead man's hands and picked him up again. She couldn't understand why they should be going to the dentist, but nothing else made sense, either.

The dentist was another inmate, although better fed and dressed than the others. He had light brown hair and a grave but friendly manner. "What are you going to do with him?" Lieserl asked.

He seemed reluctant to answer. "I'm supposed to check his teeth for gold."

She felt sick to her stomach again. "Why are you helping them like this?"

"So my father and I can eat."

Lieserl nodded slowly. "I understand."

She and the other inmate returned to the roll call, which was still proceeding at a snail's pace. The sun rose in the sky and began to burn off the fog. Lieserl's legs ached, and she felt faint from not having eaten. More inmates dropped, and again other inmates had to carry them away, although their guards kept the dogs leashed.

Finally role call was over, and kapos moved among the rows, assigning work detail. Lieserl and her mother ended up spending the day outside the compound, harvesting a crop of anemic potatoes that grew only poorly in the mushy clay of the region.

At dusk they returned to their block to a meal of thin gruel, too exhausted to think of anything but sleep. Most were already asleep in the overcrowded bunks. Lieserl found herself in the company of two girls in their early twenties, one French and the other Polish, and an older woman, Georgina, from Italy.

"Whatever you do, keep a low profile," Jeanette-Michelle told her. "Don't draw any attention to yourself." She was an elegant girl of twenty, shaved completely bald but with fine eyebrows and nice features.

"And don't ever act like you're sick," pitched in the other young woman, Paulina, dark-haired and skeletal. "Smile, but not too much. Whatever you do, don't be late for roll call. You'll go up in smoke."

"The war will be over in six months," Anna said, "once the Americans come in."

"The Americans don't want to fight another European war," Jeanette-

Michelle retorted. "They're cowards, afraid to fight for what's right. Their Franklin Roosevelt is weak, a cripple, and more woman than a man. It's no wonder they're such little boys."

"At least they don't have the Duce!" declared Georgina, referring to Mussolini. "When the war is over we're going to string him up by his privates!"

The blockhova came into the long, dark room, brandishing her whip, slapping it hard against the wall to get their attention. "Keep it down! Everybody asleep! Roll call before dawn!"

Lieserl shifted on the bed, trying to get comfortable on the planks, Jeanette-Michelle on one side and her mother on the other. They slept horizontally so they could all fit on the bed, with the result that their legs stuck off the side. Lieserl ached all over, especially in her calves from the hours of standing at attention. Thinking about physics, smiling because it made her think of Houtermans, she managed to fall into a fitful sleep.

She awoke to the sound of snoring, then of someone shifting against her. Her bladder was just about to burst. Climbing down from her bunk, she moved quietly through the long, dark room, jumping in fright when she bumped into another woman. The woman shushed her.

"Who are you?" demanded the woman.

"Lieserl Meier."

She heard an excited intake of breath. "Lieserl! It's me, Georgina," the woman said, speaking German in her thick Italian accent.

"Where's the chamber pot? I'm desperate."

"They took it away, some kind of punishment. Whatever you do, don't wake the blockhova. If you need to go, follow me. It's dangerous if you don't know what you're doing."

"We could use our mess pan."

Georgina made a quiet grunt of disgust. "I don't know about you, but I'm not going to piss in the same pot I eat out of! I'd rather get shot."

They crept to the door together and quietly opened it. The door creaked. Outside the camp was dark, although there were searchlights that periodically swept across the ground.

"Wait for the light to pass, then go to the right. At the latrines be sure to go to the far side, and bend down behind the trough if a light swings your way. I'll go first."

The woman waited for the light to pass, then moved quickly and quietly out into the night. Lieserl watched as she bolted around the back end of the building. The searchlights probed the darkness, swinging back and forth slowly while Lieserl waited, her heart pounding. Long minutes passed. Had Georgina been caught?

Suddenly she heard the sound of steps on gravel. Lieserl risked sticking her head out the door and saw Georgina, bent over against the side of the building, quickly moving toward her.

"Okay!" she whispered as she slipped inside the door. "Nothing to it.

Your turn, now."

She took Lieserl by the arm, holding her. The searchlights moved across the camp, across the front of their block, briefly dazzling them.

Georgina squeezed Lieserl's arm and whispered fiercely, "Now!"

Lieserl slipped out the door and ran around the corner of the block as the searchlight swung back toward her. But by then she was in the shadow of the back of the building in a blind spot, safe from the probing eyes.

Running through the dark, she reached the latrine and unceremoniously thrust down her pants, allowing a blessed yellow stream to arc into an open pit. The cool night air made goose bumps rise on her exposed skin. The smell of excrement, death and decay was horrific.

When she'd finished she headed back, bent over, moving quickly but prudently. A searchlight beam headed her way, and she had to drop down and slide halfway under a low temporary building that rested on concrete blocks. The light stabbed at her as she recoiled further under the building, her heart pounding in her chest. It passed by, but she'd barely moved when it suddenly swung back and stopped. She pushed deeper into the dark shadows under the building.

The light passed on and she breathed a sigh of relief. She waited there for another fifteen minutes. She became aware of something else shifting nearby, the faint rustling and squeaking of rats. There was a stench, as if something had died in the darkness, something the rats were feeding on.

She couldn't wait any longer. Creeping out from under cover, she began moving back toward her block. The searchlights still swept the compound, and she froze when one passed over her, but somehow the operator failed to see her.

Georgina was waiting for her just inside the door to the block. "Where were you?" she hissed. "You nearly worried me to death!"

"It was nothing. I thought they saw me, so I hid under a building."

"They aren't usually so alert at this hour. I don't understand it. Nobody tried to escape, or else there would have been some shooting."

Lieserl found her mother still asleep and curled up next to her, Jeannette-Michelle on her other side. She'd hardly passed out into tortured dreams when the blockhova began shouting at everyone to get up for roll call.

* * * * *

The Auschwitz kommandant transferred Lieserl and her mother to Buna, one of the many smaller satellite camps. At Buna they were making synthetic rubber using butanol. With her technical training, Lieserl was put in charge of the cultures, huge vats of soil bacteria that fermented a slop of corn and wheat, creating butanol as a side product. All day long she supervised the brewing, then the distilling, sweltering in the heat of the furnaces, receiving an additional allowance of food that she shared with her mother.

They lived in a block reserved for women. The blockhova, Klausa Koch, was a lean, mean-spirited woman in her mid-fifties with a hatchet face and great bushy eyebrows. She'd lost three sons in the Great War, a fact she seemed to hold against the inmates, as traitors to Germany. She carried a cat-of-nine-tails and used it liberally, her wiry body uncoiling like a spring whenever she lashed the whip, bringing it to bear with malice on her charges.

The block was a single large room with narrow bunks three beds high. Anna and Lieserl shared a bunk in the middle of the top row. Anna worked in fields near the camp, harvesting wheat and other grains. Sometimes she was able to smuggle some extra food back to camp, usually just a small onion or a couple of carrots. Penalties for stealing food were harsh, but slow starvation was the only other option.

They bore the daily abuse, waiting for Heisenberg to come.

Chapter Ten

Carinhall

Haberditz drove out alone to Carinhall.

Goering had called him, indicating a matter of some urgency, refusing to discuss it on the phone. That troubled him only slightly, because while Goering was a powerful man, Haberditz had an ace up his sleeve, one he could play at any time to leverage an advantage.

And he thought he knew why Goering wanted to speak to him.

Haberditz found the hulking Reichsmarschall in his study overlooking the *Dolln Zee*. He was dressed in his finest field uniform, so many gold and silver medals adorning his chest that Haberditz was afraid he'd tip over and fall on his face. His art treasures were lovingly displayed in cases here and there around the study, canvasses on the wall, statues in corners.

Goering, hearing him enter, turned his head and favored him with one of his wry, knowing smiles. Walking over to him, he flipped open the top of a box of fine Havana cigars.

"Do you indulge, Admiral?"

"I prefer cigarettes, but could never refuse such a luxury." He took one of the cigars and allowed Goering to light it for him. "You wished to speak to me, Reichsmarschall."

Goering lifted his great head, nodding. "We have discussed your pet, this Heisenberg, before. I recall you promised some wonderful new weapon that would destroy our enemies in one titanic blow."

"There has been research in that direction, but so far there isn't any weapon. It's a matter of time."

"Time," muttered Goering. "Time is what we don't have."

"Your confidence seems shaken. Not long ago at the Berghof you seemed to believe victory was imminent."

Goering blew a large puff of smoke and waved his hand, sticking his tongue out briefly as if he'd tasted rotten egg. "I always put on an act for the Fuehrer. He doesn't like bad news, and often takes care of those foolish enough to tell him the truth."

"I don't understand. Our offensive through the low countries came off flawlessly. You've routed the French, the Dutch, the Poles, and the Belgians. No one stands between us and England, and once they're gone, we'll be the undisputed rulers of Europe."

"Yes, yes, of course we shall be." He turned and trudged over to the window, sucking smoke from his cigar. "But once we attack the British," he turned, motioning with the cigar to Haberditz, who joined him, "America will enter the war. Then it will be over."

"America's too far away. We have agents in place molding public opinion against their getting involved. They're isolationists, content with their empire in the New World."

Goering smiled cynically. "There's only one problem."

"What's that?"

"Roosevelt is almost as big an asshole as Churchill."

Haberditz laughed harshly. "An impotent old cripple! Surely you don't expect much resistance from him. His wife won't let him get into a war, not with his delicate health in the balance. He'd die of the stress in a matter of months."

Goering turned, his eyes smoldering. "Be careful with that word."

Haberditz raised his eyebrows, taken aback. "Which one?"

"Impotent." He winked, his mood swinging. "Still, she was a miracle, my little girl." He shook his great head and took another pull on his Havana, blowing smoke. "America is going to kill us. That's not a theory, mind you, that's a statement of fact." He looked sharply at Haberditz. "Any suggestions, Admiral?"

"Preparation and discipline," Haberditz said carefully. "That's German, and will be the key to our victory."

Goering stepped closer, conspiratorial, and said softly, "Just between you and me—and I'll kill you myself if you repeat this to anyone else—I think we should make peace with Britain. Consolidate our gains. America's industrial backing will make the Brits difficult to defeat."

"Thus far they haven't put up much resistance."

"They haven't capitulated, either. And they won't, unless you give me a weapon so powerful that God will piss in his pants."

"I can't guarantee scientific breakthroughs. That's not how science works."

Goering suddenly reached forward and grabbed Haberditz's collar with one meaty hand, jerking up and twisting. "If the scientists don't get the breakthroughs," he said through his teeth, "then you break the scientists. Do you understand me? They are no use to us, otherwise."

"Herr Reichsmarschall," Haberditz spluttered, his face red, "please unhand me."

Goering let him go slowly and then shoved him slightly, turning as if in disgust. "You're too weak to get results from that collection of prima donnas. You need to be firm with them. You don't even have to hurt them very much, they scare easily."

"How can I get them to build something that may not even be possible?"

Goering's florid lips curled into a snarl. "Are we talking about German scientists, or a pack of Jewish asses? Of course they can make a bomb. My informants tell me that Britain and America have already embarked on an ambitious program. We need to make sure we get there first."

"We'll do everything in our power, of course."

Goering's eyes burned. "That's not good enough! Find the key personnel and motivate them! If it takes money, give them money! If it takes whores, go hire a string of them! Promise them anything, but they must deliver!"

"They'll deliver," said Haberditz grimly. "You can count on it. I'll pistol whip them myself if need be."

Goering breathed a sigh of relief, and relaxed, nodding affably. "That's much better. And meanwhile, we should commence covert negotiations with England. That will buy us time, do you agree?"

"Do you have the authority of the Fuehrer?"

Goering spread his hands. "Am I not second in command? Did I not support him in the putsch, where I suffered a disfiguring injury to my privates?" His face fell into a wooden death mask of contained fury. "Listen to me. Not a word of this goes out of this room."

"Of course not."

"You understand? Not a word. I'll hang you by the balls on a meat hook if this gets out."

"I assure you, Reischsmarschall..."

Goering waved his assurances away with one meaty hand. "I need you to find a way to get an emissary out of the country, someone they'll believe, someone who can open secret peace negotiations."

"I thought you wanted to bomb the hell out of them."

"If we get the bomb, we'll use it. If not, we negotiate for peace. Even if we move ahead with the war, a peace offer will put them off their guard, so there's no harm in pursuing both possibilities, do you agree?"

"When you put it like that, yes, in principle."

"Good. Now think, who could make a convincing case? Whom would they trust, Churchill and the rest of them?"

"Among the high Nazi officials?"

"No, not necessarily."

Haberditz sighed and puffed his cheeks. "I'll have to think about it."

"How about one of your scientists?"

"That's out of the question, Reichsmarschall. They're needed on the project."

"I'm not suggesting you send one of the good ones. What about Heisenberg's assistant? That girl, what's her name? Send her."

Haberditz shook his head. "Absolutely not. First of all, Meier knows too much. And second, she's far too valuable to the project."

"She's a woman, how much could she know? Besides, she knows enough to scare the hell out of them so they'll be willing to negotiate. Does she have contacts in England?"

"She trained a year at Cambridge. She knows Chadwick and that Jew, Weizmann, among others. But I need her here, and I don't agree that giving them someone who can describe all of our reactor work is necessarily a good idea."

Goering grunted. "Of course, there's that. But didn't I hear that her mother is in one of the camps? That gives us leverage, doesn't it?" He raised his eyebrows.

"I insist, Reichsmarschall, that there are better candidates."

He grunted again. "Well, let's think about it, shall we? You're right that she knows too much. In any case, I'm worried about her patriotism. She's a malcontent. I suggest you put the woman on a less sensitive project. Keep her away from Von Ardennes' lab, and split her off from Heisenberg. I've noticed she has a certain lack of enthusiasm for advancing the goals of the party, would you agree?"

"I think Professor Heisenberg…"

"I've decided the issue," he snapped. "Just do as I say, Admiral."

"As you wish, Reichsmarschall."

Goering walked Haberditz to the front door of the mansion. "Your ships are all over the seven seas, Admiral. Surely you can smuggle one person over to the other side."

"No doubt."

"Work on it. And at the same time, get those scientists off their asses. In three months I want another full report, and I expect it to sound a hell of a lot better. If not, well, we don't have to spell out the consequences, now, do we?"

Haberditz shook his head stolidly. Goering grinned. "I'd like to destroy those British bastards," he said deep in his throat. "I need your help, Admiral."

"I won't fail you, Herr Reischsmarschall."

"See that you don't." He pointed imperiously at Haberditz's limousine. "Now get the hell out of my house and off my property."

Berlin

Heisenberg strode importantly into Haberditz's office at noon. Haberditz couldn't help but think what a cocky bastard he was, and was glad he'd made him stew for two hours in the waiting room, although there was no particular reason for the delay.

"Please sit down, Professor Heisenberg," Haberditz said cordially, rising momentarily and indicating a plush leather chair. "I'm happy you stopped by. What can I do for you?"

Heisenberg sat down, frowning, his blue eyes hard. "I've come to resign my position."

Haberditz stared at him a long moment, then slowly withdrew a Turkish cigarette from a box on his desk, lighting it with his monogrammed gold lighter. He snapped the lighter shut, replaced it on the desk in front of him, and blew a large cloud of blue smoke into the space between them. "If you mean to say you're not competent to lead the research, I can always get Harteck or Von Weisacker to take your place."

Heisenberg frowned more deeply and cleared his throat. "They're not in the same class as I am and you know it."

Haberditz widened his eyes and shrugged his shoulders. "If you're resigning, I don't have much choice, do I?"

Heisenberg shifted in his seat, leaning forward. "It's just that I can't be expected to move ahead with the project while the issue of my assistant, Dr. Meier, remains unresolved. My understanding was that you were to make locating her your top priority."

Haberditz waved his hand dismissingly. "These things take time. Goering has alerted his people, as has Himmler, I assure you."

Heisenberg allowed himself a brittle smile. "Interestingly enough, my mother has spoken with Himmler's mother, and it appears no search is underway."

"Himmler's mother doesn't know everything there is to know in the Reich," Haberditz huffed. "And Himmler himself is little more than a clerk with an oversized ego." He leaned forward and stuck his cigarette in Heisenberg's face. "What I want to know is when you are going to move forward on the *wunderwaffen*. I compromised my position, putting my support behind you, and you've failed me miserably. When can we expect some progress?"

"We're moving ahead as quickly as we can."

Haberditz's face twisted, and he struck the table violently with his fist, making a loud thump. "God damn it, I want results! Do you understand me? All this sniveling about your assistant! You're a Nobel laureate, for God's sake! You shouldn't *need* anyone else! Where's the goddamned bomb?"

Heisenberg sat back and gazed reflectively at Haberditz, composed, again confident. "I'll need more money. A lot more."

"How much more?"

"A hundred million Reichsmarks."

Haberditz settled back in his chair and took a long drag of his cigarette before stubbing it out in his cluttered ashtray. "You've got neutron multiplication in your piles?"

"Yes. Not as much as we'd like, but it's there."

"So how are you going to build a bomb? How do you know it will even be possible? You can't even heat up a glass of water and here you think you can level cities!"

"We've virtually proven feasibility. It's just a matter of scale, having enough $U-235$ in a large enough mass. The neutrons escape, otherwise, and the reaction subsides. With sufficient mass the chain reaction will be inevitable, even with lower grade uranium."

"You've been harping on this for two years. Why should I believe you, now? What do you have that's new? Or are you shooting wind?"

"We have two new methods. One of them is something of a long shot, I'll admit: it involves pitchblende. According to my calculations, a critical mass can be achieved with uranium-rich pitchblende. We can dig a large pit and arrange a conveyor belt that places canisters of pitchblende in the pit until the accumulation reaches critical mass."

"Sounds too easy. Do you have enough pitchblende?"

"At present we don't have any."

"And once we have the pitchblende, you think the English will let us land at Dover and dig a similar pit and spend two days loading it with pitchblende so we can blow them all to hell?"

"A battleship could carry it and self-destruct outside of London."

Haberditz shook his head resolutely. "That's insane. Pitchblende is not an explosive. Pitchblende is a tar suitable for sealing the cracks between boards on ancient sailing ships, that's all."

"Maybe so," Heisenberg admitted. "But if it worked, it would be a way around the purification problem and would demonstrate feasibility, which could help us get more funding."

"And you claim you need Meier for all this."

"She's essential to the project. Absolutely essential."

"Even for the great Nobel laureate, himself," Haberditz said sarcastically. "What about your other idea?"

"We would use a new element created in piles, one that could be chemically separated and also fission readily."

"More pie in the sky?"

"Houtermans mentioned the possibility, actually. It has a much higher probability of success."

"Give me estimates."

"One chance in ten for the pitchblende, and a virtual certainty for the transuranic element, if we can create enough of it."

"I see." Haberditz stared out a window for a moment, thinking. He stood up and walked around the desk. "Stand up," he ordered. Heisenberg stood up, and Haberditz stared at him, eye to eye. "I'll get Meier for you, one way or another. You will put her on the pitchblende problem, somewhere well outside the mainstream of your work. You need to get her away from Berlin, somewhere away from prying eyes. I'll arrange it. And then you'll do it. Start the weapons work, in earnest."

Heisenberg nodded. "That's fine. Just get her back."

"You and Von Weizacker, and anyone else you need, shall work on the new element angle. As far as getting Meier back, I can't guarantee anything. I'll get her back if I can."

Heisenberg shook his head. "I can't agree to this. I need her full participation."

"You shall agree or face severe consequences. Is that understood?"

Heisenberg said nothing for a moment and then barely nodded his head. Haberditz nodded in return. "Good. If you fail, I can make no guarantees concerning your future welfare, either. Do I make myself perfectly clear? Anything could happen. You might even be pulled off the project and put to work on ballistics, or armor. You and the rest of your fair-haired assistants might even be shipped to the front."

"I understand," Heisenberg replied stiffly. Then he turned and left without shaking hands or excusing himself.

Haberditz watched him go, and when the door closed, he sighed, picked up the telephone and began dialing. Heisenberg was beginning to annoy him; he wouldn't be surprised if he had Jewish blood.

It was time to rescue Meier from hell.

Berlin, two days later

They reached the Kaiser Wilhelm Institute in Dahlem shortly after sunset. Haberditz ordered the driver to keep going, and soon they arrived at Lieserl's apartment building.

Haberditz escorted her upstairs, surprising her by producing a key to her door. "I spoke to the landlady and took the liberty of preparing your quarters."

She found her apartment immaculately cleaned. A bouquet of roses graced the kitchen table, and the pantry was well stocked with food.

"I trust you'll be comfortable, here. If there's anything you need, just let me know."

"I need my mother."

He shook his head. "I did the best I could. The Reich values you, but she's expendable. She'll receive special treatment at Ravensbruck, extra food rations and light assignments. I'll drive you out there next week if you wish to check for yourself. It's not that far north of Carinhall."

"She's nothing but a hostage."

"Even if that were true, there's nothing you or I can do about it." He reached in the pantry and brought out a loaf of bread and some preserves. "You'll feel better in a couple days. I'll check back."

"Thank you, but you don't need to bother. I'm perfectly capable of taking care of myself."

He put the food down on the table and looked her in the eye. "I need some updates on the uranium bomb. The Fuehrer is contemplating some risky military moves. Goering's air attack on England was a total failure, and Hitler is making no moves to mobilize Operation Sea Lion. I think maybe he's lost his nerve. Anyway, I'm depending on you to deliver a viable weapon, one that will bring Britain to its knees and the world to our feet. I can't trust that stupid bastard Heisenberg to deliver on his own. He virtually said as much, himself."

"I doubt that."

Haberditz grinned out of the side of his mouth. "Well, let's say I read it in his body language."

Lieserl shrugged and looked away. "You can get the updates from him. He's my direct supervisor."

He smiled slightly, and his eyes began to smolder. "There are some things Dr. Heisenberg can't give me."

He stepped over to her and took her by the shoulders, pressing his body close to his. She trembled: she could feel him becoming aroused, she could smell the smoke and liquor on his breath. One of his hands moved to her breast.

He brought his mouth down on hers. Lieserl felt so compelling a revulsion that she became sick to her stomach and feared she would vomit. She twisted her mouth away from the horrible clench of his lips. "Your wife..."

He snorted. "My wife can't give me what I need. Even Marjot is getting tiresome."

He pushed and guided her to the bedroom. "Take your clothes off," he commanded as he shrugged out of his coat.

She complied, although it was cold in the room. She sat on the edge of the bed in her underwear. Out of the corner of her eye she saw that Haberditz was stripping all of his clothes off. He was developing a paunch. She turned her head away.

Haberditz moved over in front of her, his massive erection bobbing in her face. "God, but you've lost weight. Nothing but skin and bones."

"They kept us on a thin diet."

"Can't expect fine dining at a camp." He exhaled unevenly. "Time to do your duty, Dr. Meier."

She looked up at his face, trying not to notice the engorged organ just inches from her lips, seeing the animal anticipation in his eyes, his jaw slack as he stared at her. Not lowering her own gaze, she eased away from him, lying flat back down on the bed.

"What's wrong with you?"

She only shrugged, and Haberditz stood there uncertainly for a moment, disappointed, then grunted, "I suppose I'll have to teach you everything, you frigid Jewish bitch." He climbed on top of her.

When he had finished, he got up and dressed while she remained in the bed, pulling the covers over her still naked body and waiting.

"I never cease to be amazed," he said as he brushed lint off the shoulders of his coat and peered in her vanity mirror to check his appearance, "that one of the most famous Jews of all time, second only to Jesus Christ, should have fathered my mistress." He smiled at his reflection, then glanced her way. "You could show a little more enthusiasm, you know." When she didn't answer, he shrugged. "You'll get used to it. I'll see you in a few days. Try to get yourself fattened up a little. There's plenty of food in the larder, I made sure of that."

Turning on his heel, he strode out of the room. Lieserl, surprised, rose quickly and followed him out into the living room, the bed sheet clutched to her body.

"You'll make sure my mother is comfortable and well treated at Ravensbruck, won't you?"

Haberditz paused and lit a cigarette. "Stop worrying; she'll be fine." He studied her. "If I didn't know better, I'd say you never had a man." Then he turned left the apartment.

When Lieserl heard the door to the apartment close she got up and went to the bathroom and washed thoroughly. She dried off, dressed in a nightgown, and went to the kitchen. She found the refrigerator well stocked, and poured a glass of wine. Sitting down at the table with a stack of paper and pens at hand, she sketched formulae on a fresh sheet, her eyebrows knitted in a vain attempt at concentration.

In two or three days he'd be back for more. At best she could avoid him for a few days here and there, but not for long. It was a small sacrifice; many others had suffered much worse. It would buy her time to find a solution, to free her mother and escape Germany.

Einstein's Daughter: The Story of Lieserl

In the meantime she'd have to give him whatever he wanted.

* * * * *

Weisz watched Haberditz leave the building and get into the back of his staff car. He'd seen Meier's too-thin form when she'd arrived, and guessed she'd been interned somewhere. Routinely he memorized the license plate of the car, filing it away for future use. Something wasn't right about the way Haberditz was operating, and for a moment Weisz thought of lying in wait for him at his house, but decided that would be too dangerous.

He walked to the nearest subway station and headed across town. In half an hour he picked the lock to the front door and walked unchallenged into Von Ardenne's complex of laboratories.

The lax security was no doubt due to the fact it wasn't an official government lab, which was a lucky break. He checked the bulletin board in the lobby, finding the location of Houtermans' lab. A moment later he was inside it, passing a pencil-thin beam of light around the room, he caught glimpses of beakers and retorts, obsidian lab tables, cluttered stacks of papers, and ashtrays full of cigarette butts. Toward the rear of the lab was a desk and pair of massive file cabinets. He moved quietly back to them, finding them locked.

The locks were just standard office locks, and he picked them in seconds. Quickly but methodically he began going through the files. Goudsmit had briefed him on the physics, what to look for, but he wasn't a physicist and couldn't evaluate the material on the fly. So he snapped away with his tiny camera, photographing every paper that looked remotely related to uranium fission.

Suddenly the door of the lab opened and the lights went on. Weisz froze, fighting down an instinct to turn and draw his Walther. At the doorway stood a tall, gaunt man with dark, sharp eyes and bushy eyebrows, standing there stunned and disbelieving. Weisz recognized him from photographs: a much-aged Fritz Houtermans.

"May I help you?" Houtermans said, his voice measured and cordial.

"I have an interest in your work," Weisz said, tense, still ready to draw, gauging from Houtermans' size that he could probably knock him down and make a run for it. Unfortunately, his shouts might alert the guards and awaken them from wherever they were napping.

Houtermans was nodding. "Yes, I suppose you do. Whom are you working for?"

"An official government agency."

A ghost of a smile played around Houtermans' lips. "An official agency, to be sure, but of which government?"

Weisz pocketed the camera. "I'm afraid I don't have time to chat."

Houtermans made no move to unblock the door to the lab, and Weisz was afraid he might have to use force, after all. "You're the same fellow who broke into Meier's lab, I'll wager." Weisz said nothing, and Houtermans went on. "If you'll just get on your way, I might be able to overlook the fact you've burgled my files. Did you take anything?"

"Only pictures."

Houtermans nodded slightly. "Then you may leave."

Weisz stared at the man, amazed at the ironic smile playing about his lips. He stepped carefully by Houtermans and briefly considered strangulating him then and there just to be on the safe side, but if he were caught as a result then it would compromise the whole mission. He headed for the door.

"Oh, by the way," Houtermans called after him.

Weisz stopped. "Yes?"

"Make sure those photos get into the right hands. I suggest Niels Bohr. Teller or Oppenheimer would also be good choices."

Weisz didn't reply. He left the lab, not sure he entirely understood what was going on.

Out on the street he darted into the shadows of an alleyway, then began his usual zigzagging across town, heading back to his apartment. He thought about the material he'd photographed. Was it bogus, designed to throw off Allied science? If so, Houtermans would never have surprised him, so that didn't make sense.

The papers were of great interest, even Weisz was able to see that on a cursory glance. Houtermans might be sympathetic to the Allies, but he was still working for the Germans and was therefore a significant threat. Weisz grimaced. It may be he should call for an air strike.

Sirens wailed, and a Gestapo staff car dashed up the street in his general direction. Weisz melted into the shadows, waiting for the car to pass, then came out and went on his way. Maybe he should have just shot Houtermans, but it was hard to gun someone down in cold blood, especially someone with such an excellent sense of humor. Besides, the photographs would have to be analyzed, first. He didn't want to kill on speculation and jeopardize getting the real principals.

He walked a little further, thinking furiously. The next day he would make contact with the underground and arrange to send the photographs to England. Allied physicists could better appraise the scientific content. If it turned out the papers were important, a dead Houtermans wouldn't be enough: everything in the lab would have to be destroyed.

Ravensbruck

Anna Meier sniffed the fresh, clean air, looking with approval at the neat railway station at Furstenburg, the nearest railway station to Ravensbruck. As an SS officer motioned to her impatiently with his rifle, she stepped down out of the rank, animal smells of the cattle car and onto the pavement of the station.

Not far away were sand dunes and pine trees, the air blown over nearby lakes and swamps. Ignoring the German guards and barking Alsatian dogs, she turned to a companion, a French comtesse. "The air is much fresher, here.

Perhaps the food is better, too."

Marie Dravigny was a diminutive woman with a narrow face and pouting French lips. She still had her hair; she'd come directly from Paris, France, and so had a full head of rich russet hair. "*Oui, il fait tres beau ici,*" she murmured with a distracted air.

Anna had been transferred to the train in Berlin. Most of the women with her were French. They were all disembarking, sixty out of each cattle car, although the cars were designed for only eight horses. Each of them carried a suitcase and one or two small bundles of belongings.

The guards quickly got everyone lined up in rows of five, and soon everyone was marching in unison along a sandy road. On either side of the road were nicely maintained white cottages with gardens around them. German women and children glared at them as they passed.

"Jewish trash!" shouted a boy of about ten. He picked up a rock and chucked it.

"Go away, Jewish whores!" shouted a middle-aged woman. She stepped closer, making a fist and shaking it at them. "You killed my husband!"

"Unbelievable," said Anna as they marched by. "It's all so unbelievable."

"*Boff,*" responded Marie, "what is so unbelievable is that they are so stupid. They don't even know we're French." She glanced at Anna. "Most of us, anyway."

They marched ten kilometers down the straight, sandy road before the camp came into view. It was huge and dark and sprawling, with somber stone walls ten feet high topped by several rows of barbed wire. A sign warned that the wire was electrified. In each corner was a wooden tower with an armed guard on duty.

The massive iron gates were standing wide open, almost as if waiting in welcome, eager to receive the new guests. As Anna marched through the gate she saw two smoke-blackened chimneys off to the right: the crematorium.

One of the Frenchwomen just behind her cried out in anguish: "*C'est le fin! On ne sort pas d'ici!*"

Anna turned to the woman. "Put you trust in God. He shall watch over us."

"He has abandoned us!"

Marie frowned and hissed, "*Tais-toi, pleurnicheuse.* They're watching us. Hold yourself up with pride."

The woman abruptly quieted. Just inside the camp was a broad, well-maintained road with barrack-type wood and concrete buildings on either side. To the left were the administration buildings, storerooms, the laundry and infirmary, and a Strafeblock, the punishment block. Strips of grass, brown with the cold winter air, bordered the blocks. To the rear of the camp was an industrial complex, together with a small block for the few male inmates and some isolated punishment cells behind a coal dump. On the right side of the road were the camp headquarters, another punishment block, the crematorium, and a guardhouse, as well as the housing blocks for staff.

As at Auschwitz, Anna again had to strip, parading around naked with the other new inmates while they were all given a medical inspection and treated for lice. One in six women had their hair shorn completely away, whether they had lice or not. SS officers made rude comments and jokes as they eyed the women they guarded.

A doctor was giving out anti-typhus injections as the line of naked women slowly curled through receiving. Anna noticed he was using a veterinary needle, piercing the breast instead of the arm. He had a bland, bored expression on his face as he swabbed the side of Anna's breast and then stuck the huge needle deep into her flesh. She winced, but wouldn't give him any satisfaction by crying out.

Finally the uniforms were distributed, dirty gray and blue striped shirts, jackets, and robes. Anna received a set of clothes far too small for her; inmates were forbidden to exchange among themselves. She struggled into the outfit, fastening very few of the buttons, uncomfortably pinched in her crotch and under her armpits. Shoes were wood-soled sandals that the French called *claquettes*.

On the left sleeve or chest of every garment the prisoner's number was stenciled on a white patch. Various colored triangles sewn on the clothes identified the prisoner's offense. Anna's was red, indicating a political criminal.

When they were all dressed they were led away to quarantine by the *aufseherinen*—tough, muscular woman guards who carried short whips with multiple tails. The block the new inmates were to occupy was designed for sixty inmates, but during the quarantine it would house over three hundred. Three-tier wooden bunks packed in long rows were topped by vermin-infested straw mattresses, all of them neatly stored during the day under blue and white checked covers. The only other furniture consisted of a few three-legged chairs and a table in the small area between the two main sections of the block. An adjoining washroom had half a dozen basins, a shower, and five lavatories.

To Anna, just arrived from Auschwitz, it was wonderfully luxurious.

January 22, 1941, in the North Atlantic

Admiral Guenther Lutjens, on the bridge of *Gneisenau*, gazed dourly out across the restive gray seas of the North Atlantic. In the distance he could see the pack ice, and beyond that the shadowy southern extremities of Greenland. They were heading west towards Canada while the British Fleet, short of fuel, was on its way back to Scapa Flow.

Over the past few days he'd guided the powerful battlecruisers *Gneisenau* and *Scharnhorst* on a mission through the North Sea and Arctic, deftly evading the British Home Fleet that guarded the Faeros Gap between Scotland and Ireland.

He scanned the horizon through his binoculars, looking for a telltale wisp of smoke. The hazy air played tricks on the eye. He lowered the binoculars and turned to a petty officer next to him. "Send someone up the main mast."

The man saluted, and strode off. Lutjens went to the chartroom alone, gazing reflectively at the pins that marked the last known positions of ships on both sides. In the mid-Atlantic were three U-boats, prowling for convoys just as he was. A tanker was far to the south near the Azores, and he'd likely head in that direction, particularly if spy planes caught sight of further activity by the British Home Fleet. He needed a victory, a good one, something to set him apart from Marschall, already discredited during the Norwegian campaign.

Warning bells rang, signaling action stations. Lutjens strode quickly back to the bridge, which was alive with activity.

"What is it, Captain?" he said quietly to Forster.

Forster pointed off to the southeast. "Smoke."

Lutjens raised his binoculars up, peering through them. "Change course, heading one hundred ninety degrees, twenty-seven knots. Signal *Scharnhorst* of our intentions."

"Yes, sir."

"Keep a sharp eye out for any escort. If present, we'll break off the action."

"We could take the older British ships," commented Forster. "*Ramillies* has been escorting, lately. Her upper decks are thinly armored. She's an antique."

Lutjens turned to him, a dour look on his face, recalling Forster's outspoken remarks of the Norwegian campaign and the flight from *Renown*. "As you know, Captain, our orders expressly state we are to avoid engaging capital ships."

He looked unhappy, but saluted. "Yes, sir." Turning quickly, he strode away.

Lutjens kept watch as *Gneisenau* and *Scharnhorst* ploughed through the gray waters of the Atlantic. The main masts of the enemy ships moved up over the horizon, one after the other. None of them had the telltale superstructure of a capital ship. There were sixteen vessels altogether, supply ships laden with goods, bound for England, guarded by a sole merchant marine.

"Prepare to open fire," Lutjens commanded. "At fifteen thousand yards."

Soon the eleven-inch guns of the fore turrets were booming. By the third salvo they straddled their targets, fat, slow ships that were virtually defenseless. The single Merchant Marine came boldly forward, firing a pair of six-inch guns, the salvos falling well short. Lutjens ordered a change of target, and all guns were brought to bear on the little five thousand ton defender. The very next salvo scored a hit amidships, and pierced the side just below the waterline. On the next round several shells fell true. The ship began listing to starboard, its superstructure in flames. Through his binoculars Lutjens could see men leaping over the sides. Two minutes later the ship turned turtle and sank.

The convoy had already begun dispersing, and Lutjens ordered *Scharnhorst* to concentrate on the northern quarter while he turned to the south. The two German pocket battleships moved among their helpless prey, and with

English ships in every direction, all turrets could be brought to bear on their targets. Every twenty seconds the big guns spat out another salvo, the shells arcing with deadly accuracy. Ship after ship went to the bottom, carrying thousands of tons of desperately needed food and supplies with them.

"Has a distress signal gone out?" Lutjens asked Captain Forster.

"Yes, unfortunately. The British fleet will be setting out after us again."

Lutjens nodded. "Break off the action. We'll be heading south for one of the tankers. Inform *Scharnhorst*." He pointed at a smaller ship that had thus far avoided major damage. "Let that one go. Tell its captain to remain behind and pick up the survivors."

"Yes, sir."

He turned away as Forster left him. Although outwardly he was deadly calm, inwardly he felt a deep sense of satisfaction. He'd sunk fifteen ships, massing several hundred thousand tons. If he could return safely to Brest, he'd be crowned the premier commander of German Naval forces, flying his flag on the nearly completed *Bismarck*, which together with *Tirpitz*, *Scharnhorst*, and *Gneisenau*, would constitute a squadron powerful enough to challenge British supremacy on the high seas.

February 14, 1941, Berlin.

The air in Lieserl's apartment was stifling, all the more so because it was Friday evening, a favorite time for Haberditz to come knocking at her door. She paced and fretted until finally she couldn't stand it anymore. She had to get out.

Only that morning she had returned from a visit to her mother at Ravensbruck, borrowing Heisenberg's car for the day. The conditions were only marginally better than Auschwitz, but her mother kept up a cheerful banter, pretending nothing was wrong.

Yet the female guards, the aufseherinen, marched around the camp brandishing their short leather whips, sometimes with bits of glass attached to the tails, cracking them and showering the inmates with abuse. And when Lieserl had to leave, she saw tears in her mother's eyes. She'd wept, herself, then, and all the way home she'd cried again and again.

She called a cab and got dressed in a warm coat, gloves, and fur hat. Downstairs she met the cab and gave the driver the address of Von Ardennes' laboratory. Fritz was the one man she could count on to lift her spirits.

She had the driver let her off a few blocks from the laboratory so she could walk part way. The moon was just past full and she wanted to enjoy the cold night air. As she watched the cabby drive away, she suddenly heard something. It was a faint, rumbling noise, almost like thunder but higher pitched, like a deep whine.

Suddenly the air raid sirens went off. People began pouring out onto the street, seeking news, milling around, wondering what to do next. Night fighters scrambled. The droning became louder, and Lieserl, frightened, hurried along the street.

A deep thrumming filled the air. The night fighters careened across the sky above the city, harassing the incoming bombers. Lieserl looked up; a dark shape crossed the moon, and all of a sudden she could see a dozen airplanes silhouetted across the sky. She broke into a run.

Bombs whistled through the air. One hit the sidewalk less than a hundred meters in front of her, exploding and spraying her with shrapnel. She fell down, arm protecting her eyes, shrapnel cutting her forearm and scalp. Hundreds of bombs and incendiaries rained from the sky.

She knew she should head for shelter but she couldn't stop thinking of Houtermans. Getting back up, she stumbled forward. Fires were breaking out everywhere, and the staccato crash of antiaircraft fire came from positions not far from Von Ardennes' labs.

A sudden roar of giant aircraft came overhead, so low their thrumming vibrated powerfully in her chest. She could feel them, dark and merciless, she could sense their bomb doors opening and the racks of bombs dropping off into space. Shrieks of their fall combined with her shrieks of terror, and she threw herself into a rolling dive, cowering on the concrete sidewalk, covering her head with her arms.

One explosion after another erupted in the night, punishing thuds communicated through the pavement beneath her, plaster and wood and stones falling over her. More explosions, flames shooting high into the sky as a fuel tank went up, then the roar of more planes, more bombs, splinters flying into her, penetrating her clothes, her body.

Suddenly the droning sounds began to recede. She lay there on the sidewalk, the sirens still wailing. Blood oozed from her body. She was afraid to move, afraid to try to get up and walk, because her right thigh had metal sticking in it, while another splinter had pierced her left hand, which had been protecting her neck.

She crawled to her knees and then managed to stand up. Somehow she had arrived at the laboratory in the final moment of her terrified flight. It was a smoking ruin.

"Fritz!" she cried in panic. She stumbled forward, ignoring her pain, entering the building through a ragged gaping hole. "Fritz!"

She found him lying motionless in a pool of blood under one of the heavy lab tables.

"Fritz!" She dropped to her knees beside him, tears streaming from her eyes as she threw her arms around his inert shoulders. "Oh, Fritz!"

He stirred slightly. "If this is heaven, where are the bagels and cream cheese?"

"You're alive!"

He sat up and hacked violently. When he recovered, he said, "They've got to do something about the plaster. It's everywhere."

"Are you hurt?"

"Just a little bloody. You're all right?"

"A few cuts. A bad one in my thigh."

"Those bastards! I'll hold that one against them!"

"Fritz," she said urgently, "something's wrong with your leg. Your pant leg is soaked in blood."

"It's not my leg, it's my belly."

She tore open the bottom of his shirt. There was a dark, bloody hole in his stomach just a few inches below the navel. "We need to get you to the hospital. Wait here."

"I'm not going anywhere."

She ran back outside onto the street, shouting and waving her arms, calling for help. In a few minutes she managed to flag down a passing police car.

Shortly thereafter they were in an improvised field hospital set up to administer to those wounded in the area. She sat and held Houtermans' hand throughout the operation, which was conducted with local anesthetic. He only cried out once, when the doctor, probing deeply, withdrew a jagged piece of metal.

They were transferred to a hospital a few miles away, where Lieserl's wounds were treated. Houtermans was admitted to a ward with a hundred beds in a giant hall, all of them filled. Groans echoed off the cavernous ceiling as nuns walked briskly up and down the rows of beds, tending to the patients.

"I expected he would call them in," Houtermans croaked.

Lieserl was sitting at the foot of his bed. "Who? What are you talking about?"

"I had a visitor a couple weeks ago, somebody quite interested in nuclear physics. I thought he was going to kill me."

"You mean somebody robbed the lab? While you were there?"

"Where else would I be?"

A cold hand gripped Lieserl by the throat. "Can you describe him?

"Blond, handsome, big shoulders, the perfect Aryan, except he couldn't bring himself to kill me in cold blood. He must have had a Jewish great grandmother."

"That's the one," she breathed, a tremor of intuition running through her. "That's the same one who was in my office. It must be."

"When he finds out I'm not dead, he'll send the planes back." He paused to hack. "If I were you, I'd think about leaving town. God knows I would, if I had anywhere to go."

But Lieserl's thoughts were already elsewhere, her mind processing pictures, flashing one after another, snapshots of the bakery, a man loitering on the street, another catching her as she stumbled down the steps of 26 Grossehamburgerstrasse.

"If he knew about you," she said quietly. "Then he must surely know about me. And Werner."

Houtermans raised his bushy eyebrows, tilted his head, and shrugged, his way of agreeing with the obvious.

"Werner wants me to relocate to Gottingen," she went on.

"Then you must go. You'll be safe, there. Safer, anyway."

"I'll be farther from my mother."

"I think she'd rather have you living than dead. Just a guess."

Lieserl slumped and shook her head. "Fritz, I can't take this anymore."

He sighed and reached over, patting her hand. "That's what I thought during my holiday in the Russian prison, but here I am, attracting too much attention as always. I survived by focusing on the present. One day at a time."

She moved over and knelt down next to him, putting her head on his shoulder.

Chapter Eleven

Gottingen, February, 1941

"We'll build the pit over there at the bottom of that field," said Heisenberg, pointing at the end of a long, snow-covered pasture.

Lieserl squinted. It was a bright day, not a cloud in the sky, good weather for an Allied bombing raid. Gottingen, however, was only an old university town, low on their list of priorities. "We're only twenty kilometers from the university. Will that be enough margin?"

"Of course. Pitchblende should make a very crude explosive, probably very low yield. Too easily dispersed by rapid thermal expansion."

"You're going to lose too many neutrons. If that happens, you'll get heat but not much of an explosion. The chain reaction will cut off, just like our reactor explosion at Kaiser Wilhelm."

Heisenberg put his hands on his hips. "We'll see about that."

They walked down the field, leaving their footprints in the snow, brown grass showing underneath. A small herd of deer suddenly bolted from the forest, led by a magnificent buck. They dashed across the open field, disappearing again into the woods on the opposite side.

"Did you see that buck?" said Heisenberg excitedly. "The Reichsmarschall would love to take him down!"

"I wouldn't be surprised if he had him shipped here, just so he could hunt him. He does that, you know."

"So I'm told."

Lieserl took in the beautiful expanse of pristine snow, thinking of the heavy machinery that would soon turn it into a gaping, raw wound. Then they'd stuff it with a black radioactive tar, trying to make a weapon that would kill everything in sight. She fought down a brief wave of nausea.

"When...when do we start?"

"We don't even have the pitchblende, yet. It's on order. In January, I imagine, we'll start building up the site, and by February or March we'll be ready to carry out the test."

"And the B-series, back in Berlin?"

"We'll keep working on them, of course, in the meantime."

She thought of Haberditz, waiting for her back in Berlin. She didn't want to go back there; on the other hand, it was closer to her mother, whom she worried about incessantly. "Werner..."

He stopped and turned to her. "Yes?"

"Werner, I just don't know if I can do it."

His eyebrows knitted and he stepped closer to her, half encircling her in his personal space, concerned and solicitous. "Of course you can do it. If you can't, no one can."

Tears came to her eyes. "My mother..."

"I'll make sure she's well taken care of. In any case, the Admiral has given his assurances."

"His assurances are worthless."

"On the contrary. I believe he has been very responsive."

"Werner, the Admiral raped me."

Heisenberg looked stunned. "Are you sure?"

"Oh, don't be so stupid, Werner, how couldn't I be sure of something like that?" Angry tears came to her eyes, freezing on her cheeks. "I've let him do it several times. I don't dare refuse."

"Sorry." He frowned, and his shoulders slumped, his head hanging down. "For what it's worth, I'm very sorry. And I'm angry. I never would have suspected that of him."

"He's holding my mother hostage in that awful place. He says he's trying to help, but somehow nothing ever comes of it. And he knows about me!"

"Knows you're the daughter of Einstein?"

"Yes. He knows. Did you tell him?"

"My God, what kind of idiot do you take me for? Of course I didn't."

"Then how did he find out?"

"He must have had my house bugged. Or maybe the maid overhead something and repeated it." He shook his head. "At any rate, I'm sorry. This is an absolutely terrible development."

"At any time he could tell the authorities."

Heisenberg said nothing for a long time. He stared into the distance, frowning. "I'll do what I can. I realize we've all been subject to difficult circumstances. It's not right. I'll think of something."

"There's nothing that can be done."

Heisenberg looked up, searching the gray skies. "I have certain connections. It may be there's a way."

"I don't see how. He could expose me. Or he could hurt my mother."

He straightened and sighed. "There are limits, and he's passed them. One of his enemies might want to use this against him."

"But reporting him would expose who I am."

He nodded. "Of course. I'll have to think about it and make sure it's done right."

"Don't do anything without telling me, do you understand?"

"Yes, of course, if I can manage it. You'll have to trust me."

She turned from him, throwing her arm out at the pastures around them. "You know, this isn't going to work. It's a waste."

"Still, we have to try it. If it works, we gain tremendous leverage. That's another way. Nothing could be denied us, then."

Suddenly, now that she'd released some of the fear and tension bottled up inside her, she felt ready to turn to practical matters, leaving aside what she couldn't change. "I'm to supervise the construction?"

Heisenberg seemed relieved at the question, but shook his head. "Not a job for a woman, I'm afraid. The construction crews won't be very responsive. No, I'll find somebody to help you with that, and you can supervise and direct him." He gestured at the pasture. "If you feel up to it, we can take a small hike before we start back."

Lieserl followed him across the field and into the woods, saying nothing further, feeling somewhat purged now that she'd shared her pain with someone. Heisenberg, for his part, strode silently among the trees, lost in troubled reflection.

March 10, 1941 Berlin

Grand Admiral Raeder was a distinguished-looking gentleman of moderate temper and modest looks that projected his protestant values of hard work and fair play. His measured self-assuredness made others trust his leadership instinctively. Sitting behind his desk at the naval institute, freshly returned from an inspection of the shipyards near Kiel, he stood when Admiral Haberditz entered the room, reaching over the desk to shake his hand.

"It's good to see you, Admiral," Raeder said, as Haberditz seated himself on the other side of the desk. Raeder settled back in his own chair, back erect, hands folded before him. "What is this issue you wished to discuss?"

"It concerns the Rhineland exercise, sir."

"I trust that preparations are proceeding as planned."

"Well, there is a slight problem with command."

Raeder sat back in his chair, eyebrows raised slightly. "There are no slight problems of command. Please explain."

"This is a crucial mission," Haberditz said, "crucial in the sense that pressure must be kept up on Allied shipping, and preferably from surface warships, another mode of attack that has been successful in the past, supplementing the fine job Donitz has been doing with our submarine fleet."

"Yes, I understand. Please get to the point."

Haberditz cleared his throat. "Admiral Marschall, as you know, made questionable decisions during the Norwegian campaign, handling the destroyers and the capital ships in a way that left them vulnerable to attack, resulting in lengthy repairs that have delayed our efforts. He has left the navy in a state of vulnerability on the open sea. In my considered opinion, he should not fly his flag on *Bismarck*."

Raeder frowned and shook his head. "One mistake shouldn't cost a man his career. He did sink the *Glorius*."

"True. But this mission is important not only from a point of view of pressing the war, but also in terms of bolstering the Kriegsmarine. Goering is trying to cut our funding and has great influence with the Chancellor, who has something of an aversion to action on the high seas as it is. We need to demonstrate the superiority of our capital ships, and leadership is perhaps the most important question. We need someone conservative, who can be counted on to follow orders."

Raeder nodded. "Quite right, although I fail to see how Marschall can be faulted in that respect."

"He has shown himself to be too aggressive in his deployment of the fleet. The Norwegian campaign is a good example. Lutjens followed orders, refusing to engage *Renown*. Marschall, in the same theater two months later, did not. We need someone who knows how to avoid the British fleet until we're in a position to challenge it, all the while finding the convoys and sending them to the bottom."

Raeder looked annoyed and suspicious. "Surely you're not volunteering for the job."

"God, no!"

Raeder chuckled dryly. "You'd no doubt be the prime candidate, if safety of the ship were the only criterion."

Haberditz felt his face redden, but controlled his reaction and plunged ahead. "The man I had in mind was Lutjens, who has just returned from a highly successful mission involving *Scharnhorst* and *Gneisenau*."

"Lutjens did an outstanding job, it's true, but I can't simply dismiss Marschall from Rhineland. It would be scandalous; the crew morale would plummet. That's unacceptable."

Haberditz reached into his leather briefcase, on the floor beside him, and withdrew a sheaf of papers, placing them in front of Raeder. "If morale is your concern, you may find the following Gestapo report to be highly interesting."

Raeder raised his eyebrows in surprise. "A report on Admiral Marschall? The man is a saint." He picked the papers up and began scanning them.

Haberditz sighed and shook his head, as if sorry to be the bearer of bad news. "Sadly, he has some problems associated with discipline. He is suspected of homosexual activities."

Raeder's face darkened, and he tossed the papers down disdainfully. "I know Marschall, and it simply isn't possible for any of this to be true. Damned lies, all of it."

Haberditz reached forward and flipped the first three pages off the sheaf, exposing the fourth. "A certain Jewish man—Jewish, I say—has sworn complicity in these immoral acts." Haberditz leaned back in his chair. "Perhaps, as you say, none of it is true. Still, what if it should come out during the voyage? Surely rumors are already circulating. And, on top of that, he nearly lost *Scharnhorst* during his last major command."

Raeder sighed and leaned forward, putting his elbows on the desk. "Perhaps you have a point, Admiral. It's a shame, the times we live in; no one can avoid prying eyes." He waved his hands at the papers. "This could happen to any of us. To me," he paused, "or to you."

Haberditz flinched slightly under Raeder's gaze, thinking of his own sexual escapades, realizing that if he himself were investigated he'd have a hard time keeping his own position. At least he wasn't a homosexual. To be fair, however, neither was Marschall.

"Lutjens is of unimpeachable moral character," Haberditz said. "And he has his recent success to his credit in a similar operation. Wouldn't it be simpler..."

"You're right," Raeder said abruptly. "I shall write the orders. You're dismissed." He waved at the papers on the desk. "And take those damned things with you. It's rubbish."

Haberditz gathered up the papers and replaced them in his briefcase, quickly leaving the office, inwardly jubilant. His old enemy, Lutjens, given more responsibility than he could handle, would be sent on a follow up mission that would have every ship in the British Navy on his tail.

It was a win-win situation. If Lutjens succeeded, well and good for the Reich. If he failed, not all would be lost. The holier-than-thou bastard would be stupid enough to go down with his ship, thank God.

He reached the street and stepped into the back seat of his waiting limousine, beaming, slamming the door with verve. A celebration was in order. Unfortunately Meier was out of town at one of the new test sites, so he'd have to settle for second best. Afterwards, perhaps he'd even buy some flowers and champagne for his wife.

Leaning forward, he said to his driver, "Take me to Marjot's."

Gottingen

Heisenberg drove Lieserl back to the apartment that the War Ministry had rented for her. It was close to the University of Gottingen, where they would be meeting every day, doing the mathematical work on the design of a primitive pitchblende weapon. After things were up and moving forward, he'd return to Berlin. As he stopped the car, he jumped out of the driver's side and ran around to open her door for her.

"Tomorrow at morning seven?" he asked as he helped her out onto the pavement.

"Tomorrow at seven."

"You'll have the new calculations checked and ready?"

"Yes, of course. They shouldn't take more than a few hours."

"Good. I have to go back to Berlin tomorrow afternoon, but you'll be fine here, working on the design until I assemble a team. Won't you?"

"Yes, of course I'll be fine. Why wouldn't I be?"

Heisenberg shrugged. "Just concerned, that's all. Be sure to keep me informed."

He walked her up to the door and then took his leave with a kiss on her cheek and a final wave of his hand.

Lieserl opened the door to her little apartment, shrugged off her coat and draped it in a chair. She went to the kitchen. There, piled on the kitchen table, were stacks of papers, some she'd written, others by Heisenberg, Pauli, Bohr, even Einstein. Somehow her heart wasn't in the work anymore. Her mother was still locked up in Ravensbruck, north of Berlin, and here she was in southern Germany, not even able to visit her.

She wondered why Heisenberg had isolated her from the rest of the scientists. Thirty kilometers outside the quaint town of Gottingen, Heisenberg was supposedly trying to change the course of history, but so far not much had happened. She passed her days in the university library, researching materials, experimental data, doing calculations, which Heisenberg, on his periodic visits, discussed with her, albeit without much interest.

She was fairly sure his idea of the pit wouldn't work, but if they found some easier way to enrich uranium, or simply got hold of Houterman's work on the new fissionable element, a byproduct of a working reactor based on U-238 and U-235 enrichment, then the odds of success were all the greater.

After a several hours of intense work she got up to stretch and went over to the window. She was surprised to see a man loitering across the street, a young man, tall and blond, with a solid build and a pleasant face. Almost as soon as she caught sight of him he began walking up the street, as if he'd paused only momentarily on his way somewhere.

Lieserl watched him for a moment. There was something familiar about him, about his gait, the back of his blond head. Was it the same man who had broken into her lab? She hadn't got a good look at him.

She sighed and returned to her work, hoping she'd botch the calculations, although knowing she was too good, that it wouldn't happen. If it did happen she'd be caught, maybe disciplined, and that wouldn't be any use. She reminded herself that it probably wasn't going to work anyway, and began once again tracing the strange hieroglyphics of physics on the page before her.

Hamburg

Wilfred Meier stepped in through the front door of his family home, not knowing what to expect. Back on furlough from Brest, where he'd helped build a submarine base, he had three days in which to relax and rest. But the house had an empty feel, as if it had been abandoned.

"Hello? Is anybody here?"

He moved into the middle of the living room, dropping his rucksack in the middle of the floor, noting the dust that lay everywhere. He walked over to the arched door into the conservatory and looked inside. Another bombing raid had blasted it open, wrecking the piano. Someone had done a hasty patch job, throwing a few boards across the gap in the wall.

A creaking board startled him, and he whirled around, his hand going instinctively to his gun.

"It's you again," Ritter said. "What are you doing here?"

Wilfred straightened. "This happens to be my home."

"Not anymore. I'm the owner, now."

"Who says?"

"The local party officials, that's who. And if you don't get out, I'll call the police."

"Where's my mother? What have you done with her?"

His upper lip curled in a sneer. "She's in a camp where she belongs, with the rest of the traitors."

"When did it happen? Why wasn't I informed?"

Ritter waved his hand. "You were at the front. Besides, you don't need to know. That traitorous bitch is probably dead already."

He'd hardly finished speaking when Wilfred grabbed him by the shirt. "You bastard! What have they done with her?"

"Hey, take it easy! How the hell should I know?"

Wilfred shoved him, and Ritter fell back a step. "Hey! Watch it!"

"You slimy little bastard! You rotten piece of filth!"

"She was a spy! A goddamned whore for the British!"

Wilfred's fist rocketed out seemingly of its own accord, solidly connecting with Ritter's jaw. Ritter staggered backward and he stepped forward and hit him again, this time in the solar plexus. The rat-faced little man fell to the floor, and Wilfred kicked him viciously in the face. Ritter, bleeding, began begging for mercy.

Wilfred took a deep breath, calming himself with difficulty. "I should kill you, you bastard, but you're not worth the effort."

He picked up his rucksack and left the house. He had three days to make inquiries before catching the train to the next theater of war.

Berlin

Heisenberg walked into Admiral Haberditz's office at the Naval Ministry and quietly sat in the chair across from him. Haberditz was puffing on a Turkish cigarette, leaning back in his chair.

"So, Doctor Heisenberg, what is it this time? Good news, I hope?"

Heisenberg shook his head. "Not this time, Admiral."

"You said it was extremely important. Naturally I assumed a breakthrough of some kind."

"It's very important. It regards my assistant, Dr. Meier."

Haberditz's thick blond eyebrows arched up. "Isn't she still in Gottingen?"

Heisenberg stared at him. "I know about you…you and her. Do you understand?"

Haberditz coughed and sat up straighter in his chair. "I'm not sure I know what you mean."

"I have mechanisms in place. People beyond your reach, so that if something happens to me, letters will be mailed, persons of influence will be informed. The same will happen if you dare go near her again. You'll go up on charges."

Haberditz sat back in his chair and smoked, staring at the scientist sitting on the other side of the desk. "From science to blackmail. I like that."

"Call it what you will." His lips tightened. "How could you? She doesn't love you; she detests you. The very mention of your name makes her ill."

Haberditz took a final drag on his cigarette and stubbed it out in his overflowing ashtray as he exhaled. "She has been a little slow warming up to me." He leaned forward. "But to tell you the truth, Heisenberg, I don't give a damn what she thinks or feels. I'd have her under any circumstances."

"Stay away from her."

Haberditz rose. "If you're done, I have important work to do."

Heisenberg stood. "I won't give you a second chance."

"I may not give you a second chance, either. And when it comes to influence, don't be so sure yours is better than mine. Good day, professor."

Heisenberg turned and left, closing the door behind him. Haberditz sat slowly back down at his desk and reached for his cigarette case. Whom would Heisenberg contact? Himmler, through his mother? Goering?

Then he had it. He'd contact Raeder, of course, the Grand Admiral of the German Navy. Raeder was a protestant, straight-laced and probably had never had sex with anyone but his wife. An inquiry would be extremely unwelcome, even if he could turn it aside. He wished he could have Heisenberg killed or tortured, but the Nobel laureate had just enough influence to avoid either fate.

He cursed succinctly and lit his cigarette. How could he outbox that bastard? He hadn't thought the man had any balls.

Yugoslavia

The mountain roads on the way to Belgrade from Bulgaria were treacherous for man and machine, and Wilfred Meier's job was to make them less so. He and his team of workers were in the vanguard of the Second Army under General Kleist, responding to Hitler's fit of pique after Yugoslavia's surprise coup d'etat. After annihilating all resistance there, they'd turn and run the British out of Greece, making a clean sweep of the Balkans.

For Wilfred, it was just a question of building bridges.

He'd had no luck with the Gestapo in Hamburg, interceding on behalf of his mother. They wouldn't even tell him where she was, and had nearly thrown him in prison. Only his unit commander had saved him from that fate. As an engineer, he was essential to the war effort.

All day long the Macedonians had been attacking them, just harassment, nothing serious, most of them lobbing shells at the column of tanks and men from their hideouts among the trees on the mountainsides, some of them taking potshots from hundreds of yards with virtually no chance of hitting anyone. Wilfred, still suffering from his traumatic visit to Hamburg, was tired of being on the road, tired of being shot at, and sick and tired of war. The Yugoslavs, he knew, wouldn't put up much continued resistance, nor would the Greeks after them, although they were more than tough enough to run the invading Italians back into Albania, even when greatly outnumbered. Mussolini and his soft military had been totally inept since the outbreak of war. As a result, Wilfred had to build bridges in the line of fire so Hitler could bail his ally out.

Checking the struts on the new temporary bridge one last time, he motioned to an armored car, indicating the driver should slowly cross the bridge, testing its solidity. The workmen all stood back, watching with interest.

The bridge held, hardly creaking under the weight. The first panzer rumbled across, then the next. His job was done for the moment, until the next one, probably later in the day.

Over the last weeks it seemed troops and material were all being shipped east. It didn't make sense to Wilfred, given the pact between Hitler and Stalin, but he wasn't paid to think about the strategies of war. He'd anticipated working on barges and the like for Operation Sea Lion, but the invasion of England had been mysteriously canceled in favor of the eastern buildup.

A troop transport truck slowed for him and he ran over and hopped up onto the back, pressing in next to the soldiers, who made room for him. He sat back, leaning against the side of the truck, trying his best not to think of anything.

Gottingen

Weisz wasn't making any progress.

He'd surveyed the construction site outside of Gottingen, microfilmed all of Meier's papers in her office at the university, and kept her under surveillance for days. It made him uneasy, hanging out in the cobbled streets of the little town, waiting for something to happen while deep inside he had the growing apprehension that nothing of significance was going on, that somehow it was all a bluff. Pitchblende made into a weapon of war? Goudsmit hadn't mentioned anything like that, and it wasn't credible.

Meier herself didn't seem convinced. Watching her through binoculars as she moved about in her apartment, he sensed she didn't feel like someone engaged in an important undertaking. She seemed bored: beautiful, blazingly intelligent, but very bored. And as the days passed, he began to wonder why he hadn't gone back to Berlin. There the bigger fish like Houtermans or Von Weisacker were probably up to something, while Meier had been relegated to a backwater project, something to keep her occupied and out of the way while the important work was done elsewhere.

Weisz put the binoculars down and shook his head. Maybe he was getting too close to his work. He needed to go back to Berlin and break into Von Weisacker's files, the other Heisenberg protégé that seemed to be getting all the attention, lately. And because the air strike had failed to take out Houtermans, a second strike had been ordered, but Weisz still hadn't tracked down Houtermans' new location. Eventually he'd return to his old laboratories, as Von Ardenne was rebuilding them, but that would take months.

He picked the binoculars back up and focused them on Meier again. She was at the desk next to the window, furiously scribbling her equations, a bit more passionate than usual. He enjoyed watching her when she was so intent, so concentrated on her arcane and almost magical work. It was like watching a sorceress, weaving her mathematical spells.

Although it was nearly midnight, he watched her for another hour, fascinated by her face, her beautiful blond hair and intent, hauntingly lovely eyes. The shape of her lips, as he passed his eyes along them, seemed flush with life and promise, with purpose and potential. His gaze lingered there for some time. He wondered what they'd feel like, pressed against his own.

Soon she began undressing. She unbuttoned her blouse and shrugged out of it, closing the drapes as an afterthought. The light went out. He waited another hour, then left his room, heading for her apartment.

The lock on her apartment door was old and large, easy to pick, an exercise that took him less than thirty seconds. He checked on her; she was in bed, in the bedroom, her chest rising and falling in perfect rhythm, perfect repose.

On the table in the combination kitchen and living room he found a stack of recent work. He went through the papers rapidly, photographing each page with his tiny camera. He'd have to get it to his local contact in the underground that night, if possible.

When he finished he stood in the open door of her bedroom for a long moment, gazing at the smooth curves of her sleeping form beneath the covers.

Air Ministry, Berlin

Goering pounded the massive oak desk in his cavernous office. "I told you in no uncertain terms that I needed results, Haberditz. Didn't you understand me? Results!"

Haberditz stood fearfully before the Reichsmarschall, his hands behind his back, chin up, trying to put up a brave face. "Six more months. That's all I ask."

"I need it in three."

Haberditz's eyes narrowed and he shook his head with calculated arrogance. "You can't be serious. This is science, you can't just make it happen, like magic."

Goering pounded the desk again and stood up. "I told you I would replace you, Admiral, if you failed me. And you have. I see little other choice other than to dismiss you from your duties."

"But the war is progressing well. I don't understand your sense of urgency."

Goering moved his corpulent form slowly around the desk, advancing on Haberditz until he was right next to him, his belly actually touching that of the admiral, his eyes gleaming with an odd light.

"I'll tell you why this is so urgent," he said in a low voice. "Do you really want to know?"

"If you want to tell me."

"Barbarossa."

"Barbarossa?"

"You are so low on the totem pole, these days, so pathetically incompetent that you have not been included in the planning. Barbarossa is a new military initiative: we are to attack Russia in two months with everything we've got."

"I hadn't been informed. And I'm not surprised: I don't see how the navy could be much involved in an attack on the Soviets. Whose idea was that? Bormann's?"

"It was our Uncle Adie's idea. I have been unable to dissuade him, even suggesting I might resign when he began insisting on it." He frowned and made a throwaway gesture of resignation. "You know how he gets when he starts talking about Jews and Bolsheviks." He sighed and shook his head. "I helped a Jewish family only a week ago, one of my former physicians. Some of them are quite useful. But the Fuehrer…"

"A two front war is certainly ambitious," said Haberditz. "But I expect our panzers will run roughshod over the old cavalries of the east. A blitzkrieg to Moscow could bring Stalin to his knees."

"Blitzkrieg to Moscow?" Goering laughed in his face. "Have you heard of Napoleon? How about the Great War? A two-front war is suicide!"

"If that's so, what would you suggest, hypothetically, that we do about it?"

"Close one of the fronts. It's time, Admiral."

Goering went to a picture on the wall, a priceless Monet, and removed it. Behind it was a safe. He dialed the combination and pulled the arm, opening the heavy door. Inside Haberditz could see a clear glass cup full of diamonds, tangles of jewelry studded with precious stones, wads of currency of various denominations and from various countries, stock certificates. From among the treasures Goering pulled out a thin sheaf of papers. He brought them over to Haberditz, not bothering to close the safe.

"These documents must be smuggled to England. It delineates terms of an armistice and peace agreement. If the English agree, then they must indicate their agreement by sending a night raid on Berlin within two weeks. The planes must drop only leaflets, not bombs. The desired text is indicated. I will take that to be a sign they are cooperating, and will then use the Luftwaffe to take temporary command of the government."

Haberditz sat for a moment, flipping pages, masking his dread. Was it a trap or an opportunity? "Your name isn't anywhere in it."

"I'm not that stupid. Of course my name isn't there. You can assure the English that a high-ranking officer in the Nazi party is ready to broker a deal with them." He paused, appraising Haberditz with a critical eye. "More than one of us, actually."

"Who's the other one?"

"You don't need to know. He has offered to fly across the channel on his own initiative, but I've denied his requests for the aircraft."

"They'll shoot him down."

"Of course they'll shoot him down, the English aren't idiots. He knows Lord Hampton rather well, old school chums." Goering grunted. "Maybe we'll try that if this doesn't work, but I have a better plan."

"I assume you're going to tell me what it is."

Goering glared at him. "Your wife and children, and all you hold dear, including your favorite whore, the lively temptress Marjot, will suffer terrible retribution if you betray me, do you understand that? You will be considered the traitor, not me."

"How do you know?"

"I have your signature forged on several very sensitive and very damning documents." He pointed with his eyebrows. "They're over there in the safe."

Haberditz involuntarily jerked his head around, staring at the open safe on the wall. Turning back to Goering, he said, "What sort of documents?"

"Documents my agents found at your house."

The color drained from Haberditz's face. "You planted them?"

Goering laughed. "No, my agents found them there, I assure you! But don't worry; fail me not, and I shall give them to you to dispose of as you see fit."

"Leave Marjot out of this. She's done nothing to you."

Goering smiled. "I've been sharing her name and hearing good reports on her. Wouldn't it be a shame if she suffered a disfiguring accident?"

Haberditz took a gold cigarette case out of his pocket and withdrew one of his Turkish cigarettes. He lit it and took a long drag, steadying his nerves. If he wasn't careful, he wouldn't leave the Air Ministry building alive. "Let's say I cooperate. What's in it for me?"

"That's more like it." Goering turned and put a great paw on Haberditz's shoulder, guiding him to the picture window. He gestured at the streets of Berlin far below. "If we succeed, you could find yourself promoted. You'll be one of the elite, with all the benefits that implies; a mansion, servants, obscene salary, and so forth. And you'll be a German hero."

"Tell me what I'm to do, hypothetically."

Goering stretched out his great arm, indicating Haberditz should take a seat before the desk. Haberditz did so. Goering then went back behind his desk and sat calmly down. A faraway look came into his eyes as he toyed with diamonds the size of peanuts that lay scattered on his green ink blotter.

"I understand you've been instrumental in Admiral Lutjens' rise in the ranks of the Kriegsmarine, is this not so?"

"His great skill, I believe..."

"Admiral Haberditz, I know everything about you, from what you eat for breakfast to where you like to stick your cock. So don't try to tell me Lutjens' unparalleled abilities landed him that command. You engineered the whole deal, making Marschall out to be a sexual deviant, effectively handing the command over to Lutjens."

"I did no such thing."

Goering waved his objections away. "Please. I'm not blaming you. I need you to get these papers out of Germany and into the hands of English authorities. We have naval vessels going to and from Norway. You need a courier, someone of authority or standing, someone they can believe. After he gets to Norway, he can make his way to Sweden and the English Consulate."

"Why not fly him directly to England under cover of darkness?"

"Much too dangerous. Sweden is best."

Haberditz cleared his throat and swallowed. "With all due respect, Reichsmarschall, I believe it would be far preferable to smuggle the agent into Denmark. Anyone with a small sailboat could then take him across the straits to Sweden."

Goering sighed and looked up at the ceiling as if seeking divine guidance. He looked back at Haberditz, face set in a vexed expression. "The coast of Denmark is a gigantic minefield. And further out, your own patrol vessels are blowing these small sailboats of yours out of the water. No, Admiral, the message must go out on a capital ship. You have leverage over this indecisive, unimaginative man, this Lutjens. This is the most important mission of the war and I will not entrust it to someone in a rowboat. Have you found someone to do it?"

"No, not yet."

"What the devil have you been waiting for?" he roared. "Find somebody!"

Haberditz sat up straighter. "Wait a minute. I know someone."

"Good. The papers will insinuate that Germany is on the verge of a breakthrough in atomic weaponry. With English support we will bring the war to an end and negotiate peace. Hell, maybe we can even enlist their aid against Stalin. Barbarossa may be a colossal mistake, but close the western front and we could bring it off. That two-faced, pig-headed communist bastard is long overdue for his comeuppance."

Haberditz clutched the papers more tightly. "This could be viewed as treasonous, you know. We could be executed."

Goering laughed. "I suggest you tread carefully, then. This meeting never happened, but there is plenty of evidence implicating you in the plot!"

"What will you do with the Fuehrer?"

"He'll remain Chancellor of Germany, but he'll have to cooperate fully with the new order."

"You won't get peace with England while he's still alive," Haberditz said. "He won't sit by and let you take over the government."

Goering waved the objection away. "He wants peace with England, I tell you. Hell, he loves the English! They're so much like he is, taking over the world, enslaving all the lesser races. We have a lot of friends over there, you know, people who would like Germany to act as a buffer between the civilized world and that savage Bolshevik beast."

"I don't understand," said Haberditz. "Operation Sea Lion was supposed to take care of the British."

"Shelved permanently, didn't they tell you? Maybe if the Navy hadn't been staffed with traitors and incompetents we could have brought off the invasion, but after months of preparation, what did we have? A few barges?"

"The Luftwaffe lost the air war over Britain," said Haberditz stiffly. "That's why Operation Sea Lion was put on hold."

Goering's eyes blazed. "We lost nothing! That war is still going on! Look at Coventry, annihilated! London in flames for months!"

"You should have concentrated on the factories and airfields."

Goering stood up. "We can debate all day. Now, if we are agreed, I suggest you get the hell out of here and do your job."

Haberditz stood. "Thank you, Reichsmarschall. I'm your man."

CHRIS VUILLE

Chapter Twelve

May 15, 1941 Gottingen

Lieserl opened the door of her apartment to find Admiral Haberditz standing in his trench coat, damp from the rain, water dripping off him onto the floor of the landing.

"Admiral," she said coldly. "I wasn't expecting you."

He pushed his way in and slammed the door shut behind him. "Shut up and take your clothes off."

When she hesitated, he shouted, "*Now*! Do it *now*!"

"*Go to hell!*"

He took back his hand and slapped her so hard she staggered and fell to her knees. "There isn't much time. Do as you're told."

Holding a hand to her red cheek and fighting tears, she stood and went to the bedroom, stripping off her clothes and lying down on the bed. Haberditz didn't even take his boots off. His wide leather belt dug into the soft flesh of her belly, and his breath, smelling of sauerkraut and sausage, nearly suffocated her.

She bore his grunting, thrusting weight silently, thinking of her calculations. Her luxurious, golden blond hair, grown back to several inches, was spread out on the pillow in a fan. He was heavier than ever before: he'd taken to eating too much, and was starting to develop jowls and a bigger gut. He'd protected her, as he'd promised, but she still detested him more than anyone else in the world.

He was taking longer than usual, and her thoughts drifted to Heisenberg. He had told her of new progress he'd been making, although he was not willing as yet to share it with her. That in itself was strange; he'd never held anything back from her before. The experiments she was helping design and plan she had no great confidence in, but he insisted she continue. The excavation was nearly finished, and the canisters of pitchblende were due in the next two weeks. She didn't think it would work, but if it did, it would change the course of the war.

She knew how to make a bomb, both she and Houtermans knew. Had Fritz cracked under pressure and shared his knowledge of the transuranic element with Heisenberg? That was unlikely. The bomb she and Fritz had designed didn't use pitchblende. Maybe Werner had come up with some new, viable ideas in regards the crude ore from which uranium was derived.

During her stay in Gottingen she had also designed a power plant. Unlike the B-series, it would work. She had tried not to complete the calculations, but her obsession with science had taken hold of her. Science had always been her refuge even when the knowledge she generated was dangerous.

She was frightened by Heisenberg's patriotism; he was no Nazi, but he loved Germany too much. They'd been close throughout their professional lives. Their brief, platonic affair had spanned only six weeks when he quietly withdrew. He'd had little use for women in those days, spending all his free time with his all-male youth group up in the forests and mountains. He had been their leader, the younger members looking up to him as a kind of father figure, a necessity in the aftermath of the Great War, which had left so many young boys without fathers.

Heisenberg feared the destruction of Germany and the collapse of German culture. That was his weakness. She didn't blame him for it, although sometimes she thought she should. Down deep, she was quite sure, he didn't want to work on bombs any more than she wanted to fuck a foul-smelling, overweight Nazi admiral.

Haberditz was still working at it, and she wondered if he had another mistress on the side, or perhaps was even paying attention to his wife. His breath puffed in her face rhythmically, but at least he didn't try to kiss her. She detested kissing him, feeling his heavy mustache brush against her upper lip, his thick, smoky tongue pushing into her mouth.

Finally he grunted more loudly and stiffened against her, and she knew he was done, and made a half-hearted show of gasping and groaning in feigned ecstasy. He remained on top of her for a moment, his head resting on her breasts, then climbed out of bed and started arranging his uniform.

"I have something you must do for me," he said.

"What is it?"

He tightened his belt. "You must leave the country tonight."

"I can't."

"I have documents that will help you."

"I can't leave the country when my mother's in that camp."

His upper lip curled. "Do as I say. That's the only way you'll ever see your mother again."

She sat up, fear in her flat belly, her fine breasts white and high and still shapely, with sizeable dark nipples. Feeling exposed and cold, she pulled the bedclothes up against her chest. "I don't believe you."

"Believe whatever the hell you want," he said. "Do you think the SS isn't watching you? You've had a taste of their interrogation methods, for God's sake. Wouldn't Himmler like to get his hands on you!"

Her fear was replaced by a hot surge of anger, and she stood up abruptly, clumsily wrapping the bedclothes around her lithe, naked body. "I won't leave the country without her," she said, her voice shaking.

He shook his head and said, "There's no time." He grabbed a blanket off the bed and wrapped it around her shoulders. "God damned, plugged up radiators. If I didn't know better, I'd think your landlord was Jewish. Why doesn't he keep your rooms warmer?"

He stepped over to a chair where he'd hung his coat, fishing out a thick envelope from an inside pocket. "Take this."

She accepted the envelope suspiciously. "What is it?"

"Ten thousand marks. And there's a letter for Admiral Lutjens, and another envelope containing important papers that you are to deliver to the British Embassy in Stockholm. You are to go to Gotenhafen, to the port. Go quickly, there's a train leaving tonight."

Lieserl nodded uncertainly, and said, "Why not Switzerland? It's closer."

"You'll never get across the border, they'll be expecting you to go that way. Go with Lutjens. He's an old friend and he owes me some favors. I've arranged everything."

She looked frantically around the room. "Do I have time to pack?"

He glanced at his watch. "You have little more than an hour to get down to the station. Once in Gotenhafen, go directly to the harbor. Don't delay; they shall be leaving soon, I have it from Raeder, himself."

"Who will be leaving?"

"The *Bismarck*, of course, with *Prinz Eugen*. They'll be going on a shakedown run to Norway. You'll leave the ship at Bergen."

"Will someone be meeting me there?"

"Wait near the dock. Someone will come for you. Don't worry, they'll take care of you." He leaned close, staring into her eyes. "And whatever you do, don't break the seal of the other document. Lutjens will understand you're on an important mission and will not ask for it."

"Something isn't right, here. I'm supposed to be some kind of spy?"

"Just do as you're told. If you succeed, there's every chance we'll be able to win the freedom of your mother."

"I won't do it if you won't explain what's going on."

"You'd rather be taken by the SS? There's more at stake, here. You are to be our emissary, do you understand? You must speak to the leaders in the west and end this brutal, wasteful war. Tell them we're on the verge of a super weapon, a bomb so powerful that it can lay waste to cities."

The breath caught in Lieserl's throat. "You've got one already? Heisenberg worked it out and he didn't tell me?"

"Let's just say he has made highly significant progress. In any case, it doesn't matter if we have one or not. Tell them. Make them believe. We need you alive and out of Germany, we need you to stop this war."

"Only Hitler's death could stop the war."

Haberditz stared hard at her. "Another man stands ready to take the reins of power. He is highly placed and beloved by the German people, a hero in the Great War. It won't happen unless you do your job."

She frowned, studying him. "Why now? And why me?"

"I told you, I let something slip. Now if you'll cooperate, at least we'll get something out of it. Millions of lives hang in the balance."

"Who will take Hitler's place?"

He shook his head. "I can't tell you that."

"You must tell me or else I won't be able to deal effectively."

He opened his mouth, then, and said softly, "Goering."

Haberditz put on his cap and gloves, and then eased into his overcoat. His cold, beady blue eyes swept over her one last time, and he reached up and put the back of his gloved hand against her cheek. "After the war…"

She held her tongue, a vicious retort choked off in her throat. The burst of

Einstein's Daughter: The Story of Lieserl

hatred had made her eyes smolder, and Haberditz, mistaking it for lust, smiled like a sly wolf, affectionately pinching her cheek before allowing his hand to drop back to his side. He turned and swept out of the apartment.

For a moment she stood in the middle of the room, stunned. Then she vaulted into action, running to the bathroom and washing herself quickly and thoroughly, not minding the cold water, anxious to get the last vestiges of Haberditz off her body forever. Then she dressed in a conservative gray suit so as not to attract attention, binding her hair in a bun. She pulled a large satchel out of the closet, stuffing clothes and other effects into it. Going to her desk in one corner of the room, she quickly flipped through the stacks of papers, discarding some, taking others.

She was about to leave when she decided to risk telephoning Heisenberg. She dialed his number at the University, then waited impatiently for him to pick up, desperately hoping he hadn't left town and gone home to his wife at their mountain retreat near Urfeld. She didn't want to leave Gottingen without contacting him.

"Hello?"

Her heart jumped when she heard his voice. "Werner, it's me, Lieserl."

"Lieserl! I was going to call you."

"There's no time to explain, Werner. I've got to go quickly. Do you understand?"

There was a long pause on the other end of the line, and some unusual static. Was someone listening to the conversation? If she were being investigated, that was likely.

"Yes, Lieserl, I think I understand."

She breathed a sigh of relief. "Good. Listen carefully. Destroy all the papers in my desk. *All of them*. Then meet me at the train station. You'll have to hurry; I'm leaving right now."

"Lieserl..."

"Just do it, Werner. Meet me two or three blocks north of the station. Do you understand?"

"Yes."

She hung up, worrying about the security of the line, wondering if she'd just signed a death sentence for both of them. But Heisenberg was a pure bred German, and he had the pedigree to prove it.

A moment later she was out the door, walking briskly through a cold mist along the cobblestone streets, medieval cathedrals staring down on her. Twenty minutes later she saw Heisenberg standing on the other side of the street, his reddish blond, curly hair a little mussed, his broad forehead creased in worry, looking up and down the street. She was relieved to see him; he was breathing hard and must have run all the way there. She hadn't really wanted him to risk coming, but she was glad he'd come, anyway.

"Werner!" she called out. He hadn't seen her as yet. "Werner, it's me!"

Heisenberg looked startled, and nearly stepped off the curb in front of a passing Wehrmacht staff car. The driver leaned on his horn, and Heisenberg jumped back out of the way as mud splashed up on his overcoat. Looking flustered, he made his way across the street to join her. "Thank God I caught you. I didn't have my car, and I thought…"

"We don't have much time, my train leaves soon. I don't know if they'll even let me on it, but..."

"What are you saying? Of course they'll let you on it. Why shouldn't they?"

"I'm under investigation."

"Then you've got to get out. Let me help you."

"I'm going to Norway. It's all arranged. There's no time to explain."

He hesitated, nodding. "I took the liberty of glancing over your recent calculations," he said. "That nuclear pile that you've designed is a stroke of genius."

She frowned. "You had no right to look at them without my permission. And I told you to destroy them!"

"I know. Sorry, but there wasn't enough time. In any case, your design may be revolutionary. After all we've gone through with that heavy water reactor…"

"The technology doesn't exist. It would take years to develop." It was a lie, but she wanted to derail his line of thinking.

"No, no, Lieserl, I'm quite sure it's feasible. I understand Fermi and Szilard have been working along the same lines in Chicago. With your work in hand, we could duplicate their efforts and go far beyond."

She shook her head stubbornly. "It's not practical, and may not be for years, even decades."

"Still," he insisted, "it should be investigated. I could take it up with Speer…"

"So what will you do?" she said darkly, cutting him off, disturbed that her own work might inadvertently aid the Nazi war effort. "Use it to make power plants for Hitler? Like that bomb you're working on? The one that Haberditz tells me you've already developed, on the sly, while I was wasting my time down here in Gottingen?"

He shook his head and sighed, half resigned, half exasperated. "It's more complicated than you're making it out to be. It's true that they've gone much too far, but the existence of Germany is at stake."

"You are not to use anything of mine to help them. Do you understand? Nothing."

He regarded her with his sad, gentle eyes. "I can't promise that."

She dropped her satchel and reached forward, gripping the lapels of his overcoat tightly. "You will respect my wishes, Werner," she said through clenched teeth. "Burn anything that looks the least bit important. Not everything, that would raise too many questions. That would endanger you."

"You won't be safe in Norway, you know."

"I've been led to understand everything is arranged."

"You must get to the United States. Einstein will help you."

She bobbed her head, and managed to say bitterly, "Yes, of course he will." She looked up at Heisenberg again, searching his eyes, seeing in them the secrets they shared. "Now that I have something to give him, maybe he'll help me."

"You shouldn't be so hard on him."

"You never told him, did you?" she demanded.

"I swear, never. When would I have had the chance?"

She appraised him a long moment. "There's something I want you to promise me, Werner."

He was cautious, as usual. "What is it?"

"I want you to recalculate the critical mass."

He frowned. "I've checked those calculations carefully. I believe they're correct."

"Change them. Remember Bohr's calculation? Wrong, but a good method, and no one will blame you for agreeing with him. Change the numbers, make sure it won't work."

"If I get caught..."

"If you get caught," she interrupted him, "you will die with honor, and if I survive, I'll be forever proud to call you my heroic former lover."

He colored beneath the streetlight. "We were never lovers."

She bent over and nervously checked the clasp on her satchel, then straightened again. "I know. Not like that, but we should have been. I have to go now. Goodbye, Werner."

"Goodbye, Lieserl."

She grabbed hold of his lapels and pulled him towards her, kissing him firmly on the lips, tears streaming down her cheeks. Then she turned and ran for the station as the cold rain began coming down. Only once did she glance back: he was still standing on the sidewalk in the pouring rain, gazing after her.

* * * * *

Weisz climbed up the fire escape and into Lieserl's apartment.

It was empty: he'd observed Haberditz departing earlier, followed a few minutes later by Lieserl, herself. She'd been in a hurry, carrying a large briefcase with her.

The bedclothes were in disorder, of the kind associated with sex. He quickly went through the apartment. There were no papers of any kind, not even in the wastebasket, although she had been working on them earlier. Maybe she was carrying them with her in the briefcase.

She had thrown her drawers open carelessly, tossing clothes all over the place. Her toothbrush and toiletries were missing from the bathroom. Weisz realized, then, that she wasn't planning to return.

Alarmed, he dashed out the front door of the apartment, ignoring the surprised challenge of the landlord who shouted after him. Bursting out of the door on the ground floor, he ran for the nearest train station. For all he knew she had been picked up by Heisenberg on a corner, but in that case, why had she bothered to hurry down the street, rather than wait for him in front of the apartment house?

* * * * *

Schutzstaffel officers were patrolling the train station, members of the Death's Head Regiment, the skulls on their dark blue overcoats staring at her accusingly. Lieserl purchased her ticket at a window and raced to the platform where passengers were already boarding the train. The SS were everywhere; she felt their eyes boring through her, and felt sure they could see her Jewishness through her gray suit, or maybe in the recesses of her lustrous eyes.

One of the officers, apparently in charge, was at the front of the line checking the papers of a nervous young couple. While the young man and woman shifted back and forth, he frowned, occasionally barking questions, to which the couple gave short answers that never seemed to satisfy him.

Suddenly the officer shouted out; guns were drawn and aimed, other officers converging, grabbing the young man by both arms. He resisted when one of them took hold of his girl friend, starting a scuffle that ended when one of the officers struck him in the head with the butt of his rifle. The girl screamed, receiving a backhanded slap across the face that staggered her. The officers confiscated their belongings and hauled them away.

The line moved forward. Lieserl got her papers out and stood clutching them. If it was true the SS were looking for her, then her name would be on a roster, and when she handed over her papers they'd recognize her name and take her away for interrogation. If she survived that, she'd go back to the camps.

Either of her two secrets, of course, could help her survive, even live in good style, but she'd die before revealing them. A nuclear power plant in a ship like the *Bismarck* would mean unlimited high-speed travel through the oceans without need of refueling. Submarines could remain submerged almost indefinitely. Enormous aircraft could be built, powerful enough to carry large bombs all the way across the Atlantic, if need be. Maybe that threat would delay American entry into the war, allowing Hitler to consolidate his gains before expanding further.

Her second secret would also afford her special treatment, but she would never reveal it. If she did, she would find value to the Nazis as a curiosity, at least, and possibly as a hostage. Yet her bitter pride would not allow this second secret to pass her lips, even if it meant facing the camps.

Her turn came. The SS officer was a lanky, stiff man with a brisk manner, too young for his position. He snatched her papers from her hand. He eyed her, then her photograph, then her again, his cold blue eyes penetrating and hard, suspicious, tinged with lust. Lieserl, trembling inside, stiffened her lips and drew herself up, determined not to show her fear, doing her best to smile at him.

"Pass," he said gruffly, thrusting her papers back at her.

Without a word she accepted the papers, picked up her bag and walked toward the train. With each step she felt his eyes on her, expecting him to call her back, to bark orders to his underlings and have her hauled off for interrogation in the basement of the SS offices.

She found a seat next to the window on a wooden bench. Usually the seats were covered, but the war effort had cost ordinary travelers some of their luxuries. She sat down and closed her eyes, keeping her face averted from the windows. A few minutes later the train whistle blew, and the conductors made their last calls.

With a lurch, the train started forward with a squealing of wheels, bound for Hamburg, where she'd change trains for Gotenhafen and the *Bismarck*.

* * * * *

Weisz arrived at the station, huffing and puffing from the exertion. SS guards were all over the place and a train was just moving away from the platform, blowing its whistle. He'd have to show his papers and purchase a ticket. One of the officers glanced his way, his boredom giving way to mild interest.

Ducking back out into the night, he ran around the outside of the station and then parallel to the tracks. The train was picking up speed, windows flashing by. Running up the embankment, he threw himself at a passing safety rail attached vertically on the end of one of the cars.

He thought his arms would be ripped from their sockets. His legs slammed against the side of the car and fell dangerously close to the track and the massive wheels. With desperate strength he pulled himself up into the small space between two adjacent passenger cars.

He paused to catch his breath, rubbing his shin, which he'd slammed against the side of the train. He'd have to buy a ticket on board, which would be expensive, but he had plenty of money. He didn't even know if Meier was on the train, but that was just a matter of conducting a search. If she weren't, he'd return to Gottingen.

Straightening up his clothing, he entered one of the cars.

May 17, 1941 Gdynia

The voyage by train took a grueling two days. The train stopped several times, once for repairs after an air attack, other times to fulfill some military priority. She finally reached Gotenhafen, called Gdynia by the native Poles, and had found a room in a small hotel situated over a tavern not far from the harbor. She found out from an overly talkative young member of the Kriegsmarine that the *Bismarck* wasn't sailing for a few more days due to some minor accident involving *Prinz Eugen* and a magnetic mine.

She'd arrived in the morning of the seventeenth and spent the day sleeping in her shabby hotel room. When night came, she went downstairs to the tavern to get something to eat and drink.

The tavern was packed with sailors. A burly accordion-player provided the music, and the prostitutes with their brightly rouged lips hung on the shoulders of their marks, plying them for drinks and whispering their indecent suggestions in their ears.

"Hey lady! Want to join us for a drink?" somebody called out.

"I saw her first!" someone else shouted.

Lieserl felt a questing hand on her hip and angrily batted it away, eliciting laughter from a group of merchant marines. She moved quickly away, looking around for an unoccupied table.

A waiter came and took her order. She sat alone, listening to the music, putting up with the rude, provocative stares of the sailors. She needed to find out more about the *Bismarck*; she wasn't sure she could just present herself and expect to be accommodated. Haberditz was not the most brilliant man in the world, and surely his note would do little to improve her chances.

A thick-necked drunk at a nearby table began giving her the eye. His florid face reflected the muted red light as he lifted his mug and guzzled beer. The golden liquid slopped around the edges of his lips and onto his shirt, and his friends laughed at him. He put down his mug and laughed along with them, his horse's teeth large and crooked.

The waiter brought her a small block of cheese and a cut of dark bread, along with a glass of wine. She nibbled at her food between sips of the dark, sour wine.

"Would the lady care for a dance?" he asked in German.

She looked over her shoulder, seeing the thick-necked drunk. His beady eyes ravished her, his tongue running luridly along his bottom lip.

"No, thank you."

"Just a quick turn around the floor, that's all."

He grabbed her hand and hauled her to her feet. She swung at him and he ducked, his friends laughing. "Three marks on the wench," someone cried.

"Let me go!" she demanded loudly. "I'll call the police!"

The drunk laughed and pulled her close. "Just a turn, that's all, that's a good girl."

Suddenly a tall blond man grabbed the drunk by the shoulder and spun him around. His steel-blue eyes bore into the drunk's blood-shot orbs. "I suggest you leave the lady alone."

Her rescuer was in his late twenties or early thirties. He was wearing a black turtleneck sweater, tall and trim but with powerful neck and shoulder muscles. His strong jaw and ruggedly handsome face was set in a mask of domination and authority.

With a sense of horror, she realized it was the man she'd seen stalking her apartment in Gottingen.

The drunk stood there in the man's grip, disoriented and confused. One of his friends yelled out, "Punch him, Horst! Let the bastard have it!"

Horst hauled his fist back and tossed it at the man's face. He dodged the blow easily and grabbed Horst by the arm, jerking him unexpectedly forward and sending him sprawling over a nearby table. Drinking glasses smashed to the floor amid howls of protest.

His face blazing red, Horst picked himself up off the table, shoving one of the table's occupants violently backwards so he fell to the floor. Growling like a wounded bear, he charged his tormentor.

Standing his ground, the blond man threw a hard right into Horst's jaw, and he went down. Cheers went up from the onlookers, even from the drunk's friends. The tavern's burly owner intervened, and with the help of one of the musicians dragged the unconscious man outside.

Lieserl looked at her rescuer, who wasn't even breathing hard. "Thank you."

"Wolfgang," he said, offering his hand.

She took his hand and shook it briefly. "Thank you, Wolfgang. That was very noble of you."

He shrugged. "Any decent man would have done the same. May I join you?"

She hesitated. "I'd prefer..."

"Just for a few minutes."

"Yes, all right, for a few minutes."

He sat down across from her. He signaled the waiter, who brought him a stein of beer. Now that he was seated across from her she wasn't sure whether he was the same man or not. He had blond hair and sparkling blue eyes, a devil-may-care curl at the edge of his lips.

"Not the best place for a lady," he said after a short silence.

"I'm staying upstairs."

His eyes widened slightly. She realized to her embarrassment that several of the girls in the tavern probably conducted their business in those rooms. She could see that he immediately dismissed the possibility, and was grateful he was able to tell the difference between her and the professionals working the bar.

"Where are you from?" he asked.

"Gottingen."

"You're...?"

"Lieserl Meier." She nearly bit her tongue. She hadn't meant to give out her real name.

"You work at the university?"

"Yes. How did you know?"

He shrugged. "You've got a kind of bookish look, that's all. Many people there work at the university."

"I was in physics."

He accepted the information without surprise, as if he'd already known it. "Really? That was my favorite subject in school. I wanted to build rockets with Von Braun, but one way or another I ended up in the navy, instead."

"You're not in uniform."

"Well, I used to be in the navy. No longer."

"I suppose you were getting all the ladies in trouble so they had to discharge you," Lieserl said, flirting with him, and hardly believing herself as she did it.

He grinned a little self-mockingly. "I never had that much luck with the ladies, I'm afraid."

She looked at him askance, a knowing smile spreading on her lips. "I'm not so sure I can believe that."

"It's true. What are you doing in Gdynia?"

"Why, aren't I supposed to be here?"

He laughed. "Only if you're Polish or a German sailor. So, what are you doing here?"

He was pumping her for information. Haberditz had warned her she was under investigation: he was probably a Gestapo agent, or perhaps sent by Himmler's SS, investigating her, trying to find out what she was doing and where she was going before arresting her. If he were the same man shadowing her over the months, that would explain everything.

"I'm visiting my relatives."

He smiled indulgently. "And they hadn't enough room at their house, so you're staying over a tavern right next to a string of professionals."

Somehow the way he said it left her cold. "I'm not sure what you're implying, sir."

"Sorry, that didn't sound quite right. I apologize."

"I have a brother, he's on the *Bismarck*. I came to see him. Do you know how I can go about visiting him?"

He straightened and took a drink of his beer. "There are boats going out there and back every two hours. You could probably talk your way onto one of them. But you'd better hurry."

"Why is that?"

"I saw a tanker topping off their oil tanks, today, and a lot more activity in the harbor. They'll be moving out soon."

"I see. How soon are they leaving, do you think?"

"That, I couldn't tell you. It won't be tonight, though, too many of them are on shore leave. If I were you, I'd go down first thing in the morning."

"Thank you, I may do that." She glanced around awkwardly, as if she were looking for someone, then rose from her seat. "I'm sorry, I really have to be going."

"Please, you don't need to leave so soon, do you?"

She shook her head, feeling herself go shaky inside. He was a spy, she knew it, and she'd given him far too much information already, stupidly asking about the *Bismarck*, and making up the silly story about her brother. "Sorry," she said again, and left quickly, passing by the bar and heading upstairs.

On the stairway she passed a woman and man wrapped up in each other's arms, the smell of cheap beer and even cheaper perfume mingling together unpleasantly. The woman's ruffled white blouse was unbuttoned, one sagging, powdered breast exposed, the large brown nipple erect. They were blind drunk, shifting against each other, grunting softly as they sloppily kissed and petted each other. Lieserl averted her eyes and stepped around them, passing unnoticed.

* * * * *

Weisz sat at the table, alone, thinking.

He had to get her out of the country, out of Europe, somewhere safe. He was convinced she had the answer to a German atomic bomb. In that case, his instructions were simple: kill her.

If he killed her, the mission would be over for the moment. Heisenberg, he'd decided, wasn't much of a threat. His pit out in Gottingen was the clumsiest experiment Weisz had ever seen. He couldn't believe it had any real chance of working. With Lieserl safely out of the way he could contact mission headquarters and maybe catch a sub back to England.

He signaled the waiter, holding up two fingers. The waiter scurried away, and Weisz directed his attention back to Horst.

"Come join me, my friend. A drink, to show there are no hard feelings."

Horst looked his way and grunted. "I'd kill you as soon as look at you."

Weisz waved him over. "You might as well take advantage of my pocketbook before you dig my grave."

Horst grinned and shrugged. "Sure, why not?" He got up from his table and joined Weisz just as the waiter came back with the two beers.

Over the next hour Weisz found out everything he needed to know about Horst Dorner. He was in the merchant marine, he had come to Gydnia alone, and he was going to be joining the *Bismarck* as one of the members of a prize crew, the sailors that guided captured ships back to German harbors.

Weisz plied him with beer and when the sailor couldn't drink anymore, helped him home.

CHRIS VUILLE

Chapter Thirteen

Gdynia, May 18, 1941

The harbor at Gdynia was bustling with activity: tugboats pushing barges, workers loading and unloading, machinists working on the uncompleted warships in the great dry docks. Sparks flew as welders joined metal seams. At one dock the *Graf Zeppelin* stood rusting, abandoned half finished because of the intriguing Luftwaffe commander, Goering, who opposed a separate naval air corps.

The air smelled of rotten fish and salt, of diesel fuel and rust and hot steel. Far out in the bay the *Bismarck* floated at anchor. The *Prinz Eugen*, a heavy cruiser, was further east. The ships were grand and powerful, elegant and menacing, and Lieserl couldn't help but admire them.

She found one of the ferries, an awkward-looking boat that seemed too tall for its small size. The crewmen crowded on the upper and lower decks all seemed to be young boys, blond and handsome and youthfully arrogant, pretending to be fearless and confident. Photographers from newspapers and magazines took photos and interviewed some of the men; going on the mission with the Navy men, they eagerly anticipated shots of sinking British ships.

The skipper of the ferry regarded her suspiciously when she showed him the sealed envelope addressed to Admiral Lutjens. He questioned her at length, insisting on opening the letter and reading it for himself, which she would not allow, reminding him it was from Admiral Haberditz and that it was a matter of utmost importance. Finally, worried he was interfering with someone of influence, the skipper allowed her to board.

She sat on the lower deck between a frowning reporter and a gentleman in a suit who was engrossed in reading a technical manual. On nearby benches the young sailors ogled her, elbowing each other and laughing, and she regarded them sternly so they wouldn't become too bold. The skipper fired up the engine, a tremble running through the vessel, and a mate cast off the moorings.

Lieserl gazed at the *Bismarck*, marveling at its size and grace. Sitting out in the bay on a brisk, sunny day, it looked invulnerable, powerful and menacing. She knew first hand of the awesome technical skill of German engineers and could readily believe the ship was unsinkable.

Half an hour later she was on the quarterdeck, a sailor leading her to Admiral Lutjens' private quarters near the bridge.

Admiral Lutjens was a tall, handsome man with a noble bearing, intelligent but taciturn. He had a comfortable look to him, his expression candid and somewhat sad, like a neglected family dog. Lieserl immediately noticed the absence of Nazi insignia on his uniform: he was richly decorated, among his medals the Iron Cross, but wasn't a member of the party. He sat at a small desk reading the letter from Haberditz, back erect, face calm. Unlike the Nazis she had known in Berlin he seemed free of arrogance; to her he appeared to be a reasonable man doing his duty, serving his country. She knew he had led the battle cruisers *Gneisenau* and *Scharnhorst* on a successful foray into the Atlantic, sinking hundreds of thousands of tons of the British merchant fleet, but despite that she couldn't dislike him.

When he finished reading he put the letter down on the desk and looked up at her. "Haberditz has put me in a very difficult position."

"Why so you say that?"

"I hadn't planned on stopping in Norway."

Her breath caught in her throat. "Why not? Admiral Haberditz informed me you were going there."

"The Admiral isn't up to date on the exercise."

"Don't you have to refuel?"

He nodded. "Yes, of course we do, but not necessarily in Bergen. We have tankers. We'll rendezvous with one of them."

"If you aren't taking me to Norway, then what will you do with me?"

He stared at her thoughtfully a long moment before replying. "I will send you back to shore," he said at last. "A naval vessel is no place for a woman."

Lieserl bristled. "Put me in ballistics; I can calculate better and faster than any man there."

He raised his eyebrows. "You've had training in ballistics?"

She frowned, insulted, seeing that his surprise resulted from his prejudice towards her sex. "I'm a physicist. My doctorate is in nuclear physics, from Gottingen."

He nodded respectfully. He gestured at the document on the desk before him. "The Admiral says you are an envoy on an important mission of some kind. The document looks official enough, but it's all very irregular. What can you tell me about it?"

"I can't tell you anything, Admiral."

"Can you tell me why he would use a highly-trained nuclear physicist as a courier?"

"I cannot."

He looked hard at her, and then pointed at her single large satchel. "If I searched your luggage, what would I find?"

"Clothes, personal effects, a few books and papers."

"Classified papers?"

"Yes." Her mouth was so dry that the sound caught in her throat, and she had to repeat herself. Lutjens quickly offered her a drink from a decanter. She accepted; it was a French Bordeaux. As she sipped it she felt her nerves coming together again.

He sighed and looked down at the paper on his desk. "Haberditz has created certain difficulties," he said for the second time. "If we stop in the fjords near Bergen, we risk being sighted by enemy agents. I had assured Commander Raeder only yesterday that I would avoid lingering on the Norwegian coast. The English, you understand, keep it under aerial surveillance."

Lieserl's face fell. "I understand, Admiral."

"On the other hand," Lutjens went on quietly, "I owe Admiral Haberditz a debt. And he indicates that you are on an important mission for the Reich. I suppose I should contact the SS for final clearance."

Lieserl thought furiously, trying to keep the blood from rising to her face. "Some things must be kept secret even from them."

He nodded. "And, perhaps, there is strategic justification in refueling in Bergen, especially *Prinz Eugen*, which has a shorter range. In view of that, I will make every effort to honor Haberditz's request. We could perhaps make a very short stop and refuel *Prinz Eugen* and top off the *Bismarck's* tanks."

"Thank you, sir." She felt an enormous flood of relief that she worked hard to mask.

"You shall confine yourself to quarters except when given my express permission," he went on sternly. "You shall do as I command; the same goes for any of the other officers on this ship. In Norway you will disembark and go to the address given in this letter."

"Where shall my quarters be?"

"There is a spare cabin reserved for visiting dignitaries. It's comfortable enough."

"Shall we be leaving, soon?"

He didn't answer. Instead, he got up and called a midshipman, who came and took her bag for her. Her cabin was only a few steps away, small but comfortable, the porthole giving a view of the harbor. She was exhausted by her journey, by the constant tension. She lay down in the bunk fully dressed, except for her shoes, which she slipped off. She was asleep before her second shoe hit the deck.

Naval Institute, Berlin

Admiral Haberditz nodded to his secretary and went into his office and closed and locked the door. He sat down at his desk and breathed a sigh of relief. By now the *Bismarck* had set sail, taking Meier out of the country on Goering's fool mission, one that was already doomed to failure. Heisenberg's blackmail would be moot, and life would return to normal. He'd neglected Marjot and made a mental note to have a large bouquet of flowers sent to her apartment.

The telephone rang and he answered it cheerily. "Admiral Haberditz. May I help you?"

It was Goering. "I'm calling about the project. Is it going forward?"

"Yes, Reichsmarschall."

"That's very good. Come to dinner at my estate tonight and give me the details."

"I'm afraid my duties may preclude my attendance."

"Your duties can wait. I expect you to be there at eight. Everybody's coming."

"If you insist, Reichsmarschall."

"I do. See you this evening." Goering hung up.

Haberditz lit a cigarette and sat back in his chair, enjoying a leisurely private smoke. He chuckled to himself when he thought of how he'd out boxed the corpulent Luftwaffe commander. Haberditz had followed through on his side of the bargain, but had made sure Goering's gambit would fail. The failure would occur on foreign soil, so to all appearances it would be due to bad luck rather than Haberditz's machinations. As a result, Goering would be in his debt, the Reich's real interests would be protected, and Haberditz's personal indiscretions would be rendered harmless.

It was perfect. In a head-to-head confrontation with Goering he would surely lose. This way they were allies; Goering would have to protect him to avoid opening a difficult and damaging political battle. The only real loss was the woman, but she wasn't the only beautiful bauble in the world.

Thinking about Lieserl aroused his nostalgia. He pulled a decanter out from beneath his desk and pored himself three fingers of vodka straight up. Tossing it back, he put the empty glass down on his desk with a sigh, smacking his lips and enjoying the burn down his throat. He'd enjoyed her and was sorry he would never do so, again.

May 19, 1941 The *Bismarck*

When she awoke she could hear a powerful thrumming of engines, a vibration through the thin mattress that penetrated to her very core. She got up and looked through the porthole. Dark blue water stretched to the horizon. Opening the porthole and craning her neck, she could see a large, rocky island ahead, along with several other ships, one of them the *Prinz Eugen*. She guessed they were somewhere in the relatively narrow waters separating Norway and Denmark. She used the head, then looked around the tiny cabin. A tray of food was parked on the floor next to the door; a sandwich, an apple, and mineral water. She picked tray up and put it on her bed and began eating ravenously.

Haberditz indicated that someone would contact her at Bergen. If they could help her get to Sweden she'd be reasonably safe. From there she could arrange transport to Britain, then America.

She thought about Einstein, and although she was a grown woman, tears came to her eyes. And she thought of her mother, in Switzerland near Zurich, taking care of her deranged son Daniel, Lieserl's brother. She wanted to confront her and find out how someone of her own sex could have abandoned her child. Heisenberg had said the mad son was God's punishment, but despite her feelings she thought that was too cruel. For Lieserl the only punishment was hell, usually created on Earth by its politicians. She still remembered the cheering, the bands and military hymns when trainloads of young German soldiers went off to fight in the Great War. And history was repeating itself, except that this time the devil himself was in command of the German forces.

Someone knocked politely on her door, bringing her out of her reverie. She opened the door and found a tall, retiring man, his face sensitive and kind, standing at respectful attention. He was a good decade older than most of the crewmen, who were in their early twenties.

"Admiral Lutjens requests the honor of your presence at dinner, tonight."

"You may inform him I accept with pleasure."

"Very good. I will come for you at six o'clock."

"What time is it now?"

"Eleven o'clock in the morning. The Admiral instructed me not to disturb you."

She'd slept all afternoon and then the entire night. "And what is your name, steward?"

"Claude Ritter, Doctor."

"That's an unusual first name for a German."

"My mother's fault, I'm afraid. I grew up in Strasbourg."

"Thank you, Claude. I'll look forward to seeing you at six o'clock."

Claude bowed slightly, a gallant gesture, and left her. She sat down next to her small desk and composed her thoughts. Admiral Lutjens had indicated she should remain in her cabin unless escorted; that was a shame, because she was intensely interested in visiting the different parts of the ship, especially gunnery control and the engine rooms.

For a while she mentally designed the nuclear piles that would replace the enormous diesel furnaces of the steam engines. It was almost unimaginable: a great battleship like the *Bismarck*, capable of circling the globe at top speed without refueling. That power alone would make Germany invincible on the high seas and enable an early invasion of Britain.

The sun had long set when Claude returned to her door. As he escorted her down the hall to Admiral Lutjens' cabin, she chatted with him. He was a nice-looking man, with a broad smooth face that was almost painfully sensitive. In response to her questions he shyly volunteered that he was on his first sea voyage, and that he was from Hamburg. Lieserl listened with interest, but offered nothing in return other than a polite nod of her head.

Admiral Lutjens rose from the table as she entered his cabin. The table was already set for two, a bottle of wine in a bucket of ice to the side. For a brief instant she was dismayed: it resembled a scene of seduction, and she wondered if Haberditz had offered her to him, a final humiliation for her to endure.

Lutjens' gentlemanly manner, however, quickly dispelled her fears. "I hope you've rested well, Madame," he said formally.

"Yes, thank you, Admiral."

Claude seated her at the table and then quietly left the cabin. The dinner consisted of lamb, sauerkraut, potatoes, and green beans, all very basic but hot and cooked to perfection. Lieserl ate enthusiastically. Lutjens said nothing, absorbed in his thoughts, picking at his food.

When her appetite was satiated she looked up and said, "Do you have a wife, Admiral?"

"Yes, of course."

"Children?"

"Two daughters."

"It must be difficult, your going to sea and leaving them behind."

"I've put my affairs in order. I don't anticipate returning from this mission alive."

Her jaw dropped. "This is the greatest battleship ever built! How could you have any doubt?"

He took a drink of wine and cleared his throat. "The British Navy, taken as a whole, is considerably stronger."

"I doubt that Hitler would risk such a mission if he knew you felt this way."

"Raeder assured him that the risks are minimal. I reassured him on that point as a favor to Raeder: I don't entirely share that point of view, but have little choice in the matter."

It dawned on her that the point of this strange and tense dinner together was to confide in her. He was expressing his private doubts, something he couldn't and shouldn't do with any of his men.

"You could have resigned your commission."

He shook his head but offered no verbal response. She understood that a complex of conflicting emotions were tugging at him: patriotism, the call of duty, fear for his life, love of his family. Under similar circumstances she was sure she would be in a virtual paralysis of indecision.

"Do you believe in the war effort? Do you believe in Hitler's vision for Germany?"

He sighed. "What I believe is of little consequence. I'm a patriot, and have a professional duty to perform, that is all. I receive my orders, and I execute them to the best of my ability."

Her face darkened. "That's what I hate about the military." She threw her arm out in a grand gesture. "You're always doing your damned duty while the world burns!"

He was unperturbed by her accusation, but apparently wished to cut the evening short. He rose. "We arrive in Bergen tomorrow morning. You will want to rest, and I have my duties, of course."

"Of course," Lieserl replied, her voice dripping with sarcasm. She expected him to reply, but he simply grimaced stoically and saw her to the door. Ritter was waiting for her there, and escorted her back to her cabin.

Because she had slept through the day, she was restless and couldn't sleep. Taking out some paper, she began sketching equations. She passed a couple hours that way, alternately looking at the papers and gazing out the porthole at the inky darkness of the Baltic Sea. After a while the equations began dancing obsessively through her head, and she was able to lie down and watch them weave their hypnotic spell on her.

May 21, The *Bismarck*

Two days later, at about nine o'clock in the morning just off the island of Marstein, the *Bismarck* and *Prinz Eugen* together with their destroyer escorts turned to starboard and entered the calm waters of Korsfjord. The fleet then split up, the destroyers going to Bergen, *Prinz Eugen* to Kalvanes Bay, and the *Bismarck* to Grimstad Fjord, south of Bergen.

Lieserl, peering from her porthole, watched as merchant ships were commandeered and brought up broadsides of the *Bismarck* to act as shields against torpedo attack. There was a tremendous amount of activity on the wharves, and she wondered when she would be disembarking. Her satchel was packed and she sat ready to go at a moment's notice.

Something far below caught her eye, then, and a cold hand clutched the pit of her stomach. Surely it was just a routine inspection of some kind and had nothing to do with her.

Schutzstaffel officers were swarming from their black cars and marching up the docks. Launches were waiting for them. As she watched, they began climbing aboard the boats, heading for the *Bismarck*.

For all she knew Haberditz had gotten drunk and revealed everything. Or perhaps Heisenberg had undergone a change of heart and tipped off the authorities, or been forced to reveal what he knew of her whereabouts. He wasn't strong enough to stand up to torture.

She had no idea what was inside the documents given her, but she took them out and looked desperately for a place to hide them. Finally she tore them into little bits and flushed them down the commode.

Glancing outside the porthole she saw that the first launches had come up alongside the *Bismarck*. Should she sit tight and hope she wasn't the object of their visit? She looked nervously around the room, at a loss. Finally she jumped up from her bed and went out the door of her cabin.

She walked briskly down a passageway. She was on the quarterdeck; she quickly found a stairway leading downwards. A junior officer mounting the stairs gave her a surprised look but didn't stop her.

As she passed the main deck, still going down, she heard loud voices and shouts, and the clunking boots of men in a hurry. She descended one more level, passing a couple of low-level mates, one of whom she recognized from her boat ride out from Gotenhafen. He made a snide remark, and his friends laughed, but she was already down to the next level, ducking into and then quickly out of a mess hall, trying not to hurry too much, trying to look natural. But she was the only woman on a ship of thousands of men, and every eye was on her.

She heard a shout not far behind her, and some commotion, the sound of pursuing footsteps. She broke into a run. The corridor she was following bent once, then again, and she brushed past a surprised petty officer who shouted at her and grabbed at her shoulder. She turned and pushed him hard, and he went sprawling. She turned and raced away.

She bounded down to a lower deck and found herself at the end of a corridor at a door with a heavy handle. She yanked the handle down and shoved the door open with her shoulder, entering the chamber and slamming the door shut behind her.

Wolfgang looked up from a desk, and they stopped and stared at each other. He was the only man in the room, and the last man she wanted to see was a suspected Gestapo agent. Calculating machines were everywhere. His eyes widened when he recognized her. She turned immediately, tugging at the door, but it was jammed.

"Did you lose your way, Doctor?" he inquired politely.

"This goddamned door," she said, her voice tight and close to breaking. The door came ajar, but Wolfgang had grabbed her arm. She spun around and struck him in the face.

"Let go of me!"

He tightened his grip. "Listen, I'm trying to help you. Tell me what's wrong."

"Help me?" She bit her lip, her back to the door. "Is there...is there somewhere you can hide me?"

His eyes narrowed. "What's the matter?"

"The SS are here," she said in a harsh whisper. "They're on the ship. I believe they've come for me."

For a few seconds he said nothing, and she feared he would turn her over to them. He turned his head sharply when he heard footsteps in the passage outside, looking at the door.

"Quick," he said, pointing across the room. "There's a cable conduit behind one of the desks."

He leaped up and took her hand, guiding her across the room and under one of the desks. Sure enough, there was a narrow passage with pipes and bundles of wires going through it, barely large enough for her to squeeze into. She wriggled in as far as she could, afraid her feet were showing.

She lay in the crawl space, smelling the oil and insulation, electrical smells, hardly able to breathe, curiously wondering, despite her predicament, what Wolfgang was doing there, how he'd boarded the ship, why he hadn't turned her in. Either he didn't work for the Gestapo or there was some price on her head that he was planning to collect for himself.

The door clanged open, boots slapping the floor of gunnery control, angry voices demanding her whereabouts. Wolfgang calmly feigned ignorance, deflecting their pointed inquiries with a few vague words.

Abruptly they decided they'd erred and hastily exited, pounding off down the corridors. Lieserl remained where she was, not daring to move.

Wolfgang sat down in a chair almost right next to her. Looking back, she could see his boots. "You'd better stay a while," he said in a low voice. "We'll be lifting anchor in a few hours. Once we're in the North Atlantic there won't be anything they can do to you."

"But I'm supposed to get off here!" she whispered urgently.

"Maybe after nightfall. I'll try to get you off the boat, if I can. Whatever you do, don't come out until I tell you it's safe."

The hours passed, and Lieserl tried vainly to sleep, but she was too tense, and the conduit too uncomfortable. Other men entered the control room, took up their stations, talking and joking and smoking cigarettes. Once Wolfgang left for an extended period and she feared he'd been relieved of duty, that she'd be stuck in the crawlspace overnight. He came back half an hour later. When his crewmates finally left, he crawled down under the desk.

"They've been going all over the ship, everywhere. I don't think I can get you to shore. Here, I've brought you something."

She reached back, feeling a cup. She managed to bring it to her lips without spilling too much. The cup contained water, and it felt good going down her throat. He also handed her a ham and cheese sandwich on dark bread.

"I go off duty soon. Stay quiet until I return."

"I have to go to the bathroom."

"Can you use the cup?"

"I think so."

She was acutely embarrassed, but she'd been stuck there several hours and desperately needed some relief. Somehow she managed to do what was necessary and hand the mug back to him. She was afraid he'd make a joke about it, but he didn't, taking the mug and quickly leaving the room.

The door banged open, and two other crewmates came boisterously into the computer room, one of them singing a beer hall song. Lieserl, her joints aching but otherwise feeling much better, settled down to wait.

Somehow she fell into a light, tortured state that was half wakefulness, half sleep. Time crawled by in this nether world of darkness and muted light, the smell of oil and stale cigarette smoke.

Later she awoke to the sound of engines thrumming, to a rocking, surging motion. The *Bismarck* had put to sea again. That meant there'd be no getting off in Norway, as planned, but at least for the moment she was safe. She decided to wait another hour or two before coming out of hiding, to make sure they were too far from port to put her off the boat and into the hands of the SS.

The two crewmen were joking back and forth, young men who, she was sure, had never been in a sea battle before. Lieserl had never been to England, but Haberditz had told her about the British Fleet, the mighty *Hood*, a legendary battleship left over from the Great War, and the large numbers of British destroyers and cruisers that roamed the seven seas. If the *Tirpitz* had been ready, and if British air attacks hadn't disabled *Gneisenau* and *Scharnhorst*, stationed at Brest, the Germans would have had an invincible force, too strong even for the British Navy.

The knowledge of the German vulnerability was distressing, because it was her own vulnerability. Yet the armor of the *Bismarck* was the strongest in the world. Haberditz had claimed that torpedoes couldn't penetrate its thick armor plates and that its formidable anti-aircraft batteries could shred any attacking airplanes. And, in the vast Atlantic, two fast warships would be difficult to find.

Something clattered on the floor behind her, a cup of coffee, some of the hot liquid splashing on her legs. She tensed as the crewman cursed, the other laughing. She could hear the man getting out of his chair to retrieve the cup, crouching down, and she tried to make herself as small as possible.

"What have we, here?" he said, seeing her shoes and legs. "Mark, there's someone in there. I think it's a girl!"

"Is it a stiff?" asked Mark, instantly on his knees with the other man.

"Hello, are you all right?"

"Yes," Lieserl replied. "Yes, I'm fine."

"Well, come on out of there. We won't hurt you."

Lieserl wriggled slowly out of her hiding place, the two crewmen helping her into a chair and steadying her on the swaying deck. She was relieved it was over, but desperately hoped they were too far from shore for her to be put off the ship.

"How long have you been down there?"

"A few hours."

The men looked at each other. One of them said, "We'd better call the captain."

Lieserl said, "I'd prefer you contact Admiral Lutjens."

The two men discussed the issue a moment, finally deciding the captain should be informed first. Mark called the bridge, and a few minutes later a pair of guards escorted her away.

Captain Lindemann was not pleased to see her. He paced on the bridge, chain-smoking cigarettes, looking her over. He was a tall, gaunt man with slicked-back dirty blond hair, his round, fleshy cheeks contrasting with his hard, gray eyes and stiff demeanor.

He stopped dead in front of her, piercing her with his gray stare. "We're at war, Madame Meier. I would have every right to toss you overboard."

"Dr. Meier," she corrected him. "I wish to speak to Admiral Lutjens, sir. He can explain everything."

"He'll have a lot of explaining to do," Lindemann huffed. "And to Raeder more than me."

"It wasn't his fault. I saw them coming and hid from them."

"How did you get by the men in the computer room? It's manned twenty-four hours a day."

She shrugged. "It was empty. Someone came just after I went inside. That's why I hid in the crawl space."

Lindemann scowled. "Mueller coming back from the head, I guess. He shouldn't have left his station without getting someone to cover for him." He tossed his cigarette to the deck and crushed it out with his foot. Claude appeared out of nowhere, hurrying over in a way that was almost effeminate, retrieving the butt and disposing of it. Lindemann lit up a fresh cigarette, blowing smoke in Lieserl's face and making her cough. "I should have him horsewhipped. And you with him."

Lieserl reddened. Was Lindemann speaking of Wolfgang? It alarmed her that he might suffer as a result of protecting her. She raised her voice. "If security had been more thorough, this wouldn't have happened in the first place."

He backhanded her across the face so hard she stumbled. "That's for the trouble you've caused me."

She straightened slowly, hand on her cheek, tears streaming unbidden down her face. "So much for the nobility of German naval officers."

He snorted and took another drag on his cigarette. "But you're right about security. Damned amateurs." He snapped his fingers at Claude, who was standing unobtrusively a few feet behind him. "Claude, take her to the Admiral. She's his responsibility, not mine. Thank God."

Claude bowed, his eager young face full of hero worship. Lieserl thought she read something else in his posture, in his eyes: a painful sensitivity, a shameful secret. She cast a glance back at Captain Lindemann, her eyes narrowing slightly in suspicion.

Lindemann flushed darkly and shouted, "You heard me, Claude! Get her off the bridge!" He turned on his heel stalked away, looking to the fore where the *Bismarck*'s bow ploughed a violent furrow through the North Sea.

"This way, Dr. Meier," Claude said in a kind voice. "If you don't mind."

"Thank you."

They walked along the corridors of the swaying ship. "Pardon me for saying so, but you don't look much like a sailor."

Claude smiled. "You're very perceptive. Until a few weeks ago I was a waiter at Captain Lindemann's favorite restaurant in Hamburg."

"He drafted you into service?"

"You might say that. I've been serving him for several years. He wanted me on the mission with him." His brow wrinkled. "You shouldn't take his anger to heart. He's not always like that."

"It's understandable. There's a war on."

Admiral Lutjens was in his stateroom, maps spread out on his desk. He ordered her to a chair with a glance, then went back to the maps, studiously ignoring her.

Finally she could stand it no longer. "I'm sorry, Admiral."

He glanced her way, his face like a thundercloud on the horizon: distant but threatening. "Thank you for saying so. You have created a distraction."

"Because I hid from the SS?"

"The SS received an anonymous tip that a female stowaway was carrying state secrets. They had orders to shoot you on sight."

"Admiral Haberditz gave me the document in question."

"He denies writing the document."

"Didn't it carry his signature?"

"His signature was there, but I must presume it was forged. Pursuant to his instructions, I burned his letter." He straightened and walked over to a porthole, peering out into the night at the dark shape of the *Prinz Eugen*. He turned to her. "Captain Lindemann would like to throw you overboard. One way or another we must return you to Germany to face justice."

"Admiral, please believe me. I'm a victim of circumstance."

"In what capacity did you know Admiral Haberditz?"

"I worked for him on the German atomic project. And I was his mistress, although not by choice. He forced me. My mother is at Ravenbruck and I couldn't refuse..."

Tears came to her eyes, and she fought them back. Lutjens noticed, and came over and sat across from her, offering his handkerchief. She accepted it and dabbed at her eyes.

"You're Jewish?"

"Does it matter?"

"You don't look it, except perhaps in the eyes." He took out a piece of paper and pencil and gave them to her. "Show me the ballistics equations for projectile motion."

"They're elementary." She took the pencil and quickly sketched them in three dimensions, with corrections for air drag and the Coriolis force. She moved the paper a few centimeters towards him. "What else would you like to know?"

He glanced at the paper. "I was just checking your story. It looks like you know more physics than I do." He took the paper and crumpled it, tossing it into a waste can. "I don't consider Jews a problem, Dr. Meier. They are no different than anyone else, except for a few of their customs, which are of negligible importance, and their choice of religious reading material."

"Thank you, sir."

"As for Captain Lindemann, I don't agree with him. You're too valuable to throw overboard, and there is no convenient way of getting you back to Norway. British aircraft spotted us at anchor at Bergen, and turning back would seriously compromise our mission."

"What will you do with me, then?"

"Nothing, for the moment. You may return to your quarters."

"You aren't going to have me executed?"

"The SS requested as much."

"And?"

"I informed them I would return you to them should I discover your whereabouts, but that I would do so at my convenience and discretion. At the moment, it's not convenient, and I'm not satisfied that doing so would be the proper resolution to this matter." He stood up and gestured at the door. "You're dismissed to your quarters, Dr. Meier. I would appreciate it if you would remain there unless summoned."

"Excuse me, Captain, but shall I be permitted to walk the decks for exercise?"

He nodded briefly. "Claude can escort you."

Claude was waiting outside, and Lutjens exchanged a few words with him and reentered his stateroom, closing the door. Claude led her down a few doors to her own room, letting her in, then fastidiously smoothing the bed covers for her and straightening up her few belongings.

"Is there anything else I can do for you?" he asked cordially as he stood next to the door.

She looked over at him, the image of humble nobility. "Yes, Claude, there is. It's rather a large request."

He bowed slightly. "Please ask. I'll grant it if I can."

She wanted to get a message to Wolfgang, but wasn't sure that was entirely wise. If it were known he'd aided her, he'd surely face disciplinary action. "Can I trust you, Claude?"

"Yes, Doctor."

"There was a man on this ship, by the name of Wolfgang. I don't recall his last name, but he's a merchant marine, part of the prize crews. He might be associated with computations. I'd like to see him, but I'm afraid he might be compromised."

Claude bowed slightly, favoring her with a judicious smile. "I'll be happy to take care of the matter, Dr. Meier. And don't worry; I'll be discrete."

"Thank you, Claude."

After he left she found she couldn't sleep despite her great fatigue. The rolling of the ship and the thrumming of the engines penetrated to her very core. She kept remembering what Lutjens' had said about being ready to die. A death's scythe hung over him, ready to cut him down, and her with him. That thought left her feeling empty and lost. She hadn't even lived as yet, no more than the two thousand twenty-year-olds manning the ship.

She wasn't ready to die.

Einstein's Daughter: The Story of Lieserl

Chapter Fourteen

May 22, the *Bismarck*

When she awoke the next morning Lieserl washed as best she could in the sink, then lay on the upper bunk looking out the porthole. A fog thick as soup reduced visibility nearly to zero. Fog meant safety: the British wouldn't be able to find them. On the one hand, that was a relief. On the other hand, she couldn't stand the thought of what would happen out in the Atlantic when the *Bismarck* and *Prinz Eugen* began attacking the convoys.

Claude came to take her for a morning walk around the decks. They walked back along the quarterdeck to the stern, where the powerful screws were throwing up an enormous plume of water. Claude told her that two British destroyers were shadowing them despite the dense fog, using an advanced radar set that had a far greater range than the standard equipment.

The rest of the day was spent in similar monotony, but shortly after dinner Wolfgang showed up at the door of her cabin. He was carrying a small brown sack.

"Thank you for coming," she said as she let him in. "I didn't expect you; Claude told me everyone had to stay at their action stations."

"I've helped out in the computer room, but most of the time I hang out deep in the ship with the other prize crews. I won't be missed."

"Why don't you sit down?"

He sat in a small metal folding chair, while Lieserl sat on the bed. "I wanted to thank you for helping me."

He shrugged with one shoulder in an American way. "Any decent man would have done the same."

She regarded him cautiously. "I thought you were with the Gestapo."

He smiled. "Sorry. Not my branch of service."

"I thought I'd seen you in Berlin, then Gottingen. I was sure you were tailing me."

"I've lived in Hamburg my whole life. I have a rather common face."

"You lived in Hamburg?"

"South side. The whole family, except for those called up."

"So you're saying I'm mistaken."

He shrugged again. "It happens." He glanced out the port as if looking for something. "The *Hood* has left Scapa Flow, according to intelligence. Half the British Navy is steaming our way."

"Are you worried?"

He waved his hand in a dismissing gesture. "The cruisers aren't much to worry about; we can handle them. Six and eight inch guns, that's all they've got. They'll shadow us from a respectful distance. The *Hood* and the *King George*, on the other hand, are dangerous. They're nearly as big as we are."

"What about an air attack?"

"The word is their torpedoes would be like bee stings that hurt but don't do any real damage."

Her eyes narrowed. "I can hardly believe that."

"Just the standard party line. But fifteen inches of steel around the waterline is serious protection. It would take a big torpedo to break through that."

"And bombs on the superstructure?"

"First of all, we're a moving target, and it'd be hard to hit us. And second of all, our flak crews will nail them when they're still miles away." He spread his arms. "You've got nothing to worry about."

"I wouldn't say that."

He pulled a bottle of wine and two small glasses out of his sack. He gave her a glass and popped the cork off the bottle. "Don't worry," he said as he poured the drinks. "Nothing will happen to you. They'll put you on the war effort, that's all. You should be working with Von Braun."

Her eyebrows tightened, her voice hardening. "I'll never work for them again. I don't care what they do to me."

"I heard that there are groups working on a new kind of power plant, a reactor. Were you involved in that?"

She sipped her wine, regarding him suspiciously. "There are some theoretical calculations. I know something of them, but it was mainly Heisenberg's project."

Wolfgang nodded. "Of course. The great man, himself." He downed the rest of his wine and reached into his sack, pulling out a smaller sack of wooden chess pieces and a checkerboard. "Do you play?"

"I thought you wanted to talk science."

"Later. I need to relax."

They played chess for two hours straight. Wolfgang was good, beating her three games in a row before she managed to gain a draw. She noticed he was very adept with his knights, always finding good outposts for them, penetrating her position, limiting her options. In the last game she sacrificed both her bishops, however, and delivered a classic checkmate with queen and rook. Wolfgang leaned back against the wall and applauded.

"Bravo!"

"You let me win."

"Why would I want to do that?"

"To get on my good side."

"If that were the case, I'd have let you win all five games."

They sat on opposite sides of the lower bunk, looking at each other, sipping wine, not saying anything, trapped in an awkward silence. She wondered if he had been given specific instructions on what to ask her, or if he was truly there only because he wanted to be. She wanted to question him further about his background, because of his similarity to the man she thought had been following her, but somehow she couldn't bring herself to start.

"Well, what would you like to talk about?" she asked him. "Physics?"

"No. I've had enough of that."

"You're sure? I don't mind."

He shook his head. "No, please, no more talk of science."

"What do you want to talk about, then?"

"You."

She blinked, and said guardedly, "What about me?"

"Well," he said, pausing awkwardly. "Are you married? Do you have a family?"

"No. I never married."

"I find that surprising."

"Why?"

"You're obviously a very attractive woman. A great many men must have been interested in you."

She gave him an annoyed look. "That's rather personal."

He shrugged and went on. "What about your parents? Are they still alive?"

The question struck a bitter chord deep inside her, and she said, "Yes. Unfortunately."

Wolfgang's eyes widened. "No love lost, sounds like."

"They abandoned me. I never really knew them."

He looked puzzled and curious. "Then how do you know they're still alive?"

"Because...because..."

The ache in her chest deepened, and she decided she had to change the subject. "That's neither here nor there. I mean, it's none of your business."

She'd said it too harshly, and he was instantly contrite. "Sorry." He sat up, putting his hands on his knees. "Well, perhaps I should be going." He stood up and stretched.

"Sorry, Wolfgang. Please stay."

He hesitated, and then sat slowly back down. "With pleasure. You don't have to talk about your past, if you prefer not to."

"That's all right. I was adopted. My foster parents were kind to me, and I loved them."

"They're alive?"

"My foster father died in the Great War. My mother is at Ravenbruck."

He nodded, lips pressed in a line. "I see. That's very difficult." He turned towards the door. "I really should be..."

She stood up. "Thank you, Wolfgang. Thank you for coming."

He didn't say anything for a moment, staring at her, looking slightly confused. Then he started putting everything back in his sack.

"Maybe you can come back tomorrow."

"I'll check the schedule. I may be on duty."

She followed him to the door and touched his shoulder briefly in a gesture of farewell, which he only barely acknowledged. When he had gone, she sat back down on the bunk, realizing she'd been too abrupt with him. She sighed, swaying with the movement of the ship, trying to remember what men felt, how they thought. He wasn't a child, not like most of the men on the ship, who were barely twenty. She felt mixed emotions about him, like what she'd felt for Heisenberg.

Changing into a nightgown, she lay down in bed and snuggled deeply under the covers. The ship, as always, swayed in the growing swells of the North Atlantic, and the engines droned, the bulkheads vibrating. She held herself, arms crossed, wondering how it would feel to have someone there in bed with her, a strong and muscular chest pressing against her soft breasts.

She lay awake until the sound of the engines and the rock of waves had her in visions of penetrating knights and dying bishops.

May 23, the *Bismarck*

The two ships steamed well north of Iceland, then turned south to pass through the Denmark Strait separating Greenland from Iceland. Claude came regularly to escort her on walks around the decks. It was cold; sometimes they could see the Greenland ice pack through the mist to the west. To the east were the minefields. *Bismarck* and *Prinz Eugen*, according to Claude, were foregoing a run to an Arctic tanker so as to take advantage of the foggy weather for as long as possible. Refueling would take place somewhere north of the Azores.

At these latitudes the sun hardly set and Lieserl, late in the evening, was tired, only barely awake. She was in the middle of a calculation, a harmlessly impractical one, concerning the fusion reactions in the cores of stars. Lying in the spartan bunk, she drowsed, nodding off, finally dropping her calculations to the floor and, reaching up, turning off the light.

Suddenly a soft, urgent knock came at the door, barely audible about the thrum of the engines. Lieserl turned the light back on, and pulling on her robe, went to the door.

Wolfgang was standing in the hallway, a bottle of wine in one hand and a pair of thick sandwiches in the other.

"May I come in?" he said with polite urgency.

"Yes, of course," she replied at once. He entered, and a moment later they were drinking wine out of shot glasses and eating ham and cheese sandwiches.

"Isn't it irregular for you to be visiting me all the time? Someone might suspect your motives. It might be dangerous."

He shrugged and grinned. "It's dangerous to be on this boat."

"They could throw you in the brig."

He nodded, unconcerned. "They wouldn't do that. I've been too useful to them down in the computer room."

A smile tugged at the corners of her lips. "Are you, now? And how many ships have you sunk?"

"Well, none, actually. Merchant marines don't usually carry guns. There was the barge."

"Barge?"

"We were taking target practice, the morning before we left, shooting at a barge."

She couldn't quite laugh. "And how many rounds did you have to fire?"

"We straddled it with the first salvo and hit it dead center with the second. It never had a chance."

"Not bad."

He looked over at her desk, where her afternoon of calculations lay strewn in disarray. "Can't leave the science alone, can you?"

She took another sip of wine. "Not when I'm working on an interesting problem."

"When I was a student I dreamed of building space ships, of traveling between worlds. I still do."

"You know something about rockets?"

"The basics. I never wanted to join the navy, but here I am, technically a civilian sailor but still on a warship. What do you think of it?"

"It's a very terrible and beautiful ship."

He gestured at the papers again. "Show me what you're doing."

She shook her head ruefully. "I'm afraid you couldn't begin to understand."

"I was first in math in school. I'll bet I can follow."

"Well, all right."

She spent the next hour tutoring him in the basics of the theory of stellar fusion she was working on. It crossed her mind once more that perhaps he'd been sent to pump her for information, but she was starved for company and loved to tell people about her work. At any rate, fusion power would never be a reality: the fission piles, of course, were another matter, and she carefully avoided references to them. Wolfgang was an excellent student, intuitively grasping the equations and asking good questions.

Suddenly the alarm bells began ringing.

"That's it!" he shouted, jumping up from the bed. "I have to go to my station!"

"I thought you were off shift," she protested.

"Not anymore. Thanks for the lecture, Professor." He hesitated for just a moment, looking her in the eye, and she couldn't help but think what a handsome man he was, and how in the next hours or days he might have to die.

Then he was gone, out the door, on his way to his station in computing.

She could see nothing outside her porthole but the gray, restless slate of the sea. Checking her door, she found it unlocked, and the corridor outside empty. Contrary to her orders, she made her way to the nearest exit and stepped boldly out onto the open deck, the vast Atlantic before her to port.

The great gun turrets were already turning, the enormous maws of the fifteen inch barrels pointing towards the horizon. The guns were monstrous, yet the turrets moved them with effortless grace, a miracle of German engineering.

In the distance a ship came out of a fog bank, a British cruiser with three funnels plying through the restless gray seas. Lieserl moved to cover her ears as the *Bismarck*'s guns fired in anger with a deafening roar, the recoil jolting the entire ship and staggering her, black-brown cordite smoke filling the air. She choked on the smoke and stumbled back inside as an answering salvo tore through the skies, sounding like an approaching express train. The shells exploded harmlessly on either side of the ship, sending up towering fountains of water.

As she reached her cabin another departing salvo shook the ship, like a giant's fist against the hull. She slammed her door shut and threw herself onto her bed, covering her ears with her pillow, terrified that in the next moment a British shell would find her cabin, tearing through the wall and exploding over next to the wash basin, mutilating her body and mind.

A moment later it was all over. Lieserl got slowly up out of bed and peered out the porthole, seeing smoke on the horizon, not knowing if the British ship had been destroyed or had merely put up a smokescreen and escaped. She heard no cries of jubilation, so she suspected the latter.

She sat back down on the bed, still trembling from the experience, knowing that more was to come and afraid that it would be far worse.

May 24, early morning

She awoke to alarm bells and the sound of shouts and of boots pounding against the decks.

Leaping out of bed, she threw on a robe and opened her door, peering out into the hall. An officer ran by, not even looking at her. She slammed the door shut and ran to the porthole. The luminescent hands of the clock next to the bunk told her it was two in the morning, close to sunrise at these latitudes.

She looked east through the port and there, silhouetted in the pre-dawn light, she saw the upper works of two enormous ships on the horizon, each at least as large as *Bismarck*, herself. One of them was surely the mighty *Hood*, the largest and most feared battleship in the British Home Fleet.

The giant ships slowly turned as she watched, presenting their beams. Suddenly a ripple of fire ran along them. She counted the seconds, and half a minute later came the roaring sound, the sky tearing apart. The entire ship lurched, then the *Bismarck*'s big guns gave answering fire, the explosion of sound deafening her. Lieserl held her hands over her ears, bracing herself against the port, too stunned to be afraid. Every twenty seconds came another violent eruption, and in between the screaming of incoming shells.

Horrified, she saw spray leap up as an enemy shell hit the water not one hundred meters in front of her, skipping up like a thrown stone from the sea, heading inexorably towards her as if it would enter her porthole, a fraction of a second expanding into a lifetime.

Then it was gone, too high, over the top deck and down on the other side. Lieserl almost fainted with relief, but a loud thump jolted her back; a hit, although there had been no explosion.

She couldn't think about it, because return fire erupted again along the length of the *Bismarck*, and from the *Prinz Eugen*, which she could now see out in front not a kilometer away to the southeast. She thought of Wolfgang down in the computer room deep in the bowels of the ship, calculating the angles, taking into account the wind, the movements of the *Bismarck* and of the British ships. She prayed fervently that he'd find the range, straddle the targets and neutralize them, prayed for German victory although she hated the German nation, hated Hitler, and prayed although she wasn't sure she believed in God. She knew, in her heart, that it wasn't a battle between the Germans and the British, it was a battle between old men, using the young as their surrogates, pawns in a deadly game of chess, the fruit of their daughters' wombs. It seemed unspeakably cruel, and she cried tears of empathy and rage.

Suddenly a tremendous column of flame shot up from the British battleship on the right. The flame was deep red and full of turbid smoke, a bolt from hell reaching for the heavens. Strangely, the explosion seemed to make no sound, the black and gray smoke, laced with fire, streaming up and spreading into a mushroom higher up while the two halves of the ship—was it the *Hood*?—gracefully pointed to the sky before slipping too quickly beneath the waves.

Stunned, relieved, and horrified, she stared at the slowly shifting cloud as the *Bismarck* roared again, targeting the remaining British battleship. She counted seconds silently, and she saw distant return fire through the cordite smoke, then a terrible hit on the last British vessel, then another one. Was it true that *Bismarck* was invincible? In the next moment the remaining British ship made smoke and fled, unable to stand up to the concentrated fire from both German warships.

She could hear the faint sound of cheering over the still-powerful thrumming of the engines. The mixed emotions left her confused and saddened, exhaustion mingled with a relief so powerful it was exhilarating. She collapsed back down on the bed, her feelings pulsing madly within her.

Claude came to her room a few hours later, awakening her with a polite rap that she barely heard above the continuous noise of the engines. She opened, and he offered her a breakfast of bread and water and two strips of cold, greasy bacon.

"Please come in, Claude."

He bowed slightly, smiling in self-effacing embarrassment. "Only long enough to arrange your breakfast, Doctor."

"You don't have to call me 'Doctor'. Call me by my first name."

He hesitated nervously, as if choosing his words carefully. "If you don't mind, I would prefer to address you with proper respect. You're a person of exceptional knowledge and achievement, and deserve to be treated as such."

She shrugged, and gestured at the writing table, where he deposited the tray of food.

"What happened last night?"

"One of our shells hit a magazine in the *Hood*."

"So the British are gone?"

"I'm afraid not. A cruiser is still shadowing us."

"Is Captain Lindemann concerned?"

"We all are, I'm sure. Now, if you'll excuse me..."

"Something's not right with the ship," Lieserl went on. "The angle of the deck..."

"We've taken on some water; an enemy shell hit one of the oil tanks. We were fortunate the shell didn't explode."

He moved to the door, bowing on his way, but Lieserl got up and went over to him. "I have a message for Wolfgang. Will you deliver it?"

Claude assumed a careful, attentive expression. "By Wolfgang, you refer to the merchant marine, one of the prize crew members. The one I contacted for you, before."

"Yes. Tell him he is to come to my cabin when he's off duty, no matter what time it is."

"And should you be indisposed?"

"Just tell him to come. Will you do that?"

"Yes, certainly, if I have the opportunity to do so. That's less certain, now that the British have found us."

"Do your best."

"I certainly shall, Dr. Meier."

Claude left. Lieserl went back to the small writing table and began eating her breakfast, but ended up pushing most of it aside. The beast was wounded, now, and the British warships would soon be circling like hungry wolves.

An unexpected knock at her door interrupted her dark thoughts. She opened, finding two stern-looking marine guards.

"Admiral Lutjens requires your presence in the chartroom," one of them said. "Immediately."

They were both young; only a year or two before they had been carefree students somewhere, carousing with the frauleins. "Yes, of course." She was taken off guard: why would the admiral want to see her when his ship was damaged and in danger?

Lutjens was poring over the charts with Lindemann standing nearby, arms crossed, smoking as usual. Lutjens seemed only a little worried, the forehead of his hound's face creased more in concentration than fear. He looked up as she entered, bracketed by the two guards. "You're dismissed," he said to the guards.

When they'd gone, Lindemann said, "You lied to us."

She shot him a furious glance. "Whatever are you talking about?"

"We have more information about your role in the German program, Dr. Meier," said Lutjens calmly. "A number of scientific documents were stolen from your office in Gottingen. It has been suggested that you were to turn them over to the enemy."

"I didn't steal anything. I destroyed some documents, yes, but they were my own."

Lindemann said, "They were the property of the Reich and you know it."

Lutjens said, "Do you have any of your calculations among your personal effects?"

"No, I don't."

Lindemann scowled, sending dual streams of smoke out his nostrils like a dragon. "You could be shot as a traitor," he snarled. "Not only did you destroy papers important to the war effort, but your interfering presence in Bergen caused us to miss our refueling. We've lost three hundred tons, and..."

"Captain," the Admiral interrupted sharply, a look of warning in his eye.

Lindemann nodded stiffly, although he wasn't truly contrite. "I'm sorry, Admiral."

"That's fine, Captain. Perhaps you'd like to leave us alone for a few moments."

Lindemann left the room without another word. Lutjens went back to studying his maps, bracing himself against the shifting of the deck.

"Surely you didn't call me here to help you chart your course," she said at last.

He looked up. "No, I didn't. The oil situation is bothersome, but we have enough. We took a shell in one of the tanks. Thank God it didn't explode."

Lieserl crossed her arms. "Well? What are you going to do with me?"

He straightened, turning his mind from his charts with a conscious effort. "I've received instructions from Raeder, the Commander-in-Chief of the German Navy. The instructions are specific. I am to extract the desired information any way I can, using any means at my disposal."

She stiffened. "You mean you'll torture me?"

He sighed and walked slowly around the table. "That's not my first choice. Others may not be so hesitant. I would rather persuade you to voluntarily reproduce those papers from memory."

She looked away, taking a deep breath. "The calculations are very complicated. I could never redo them without a proper library. Even then, it could take months."

Lutjens regarded her candidly. "Dr. Meier, reliable sources have informed me that your memory is virtually photographic."

She lifted her chin and met his gaze defiantly. "Then I suppose you'll have to torture me. Will you do it yourself or assign the task to an underling?"

"You're not being reasonable."

She nearly laughed in his face. "And you think the Nazis are reasonable?"

His face darkened, and he seemed troubled. "I didn't join the party. They have used excessive force, at times. All the same, I'm an officer and will do my duty."

"You are so controlled, Admiral. And, you didn't answer my question. Are you or are you not going to torture me?"

"Raeder is persuaded that what you know could change the whole course of the war in our favor."

"As you say, you're not even a member of the party. Why should you want the Nazis to rule the world?"

"I may not agree with them, but nonetheless my duty is to the Fatherland and to the Fuehrer. I will carry that duty out to the best of my ability."

Her lips compressed into a tight line. "Well, go ahead and do your duty, then, you cold-hearted bastard."

He stood before her like a statue, his eyes smoldering, and she wanted to strike him with her fists, anything to crack his reserve.

The air raid siren began howling.

Lutjens walked quickly to the door and called a midshipman to escort her back to her quarters. "We'll continue this discussion later," he said.

"If the torpedoes run true we may not have to bother."

"I'm not afraid of torpedoes." Then he was gone down the corridor, heading for the nearby bridge.

Her cabin was in the complete disarray associated with a thorough search. She lay with her head buried in her pillow, trying not to hear the explosive chatter of the antiaircraft batteries. Airplanes passed overhead, and once the entire ship shuddered, as if a bomb had gone off nearby. Within minutes, however, the guns fell silent, and the *Bismarck* and *Prinz Eugen* were once again alone in the dark Atlantic.

Evening, May 24

Weisz lay in his bunk in the quarters he shared with one other merchant marine, deep in the bowels of the ship. Earlier in the day he'd spoken to Claude and discovered Lieserl's difficulties with Lutjens. Submarines prowled the waters of the Atlantic, and it was possible Lutjens would put her off on one for transport back to Europe. If that happened, she'd be permanently beyond his reach.

He had to complete his mission.

She knew how to do virtually everything. She knew everything Houtermans had known and more. She was the most dangerous person in the world.

The Walther PPK was underneath his pillow. He reached for it, touching its sleek coldness, the hard metal a symbol for his heart, or what his heart had to become. The many required the sacrifice of the few.

Time was running out.

Chapter Fifteen

Evening, May 25

She didn't see Wolfgang for over a day and Claude, bringing her dinner, had no news of him. He told her that *Prinz Eugen* had broken off on her own to go in search of convoys, while Lutjens had ordered the *Bismarck* into a broad turn. Those maneuvers would hopefully have the effect of losing the shadowing British cruisers, and everyone was optimistic of the *Bismarck*'s chances of reaching Brest, where the forward fuel tank could be repaired.

"Claude," Lieserl said as he was fastidiously preparing her tea, "how well do you know the Admiral?"

"The Admiral I know only a little. The Captain, I know well."

"Has Admiral Lutjens ever tortured anyone?"

He nearly jumped. "I don't believe he would be capable of that."

She nodded. "I see. What about Captain Lindemann?"

He looked away, around the room, anywhere but at her. "No, of course not. Excuse me, Doctor, but I must be going. I have to keep the coffee hot up on the bridge."

She ate her dinner slowly. The soup was cold and the rolls stale, but at least the tea was good. She smiled at the irony, thinking it was probably British tea. Lutjens, she decided, was not the type to torture anyone, but Lindemann had more of an inclination to inflict pain, if her judgment of Claude's reaction were accurate. She tried to remember the physical pain she'd suffered in her life: a broken toe, an operation to remove her appendix. She didn't fear pain: not as much as Heisenberg, anyway. Maybe that was because she carried a deeper pain with her always. Maybe she'd always known, in her heart, that she'd been abandoned, maybe that was why she'd gone into mathematics and science. Only when she was immersed in a difficult problem did all the pain go away.

Drinking her tea in her tiny stateroom on the swaying battleship, she wondered if the pain of childbirth would have cancelled her secret pain, her pain of abandonment. She'd had few relationships and never made much effort to get married and have a family. She didn't remember anything before the age of three, but perhaps somewhere inside her the memories lived, eating away at her, driving her, controlling her, creating ill-understood feelings.

She finished her meal and took the tray outside her door, setting it down on the deck. A guard eyed her; that was new, they hadn't bothered before.

"Are you going to be stuck there all night?" she asked him.

"Yes, Doctor," he replied stolidly.

"You're to see to it I stay in my cabin, is that right?"

"Yes, Doctor."

She tried to flirt with him, warm him up, but he refused to answer in anything but monosyllables. She gave up and went back into her cabin.

She had difficulty sleeping. Every time she closed her eyes the equations went flitting across her darkened vision, taunting her. How would they hurt her, she wondered, and how much could she take before cracking? She could buy time, of course, by giving them plausible but flawed work. The retribution would be all the greater when she reached Brest.

The seas were high, and the incessant shifting of the deck made her feel slightly nauseous, although she was lying in bed. As the hours passed she heard no more airplanes; it gradually dawned on her that perhaps Lutjens' maneuvers had finally allowed *Bismarck* to slip off the British charts. That notion made her feel safer.

She dozed off, and began dreaming of ice skating with Heisenberg on a pond near the University of Gottingen.

* * * * *

With a soft click, barely audible above the incessant rumble of the engines, the door to her stateroom swung open. A dark form entered the room. The door swung shut again.

Wolfgang took out the Walther. A bullet was in the chamber and seven in the magazine. Lieserl lay on the bed before him, oblivious to his presence, looking as if she were dead already, wrapped up in her sheets and bedding like a shroud, facing away from him. That was good.

Suddenly she took a deep breath, shifting, turning toward him. Muted light from the Aurora Borealis came through the porthole, playing on the fine skin of her face, and all at once she was alive again, vibrant and beautiful.

Wolfgang slowly lifted the gun, cursing the fact she had turned: it would have been easier to shoot her in the back. The sound of the report would bring men running. He'd put three bullets in her, then pop the blue rubber pill he was carrying in his pocket. Biting down on it would release the cyanide, killing him almost instantly. His death would save a dozen other operatives on the continent.

He returned to the problem at hand. Where should he put the bullets? A head shot was surest, but he couldn't bare putting a hole in her face or in the back of her head, where blood would soak into her blond hair. He decided he'd shoot her three times in the chest, in and around the heart.

His hand was shaking. His finger tightened on the trigger.

She yawned and sat up in bed, golden hair spilling forward, peering through the darkness, pulling the bedcovers up in front of her although she was fully clothed. She saw a dark shape, and her breath caught in her throat.

"Who's there?"

Wolfgang gritted his teeth, sweat breaking out on his forehead, his gun hand slippery. "It's me, Lieserl. Don't be afraid."

"Wolfgang!" She wanted to jump up and run into his arms, but it was dark and she could only barely see him, and was unsure of his intentions. "How did you get by the guard?"

"Claude relieved him an hour ago."

"Won't they notice you're not at your post?"

"We've given the Brits the slip. At least, that's what everyone thinks. I've got the next six hours off."

The thrumming of the engines filled the silence. "You're...you're tense," she said. "Something's wrong."

"Everyone's tense. For God's sake, Lieserl, the entire British Navy is after us!"

She lowered the bedclothes and fumbled for the light switch, but before she could locate it she heard something metallic clatter to the floor. He found her, his strong hands closing around her upper arms, gripping her.

"What...what are you doing?"

He didn't reply. She felt weak and dizzy, but when he drew her up off the bed and into his arms she felt a surge of strength run through her. She pressed herself hungrily against his chest and kissed his cheek. He returned her kiss, and kissed her again and again, circumspectly avoiding her lips, kissing her on her neck, on her soft cheek, beneath her eyes. She didn't know who he was but it didn't matter, nothing mattered anymore. She felt her body warm under his touch, and finally his lips found hers.

They fell back down onto the bed and wrestled there together, somehow in the process managing to get their clothes loosened; it was too cold to take them completely off. She felt a terrible urgency deep inside her, a desire to be taken and transported away. She fumbled with his zipper and his underwear, freeing him, feeling his warm shaft in her hand. He groaned, and it was like the *Bismarck* groaning, and he pressed into her, tugging down her underwear.

The tiny room seemed to warm, and they worked out of their clothing. He kissed and caressed her, cherishing her touch, bringing her body into a heightened sense of aliveness with his strong and sensitive hands. He kissed her breasts, her nipples, moving downwards across the flat plain of her belly to her dark nexus, awkwardly inverting his body on the bunk until they faced opposite directions.

She was slightly alarmed. Hans Bauer, her teenage lover in Hamburg over two decades before, had never dared something so unhygienic, nor would she have expected him to, but her breath caught in her throat as Wolfgang's face nestled in her lap and he began kissing her there. She felt his erection brush against her cheek as his warm tongue explored her secret contours, and she kissed and caressed it, running her tongue around the rim. She felt his arms slide around the small of her back and a wave of pleasure rippled up her body, then another. Instinctively she took him into her mouth and held him, and it was excruciatingly daring and erotic, delicious as he drew himself partly out, then eased back in. Something suddenly gave way inside her, and she turned her head to the side, releasing him with a gasp, and she began thrusting against his face, emitting a tight moan with each thrust, panting for air and clawing at his buttocks as she came to a shuddering climax.

For a moment she could only lay spent on the bed as he gently kissed her thighs. She felt a curious void, something left undone, and as she got her breath she pulled at him, turning him around. She guided him inside her, and it felt completely natural, like he had always belonged there. She rubbed his chest and back and kissed him as he fell into a rhythm of unhurried thrusting. It was as if they were on a long, leisurely voyage to a forgotten exotic land, to Katmandu or Eden. "It's all right," she said to him softly, sensing he was holding himself back. He quickened then, and she felt something begin to open up inside her, opening like a flower blossoming or like dawn slowly gathering, growing brighter, something inexorable and beyond her control. She sucked in a deep breath involuntarily, and he answered her, until both of them were breathing in long, deep gasps. Finally, straining at the peak of her being, she cried out, so loudly he stiffened, afraid he'd hurt her, but she cried out again, a paroxysm wracking her body as she dug her nails into his back and arched up into him, and he thrust himself powerfully inside her, again and again, his climax an echo to the final waves of her own.

He lay beside her, holding her close. Tears began streaming down her cheeks, and he felt them with his lips and tasted them.

"Did I hurt you?"

She sniffed and tried to wipe her eyes dry. "No, of course not. Don't be silly."

"Then why are you crying?"

"I...I was thinking about..."

She fell silent, and Wolfgang propped himself up on one elbow. "Are you going to share it with me?"

"I can't."

"It's your mother, isn't it? You're afraid she's going to spank you."

She laughed through her tears. "How did you guess?"

"My mother's going to spank me, too."

"I think you might have grown too big for her."

"You haven't seen my mother!"

Lieserl laughed again. "If she could hear you!"

"I wish she could."

His abrupt change in tone made them both fall silent a moment. Then Wolfgang said, "Were they really so bad?"

"Who?"

"Your parents."

Somehow she began to tremble. Despite Wolfgang's warmth she felt suddenly cold and empty again, like a chasm was yawning open within her. "I don't want to talk about it."

"Do you ever write them? Do they write you?"

"Wolfgang, I told you I didn't want to talk about it."

"Why not?"

"This...this is silly."

She sat up and fumbled for a handkerchief. She found one on the table next to the bed and blew her nose. "I was born out of wedlock," she said, still clutching the handkerchief and holding it close to her face. "When I was little more than a year old they put me up for adoption."

"Do you know who your real parents are?"

"Later, much later, I found out. My foster mother, before she was sent away to the camps, gave me a locket with a woman's picture in it. The woman, my true mother, was holding me in her arms. My father had insisted on giving me away over my mother's objections."

"Did your foster mother tell you who they were?"

"She didn't know." She stopped to catch her breath. "After I found out from Heisenberg, it was as if some deep hurt had been uncovered inside me. I could never forgive my biological father for abandoning me, nor my mother for allowing it."

"You should talk it out with him and clear the air. Do you know where to find him?"

She gave a short, broken laugh. "He's easy to find. I even know where he lives."

Wolfgang sat up in surprise. "Where is that?"

"Princeton, New Jersey. In the United States."

"You mean he's a professor like you are?"

She nodded her head, feeling a strange sense of relief that at last her secret was to be revealed and shared with someone. "My true father is the physicist Albert Einstein."

Wolfgang stared at her for a long moment, then lay carefully back down.

"Well? Aren't you going to say anything?"

"That's unbelievable."

"I don't believe it myself, sometimes."

"How do you know it's true?"

"Heisenberg knew Einstein's secret, and when he saw the picture in the locket he recognized my mother and knew instantly." She sighed. "He's a clever bastard."

"Does Lutjens know this?"

"I don't think so."

"Don't tell him. There's a reward out for your father, dead or alive. They'll try to blackmail him, or use you as some kind of propaganda tool."

"It hardly matters, now. They already want something from me."

Wolfgang nodded in the darkness. "Yes, the nuclear reactors, of course. And nuclear weapons."

She shot him a glance, thinking that he seemed to know more than she had expected, that someone else must have briefed him. "They might not work."

"But if they did..."

"Hitler would win the war. Is that what you want?"

"God, no! I just want it to be over, that's all."

"That's treason, you know. You could be shot."

"The devil with that. We're all going to die."

"Yes. I'm afraid we are." She shifted in his arms. "Now it's your turn.

Who are you?"

"The less you know about me the better."

"Tell me," she insisted. "You said yourself that it doesn't matter."

"It's better you don't know."

"You're Gestapo, aren't you?"

"God, no!"

"You made love to me," she said, quiet urgency in her voice. "You must tell. I know you; I didn't really believe your denials. You were in Berlin and you were in Gottingen, and now you're here. You were watching me. Why?"

He sighed. "I have watched you for months. I was the man who broke into your apartment and your office. I called the air strike that took out Manfred Von Ardenne's laboratories. I had orders to kill anyone who possessed the secret of an atomic weapon, a bomb."

She tensed. "You're supposed to kill me?"

"Yes. That's what I came here to do. It was something I should have done a long time ago, my duty. I was going to do it tonight."

"But you didn't. Why not?"

"I don't know, I just couldn't. The longer I waited, the harder it got."

"So you failed in your mission."

"Yes. I failed the Allies, and I failed myself. I think I'm in love with you."

She paused, creating a silence in which anything could happen. "I see."

"Well?"

"Please, Wolfgang. I'm not sure what to think. Don't ask until I've had time to sort it out."

"All right."

They settled in against each other, neither one of them quite comfortable, uneasy, dozing off to the powerful thrumming of the *Bismarck*'s engines.

May 26, 5 AM

The pounding jolted Lieserl out of a dead sleep, ripping her from calm repose to heart-racing fear. Frantically she pulled on her clothing, rolling to her feet and fumbling through the dawn light for the door handle.

She cracked open the door, finding three guards, one at the door and two more behind him.

"We must search your cabin, Dr. Meier," he said.

"You've already searched it. Come back in the morning."

"We must search it again."

"Can you give me five minutes?"

The man nodded. Lieserl began to close the door, but Wolfgang called out to her, and in the same instant the MP stuck his foot in the door and blocked it, pushing it open. His eyes swept across the room to the bed where Wolfgang lay, squinting against the light that streamed into the room.

"What's this?" the guard bellowed. "A breach of discipline?" Then he saw the gun on the floor and drew his own sidearm. "Get your hands out where I can see them!"

"No," protested Lieserl, "it's not what you think."

He moved quickly into the room, kicking the Walther out towards the hallway, keeping his own weapon trained on Wolfgang, who was sitting paralyzed in bed. "Men! Take him to the brig!"

The other two men barged in past her and went over to the bed, grabbing Wolfgang by both arms, hauling him out of bed. He was still naked.

"At least let him get his clothes on!" shouted Lieserl.

"All right," said the guard. "Get dressed and be quick about it." Wolfgang threw his clothes on and the other two guards hustled him out the door.

"Admiral Lutjens will hear of this outrage!" she shouted at the guard.

"Captain Lindemann gave the order," the guard replied stiffly. "He'll answer to the Admiral."

"He's done nothing wrong! You have no right to take him!"

"Sorry, Doctor, but you can continue your protests in the morning. Good night."

"I demand to see Admiral Lutjens."

"That won't be possible. You're confined to quarters. Again, good night."

He left her, shutting and locking the door. Lieserl went back to bed and lay down, still smelling Wolfgang among the sheets, feeling helpless and small. In a few minutes she began thinking through her options, the cards in her hand, trying to decide which one would be valuable enough to win Wolfgang's release, yet not so valuable as to give the Germans military advantage. She couldn't bear the thought of Wolfgang being interrogated, probably tortured for information about her, although she was sure he wouldn't say anything.

On the other hand, if he were a plant, a member of the Gestapo...

The notion grew inside her, slowly, until she felt she could scream. Had Wolfgang simply used her, gained her confidence for the purpose of getting information?

That didn't completely make sense. After all, he had been taken into custody. Surely they would have left him with her longer in hopes of getting even more information out of her. On the other hand, perhaps they would hold him hostage to ensure her cooperation.

Dark thoughts swirled through her head as she lay on the bed, trying to sleep, never managing more than a few fitful minutes at a time. The sun never came up; it was hidden behind the leaden overcast. Lieserl stayed in bed, because the heavy seas made it hard even to sit at a desk. The weather worsened until the *Bismarck* was bludgeoning through fifty-foot seas.

Claude brought her breakfast, and she spoke with him a few moments. Morale was higher, because they'd be within range of the Luftwaffe by the next morning. No doubt there would also be a line of U-boats waiting to take out any British warships that might have picked up their trail. A day later she'd be in Brest, and from there, rapidly transported to Berlin. For all her bravado, she wasn't certain she could resist any serious inquisition. She wondered if Heisenberg would help her torturers, telling them when the equations she babbled didn't make any sense. Sometimes she felt she hated Heisenberg more than Haberditz. Heisenberg, at least, was brilliant enough to make an intelligent choice, but had failed to do so.

Shortly before nine o'clock in the morning someone rapped loudly on her door. She opened up, finding the same marine guard that had ordered Wolfgang off to the brig.

"What do you want?" she asked crossly.

"Dr. Meier, you shall go with me to the flight deck. You have five minutes to prepare yourself."

"What did you do to Wolfgang?"

"His fate will be up to Captain Lindemann."

"He hasn't done anything wrong. I invited him here."

"Please hurry. If you are not ready in five minutes, you will go as you are."

"Go?"

"No questions, please."

Ten minutes later they were up on the flight deck, a platform amidships equipped with steam catapults. Lutjens was there, along with a number of sailors who were preparing the airplane. Lieserl could feel the envious stares of the sailors, which she didn't quite understand, except that she and the pilot would be escaping, leaving behind the *Bismarck* to its private fate.

"He's innocent," Lieserl protested to Lutjens as he greeted her.

"Who?"

"Wolfgang, the computer operator in ballistics."

"I don't understand."

"He was in my room at my invitation. He's been thrown into the brig."

He nodded and said, "I'll look into it. You'll be returning to Brest by airplane."

"Why?"

"We're still in considerable danger. It's essential that you be returned to Berlin in good health."

"You know I won't cooperate with them."

"I know. But that won't be my problem, anymore."

A nearby aide gave the ship's log to the pilot. Another man helped Lieserl up into the copilot's seat. The pilot, not looking at her, went through a rapid check of the cabin instruments, then fired up the port and starboard engines. He gave a thumbs-up to the catapult operator, who pulled the release.

A great puff of steam billowed out, but the plane didn't budge. Confused, the operator and his assistants prepared for another try. Again nothing happened.

Everyone started milling around, checking the steam conduits, scratching their heads. Lieserl felt sick to her stomach, the adrenaline of having awakened badly, the excitement of escaping the ship, then the confusion and disappointment of failure.

A sailor ran up alongside the pilot's side of the plane. "Shrapnel in the conduits. She can't hold the proper pressure."

The pilot cursed. "Can it be fixed?"

"Yes, but only back at port. We'll have to ditch the plane. It's nothing more than a bomb with all that fuel."

"God damn it!" The pilot glared at Lieserl, as if daring her to correct his language. Then he flung open the door and climbed down out of the plane.

Lieserl reached over to the control panel and turned on the radio, then picked up the mike and squeezed the send button. "This is Dr. Lieserl Meier on the *Bismarck*," she said in her thickly-accented English. "Repeat, this is Dr. Lieserl Meier on the *Bismarck*. RAF, come in, repeat, this is the *Bismarck*..."

Someone jerked her door open and yanked her down out of the plane. She stumbled and fell to the deck, landing painfully on her left elbow and hip. "What the hell do you think you're doing?" a sailor roared in her face.

"That will be all, Dorfman," commanded Lutjens in an iron voice.

The man turned, still holding Lieserl's arm in an viselike grip. "But she was calling the RAF, for Christ's sake!"

"Let her go, mister."

Dorfman threw her arm down in disgust, walking away angrily. Other men were pushing the plane down the ramp. It fell into the shifting cold waters of the Atlantic.

Lutjens stared at her, not in anger, but with an air of tired defeat. She felt sorry for him, and strangely ashamed of her action; if her brief transmission had been picked up by British radio operators at two different locations, their position could be exactly determined and she had assured a death sentence for everyone in the crew, including herself. "I'm...I'm sorry," she stammered.

He made a curt gesture of his hand to a nearby crewmember. "Take her back to her cabin. Make sure she stays there."

Back in her cabin she tried to nap, but the excitement of the aborted flight kept awake. She wondered if her message had been picked up, whether Wolfgang were a plant, or Heisenberg a traitor to her as well as to the rest of humanity. The thoughts kept spinning thickly through her mind until at last she fell into a fitful sleep.

May 26, 9 PM

She was lying in bed, bored and turning physics problems over in her head, when the alarm sounded.

She'd spent most of the day in bed, nervous and tired, moving into and out of tortured dreams. The deck was heaving from the heavy seas and she felt a little ill. Several times she second-guessed herself on her distress call to the RAF, but in the end decided she'd done the right thing, although she may have signed her own death warrant.

She reacted slowly to the alarm, finally getting up and going to the porthole, careful to keep her balance. It was still light out, although gray and overcast. The antiaircraft batteries opened fire; it was a torpedo run, with eight or ten slow-flying planes that were more suited to reconnaissance than to combat. She recognized them: they were Swordfish, relics from the Great War.

Every gun on the ship joined in, even the big fifteen-inch guns came to life with their deafening, mind-numbing roars. The air was thick with cordite smoke; but still the clumsy planes came, miraculously unharmed, dropping their torpedoes into the fifty-foot seas.

The ship turned violently to port so as to present a more slender profile to the torpedoes, drilling their way mindlessly through the water. The batteries continued their rapid-fire hammering of the sky. A tremendous thump nearly threw Lieserl onto the floor, then the fifteen-inch guns roared again, and she was hanging on for dear life on the edges of the porthole.

Then the planes were gone, and the batteries fell silent.

Twenty minutes later someone began pounding on her door. She opened up, still in her nightgown, finding a guard.

"What do you want?" she asked sharply.

"Admiral Lutjens requests your assistance on the bridge."

"Tell Admiral Lutjens he may call upon me tomorrow, no earlier than noon."

"Please, Dr. Meier. I have been instructed to insist."

"Oh, all right. Give me a couple minutes."

She washed her face in the basin, brushed her hair, and then got dressed, taking her time. When the guard again knocked on the door, more urgently this time, she finally joined him in the passageway.

Lutjens wasn't on the bridge anymore; they found him in the chart room with Lindemann, sitting before a large nautical map on the table before them. Leserl took a seat on the opposite side of the admiral.

"Thank you for coming," Lutjens said cordially.

"Yes, thank you very much," Lindemann said, his voice dripping with sarcasm. "Thank you for giving our position to the British so their planes could torpedo us."

"Is the ship badly damaged?"

Lutjens shook his head. "Not too badly. A torpedo exploded off the stern, slightly compromising the hull, flooding one of the engine rooms. We've got that problem taken care of; now, we must free the rudder. It's stuck at a fifteen degree angle."

"So we're going in circles."

"Yes, God damn it," snarled Lindemann. "Yes! That's exactly what we're doing."

Lutjens shot a warning glance at Lindemann and then continued. "I thought that you might be able to help us think of a solution."

"Don't you have an access from the inside?"

Lutjens nodded. "Yes, but it would be suicide to send a diver through.

We've tried; they were nearly pounded to death against the hull. The seas are too high."

Lieserl pursed her lips. "I see. What about explosive charges?"

"They would have to be placed carefully, so as not to damage the ship. The divers couldn't possibly handle them under these conditions."

"Have you tried a system of sea anchors? Deploy them off the starboard side, and you may be able to create a net vector to the east, although at greatly reduced speed."

Lutjens glanced at Lindemann. "I suggest you see to it at once."

Lindemann, still puffing on a cigarette, got up and left the chart room. Claude came in a moment later, carrying an urn of coffee. Lutjens accepted a cup from him, distracted, poring over the maps, keeping the coffee level as the ship deck shifted.

"Just another three or four hours," Lutjens said in a low voice. "That's all we need to get under the protection of the Luftwaffe."

"And if the problem isn't fixed?"

He took a deep breath and said tightly, "Half the British fleet will be on top of us: *Prince of Wales*, *Repulse*, and their destroyer escorts. And the aircraft will be back with more torpedoes."

"Mere bee stings," she said, quoting him.

He shot her a sharp glance, and for a moment she thought he was going to get angry. His eyes were bloodshot from lack of sleep, his face drawn, far more gaunt than when they'd left Gdynia. He looked ten years older.

"There remains the question of what to do with you."

"Assuming you don't reach Brest?"

"Yes. I've contacted Donitz, the U-boat commander-in-chief. He has ordered every available U-boat into the area. You shall be placed aboard one."

"I won't go."

He looked up, surprised. "What do you mean?"

"I won't go unless Wolfgang goes with me."

Lutjens straightened. "He was absent from his post, suspected of treason, and must remain in custody. I can't grant your request."

"Then I won't go."

Lindemann strode back into the chart room, taking heavy drags off a new cigarette. "We've deployed the sea anchors, Admiral. I've ordered them to experiment with the placement, with a view of maintaining the maximum speed possible."

"Are the anchors effective?"

Lindemann shook his head. "It's too soon to say. The men are working on it. If it doesn't work, I have several volunteers willing to carry explosives strapped to their bodies down to the rudder."

"Commit suicide? I won't allow it."

"We should consider it," Lindemann replied stubbornly. "The men are volunteering for the job."

"Why couldn't the explosives be lowered down by rope?" asked Lieserl.

Lindemann turned to her, his face sour. "In these seas, someone would have to position them properly near the rudder and hold them in place during the detonation."

"You'd probably end up putting another hole in the stern," Lieserl said. "And flood your engine room again."

"Unfortunately, Dr. Meier is correct," Lutjens said. "That isn't a good solution." He cleared his throat. "I'm afraid that we should start working on contingency plans, should the sea anchors fail to resolve the problem. If we are not to survive this mission, it's imperative that my log, together with Dr. Meier, be returned safely to Naval Command."

Lindemann nodded. "By submarine, of course. Shall I radio Donitz?"

"I told you I wouldn't go."

Lindemann and Lutjens exchanged a long glance. Lutjens sighed heavily, looking resigned. "Captain, take care of the situation, please. I need a few minutes of rest."

Lindemann straightened and saluted. "At once, sir."

Lutjens left the map room, leaving Lieserl alone with Lindemann. Lindemann took a long drag on his cigarette, then pulled another out of a gold cigarette case and lit it from the stub of the first. He then neatly placed the stub in an ashtray. His predatory eyes never left Lieserl's face.

"You have two choices, Dr. Meier," Lindemann said. "You can make it easy, or you can make it hard."

"What do you want?"

"First, I want you to write down everything that was on those papers you destroyed."

"Impossible. I can't remember it."

"According to our informants, you have a photographic memory. After we have the papers, you will be evacuated via U-boat. Your lover Wolfgang will go with you and face trial in Germany."

Lieserl began trembling. "And if I refuse to cooperate?"

"You will be persuaded until you cooperate." He shrugged. "And, of course, if you agree to help us, we may be willing to commute Wolfgang's sentence."

"Sentence?" she echoed, unable to keep her voice from quavering.

"As it stands, he will be put to death as a traitor for abandonment of his duty during a wartime engagement. We'll carry out the sentence right here, immediately. Choose, Dr. Meier. A woman of your intelligence should have no difficulty making the correct decision."

His eyes bore down on hers. She felt like a rabbit before a snake. As the seconds ticked by, she realized she was at a crossroads, where her actions, by themselves, could determine the fate of others, perhaps even the fate of nations. She also realized that she loved Wolfgang more than anything else in the world, and that her choice could end his life.

But all of a sudden the answer was obvious. "Do what you will, Captain. I won't cooperate."

He frowned and picked up the phone. "Well, perhaps we'll try some physical persuasion, first. You'll cooperate, Dr. Meier. I assure you of that."

*****

Half an hour later she was filling sheet after sheet with equations while a pair of guards looked on. She was defeated, and she knew it. She could only hope that somehow the British would stop them. She was no braver in the face of pain than Heisenberg had been.

Periodically Lindemann dropped in to warn her against treachery. They were holding Wolfgang; and if it were discovered she deliberately falsified the work, they would execute him. They counted on Heisenberg, when provided with her notes, to complete the reconstruction of her theories.

She debated making deliberate errors, but she had lost all will to resist. She had a black eye, assorted bruises and contusions, a bloody nose, and she was so tired she could barely hold her pen steady. All she wanted was to be left alone.

Her own weakness repelled her. The most she could manage was a deliberate error on the reaction energy. Heisenberg would probably notice it, however, and correct it. She couldn't even hate him for cooperating; she understood, now, how difficult it was to resist when there was a war going on and no one cared how much they hurt anyone.

She finished shortly after midnight and handed the papers over to one of the guards. The other one led her back to the bridge, where she took a chair and sat exhausted while Lutjens sent a statement to Hitler over the wireless. She rolled her eyes when she heard the proud bravado, talk of fighting to the last shell for Fatherland and Fuehrer. Lindemann paced the bridge like a caged tiger, chain-smoking and drinking cup after cup of coffee. The ship's steerage was still out; the *Bismarck* was heading northwest at fifteen knots, away from Brest, away from salvation, and there wasn't anything that anyone could do about it.

Chapter Sixteen

May 27, 1:30 AM

She awoke from a doze to a general alarm. Groggily she rolled up out of her chair, standing up. It was not yet dawn; outside she could see nothing. The seas were still heavy; the deck swayed beneath her feet.

Lutjens was still in his chair, uncharacteristically smoking a cigar. He glanced at her as she walked over close to him, and said, "The submarine hasn't yet arrived. We expect it shortly after dawn. When it gets here, we'll put you on board."

"And Wolfgang?"

"He will go with you, as we've promised."

A sudden report came over the intercom system: "Attention! Destroyer off the port stern", and a moment later, "Attention! Destroyer off the starboard bow."

Claude served everyone hot coffee and biscuits as if nothing was happening. Lindemann smoked and paced up and down. Lieserl exchanged a glare with him. The seas were fifty-foot hills of water; hardly anything could be seen through the spray and darkness.

Suddenly Anton and Bruno turrets, on the foredeck, began a massive turning, the mighty fifteen-inch guns raising up, seeking their proper elevations. They exploded into action with a deafening roar, the fire from their muzzles lighting up the angry ocean.

Lutjens still seemed unconcerned. "These are the picadors," he explained to Lieserl. "They can't hurt us much."

"They'll weaken you."

"Perhaps. If our U-boats arrive..."

His voice trailed off, as if he didn't believe it himself. Again, over the intercom, came another announcement: "Second destroyer off the starboard bow."

Sparks of fire winked on the horizon, followed moments later by the shrill whistling of six-inch shells, while *Bismarck*'s batteries fired another deafening salvo. Geysers of water erupted all around the ship, one of them washing over the bridge in the high winds.

"Perhaps you'd be better off in your cabin," suggested Lutjens. "It's going to be a long night."

"No, I couldn't stand that." The prospect of returning to her solitude seemed oppressive. "Can you have Wolfgang released?"

He shook his head. "That would be bad for discipline." He shifted uncomfortably in his chair. "I apologize for any discomfort you may have experienced, particularly due to the fact that it may have been in vain."

"Your apology," she said acidly, "is most decidedly not accepted."

He frowned at her. "I'm sorry, Dr. Meier. I had my orders."

Claude came over and offered her a cup of coffee and a stale pastry, which she accepted. She found an unoccupied chair nearby and sat down, staring out at the violent darkness.

All night long the battle raged, exchanging fire with the British destroyers, repelling weak torpedo assaults by the ungainly Swordfish biplanes, originating off an aircraft carrier that only once made the mistake of coming within range of the *Bismarck*'s guns. The vintage carrier suffered a devastating hit amidships before withdrawing. Five destroyers tormented them, periodically breaking off just when the *Bismarck* gunnery control was finding the range, only to return later, materializing at a distance, cloaked in darkness and mist.

Then, through the clouds of cordite smoke, dawn began to break. The seas calmed and the destroyers withdrew.

"Looks like they're breaking off the action," said Lindemann in a gravelly voice. His eyes were bloodshot. "The weather's clearing; maybe we can get the divers down for another go at the rudder."

"Get the men on it immediately," ordered Lutjens. "Three hours south at full steam and we'll pick up some air cover."

Lindemann grabbed the telephone and made the call. Lutjens stood up and gripped the railing, peering grimly off to the northwest through his binoculars. Lieserl quietly joined him at the rail.

"They must have run short of fuel," he muttered. "Or perhaps the U-boats have been sighted." He paused, lowering the binoculars, allowing himself a sigh of relief. "We have a chance, now, after all."

"May I, Admiral?"

Lutjens handed her the binoculars. For several minutes she scanned the horizons. Indeed, there was no trace of the British ships that had hounded them through the night.

Lindemann stepped back to the railing. "Divers have gone over the side with welding torches. I've instructed the engine room to disengage the screws when we've come about to a southeastern heading. In half an hour, at most, we'll be able to make forward progress again."

"And if we should drift off course?"

"The sea anchors should be sufficient to bring us back in the proper direction, once the rudder is gone."

"Excellent, Captain. Inform me when the work is complete."

Lindemann left them. Lutjens said, "We'll be safe in Brest in a few hours," he told her. "And I give you my word: you shall be treated fairly, so long as you cooperate. I shall personally see to it."

Lieserl didn't answer. She was still staring intently at the horizon. Lutjens squinted in the general direction she was looking. "What is it?" he commanded. "Do you see something?"

She lowered the binoculars and handed them to him. He put them up to his eyes for a moment and lowered them again.

"Captain!" he bellowed, turning. "Come here, please!"

Lindemann strode over. "Yes, sir?"

"I believe I see a mast."

Lindemann immediately snatched the binoculars and peered through them.

"There are two of them," said Lutjens. "Would you agree they're both battleships?"

"Yes, they are," announced Lindemann. "Most definitely."

Lutjens took the binoculars back again and studied the ships for a long moment. "It's the *King George V*," he announced. "I had lunch aboard her in '24. And the other one is *Rodney*. Three turrets with sixteen inch guns, all in front." He handed the binoculars back to Lindemann.

Lindemann said, "We took the *Hood*. We can take them, too."

Lutjens ignored the comment. "How are the divers doing?"

"They need another quarter hour."

"With the water we've taken on, I doubt we can outrun them, even if they succeed in disengaging the rudder."

"Every kilometer closer to France will mean more air support."

Lutjens shook his head, his face gray. "We don't have enough time; but no matter. We will fight to the last shell. I will address the crew."

He took up the microphone of the public address system and began speaking to the crew in a voice that was tired and defeated. He praised the men for their courage, and told them they'd be heroes, but it was obvious to everyone that he didn't expect *Bismarck* to survive the engagement. Lieserl was shocked that he would make such a speech, destroying in a moment any last shreds of crew morale.

"I must insist that you seek comparative safety, Dr. Meier," he said when he finished. "When the U-boat gets here you must be ready to leave immediately. Do you understand?"

"Yes, sir," she said. "Can you release Wolfgang, now?"

He looked distracted for a moment, consulting a sheaf of papers, then suddenly picked up a telephone, quickly dialing a number. "Release Wolfgang Mueller to his duties."

He hung up. "He'll be going back to the rear computer room. I regret I can't free him from duty. We'll need him to assist us during the engagement."

"Thank you all the same, Admiral."

As she turned to leave, the first salvo roared from the fifteen-inch guns.

No one stopped her on her way below decks. She had no difficulty finding the rear computer room. Inside, in the green light of the radar screen, a dozen men were busy with their computations, sending the results to the crews manning the guns. It was quiet there, the sound of the guns muffled, from a different world. Hardly a head turned as she moved through the room looking for Wolfgang, so engrossed were they in the work that was crucial to their survival.

She went to the far end and started back, wondering if she should go check the forward computer room on the opposite side of the ship.

Then the door opened and Wolfgang walked in. When he saw her there, bathed in green light, he froze, his face stricken with a mix of conflicting emotions. In that awful moment Lieserl feared that she'd been right, that he had used her and cared nothing for her.

The duty officer stood up. "You can't stay here, Dr. Meier."

"Just a moment..."

"I must insist."

The officer took her firmly by the elbow and led her out the far door. She kept looking over her shoulder, trying to read something in Wolfgang's stance, his expression, but the light was too dim and her heart too conflicted.

She climbed back up to the quarterdeck, back into a choking hell of sound and fury. Salvo after salvo exploded out and screamed back as she ran the length of the ship.

Suddenly the bulkhead tore open before her in a blaze of fire and smoke, the explosive shock throwing her to the deck, struck by shrapnel and debris and choking on hot smoke. Lieserl hardly dared move, and then found, miraculously, that she had only a couple of bloody gashes, one on her forehead and the other on her leg. She crawled on all fours, picking her way over the body of a young man without a left arm or face, still breathing fitfully as his blood pumped languidly onto the deck. An entire section of bulkhead was gone, and she felt the ocean breeze. It was a beautiful, sunny day, the first since they'd passed through the Arctic, and out on the shining blue waters, so close now she could clearly see them, were *Rodney* and *King George V*, not more than five thousand yards away, firing repeatedly at virtually point blank range.

The moaning and the dead lay scattered all around her. Getting up, she stepped over the casualties and ran through smoke and flame, heading for the bridge.

No one stopped her as she climbed the last steps and entered the bridge. Lutjens was talking calmly on his telephone, while Lindemann and Claude were standing next to each other, quietly reminiscing. The other officers were going about their business, helmsman at his station, although the rudder was still jammed, the radio operator coding messages. Below the bridge, she could see that Anton and Bruno, the forward gun turrets, were out of action: Anton's gun barrels were drooping drunkenly at an impossibly low elevation, and Bruno's were twisted upwards, as if a giant hand had gripped and bent them.

Lieserl marched over and planted herself in front of Lutjens as he hung up the phone. "Pull your colors," she demanded. "Raise a white flag."

He frowned at her, his face lined with fatigue, looking more than ever like a tired, worn out family dog. "That's unacceptable."

"You're condemning two thousand boys to their deaths!" she shouted. "Don't you realize that?"

"They'll die with honor."

"What honor? What does honor have to do with anything? What about their mothers, their fathers, what about their dreams?" She threw out her arm, taking in the whole ship in a gesture. "Your ship is on fire," she said in an acid voice. "Your guns are no longer operational. Don't you understand? The British hate your guts, they'd just as soon sink your ship and send you all to the bottom with it, but they'll respect a white flag and cease fire. Do it! Do it now! Surrender!"

Lutjens was slow in replying, and he refused to look her in the eye. "The rear turrets are still in operation."

Her mouth dropped open, her face reddening in fury. "Are you mad?" she cried over the din and chaos. "Have you lost your mind?"

His voice found its timbre then, and his eyes hardened to steel. "We will go down with our colors flying!"

"You bastard! You egomaniacal bastard! You think that by doing that you'll reserve your place in Valhalla?"

Anger flashed in his eyes and he clenched his fists, but the sound of an express train had them diving for cover. In the next instant the shell struck just beneath the bridge, shattering glass, spraying shrapnel and fire.

Lieserl crawled out from beneath an overhanging piece of bulkhead, seeing that Lindemann was still standing arm in arm with Claude, both of them bleeding. The helmsman crouched over Lutjens, feeling the admiral's neck for a pulse.

The helmsman looked up. "He's dead."

Gone to Valhalla, she thought bitterly.

She turned to Lindemann. "Run up the white flag!" she shouted, but he pulled his sidearm out of its holster and she turned and ran, the shot errant only because Claude grabbed his captain's wrist and spoiled his aim.

As she ran through the smoking ruins of the superstructure, the general call to abandon ship came over the intercom system. She hesitated, not knowing what direction to take, thinking she needed to find Wolfgang, when she heard someone calling her.

"*Fraulein*! Over here! Take this!"

A sailor was holding out a yellow life jacket. She accepted it gratefully, and he helped her put it on.

The ship was listing heavily to port. She went to the railing; men were milling around on the main deck, shouting at each other, many of them burned or mutilated. She watched as a man not ten meters from her stood ready to jump, but decided to take his pants off, first. She was thinking the water would be cold, that he ought to keep them on, and suddenly there was the explosion of an incoming shell, knocking her back against the deck. The man fell, legless, to the deck, and rolled off the edge, falling into the frigid North Atlantic.

She turned from the horror, vomit coming up into her gorge. Coughing violently, she stumbled to her feet. "Wolfgang!" she shouted futilely against the furious sound of the engagement. She shouted his name over and over as she moved through the smoke and flames.

Someone grabbed her from behind, tearing at the straps of her life jacket. She screamed and struck at her attacker, but he shoved her brutally to the deck and then was on her again, crushing her beneath his weight as he worked to loosen the straps.

Suddenly the weight left her. She scrambled to her knees. Another man had pulled him off, and the two were locked in a brawl, going down and rolling in a vicious wrestling match on the deck. Too frightened to help her rescuer, Lieserl stood up and ran toward the rear turrets, choking on the thick smoke.

A battered lieutenant commander was trying to organize a ragged detachment of survivors. Lieserl found a dead man with a gas mask, which she removed and put on. The ship listed more to port, and suddenly everyone left on deck began throwing themselves into the water. She hesitated on the railing, terrified of the rolling seas, not knowing whether to stay put or take her chances in the ocean.

Another exploding shell decided her and she jumped, falling through a dozen meters of space.

She hit the water and plunged down several meters, then bobbed to the surface. Her gas mask was impeding her respiration, and she tore it off. The *Bismarck* was listing to port at a deep angle. She struck out, swimming as hard as she could through the heavy oil slick so she wouldn't be sucked down and drowned when the ship sank. The water was full of men, all of them struggling, crying out in pain and confusion.

"Look!" someone cried. "It's the captain!"

The *Bismarck* had turned so the main deck was almost vertical. Lindemann was there, near the bow, Claude with him. Lindemann was gesticulating violently towards the water, trying to convince him to dive into the sea and save himself, Claude just as steadfastly refusing with resolute shakes of his head. The deck eased underwater so they climbed up on the starboard side, walking up to where the keel was heeling up out of the sea. The ship slowly turned completely over, and Lindemann, with Claude hanging on to him, climbed up and sat against the keel.

Lieserl, swimming an awkward backstroke away from the ship, watched the two men, sitting resigned on the keel as the ship settled. It was fantastic, tragic and heroic, and mesmerizing, despite the danger.

The ship settled lower in the water and then the bow began to heel up as the stern sank. Lindemann managed to lurch to his feet one last time, Claude clutching his leg with one arm and the keel with the other. Lindemann snapped off a final salute as the *Bismarck* disappeared from view, headed for the bottom of the Atlantic two miles below.

A British frigate loomed through the smoke, and Lieserl turned onto her stomach and began swimming freestyle, angling for it. The frigid waters had already numbed her legs, and soon she couldn't feel her fingers or hands, either, and could barely lift her arms. She rolled onto her back again and began doing an improvised rowing stroke, lifting her arms totally out of the water; only her shoulder and chest muscles seemed capable of movement. All around her wounded men floated in their life jackets, moaning, some of them calling for their mothers, the more robust swimming for their lives.

In only moments Lieserl found she couldn't move her arms anymore. She cursed at herself, willing her arms to move, but it was too cold, she was too exhausted, her arms refused to move in more than impotent circles. Hot tears came to her eyes. She felt the cold creeping up her torso, striking deep within her, and she wanted to cry for her mother, too, and for her father, but only bitter, angry memories arose as she thought unwillingly of Einstein and Mileva. She bit her tongue, stifling a cry of angst, knowing that the end of her life would be like the beginning: bitter, empty, and alone.

Then a strong arm swept around her, and she was moving again, her hip bumping against someone else's, someone still alive and still strong.

"Lieserl, it's me! We're going to make it, do you hear me?"

She squeezed her eyes shut as tears of relief came pouring out and the knot of pain warmed. "Wolfgang! Thank God!"

Wolfgang was a strong swimmer, but the cold began to get to him, too, and he slowed. After what seemed like an eternity, Lieserl turned her head, and to her surprise the frigate was enormous, she could see the name *Dorsetshire* stenciled on its side.

Hundreds of men were in the water next to the ship, climbing up the ropes the British crew had tossed down to them. Wolfgang caught hold of one.

"Hold on tight. I'm going to help pull you up with me."

He began climbing up, and she reached out and took hold of the rope. They struggled up together as a pair of British sailors hauled from above. As they gained the railing, one of the sailors reached out and caught hold of Lieserl, drawing her on board. During the exchange the ship shuddered and Wolfgang lost his grip on the rail. His arms waving and a look of shock on his face, he fell backwards, plummeting far back down into the sea.

"Wolfgang!" she cried, for the ship was moving forward. She watched as he resurfaced, realized what was happening, and struck out for one of the trailing ropes.

"Stop the ship!" she shouted at the sailors. "Please, you've got to stop the ship!"

"U-boat, milady," muttered one of them apologetically, a weather-beaten man with a cockney accent. "Can't stay any longer."

She threw herself against the railing, shouting desperate encouragement. "Go!" she cried. "Go, Wolfgang!"

He narrowly missed regaining the rope and then went under in the wash when another rope went by, missing it also. Then he was scrabbling at the sides of the ship like dozens of other luckless boys, watching their salvation slide inexorably away.

Lieserl wanted to die, and her rescuers knew it because they pulled her away from the railing as she cried Wolfgang's name over and over again. The cries of the abandoned men faded as the *Dorsetshire* pulled steadily away.

Einstein's Daughter: The Story of Lieserl

Epilogue

Berlin

The Gestapo agents hustled Haberditz down into the basement of 26 Grosse Hamburgerstrasse, ignoring his protests, tying him down on the table and then cutting off his pants and underwear with razor blades. A naked light bulb swung overhead. Haberditz, struggling futilely, caught sight of Dobberke. He was sneering at him, smoking a cigarette in a corner of the room.

"What is the meaning of this?" he shouted with all the vehemence and authority he could muster.

Dobberke walked over to the table, smiling, his eyes glinting with a strange, cruel light. "This is an interrogation, Admiral. There are some who believe you passed secrets to the enemy through the traitor, Dr. Lieserl Meier. I have been charged with finding out the important details of this matter."

"On whose authority!" demanded Haberditz, his voice nearly cracking in fear.

"Himmler requested it, and after what your man did to me a few months ago, I accepted the assignment with pleasure."

"What are you talking about? I didn't send anybody after you."

Dobberke blew smoke in his face. "You'll pay all the same, you cock-sucking bastard."

He put his cigarette out on Haberditz cheek, eliciting a howl of pain. He glanced at his two men, flicking his eyes toward his victim. "Soften him up for me."

Dobberke stepped back and leaned against the wall, watching the proceedings with keen interest. Within a couple hours he'd know everything in Haberditz's head, at which point, as Himmler himself suggested, no one would have any use for him anymore.

Berlin, July 1941, Air Ministry Building

Goering sat at the head of the heavy oak conference table, his florid lips curled in an ironic smile. He gazed shrewdly at Udet, who was doodling on a notepad. Goering's smile turned, bordering on a sneer. He looked around at the others.

"The Fuehrer has declared a state of total war against the Bolsheviks," he said.

"Of course," said Levholk. "There's no other kind."

Goering gave him a hard look, simmering with malice. "Total war means total war. There will be no mercy. We take no prisoners, nor do we tolerate the slightest infractions on the part of the conquered Slavs."

Udet glanced up from his drawings. "What will become of them?"

"They will service the farms, as they always have. They will work for us, doing the labor of beasts." He leaned forward, fire in his eyes. "As a matter of policy, the Russian people should be subdued by any means, no matter how brutal. Jews and commissars are to be shot without trial, without delay. Their children should not be spared, for when grown they will turn against us."

Udet, looking flustered and alarmed, shot to his feet, his pencil rolling off the table and dropping to the floor. "Children, you say! Women!" He spluttered in confusion, finally finding his tongue again. "That is unacceptable, totally unacceptable! That is contrary to the Geneva Convention!"

Goering waved the objection away. "The Soviet Union was not a signatory, so the Geneva Convention doesn't apply to them."

"But women...children...and this persecution of Jews, that's illegal! Worse, it's immoral!"

Goering shook his head and sighed in disgust. "Where have you been the last ten years, Udet? Did you have your head up some whore's skirt? Don't you know what's happening in the camps at Buchenwald, at Auschwitz, right under your stupid nose?"

Udet stuttered. "But these people...these are detainees. They are suspected enemies of the state, awaiting deportation to countries more in keeping with their beliefs, more accepting of their ways. Wasn't that the purpose of the Final Solution?"

Goering laughed harshly. "Buchenwald and Auschwitz are death camps for the Jews! We are slaughtering them by the thousands every day, shooting them, gassing them, starving them, beating them to death. The young and healthy work the mines, on the railroads, on our munitions, while the old, the sick, the children, our medical scientists experiment on them like lab animals and then dispose of them just as quickly. That, my poor, naïve, drink-sodden Udet, is the Final Solution!"

Udet's breath went out of him and he felt faint, staring in utter disbelief, unable to arouse any further righteous anger.

Goering, seeing his discomfort, softened. "I admit I have no great love of this business, Ernst, but this is war. Surely you understand that." He glanced around the table at the others and then went on, his demeanor hardening. "The fact of the matter is, you have been causing some slowdown in production, dragging your feet, arguing for more long-range bombers. This must stop. I am therefore suggesting you take several weeks vacation, effective immediately. The rest will do you good."

"The long-range bombers are quite necessary if you are to attack Moscow from the air."

"We'll have advance bases in the Ukraine within a matter of weeks. Long-range bombers won't be necessary." Goering gazed imperiously around the table, gesturing at Udet as if he were an odd piece of furniture. "You see, my friends, the Reichsmarschall of production hasn't the slightest idea of how to conduct a war. He'd be better off back in America, walking wings in his flying circus!"

"So you're dismissing me?"

"Just a vacation, that's all. Take care of your health. Try to lay off the liquor and pills. You may return to work when your nerves have recovered."

"And when will that be?"

"That, Udet, is up to you. I might suggest you reflect deeply on your views on race, you don't seem to understand the kind of people we're dealing with."

"But to slaughter them...like cattle..."

"Exactly, I see you understand completely." Goering waved his hand in a conciliatory gesture. "If it's of any consolation, these orders come from Himmler himself, endorsed by the Fuehrer. Himmler has assumed full responsibility. It's not for us to question our leaders; we must do our German duty, even when that duty is distasteful to us. As for you, Reichsmarschall Udet, I dismiss you as of this moment for recuperative leave."

Udet turned and left the room, moving like an automaton, passing out of the conference room without another word.

Outside the massive Air Ministry Building Udet stumbled and weaved as if drunk or ill. The orders from Himmler, endorsed by the Fuehrer and now by Goering, were still echoing through his mind with a terrible, irrevocable clarity.

They were to attack deep inside Russia without the benefit of a long-range bomber. That was bad enough, tantamount to a suicide assault. Worse, incomparably worse, had been the orders for a war without mercy.

The revelation about the camps shamed him to the very core of his being. He realized he'd known it all along, he just hadn't wanted to admit it to himself. He loved flying, he loved airplanes; he simply hadn't wanted to believe the rumors. He couldn't believe Germans could do such things.

An adjutant gave him a ride back to his posh home in a still untouched, wealthy suburb of Berlin. No one was there, not even the servants; they'd left for the country.

Udet went to his bedroom and took a long draught form a bottle of Scottish liquor. He sat on the bed, staring at the wall, clutching the bottle. For the first time in years he had nothing to do, nowhere to go. He thought about the Jews at 26 Hamburgerstrasse. Dr. Meier had tried to tell him of the abuse, but he hadn't believed her. How could he have deceived himself? It was all so painfully obvious, and he was one of them, a member of the party, an official no less, one of the responsible. He'd been too afraid to believe it, afraid of the responsibility that conveyed, of what he could not change, of what he might lose.

He remembered Meier's mother and the day Meier had wept, begging for his help.

Getting up, he threw the bottle against the wall; it hit with a thunk and fell to the floor, liquor spilling onto the carpet. Then he went and washed his face in the bathroom and shaved carefully. For a long time he looked at the face in the mirror, thoughts spinning uncontrollably through his mind like leaves in a whirlwind.

Returning to the bedroom, he took a red grease pencil out of his briefcase and, with shaking hands, scrawled a message on the wallpaper over the bedstead: WHY DID YOU BETRAY ME, GOERING?

Also inside his suitcase was his gun, the standard issue Luger, which fired nine-millimeter shells. He checked it carefully, testing the action, putting a bullet in the chamber. He lay down on the bed, gazing a moment out the window, looking at the clouds where he'd lived for so many years.

He couldn't do it. He sat up and picked up the phone, calling his mistress.

"Marjot!" he cried tearfully when she picked up. "Marjot, they're killing women and children, they're killing everybody!"

"What are you talking about, Ernst?"

"Goering, Himmler, Hitler, all of them, they're killing the Jews, the Gypsies, everybody! I can't take it any more, do you understand me? And Goering, he's turned on me! Please, Marjot, please come right away!"

"Ernst, you have to get hold of yourself. War is war, nobody likes it except the leaders, maybe not even them. It's not your fault."

"I'm one of the leaders," he sobbed. "*I* killed them! She begged me to help her, and I did nothing, I kept telling her I could do nothing."

"Who?"

"Meier! That woman, you know, that woman who was working on bombs!"

"Meier? You mean that scientist that Franz had the hots for? Ernst, I don't know what you're talking about, but you've got to calm down. Do you understand me? I'm coming, I'll be there in half an hour. Are you at home?"

"I've got a gun, Marjot." He picked up the Luger and put it to his head. "Goering betrayed me, they all betrayed me. I was only doing my duty as a German, because I loved flying, and I loved Germany, and now, now it's all wrong, do you understand?"

"Ernst, listen to me, put the gun down. I'm coming over, I'll get a cab and be there in twenty minutes, okay? A drink and a massage, dear, that's all you need."

"Goodbye, Marjot. I love you."

"*Ernst, no!*"

He put the gun's hard, cold muzzle to his temple and squeezed the trigger.

January 1943 Stalingrad

The remains of the Sixth Army huddled in among the ruins of Stalingrad. They'd taken the city, and it had become their prison.

The capture of Stalingrad had commenced as a rout in late August of 1942. In the suburbs, where the buildings were predominantly made of wood, the Panzers annihilated everything. Toward the center of the city the buildings were mainly of brick and concrete, and the action degenerated to a series of street battles. Weeks passed as the Germans slowly captured the city street by street, building by building, stopped for days at a time by a few snipers.

Then, after the Germans had captured the city, the Russian army had surrounded and trapped them. Their only chance at escape came when the 4th Panzer Army, dispatched in December by Manstein, had arrived within thirty kilometers of the city. Rather than fight his way out and join the salient Manstein had created, General Paulus elected to follow the Fuehrer's stern recommendation, that of keeping the army in place, resisting the stubborn, counterattacking Soviets to the cold, bitter end.

Planes flew in regularly, bringing tons of supplies, but far less than needed for an army of a quarter million soldiers. And as the days passed, more and more young German soldiers lay down their lives, picked off by snipers or dying from their injuries, from semi-starvation.

Wilfred Meier was on guard duty when he heard a woman's muffled shriek coming from inside a ruined apartment building. Shouldering his rifle, he glanced at the rooftops for snipers and then zigzagged across the street.

The front door of the building was hanging at an angle, and he carefully stepped past it. More female shrieks came from upstairs, accompanied by men's laughter. Taking the steps two at a time, he charged up to the fourth floor. He heard sounds of struggle and a hard slap, coming from behind an apartment door. Drawing out his Luger, he opened the door and stepped into the room.

"Don't move!" he shouted, gun muzzle pointed at the ceiling.

A beautiful Russian woman was tied spread-eagled on the bed, her dress pushed up around her waist, her underwear gone. The pink imprint of a hand was on her cheek. A German enlisted man knelt between her legs, his pants pulled down to his knees, his male member somehow looking ridiculous, standing at attention while he and the other three men stared at Will in stunned surprise.

"Would you like to have a turn?" ventured the man on the bed.

"Get out of here. Leave her alone."

The woman shouted another stream of invectives in Russian. Wilfred motioned with his gun. "Get away from her, all of you."

The man on the bed said, "She's nothing but a Russian slut! Look at her hair, a Jewess no less!"

"Leave now and get the hell out of here. German soldiers don't rape the enemy."

Disgusted, the three standing men left the room. The one on the bed managed to get up and pull his pants back on. "I'll report this to your unit commander," he snarled as he passed Will.

"I'm counting on it."

"You'll get yours!" he shouted over his shoulder.

When he was sure they were gone, Will holstered his gun and cut the woman's bonds. She was a big girl, buxom, with large bones and tawny hair. She quickly arranged her clothing and, muttering a hurried thank you, fled the room.

Days turned into weeks, weeks into months. The Russian winter descended on them. Supplies became ever more scarce as weather worsened and the airlift slowed. Daily guerrilla attacks winnowed the German ranks. Will spent his days improving fortifications, his nights on guard duty. His daily ration had been reduced to a slice of bread and half a can of beans. He became gaunt, his eyes sunken in his head, skin hanging on his bones.

On the day General Paulus finally surrendered, against Hitler's orders, Wilfred Meier was unconscious in the ruins of the same small apartment on the fourth floor where he'd rescued the Russian Jewess, where he had been ordered to serve as a sniper. He was a victim of a grenade that a Russian soldier had launched into the apartment through the window. His wounds were not serious in themselves, but they were infected. He was feverish and starving. Somehow everyone had forgotten about him, and when the remaining Germans walked out in surrender, those few strong enough holding their hands up high, he remained behind on the cot in the wrecked apartment, cold air blowing on his face through the shattered windows.

Two days later Tatiana Gorchenka found him still lying there. The apartment had belonged to her before the general evacuation, and now it was hers again. It horrified her to find one of the monstrous Germans lying in her bed. And still alive!

She took out a knife, grabbed him by the hair and jerked his head back, exposing his throat.

Something in her Eastern Orthodox upbringing stayed her hand. She couldn't kill in cold blood, even a hated German. Then, looking again into the German's face, she suddenly recognized him and gasped. She had almost dispatched her rescuer!

Tatiana was a nurse by trade. She stretched Will out on the bed and examined his injuries. Getting her kit of medical supplies and a pot of water, she began cleaning and dressing his wounds. When he was stronger she'd turn him over to the proper authorities.

When all the other Germans were long gone, Will remained hidden in Tatiana's apartment. As he grew stronger she began teaching him Russian, which he had already studied in school, so he learned quickly. Soon he was well enough to get out of bed and move around the little apartment. When help was needed in the hospital she arranged for him to work there, getting her friends to fix his papers. He was handsome and intelligent and kind, and she liked him. He did his work well, keeping the hospital machines all up and running, getting along with everyone. He wasn't anything like the terrible creatures described in the newspapers and on the radio. To all appearances, he was just a healthy young man, with all the usual interests men had: soccer, good beer, and beautiful women.

At the end of the third month she began sleeping with him, and then, at the end of the summer, they married. Within a year the twins were born, a boy and a girl, both of them healthy. By the end of 1944 Wilfred was a supervisor in the hospital and spoke Russian so well that even Tatiana's closest friends had forgotten his unusual origin.

May 1945 Germany

The train broke down under allied attack. Heisenberg, finding an abandoned bicycle, began a perilous journey across the ruins of Germany.

It took him three days to reach his family, ensconced in a cottage in the Bavarian mountains, hungry but safe. On the way there a die-hard populist militia had stopped and nearly executed him, thinking he was a deserter. One of the men recognized him, and he was saved a bullet in the brain.

Three days later, an American physicist, Samuel Goudsmit, knocked on his door. Heisenberg opened. Goudsmit was Dutch by birth, Jewish, with dark curly hair and an open, guileless face. A few years previously he'd written to Heisenberg, asking him to intercede for his parents, incarcerated at Westenbork in Holland. Heisenberg had taken seven months to respond, and then it was only in the form of a letter informing Goudsmit he could do nothing.

Goudsmit's parents, transferred to Auschwitz, died soon after.

Heisenberg was eager to cooperate. Goudsmit listened to him prattle on about his feeble, failed experiments, finally stopping him.

"You are under arrest, Dr. Heisenberg."

"That won't be necessary. I've assured you, I will cooperate fully."

Goudsmit gestured to the OSS team that stood at ready outside. "Come on, guys, put him on ice."

As they moved forward, Goudsmit turned back to Heisenberg. "You don't know anything of any use to us, do you understand? You're strictly an amateur."

Goudsmit turned away, unable to bear the sight of the man another minute, knowing that later he would have to depose him for several hours. He also knew that Heisenberg, regardless of his excuses, would carry a stain to his dying day, something even a Nobel prize couldn't erase from the minds of men.

New York, 1950

Lieserl spent the post-war years in a suburb of New York. Every day she visited her mailbox in front of the little white house and picket fence, hoping for some news of her mother or brother. Every day she was disappointed.

Most of her free time she spent preparing science lessons for her students at the high school. She hadn't done any of her real work in nearly a decade, and didn't want to, ever again. Hiroshima and Nagasaki had traumatized her, filled her with shame, burned out the last of her passion for science.

She had visited her biological father only once, at Princeton, sitting in the back of a lecture hall and watching him scribble equations on the blackboard. After the lecture she watched him walk away down a snowy sidewalk, and was on the verge of calling out to him, only to find that her voice had failed her. She'd gone home and never returned.

On a bright, cool Saturday morning in the spring of 1950 she heard the front door bang open. A boy came running through the house, calling her name. She looked up from her desk as he burst excitedly into the study.

"Mom, come quick!" He spoke in English as she did; she only rarely spoke her mother tongue.

"What is it?"

"There's a man standing next to the mailbox."

"The mailman? He's not due for a couple hours."

"Not the mailman. A stranger, he's just standing there. He was looking at me."

Lieserl rose at once, alarmed. "Let's go find out what he wants."

She accompanied her son back through the small living room, stepping through the front door onto the screened porch. Sure enough, near the mailbox stood a man dressed in an expensive leisure suit, looking away with one hand in his pocket as if deciding what he should do next. Lieserl opened the screen door to the porch and stepped down to the walkway.

"Can I help you?"

The man turned, his eyes widening. He was handsome, blond, worldly, but there was something boyish about his blue eyes, a muted twinkling, as if something or someone he treasured had been lost for a long time and suddenly, unexpectedly, found. Lieserl stood transfixed on the little sidewalk, memories from the *Bismarck* flashing through her mind, mingling with the sweet smell of blooming spring flowers and the fragrant earth of her garden.

Her son tugged at her hand. "Who is he, Mama?"

Lieserl found her voice, tears clouding her eyes. "That man, Jimmy, is your father."

Wolfgang Wiesz walked slowly up the sidewalk. "Lieserl Meier?"

"I'm she." They stood looking at each other for a moment. She felt as if she were in a dream; he stood before her, smiling.

"You survived."

"I found a rubber raft floating nearby and spent five days out on the ocean with two other survivors before a U-boat picked us up."

"But you were a spy! They would have shot you!"

He shook his head. "The people who knew anything about me all went down with the ship. I spent the rest of the war working the dockyards in Brest, sending intelligence to the Allies through the French underground. After the war I searched for you all over Britain and Germany. I finally got access to the proper records and found your address." He nodded to the south. "I've been living in New Jersey for the past several years, not fifty miles away."

She looked down at her son, still clinging to her dress. "This is your son, James Meier."

Wolfgang took a cautious step forward, his face uncertain, one hand stretched tentatively forward. But her son retreated behind her, holding tightly to her dress, shy and embarrassed.

Wolfgang lowered his hand and straightened. "He'll have to get used to me. And the rest of the family."

She turned back to him, looking into his eyes uncertainly. "Are you married?"

"His grandparents—my parents—live near me, in the same town. And no, I've never married. And you?"

"After the *Bismarck* went down I never wanted anyone else."

Jimmy peered tentatively from behind his mother. "Do you play baseball?"

"Sometimes. Usually I play soccer."

The boy nodded grudgingly. "Soccer's okay."

Wolfgang looked back at Lieserl. "May I come in?"

They stood facing each other, mother and son and her son's father, separated by two short steps and years of time. Lieserl briefly closed her eyes, remembering that cold night in the North Atlantic, the night of passion that had given her a son, the night that had given her life true meaning, meaning that could not be written down in an equation.

"Yes, Wolfgang. You may come in. Please do come in."

He smiled and they mounted the steps together, Jim running inside ahead of them. At the threshold she paused and turned to him. They were almost touching.

"I'm much older, now," she murmured, the scientist in her demanding a confession, an obligatory protest to the road that was suddenly and irresistibly opening up within her.

He leaned forward slightly, and she found herself doing the same. "It doesn't matter. So am I."

Putting his hands lightly on her hips, he kissed her soft cheek. She turned her head, then, and kissed his mouth.

Easing back from her, he said, "It's nice to see you again."

"Likewise."

As they entered her home together, hand in hand, the last of her bitter memories faded into a soft warm light.

CHRIS VUILLE

ABOUT THE AUTHOR

Chris Vuille, Ph.D. is a physicist working at Embry-Riddle Aeronautical University in Daytona Beach, Florida, teaching a variety of physics courses and conducting research in general relativity, quantum theory, and cosmology. He is a co-author of *College Physics* and of *Essentials of College Physics*, Cengage Publishing, and has published articles in *Analog Science Fiction/Science Fact* and in a number of scientific journals throughout the world. His other books include *Thin Walls and Space-Times with Stress-Energy* and a spiritual self-help book, *Entering Light. Empires of Light Part 2: Chaos Ascending*, is due out in 2014.

Printed in Great Britain
by Amazon